S0-BZP-971

DOUBLE EXPOSURE

Other books by Blaine M. Yorgason
and/or Brenton G. Yorgason

Seeker of the Gentle Heart
The Krystal Promise
A Town Called Charity, and Other Stories About Decisions
The Bishop's Horse Race
The Courage Covenant (Massacre at Salt Creek)
Windwalker (movie version)
The Windwalker
Others
Charlie's Monument
From First Date to Chosen Mate
Tall Timber (private printing)
From Two To One*
From This Day Forth*
Marriage and Family Stewardships*
Creating a Celestial Marriage*

*Coauthored with Wesley R. Burr and Terry R. Baker

DOUBLE EXPOSURE

A NOVEL

Blaine M. Yorgason
Brenton G. Yorgason

Bookcraft / Salt Lake City, Utah

For Tom Ballard
who never lost faith

Library of Congress Catalog Card Number: 82-72273
ISBN O-88494-464-6

6th Printing, 1988

Lithographed in the United States of America
PUBLISHERS PRESS
Salt Lake City, Utah

Acknowledgments

For their selfless contributions toward making this a better manuscript, we would like to acknowledge the following friends: Richard L. and Linda Baird Jamison, Francine Shumway Sumner, Joseph O. Eggett, Jr., Max W. Smith, Peter N. Johnson, Michael O'Hara, and Susan Miller Beck.

Glossary of Mountain-Man Terms, circa 1848

Air: Used interchangeably as "are," "as," or "is." It also meant "there" when preceded by thet or them; thet-air, them-air.

Ary: Any.

Boudins: Intestines, preferably buffalo. Lightly browned over the fire, they were considered a great delicacy by the mountain men.

Brownskin: A name given to all Indians.

Cache: A place of concealment. As a verb, to hide or protect one's self or possessions from anyone else.

Catamount: An American mountain lion. See Painter.

Child: See Hos.

Come, Make someone come: Kill, overcome, be victorious over.

Coon: See Hos.

Fandango: Any dance or celebration, not the specific Spanish dance of that time.

Fat cow: Good living. See Poor bull.

Fleece: Strips of meat from along the backbone of an animal, preferably buffalo. Considered choice.

Flutterin' fantods: An expression meaning great nervousness.

Fofarraw: Fanciments, trimmings, decorations for personal adornment. As an adjective, fancy, affected.

Go under: Go under the sod, die.

Hos: One of the many mountain-man terms for self. Interchangeable terms were child and coon.

Hos and beaver: Everything, the works. Through gambling, disaster, or Indian raids, a trapper might lose his most valuable possessions: his horse and beaver pelts. Hence the expression.

Hump rib: Meat from the buffalo's high shoulder hump. Much esteemed.

Hyar: Here, this place. Also used for hear, to hear.

La: An expression of surprise or exclamation.

Mulada: Herd of mules.

Painter, catamount: Two of many names for the American mountain lion.

Palaver: Discuss, talk about.

Parfleche, Parflesh: Rawhide, hide scraped to remove fat and hair, but untanned. Also articles made from rawhide, such as moccasins, pouches, etc.

Plew, Prime plew: A beaver pelt or hide, and one in very fine condition.

Poor bull: Tough meat, hard living. The opposite of Fat cow. The origin of the two terms came from the fact that buffalo cows were better eating than bulls, particularly when grazing was sparse.

Possibles: A man's personal possessions, often carried in a "possibles" bag or sack.

Poudrie: A ground blizzard, where the snow is blown up into a fine powder.

Raise, Make a raise: To "raise hair" was to scalp; to "make a raise" was to find or get possession of something.

Rub out: Kill. To be rubbed out came from the Indian sign language, and signified graphically, by the rubbing of one hand across the other, that something or someone had been done away with.

Sartin, Sartin-sure: To be certain of.

Shine: Do extremely well, be successful, make good impression, please. "That won't shine" meant that it wouldn't do, was no good, was not pleasing or understood.

Sign, Indian sign: Anything indicating the presence of game or Indians. Tracks, dust in the air, smoke, old campfires, etc., were all signs.

Thar: There.

Thet, Thet-air: That, that-there.

Top-knot: A man's hair. Also used occasionally to refer to the top of an animal's head.

Vinaigrette: Smelling salts.

Vittles: Food, anything in the least bit nourishing.

Wagh: A term of exclamation, most likely picked up from one of several Indian tribes. For each mountain man the meaning was probably a little different.

Whangs: Leather or rawhide thongs or strings, used to repair or hold together all manner of possessions. The fringes on a man's buckskins were a man's whangs, to be pulled off or cut off as needed.

Whet: What.

Wiping stick: The wooden ramrod used to load and clean rifles. Also used as a support to steady the aim while firing. Most mountain men preferred hickory wiping sticks.

Yarrow, Yarror: A strong-scented herb (*Achillea millefolium*), widely used as a pain-killing medicine.

PROLOGUE

I

The land lay empty around them, frozen and still. The wind, coming down off the flanks of Pool Table Mountain, blew cold, sweeping the dry snow ahead of it, filling the twisting canyon of Alder Creek with fifteen-foot drifts, whipping the aspens along the slopes, and chilling to the bone the men of John C. Fremont's fourth expedition.

Under a ghostly, lightning-struck pine, Old Bill Williams, mountain man and guide, paused and looked around. Past sixty, he was still nursing a bullet-shattered arm which he had received fighting the Utes, and now he was back in their country. But it was winter and he had seen no sign, so he gave the Indians little thought. His worries now concerned the expedition, for these men were out in one of the worst winters Colorado had ever known, and Old Bill sensed that there would be trouble.

Although the slope where he stood was steep, he ordered camp made there, and then he climbed through the deep snow to a rocky outcropping above. Before him the view opened up, showing a mighty panorama of rugged mountains and deep canyons now lost in darkness, of forests blasted by lightning-spawned fires, and of the gray bleached bones of long-dead trees. Under the low, dark clouds the scene was strangely somber and majestic. The higher ridges and peaks vanished in the clouds, and before him the bleak hillside stretched upward, bare and unpromising. It was a terrible place to be, that winter of 1848, and Old Bill knew it.

Later, as the thirty-two men sat huddled around their fires, snow began to fall. Not the intermittent flakes they had dealt with for two days, but fine, icy particles, the accumulation of which added yet another layer to the deepening white blanket. The wind whipped the strong pine smoke into their eyes, a wolf howled somewhere out in the forest, and one of the mules shifted its feet uneasily. Alexis Godey spoke to the mule softly, calming it, and then stretched his hands toward the dancing flames. From time to time fuel was added to the fire, and the night was very cold. The wind came hard around the boulders and down through the trees, plucking at the fire and stirring it with irritated fingers, chilling even further the already cold men.

No one talked much, for lips were cracked and bleeding, and there was not much to say that was worth the pain. The men made beds, under Old Bill's direction, by cutting down trees and banking up against them with pine boughs, forming relatively flat areas on which to sleep.

For days the men had battled the cold, the snow, and the wind, had crossed two ranges of mountains, and were now beginning their ascent of the third. Sadly, they were in no condition to do so, and Old Bill knew it. The weather had worn them down, and though there was no complaining, Old Bill could see their suffering. Like Doctor Benjamin Kern, who, upon removing his boots, found his stockings frozen to his feet. He was now thawing them at the fire so he could get them off, and he would be ready to go tomorrow. Even so, Old Bill knew that this kind of suffering could not go on indefinitely. It was already December 12, and they were behind schedule. They had been climbing toward Wagon Wheel Pass for just one day, had traveled only half as far as they should have because of the deep snow, and Old Bill knew that they were in trouble.

The expedition, privately financed, had been encouraged by Fremont's father-in-law, Missouri Senator Thomas Hart Benton, who, caught up in the doctrine of Manifest Destiny, envisioned a national roadway that would run from St. Louis to the bay of San Francisco. On that mile-wide road he hoped to place a railway, a plank track, a newfangled magnetic track, a macadamized (concrete) road, and a plain old dirt path. All that remained, before he could get governmental approval, was proof of the practicality of the route in winter. Thus his son-in-law's expedition, which was superbly organized and equipped and ready for anything. Almost.

Leaving St. Louis on October 3, the men reached Pueblo on November 21, passing the deserted log cabins built by the Mormons two years earlier. The Pueblo was not impressive to the men, for it was a menagerie of Spaniards, cows, horses, mules, dogs, chickens, and bad stench. On the twenty-fourth they arrived at Hardscrabble, a home-base community of mountain men and hunters, which consisted of about a dozen cabins and some corncribs. There they shelled and sacked corn, one hundred and thirty bushels of it, to feed the mules should they find no grass in the tops of the mountains. There they also picked up Old Bill Williams.

Two days later the expedition moved out, on foot, and crossed over the Wet Mountains. Then, on the thirtieth, near the summit of the Sangre De Cristos, two men from Pueblo caught up with them, asking permission to join the company. However, when it was learned that one of them was the man who was known as the Preacher, Old Bill made a fuss, and so the two men were turned back.

Now, as Old Bill shivered beneath his blanket, he felt badly. The one man, the Preacher, who had wanted most badly to accompany the expedition, was actually an old friend of his, one he'd trapped with for several years. He was a good ol' hos too, but Bill felt the man had snubbed him a couple of years back when he'd gone and got religious and then married that little gal down to Pueblo. Bill, who never forgot those things, was still miffed.

Trouble was, the ol' hos had given him a look, as he had turned to go back, that was cold enough to make an icicle feel feverish. And, he had threatened to follow them anyway, making his own way on their backtrail, for he wanted in the worst way to get into the valley of the Salt Lake. The look itself hadn't bothered Old Bill, but the threat had. This trip was bad enough with a well-equipped party. But alone, on a winter trail? Well, it was enough to make an old hos worry. It—

"Hyar, Bill? Air ye awake?"

Williams, startled by the whisper, took a moment to identify it. *Tom Breckenridge,* he thought quickly. *Thet-air be Tom's whisper.*

"Wagh," he whispered back. "Be that ye, Ol' Tom?"

"Aye, thet it be. Bill, this child were talkin' with the Frenchie, Proue, tonight, and thet coon's got 'im a bad feelin'. Air ye sartin-sure this hyar creek be Willow Creek?"

"Sartin-sure as tomorrer be Wednesday morn, ol' hos. This child's bin here afore. Found this pass onct, and I've found it agin. Course the snow's considerable more than I reckoned, and like I told the Colonel Monday last, nothin's sure-fire sartin in the winter. I reckoned we'd ought to skirt these hills to the south. But the Colonel, he air a stubborn man, and he'd have none of any detours. He says we're goin' up, so that's where this ol' hos be takin' 'im. You fellers'll just have to go along fer the ride."

"Yeh, I reckon. Only I wisht it weren't such a blamed cold trip. I never seed such snow. The good Lord sartin must've pulled out the cork when he started *this* storm. Some of the boys made mauls tonight. Reckon tomorrow we'll beat us a trail with 'em so's the mules don't sink through. Night, Bill."

"Night, ol' hos."

The next morning Old Bill realized that he had never seen, in all his forty years in the mountains, anything like it. The hill did not look steep, nor did it look particularly rough, but still it had taken the men nearly two hours to climb approximately three hundred feet, beating out a trail with their mauls and dragging the mules up behind them. And now, near the top, this.

The mule had accidentally stepped off the trail and had gone belly-deep in the snow, then deeper. Floundering desperately the animal fought for a foothold, jumping and plunging until it finally vanished from sight, simply sinking beneath the snow. For a short time the snow continued to shift above where the mule had disappeared, but then even that stopped, and all was still. The men stared in uneasy horror, each of them mentally taking the place of the unfortunate mule.

But then Fremont, in a voice of thunder, ordered them forward, and the spell was broken. The mule and what it carried would be abandoned, he told them. But the men, at whatever the cost, would move forward. That had been his way for years, and he was not about to become a quitter at this point in his life. Not by a dogged sight he wasn't!

On the fourteenth the men finally reached the top of the first ridge, near Pool Table Mountain, moving always into the face of a howling ground blizzard. In the minus-twenty-degree temperature the blood from their bleeding noses congealed and froze into their whiskers, giving them a gruesome appearance. Under terrible conditions the party struggled down off the ridge and into a stand of yellow pine where they made an early camp.

That day eight more mules and one pack of macaroni were lost, and Fremont detailed six men to recover the equipment. It was nearly morning when the recovery party finally arrived back at camp, exhausted, and without the equipment. One of them, as he was dropping off to sleep, reported hearing what might have been a rifle-shot from down canyon.

Old Bill Williams, hearing that, thought immediately of the Preacher, of his scriptures, of his journal, and of his misplaced faith in a loving God. For the rest of the night he tossed and turned in his sodden bedding, listening to the sorrowful braying of the hungry mules and worrying about his old friend. If there was only something he could do—if only he had not refused the man. But he had. He had, and there was nothing he could do about it now, nothing at all. And the snow was falling, again.

II

Night came like a ghost to the mountain, quick and silent, and the lone man felt fear. It was cold, bitter bitter cold, and the wind from the high-up peaks cut through even the warmest clothes, chilling, draining precious body heat, killing.

With a shiver the man rolled over, winced with pain, and broke a few small branches from the huge dead tree that comprised his only shelter. Rolling back he grimaced with agony once more, controlled the expression on his face, and fed the sticks into his hatful of a fire.

It helped, it helped a lot to feel that heat. But it was not enough, and the man knew it. He also knew, with a quiet resignation, that he could do no more. His animals and packs were gone, his leg was badly broken, and there was something else wrong inside him, something that caused him to spit blood each time he coughed. No, the fire helped, but it was only temporary, and the man knew it.

Nor was it as if he'd not been warned. Bill Sharp'd given it to him straight, with no beating around the Juneberry bush. "Ol' hos," Bill had said, "if'n they don't want us, it be plumb foolish tryin' to foller 'em. The snow be too deep, the animals be all gaunted up, and a man or two alone won't make it. Sech doin's as a blizzard like this don't shine at all. Do whet ye've a mind to, but this child's turnin' back."

Bill'd done it, too, leaving him alone to try to follow Fremont himself. And he had; for days and days of cold and hunger and exhaustion he had followed, living on almost nothing, watching his animals slowly die of cold and starvation, driven on only by the desire to be reunited with his family.

But then had come the slide, the avalanche of snow that had taken everything from him but his mule and his possibles. He'd fired his piece in the faint hope that Fremont or Old Bill Williams or someone would hear, but there had been no response. Nor had he expected that there would be. The howling of the wind was too loud, the snow too deep, and all sound was muffled and drowned out.

What followed then had been a nightmare, a horrid blending of days and nights, of cold and hunger, and of merciless pain. He supposed he had tied himself to the mule and had urged it upward into the mountain, but he didn't know. He had no memory of it. All he knew was that he had almost made it. Ruefully he looked around at the blackened and empty fire pits. Only hours had separated him from Fremont, but those hours would stretch out to forever, and he knew it.

So he'd not died in the slide, nor had he died being dragged behind the mule. But his time was about up, and there was nothing he could do about it. Actually, he was not bothered by that, not in the usual sense that a man fears death. He didn't fear, for his faith in the Lord sustained him, and that was a plain fact. He feared only for his family, for his lovely wife and infant son. They would be alone, and he wondered how they'd ever make it. The frontier was a hard place for anyone, and for a woman and child alone it would be doubly so.

A spasm of coughing wracked the man, and after it had passed he wiped the blood away from his mouth and then groped about in his possibles bag. Shortly he withdrew a small packet, untied it, removed a tiny journal, and with a blackened stick from the fire he began to write. It was a slow process, and more and more often he was interrupted by coughing and the spitting of blood. Finally, though, he finished, retied the packet, placed it back in his possibles bag, and lay back.

"Weel," he gasped as he did his best to smile, "it be done, and I . . . I hope it'll help. . . . Sarah sartin put store by writin' it."

Moments later he gasped, reached out, tried to stagger to his feet, and at last fell back into the snow by the fire. For a moment his lips moved and he seemed to be apologizing, telling someone that he was sorry for something he had done. Then his lips grew still, his eyes glazed over, and the only sound on the mountain was the lonely howling of the winter wind.

The man walked slowly down the center aisle of the Goodwill Industries store, apparently looking for something. Casually he cast his glance to his left and to his right, superficially examining the contents of the bins and the shelves he was passing.

The man stood a solid six feet from the ground, and carried the bulk of his hundred and ninety pounds in his chest and shoulders. His face was hard-boned, tanned, and clean-shaven, and though his jaw was placed firm and square, his eyes, set deep, seemed to dance with excitement. In short, he gave the impression of one who knew what he was about, and yet who walked quietly, not wanting to draw attention to himself.

His dress was, if anything, nondescript, at odds with the man himself. The only remarkable thing about it, if it was indeed remarkable, was his tweed coat. Though probably common enough, it appeared to be of European make, was obviously expensive, and seemed somewhat out of place in such a setting. Still, the man wore it in such a way that it was not obtrusive, and so it was hardly noticeable at all.

Steadily, with a soft step that made it seem more like he was gliding than walking, the man moved toward the back of the store. As he passed other customers he stepped courteously out of their way, yet none of them paid any attention to him whatsoever. For his part the man too remained silent, merely smiling and nodding in greeting as he passed.

Finally, at the very back of the store, he grinned widely, for he had found what he was looking for. An ancient and battered trunk sat on the floor, almost buried under a stack of discarded clothing. Yet the trunk was what the man wanted.

Carefully, and yet without apparent nervousness, the man looked around. He was as alone as he could expect to be, and so stooping he took hold of the pile of clothing and quickly removed it from the top of the trunk.

For a moment the man worked at the latch, which he found to be rusty and in poor repair. From the expression on his face it was obvious that the rust was distasteful to him, yet he said nothing. He simply continued to work at the latch with his fingers. Finally, after long moments, it sprang free, and he slowly lifted the lid of the empty trunk.

Again he straightened and looked around, but still no one was nearby. Bending over once more, he worked his fingers beneath the ancient, discolored satin lining of the lid of the leather-bound trunk. Pulling quickly, he tore the lining loose. Then, reaching up behind it, he fumbled for a moment and at last removed a small packet wrapped in dark oilcloth.

For a moment he gazed at the packet without moving, wondering whether or not it would work. Then he smiled again, resecured the lining in the trunk, placed the packet in his pocket, closed the lid of the old box, and replaced the huge pile of clothing. Turning then, he walked quickly up the aisle, past the cashier, and out of the store.

For better or for worse, he knew, it had started.

PART ONE

1

What she'd expected was an argument. What she got was an awfully intriguing proposal.

"If you won't sell," the man had said as he poked his head into her door, his beautiful smile playing across his face, "I have a better idea. Let's get married and merge."

Even now, in the midst of what she was planning, Angela Armstrong smiled as she recalled the ludicrous incongruity of it. The whole thing had been crazy, off the wall. But then, so had she. Instantly, almost before he had finished asking, she had accepted, surprising him almost as much as she had herself.

Slowly Angela leaned back from her desk, the empty suite of offices around her forgotten. Then, while her pen absently traced doodles around the word she had printed and reprinted across the top page of a memo pad, she let her mind slip back through the months and years to the day when she had first seen and conversed with her husband.

Nelson Thurgood Armstrong, she had realized instantly that day, was probably the most attractive man she had ever seen.

He was tall and lean, and had beautiful dark hair that waved back in just the right way. He also had Viking blue eyes that squinched almost closed when he smiled, crinkling at the corners into crow's-feet that made him look weathered and, well . . . distinguished and at the same time boyish, something she found irresistible.

Even now, after all that had happened, it was still true. She had never met, had never wanted, even, a man until she had met him — witty, incurious, restrained, somewhat distant, clever, wordlessly understanding. And somehow, with all of that, he had a way of allowing her for the first time in her life to feel needed.

Angela recalled how she had also been attracted to Nelson's mind, his quick, incisive mind. He was intelligent, he was well-read, and, like her, he was a winner. He knew what he wanted in life, and would, Angela had quickly realized, be a very good person to team up with, for he could take her far toward where she herself wanted to go. Also, he radiated an aura of invincibility, and the challenge of penetrating that aura made her instantly resolute.

In addition, Angela had learned from others who were nearby, Nelson was wealthy. The man, still in his early twenties, had inherited the presidency of his family's business, and almost overnight had turned it into a multi-million-dollar corporation. And that, Angela was forced to admit, had made him seem even more attractive.

He had moved past her that day at the ski lodge, not noticing her at all, and her interest was piqued. In a far corner he had taken a chair, relaxed, and then had begun reading a book he was carrying. After a brief but sufficient time, Angela had arisen and had moved gracefully, almost sensuously, toward him. Yet still the man had paid no attention.

For a moment Angela stood before the wonderfully handsome man, wondering what to do, wondering what was wrong with her that he had not noticed her presence. But there was nothing wrong, she knew that, and so with practiced ease she proceeded. Seating herself carefully on the footstool in front of him, she tilted her head to one side, smiled slightly, and said hello.

There was no instantaneous response, which was not normal, and Angela was a little surprised. But then, after a moment, the man looked up, gazed into her eyes, smiled, said hello, and turned back to his book.

Angela was incredulous! Men did not usually dismiss her with an insouciant hello, nor did they pass over her face with a casual glance and look away, totally avoiding the attractive territory below. She was surprised, and curious. Leaning back, she thought for a moment, glanced at the title of his book, smiled, and clasped her knee with both hands, unconsciously raising her skirt slightly but provocatively. Then, still smiling, she spoke.

"Do you think," she asked quietly, "that the Medicis acted appropriately when they put Machiavelli to the rack?"

Again the response was slow, but again it was accompanied by a smile, this time even wider. "Well, well, well," the man said, gazing at last into her eyes. "The question is not an empty-headed 'What are you reading?' which was expected, and which anyone could learn simply by glancing at the spine of my book. Instead, the lady asks, 'Did the Medicis do right?' which shows that, besides her obvious beauty, she has a finely tuned mind.

"My answer to your question, ma'am, is both no and yes. My follow-up question, divided into two parts, is, do you know the Florentine well? And, do you have a name?"

For just a moment Angela remained silent, watching him, observing the light from the fire as it played across the rugged features of his face. Oh, how she ached to reach out, to touch the masculine strength displayed before her.

"Part one," she finally replied, speaking easily, enticingly. "I am acquainted with Machiavelli's writing, but one cannot know a man well simply by reading a few words he has written down. Thoughts thus recorded are most carefully selected, and do not truly reveal the man. Part two, my name is Angela Westport. And now, I will ask one more question, which you may be sure will be my last."

The man raised an eyebrow and grinned, obviously anticipating what she would ask, convinced that he knew the direction of her thoughts. But Angela knew that he didn't, for that was one of her great talents, the ability to keep people off balance, to keep them at her mercy.

"Why," she asked, "do you read Machiavelli?"

For an instant the man simply stared, and then he laughed outright. "You're kidding," he said. "You aren't interested in my name?"

"No, not really. At least, I'm not interested until I find out why you're reading that book. At that point, I *might* be interested. I know already of your interest in me, but I have no wish to make it a mutual thing until I understand you."

Again the man chuckled as he spoke, which had the curious effect of making his voice sound almost musical and, Angela decided, very delicious. She was definitely interested, despite her protestations.

"You, Miss Westport," Nelson responded, "are truly unique, and I consider it an honor to be having this conversation with you. And I will answer your question. But first let me introduce myself. My name is Nelson Armstrong, and I am delighted to meet a woman, a truly beautiful woman, who is not afraid to show that she is well read.

"And now to your question. Idomeneous, in the *Iliad,* says that true courage is fearlessness, cowards are undone by fear, and so cowards are losers. I read Machiavelli simply because he was not a coward. He believed in winning because he knew that winning, finally, was the whole point of life. For the same reason I read with pure pleasure of Prince Andrew and young Rostov in Tolstoy's *War and Peace,* of heroes of Troy's siege, and of the courage of Leonidas at Thermopylae. These men, too, believed that winning was the ultimate in success."

"And do you also believe that?" Angela asked, her face very serious.

"Of course! For though methods change, and though lifestyles evolve, and though technology advances, the philosophy of life remains constant century after century. Life is no different for me, really, than it was for Machiavelli. And though I don't agree with all of his methods, I do agree with his conclusions.

He learned that the whole point of life was to be successful. Long ago I came to the same conclusion. My entire object in life is happiness, and achieving is at least part of what provides that for me."

"I see . . ." Angela replied thoughtfully. "I assume then that you are familiar with other winners from the past. Those written of by Plutarch, for example?"

"Yes, I am acquainted with Plutarch's *Lives*, though I disagree with him that all were as great as he claimed them to be. Besides, they were most definitely not all winners."

"For instance?"

Nelson looked once more at the woman, rather carefully, and then he smiled again, convinced that she was sincerely interested in what he was saying. "Antony, Miss Westport, is an instance. Plutarch tells us that Antony believed in winning, and he tells us of great battles that he did indeed gain victory in. Yet Antony was not competent to insure himself permanent victory. He indulged in too many vices, and so he lost control of himself. A man who is not in control is not happy. Nor is he a true success."

For a moment Angela thought about what he had said, and then she replied, "Yes, you're right. But only partially so, at least in my opinion. Antony did lose, but it was not because of incompetence or incontinence, either one. Antony lost because he met an even greater winner, Cleopatra. As you no doubt recall, Cleopatra became his lover, and as Plutarch says, the soul of a lover lies in another's body. Antony lost because he let his emotions control his actions. His feelings replaced his rational thinking. Cleopatra never allowed that to happen. Thus she succeeded while Antony did not."

"Until the end, when she needlessly destroyed herself," Nelson chided gently, still smiling, "because *she* lost control."

"Touché," Angela said, and suddenly she found herself laughing with him, laughing not because it was the best thing to do, but laughing simply because it felt good!

"Are you too a winner?" Nelson had finally asked, gasping for breath.

"I hope so," she had replied seriously, surprised at her own candor in front of this man whom she so wanted to impress. "I want to be, for there is security in winning, and right now I seek security even more than I seek happiness. However, I know little about winning, for I am only in my first campaign. Would you—uh—care to teach me?"

"Why—uh—yes," Nelson responded, grinning again. "Yes, I would like that very much. And if I became your teacher, then we would both win, wouldn't we?"

They both laughed then, and their relationship, for the remainder of that long weekend, had leaped easily forward. They had been so wonderful, those days together. If only . . . if only . . .

Tears quickly filled her eyes, tears of pain, sorrow, and regret, and slowly Angela came erect in her chair, her eyes on the word she had written and rewritten on her memo pad.

DIVORCE!

How she hated the word! How she dreaded the thought of it. How she ached when she thought of the joy and happiness she had known with Nelson. Yet divorce was the only answer now, and she knew it. Especially after what she had learned. Nor would it help to put it off. She must sever with him quickly, and not a little at a time. It was the only way she could bear to do it, the only way she could save all that she had worked so long to build and obtain.

But—Nelson did not see it yet, and had refused even to discuss it. Of course they discussed little anymore except their respective businesses, which was a great part of the problem. But this was important, this was more than—

Suddenly, Angela was not alone! The feeling had come again, as it had come repeatedly since she had made her decision—the eerie sensation that made its way in chills up and down her spine, pulling her hair erect at the nape of her neck, and bringing myriads of goosebumps to her flesh. Angela Westport Armstrong, alone in her office, was not alone—and she knew it!

Instantly she leaped to her feet and ran to the window, sobbing and beating at it with her fists, as though it held the hidden eyes that she could feel. Someone was watching her! Someone was *watching* her, emotionally caressing her with . . . with a sort of love!

A sudden knock on the office door brought her around once more, and she was moving to answer it when the feeling came again: the unspeakable emotional horror of a presence not seen, but nevertheless real—a presence she could not reach, but one that she could feel with every fiber of her being.

Choking back a sob she whirled around, and again found herself alone in her office. What was going on?

Breathing heavily, she stared at her terrified image in the mirror on the far wall. She was alone! She knew that she was alone! And yet, just as surely, she knew that she wasn't. Someone else was there.

Suddenly she realized that she had to get out! She had to leave, to tell someone, to talk about it with someone—

Nelson! That was it. She could talk to—but no, he wasn't back yet. His secretary had told her so. But the board meeting had started, and he was supposed to chair it.

Again the knock came to the outer door, this time more loudly. Angela, doing her best to regain her composure, purposely ignored the incessant attempt at interruption. Instead, she turned slowly back to the window where she gazed down at the street below.

What could it be? What could possibly be giving her such an overwhelming feeling of . . . of whatever it was that she was feeling? She had never felt this way before, and—

"Mrs. Armstrong?"

Angela screamed, spun around, and was shocked to find herself facing a man, a complete stranger who had somehow gained access to her office.

"I'm sorry, Ma'am," he drawled apologetically, his voice filled with genuine concern. "I didn't mean to startle you, but—"

"Who . . . what . . . how . . . how did you get in here?" Angela shouted, her fear turning to quick anger.

"There was no one in the outer office, Ma'am, and I did knock. But you must not have heard me."

"Who *are* you?" Angela demanded, suddenly feeling very alone and frightened once more. "Who are you, and what do you want?"

"Are you Angela Westport Armstrong?"

"Yes, I—wait a minute! *Wait* a *minute!* I demand that you tell me who you are and what you are doing in my office!"

"I was told that you were lovely," the man said, his voice ringing with sincerity, "but I had no idea—"

"You have three seconds to leave—three seconds before I start screaming!"

"Yes," the man mused, smiling slightly. "The temper too is evident." Then, with his grin growing wider until it engulfed his entire face, he spoke again to Angela. "Your scream won't be necessary, Mrs. Armstrong. I'm leaving. But I did want to return this packet to you."

"*Packet?* What packet? I haven't lost any packet!"

"Oh, I'm most sorry. I was told that it was you who had donated the old leather-bound trunk to Goodwill Industries. And since this was found in it, and since it is extremely valuable—"

"Well, I did donate an old trunk to Goodwill. But—"

"Then they were right! It *is* yours. It was found in the lining of the lid, and they . . . I felt that rightfully it belonged to you. Here you are. Now please excuse my interruption, and thank you for your generosity to Goodwill Industries. We hope that you'll think of them again. Good day, Mrs. Armstrong."

With that the man smiled again, brightly, bowed slightly, turned, and walked out of the door. Angela, still shaken, stared at his retreating form, at his wide shoulders, at his tweed jacket. Then, suddenly, unaccountably cold, she dropped the packet onto her desk, stood up, and walked into her closet to get a sweater.

"What on earth?" she asked herself, shivering. "What is going on? Who was that man, and why did he look at me as he did? And a packet! I thought . . . I thought . . ."

Suddenly Angela began perspiring, and then she knew that she had to get out of her office, her prison of fear. She had to leave, to go—to go home! Maybe there, after a relaxing bath, she could collect herself. Yes, a hot bath and perhaps even a nap. That would also help her to stop feeling so cold, so warm, so . . . well, so clammy. And then perhaps she would be up to discussing the divorce with Nelson.

2

Setting the telephone receiver gently back into its cradle, Nelson Thurgood Armstrong III dropped the transmission of the red Lamborghini into second and slowed for the traffic light ahead.

An amazingly handsome man, Nelson wore his designer sunglasses and his elegantly informal clothing much like a four-star general wears his uniform. Unlike most four-star generals, however, he was affected neither by his uniform nor by his good looks. His thoughts, in fact, were miles away from such mundane things.

"Angie, Angie, Angie . . ." he muttered aloud as he controlled the powerful machine that was wrapped around him. "Angie, what has happened to us? For the past few weeks you've been as cold toward me as a December wind, and I still can't figure out what I've done."

As Nelson pondered his relationship with his wife, a new Porsche braked to a stop in the lane to his right. Glancing with interest at the car, Nelson was startled to find the driver, a beautiful young woman, staring directly toward him. She was also gently revving her engine, obviously in an attempt to get his attention. Responding, Nelson politely flashed her his all-American smile. Instantly the woman smiled back, dropped her eyes, and looked away. Seconds later, when the light changed, she aggressively accelerated forward, a challenge-invitation for Nelson to follow.

Again he smiled, but then, instead of following, he made a very deliberate right turn, drove a block, and turned into the parking terrace of the Armstrong Communications Building.

Leaving the engine idling so the attendant could park the car, Nelson walked briskly toward the security guard who was seated before the bank of elevators.

"Afternoon, Mr. Armstrong," the guard said as he hurried to push the call button for the elevator.

"How's it going, Hank? Hey, you're really trimming down. No kidding. You look fit as a fiddle."

"Thanks, Mr. Armstrong. I took your suggestion and started jogging. It hurts like crazy, and the first few steps nearly kill me every time, but it's working and I'm starting to enjoy it. And this," he said, softly patting his middle, "is even starting to go down."

"That's great, Hank. I knew you could do it. Hey, see you later."

Grinning at Hank's joy with his weight-loss program, Nelson entered the elevator and stood patiently as it climbed to the twenty-first floor. As he rode, he pulled some papers from his pocket and began thumbing through them.

Leggit, he thought. *Dick Leggit. Graduate summa cum laude, Harvard School of Law, corporate attorney for Armstrong Communications, and personal friend. Dick Leggit, what am I going to do about you?*

The doors to the elevator slid open, and Nelson, totally absorbed in thoughts of his attorney, strode rapidly toward the board room.

"Mr. Armstrong? Mr. Armstrong?"

"Yes, Joyce," Nelson responded, slowing down only slightly as he passed his secretary's desk.

"A message, sir. The Board of Directors began the meeting

ten minutes ago. Some of them seem to be—uh—running a bit short of patience."

"Wonderful," Nelson responded, grinning. "Any other hot news flashes?"

"Yes," his secretary replied, obviously savoring the relationship she felt she shared with the president of the corporation. "But I'll tell it to you later, when we're . . . alone."

"Very well," Nelson responded. Then he smiled, and ignoring the obvious message his secretary had just given him, he turned and entered the board room. As he did so, he saw that Dick Leggit was speaking.

"And so, the big fear right now," Dick was saying, "is that the Supreme Court will let the decision stand. That means we'll be rewriting the rule books concerning libel laws. So please, if you have any controversial stories or gossip items, check with me first before you print them or air them."

As Nelson closed the door, Leggit stopped speaking, and all eyes in the room turned to the door. Smiling briefly, Nelson moved quickly to his chair. "Excuse me," he murmured, nodding for Leggit to continue.

As Leggit's presentation dragged on, Nelson found himself idly examining the dozen people in the room. What would happen, he wondered, if all those good people found out that he and Angie were having problems? If those problems led to a divorce, how would these people be affected? Angie of course would take *Fashion 1* with her, but her employees would remain employed. The problem would be with some of his own people, who would lose their transitional positions. Of course there were other jobs, and—

Good grief, what was he thinking of? There would be no divorce. There couldn't be! He loved Angie! Always had, in fact. Whatever the problem was, it could be resolved.

When the meeting had adjourned and everyone else had departed, Nelson and Dick Leggit remained alone in the board room.

"I missed Angela today," Dick stated suddenly. "You know, her presence adds a great deal to our meetings."

"Does it?" Nelson asked absently, still preoccupied with the distance he was feeling between himself and his wife. "In what way?"

Leggit, suddenly, unaccountably defensive, found himself struggling for words. "Why, uh . . . she's . . . she's a beautiful woman, Nelson. And it's obvious that she loves you."

"Yeah, I guess so," Nelson responded, his mind still far away.

"Hey, what is this? Do I detect a note of despair, of hesitancy? Is there yet hope for those of us who leer from afar?"

"Forget it, Dick!" Nelson said curtly, suddenly concerned that his thoughts had been so transparent. "You're as married as I am, or at least you were yesterday when I spoke to your wife. Now back off about Angie!"

"Ouch! That smarted, my friend."

"Well, maybe it needed to smart!"

For a long moment Leggit gazed at Nelson. "I'm afraid," he said at last, "that you misunderstood me. I meant to imply nothing more than that you had a lovely wife, and that in some ways, many ways, actually, I was envious of your happiness, of the beautiful relationship you and Angela seem to have. The two of you set a standard that is difficult for most of the rest of us to follow. Nevertheless, for whatever it was I said that upset you, Nelson, you have my apologies."

"Forget it, Dick," Nelson responded quickly, sincerely, feeling suddenly awkward for the way he had responded. "You said nothing that was wrong. In fact, I'm flattered that you find Angie attractive. I apologize for sounding so boorish. I'm just preoccupied, I guess. Now, what did you want to see me about?"

"Well, uh . . . actually I wanted to discuss three things: the Cable-X deal, the offer on *Fashion 1*, and the Pete Moore situation."

"Ahhh," Nelson sighed. "Sounds like a full agenda."

"Isn't it always? The Houston deal is all set up. Brenner squawked pretty loudly when I tried to change it to Monday, so I backed off. No sense antagonizing him over a little thing like that. Not yet, at least."

"Can we get back in time?" Nelson queried.

"Absolutely. When he demanded Saturday, I gave him your time parameters. He wasn't happy, but I squeezed a little, and it's set for first thing in the morning."

Nelson grinned. "You do that pretty well. Walk softly but carry a big stick, I mean."

"I try," Leggit said, pleased. "My office is finalizing some things this afternoon. I'll go over all the stats with you in the morning while we're flying down. It looks pretty solid."

"Fine. How early do we leave?"

"Well, I have to touch base with Brenner, but I'd say seven-thirty or eight would get us there in plenty of time."

"Sounds good, Dick. I appreciate your thoroughness. What's next?"

For a moment Dick Leggit hesitated, wondering. But then, feeling that all of his bases were well covered, he went ahead.

"Nelson, Multimedia upped their offer for *Fashion 1* today. They've made it incredibly attractive, and I told them that—"

"No, Dick."

"Nelson, don't let your emotions get in the way of sound judgment."

"Dick, this has nothing to do with my emotions. *Fashion 1* is not mine to sell. It's Angie's. It always has been, and always will be. That's the deal. Period. Now, you mentioned Pete?"

Leggit hesitated, but decided to continue pressing. "Nelson, it isn't going to be that easy. I sent out the signals, weeks ago. You wanted that deal in Nashville, and this is a trade option. Multimedia is responding to us, not vice-versa."

For a moment Nelson eyed his corporate attorney. When at last he spoke, his voice was calm, controlled. "Stop the deal, Dick. *Now.* Tell Nashville we've changed our minds, we're not interested. I mean it. I won't play with Angie's magazine."

"Nelson . . . ?"

"You mentioned Pete?"

Leggit, to calm himself, took a deep breath. This man might be young, he suddenly realized, but he let you know right off that he was in control. Totally.

"I know, Nelson," he finally said, temporarily dropping *Fashion 1*, "that Pete was right there with your grandfather when Armstrong Communications was founded. Even so, I'm worried about him and, well, about Armstrong Communications."

Nelson raised his eyebrows and cast a questioning glance at his attorney. "Go on," he said quietly. "I'm listening."

"Nelson, in today's world, Pete is an Achilles' heel to the entire organization. I don't want to sound callous or ungrateful for what he's done. But frankly, he's over the hill. My honest recommendation is that he be given an early retirement—with full benefits, of course. Such a course would be good for Pete, and it would certainly be in the best interests of Armstrong Communications."

Silently Nelson eyed his corporate attorney. The man was sincere, Nelson could tell that much. In fact, sincerity and good will were fairly dripping from him. Nelson thought then of something his grandfather had once said. "When a man tells another," the old man had counseled him, "that he is being frank or honest, then he usually isn't." Nelson almost grinned at the memory, but he controlled himself and spoke once again to Leggit.

"Is there any specific complaint?"

"Oh, I don't know about complaints. It's just that Pete takes so long to make decisions. He doesn't seem to grasp the fact that newspapers *make* news, not just report it. He's driving the junior editors and most of the reporters crazy. He simply has not kept pace with the age. That's why I recommend that we retire him."

"Thank you, Dick," Nelson said after a moment of thought. "You have expressed some thought-provoking things. And in fact, you've helped me make up my mind. Would you have Joyce give Pete a call? Have her ask him if it would be convenient for him to come up within the next thirty minutes. And Dick, I'd like you here when I talk with Pete."

For a moment Dick Leggit looked surprised, for he had not expected Nelson to agree so easily. But then the light of understanding lit his face, and he began to smile.

"I'll tell you something, Nelson. What the little people

around here say about you is true. Break it to them easy, but do it fast. No fooling around with suspense. You are an honest-to-goodness nice guy."

"Am I, Dick? Does a nice guy end a man's career when he's finally learned enough to really make a contribution? Particularly when that man has already given all he could give to the organization? Tell me, Dick. Is that what it means to be a nice guy?"

"Well, uh . . . I can see, Nelson, that your position is not easy. Leadership never is. But nevertheless, I'm certain that you are doing the right thing. Pete is no longer an asset to the *Daily News*."

"Perhaps he isn't, Dick," Nelson replied softly. "But if that is so, then maybe the process should be reversed. Did you know that Pete wasn't just there when the *Daily News* was founded?"

"What? I don't—"

"Dick, Pete founded it. Alone. He brought my grandfather in for capital—ten grand, I think. There were a few bad years, and old N.T. finally bought him out, because that was the only way it would work at the time. But the understanding between them, I've heard, was that it was only temporary, only on paper. Grandfather always said that the *Daily News* was Pete's."

"But that's the point, Nelson. It isn't, not any longer. Pete sold it for a fair price, it's now a huge daily, and though it's only a small part of Armstrong Communications, you've got to make some decisions regarding it. Pete can't. It's just gone past him. Why—"

Dick Leggit was interrupted by the buzzing of the interoffice telephone.

"Yes, Joyce?" Nelson asked, cradling the phone against his shoulder. "Already? Well, that's fine. Ask him to step in. And Joyce, would you come in as well? Thank you."

Nelson settled back in his chair, giving no indication that he noticed Leggit's smile, and waited. Seconds later the door opened and an older man entered, an aging man who normally had the sparkling eyes and bouncy step of a teenager, but who now looked as old as he was. Pete Moore, Nelson suddenly realized, knew full well why he had been called in. He had heard the rumors, rumors intentionally started, no doubt, by Dick Leggit's office, and he was ready.

Nelson returned Pete's smile, shook his hand, reintroduced Dick Leggit, and motioned for him to take a chair.

"Pete," Nelson started to say, when he was interrupted by the older man.

"Excuse me, Nelson, but before anything else is said, I'd like to make a statement. I reckon my years here have earned me that, at least."

"Yes, Pete, they certainly have. Please, go ahead. What's on your mind?"

"Nelson, I reckon you know as much about me and your grandfather as I do, so I'm not about to drag out old histories. Still, I've been with the *News* since day one, when it was a little ol' weekly news sheet.

"We've grown together, I reckon, the paper and me, and it's been good to us both. But now it seems that things have grown a little bigger than I thought they would. In fact, they've grown even bigger than me, and so I ought to step out of the way. I'd never want to hinder the growth of what I've fought so hard to establish.

"Now, I've heard the rumors about me getting the sack. I don't think old N.T., wherever he is, would like to see that happen. And frankly, neither would I. So it just won't! Nelson, don't take it personal, but as of today I'm resigning. I'm handing over my keys."

In the silence that followed, Nelson looked from Pete Moore to Dick Leggit and back again, noting the pleased look on Leggit's face. It was time, he suddenly decided, for him to take a stand. Hopefully, Dick would learn a lesson in the process.

"Joyce," he said quietly, turning to his secretary, "please see that the proper documents are drawn up showing that Pete Moore has resigned as and is no longer the Senior Editor of the *Daily News.*"

"Pete," Dick Leggit interrupted, arising and extending his hand, "we, all of us, are sorry to see you go. But may I say frankly and honestly that—"

"Dick," Nelson said softly and yet firmly, "sit down. Please."

Startled, Leggit looked at Nelson, started to object, recalled Nelson's tone of voice, thought better of saying more, and sat down.

"Joyce," Nelson continued, "have further documents drawn up, with each of us as witnesses, and over my signature, showing that Armstrong Communications hereby transfers full title and ownership of the local newspaper division of Armstrong Communications, specifically the *Daily News*, to the ownership of Mr. Peter Moore, and to his heirs and assignees, in perpetuity forever, for the total sum of $10,000, legal tender, payable in increments of $1,000 per annum for ten years, at no interest. Have additional documents drawn up showing that Pete is the new Senior Vice President of Armstrong Communications Corporation, the same position he held under my grandfather, and which position he vacated when I took over."

Pete Moore, halfway to his feet, sank slowly back into his chair, his face expressing his shock at the turn of events. Dick Leggit, in the other chair, gasped in disbelief. Then, following a brief pause, he spoke quickly.

"Nelson . . . gentlemen, it, uh—it appears that perhaps I have outlived my usefulness to your firm. It—uh—seems appropriate that you obtain legal counsel from someone—uh—some firm that can more easily accommodate your needs. Perhaps—"

"Dick," Nelson said softly, his voice sounding tired, "sit down and listen. You're a heck of an attorney, but I'm still president here. Decisions, you know, must ultimately be mine."

In the silence that followed, Nelson rose to his feet. Smiling, he took the hand of the still shocked Pete Moore.

"Pete," he said, gazing into the curiously young eyes before him, "Grandfather once told me that a business grows through employee loyalty. But he also said that no business was worth its salt if it couldn't give back. That's what I'd like to think that Armstrong Communications is trying to do with all of our people. As far as I'm concerned, it's why we're in business. I'll be proud to watch the *Daily News* continue to grow under your gifted leadership and hard-earned insight."

Turning then, Nelson stepped over to Dick Leggit, who had awkwardly arisen, and extended his hand to the man. "Dick," he said gently, quietly. "Joyce has my power-of-attorney, as you know, to conclude all of our dealings. If that's what you really want, we'll do it. However, it would be to our great advantage as a corporation, as well as to my own personal preference, if you would stay with us. There's no better attorney anywhere, and I know it! Nor do I have a finer friend. Armstrong Communications needs your legal expertise, and we need it badly.

"But, whatever you decide, I'd like you to drop by the house with your wife next week. Angie and I would love to get together with the two of you for dinner.

"Now," he said, speaking once more to both men, "if the two of you will excuse Joyce and me? We have to get some things ready for the bank."

With that, and with another smile, Nelson escorted his secretary from the room.

3

As Angela swiftly worked to clear her desk so that she could leave, she found that she could not shake the strange sense of being watched. It was there, as real and tangible as anything she had ever felt. It was also behind her, for she could feel it there. Quickly she spun about.

But there was no one — nothing — the glass wall of her high-rise office stared emptily back at her, a glass wall of windows that formed three sides of her exquisitely designed and decorated prison.

But there had been someone! She knew that there had been someone in her office with her. Someone besides that strange man. She had *felt* it! She had felt a sense of presence, a sense of warmth, a sense of overwhelming acceptance that was so foreign, so alien to anything that she had ever felt before, that it unnerved her. In fact, though the feeling was nonthreatening, it terrified her, and she had no idea of why, or of what to do about it.

Oh, why had she come to work? she asked herself. Why? Especially when she had known that she would be alone? For she was, totally and completely, alone! Nelson was out, one secretary was ill and the other had the day off, Hector and the rest of the staff were down in the gallery, and she was alone and all goose-bumpy with fear because someone, or something, was watching her. It was illogical, it was crazy, and yet it was true!

The chiming of the telephone jarred Angela back to reality, and with an intense feeling of relief that she could take the calls, she pushed the first of two blinking buttons.

"*F—Fashion 1*," she stammered. "May—may I help you? Speaking. Oh, Hector! I'm so glad you called. I—What? Uh . . . well, nothing, really. It's just that—that . . . oh, never mind. I'm just not feeling well. Now, how can I help you? Yes, I know she's very hot right now, but with our lead time she could be oversold by the time . . ."

For several seconds Angela listened in silence, smiling; then, with a firm ring of finality in her voice, she interrupted the caller. "Thank you, Hector, for your input. You're sweet. Let me sleep on it, and we'll discuss it Monday. And Hector, thank you especially for the call. You saved my life. Ciao."

The feeling of being watched was gone, apparently driven off by the interruption. With a sense of relief Angela took a deep breath, pushed the remaining blinking button, and answered.

"*Fashion 1*. Oh, hi, Joyce. The Mercedes isn't ready *yet*? You've got to be kidding! What is wrong with that mechanic? He promised me! And this is the chauffeur's day off, isn't it? I was afraid you'd say that. Friday is a terrible day around here. Tell me, is the El Dorado downstairs? Oh good, then I can use it. Listen, is Nelson back yet? Oh no! Well, be a doll and tell him when he gets in, will you? Tell him that I've taken the Caddy, and that I won't be riding with him. Thanks, Joyce. 'Bye."

With a sense of relief Angela hung up the telephone and sat back. The feeling, the sense of fear, was really gone, and she was certain that the intrusion of the telephone had done it. Those calls had pulled her back into her world, into the world of reality. But what was wrong? What was causing her to feel as she did?

For weeks she had found it almost impossible to keep her mind on her work. Instead, all she could think of was Nelson and the empty and lonely shell that her marriage to him had become. Why, she wondered over and over, had it once seemed so right when it was now so obviously wrong? How could she have made such a mistake?

Yet had it really been a mistake? she questioned, realizing as she did so that her mind was going in circles. She *had* loved him. She knew that. In fact, in some ways she still did, for whatever *that* was worth. He was a unique man, one of a kind, and she was certain that she would never find another like him, and would likely never marry again because of that. She had realized that the day she had met him, and it was still true. Nelson Armstrong was the *one* man in her life.

But that was part of the problem, part of the reason why she had finally become convinced that divorce was the only answer. His business dealings, his need for total control, had long since taken priority over her. She now felt like she was little more than an employee to him. His entire thought processes, day and night, were directed toward Armstrong Communications. And sadly, she admitted, she had done the same with *Fashion 1.*

Somehow their marriage had become a business, filled with shoptalk and little more. They were both ambitious people, both filled with the need to succeed, and both had. But somehow success had been accomplished at the expense of their relationship, of their love. Such a condition was far too painful for her to accept, to live with. Nor could she, any longer. Especially not after she had learned what she had about Nelson's duplicity, about his negotiations to sell *Fashion 1* without her knowledge or consent.

Yet with her decision to divorce him had come this . . . this warm, crawly feeling that she was being watched, that someone was always with her, observing her. Only each time the feeling had come she had been totally alone. There was no possible way for anyone to be watching her. And yet . . .

As she picked up her purse to leave, Angela thought again of the small packet that the strange man had given her. For an instant she considered taking it home, but then just as quickly she rejected the idea. With the awards banquet on Saturday night and all the other things she had going, there would be no time to examine it. No, it would wait until Monday.

Subconsciously turning toward her desk for a final glimpse of the packet, Angela was shocked to see nothing there. The desk was clean, its top cleared of all papers and other items, exactly as she always left it on Fridays. But—

The packet was *gone!*

Angela stared at her desk incredulously. It had been there. She knew it had! She had put it there herself. Only . . . where on earth had it gone?

As her mind scrambled to unravel the strange puzzle, Angela suddenly found herself wondering if perhaps the entire episode might not have happened at all. Was it possible that she had imagined it? There was no packet anywhere, that was certain. Was it all, the fears, the feeling of being watched, and the visit by the strange man, part of the same gigantic delusion?

Of course! That had to be the answer. There had been no man, there had been no packet, there had been nothing at all. The entire past four or five days had been filled with stress, an intense kind of pressure that her mind was reacting to. It was all quite simple. Stress was behind the whole thing. If she could get home, relax, and finalize the impossible situation with Nelson, then the fear and crazy imaginations would go away. It would be as simple as that.

Quickly Angela turned, secured the lock on her door, and walked out.

As the elevator descended to the studio level below, Angela briefly fluffed back her hair, her thoughts repeatedly dwelling on her strange encounter, and the fears that had besieged her. What was happening? she asked herself over and over. What was happening in her life? Could Nelson be behind it, Nelson with his total control? Was he somehow trying to drive her crazy so that she could not stop his planned sale of *Fashion 1*? Could that be it? It was certainly possible, for she was positive now that he did indeed plan to sell her out. There were too many rumors, too many hints, to think otherwise. But how could he have given her the fears? There was no way, no way . . .

When at last Angela walked into Gallery Three, Hector was busy with his camera and two new fashion models, getting stills for the October edition of the magazine. As she waited for him to finish, Angela suddenly thought of Hank, the security guard out front. If someone had been in her room, Hank would surely know about it. Quickly she picked up the telephone and called him. For a full two minutes she questioned him, and at last, after listening to his denials, she explained to him her experience with the strange man.

"Hank," she concluded, doing her best to be gentle with the aging security director, "I really don't know what to think about that guy in my room, but in a way it doesn't matter. We've simply got to be more careful! It's a crazy world out there, and this business especially is filled with kooks. Much of the time I'm alone with my secretary, Hank, and I need your help."

For a moment Angela listened to the sincere apology, and then she smiled, thanked the man, and hung up.

The photo session was just ending, and as the models and technicians dispersed, Hector picked up a package of photographs and brought them to her. "Wait'll you see these," he said excitedly. "Angela, they're incredible!"

Silently Angela took the portfolio and began looking through it, giving little more than a cursory glance to each of the photographs. Hector, anxiously awaiting her approval, finally verbalized his exuberance. "Aren't they marvelous? Doesn't he do absolutely fantastic work?"

When there was still no response from Angela, he spoke again. "Angela, it is by far the finest work that Marco has ever done. I'm serious about that."

Angela, still silent, reached the final print. Then, shuffling the photographs back together, she handed them back. "Yes, Hector," she said, smiling, "they *are* beautiful photographs, and no doubt they represent Marco's very best work. However, we can't use them in *Fashion 1.* They're too sexy."

"Too sexy!" Hector shouted, obviously upset. "How can you say that? Nothing can ever be *too* sexy!"

"These are, Hector. The expression on these girls' faces, their entire attitude, is wanton. In addition, Hector, you are shouting at me."

Instantly the man dropped his head, appalled at his own rudeness in the face of this woman who was the very source of his own living. "I'm sorry, Angela," he stated sincerely. "I didn't mean to shout. But the difference here is the whole point. Surely you agree with me on that. These are controversial, they are exciting, they are—"

"Not for us," Angela concluded with finality.

"Please, Angela," Hector pleaded, "be realistic. If we say no, then you know exactly what Marco will do. He'll turn right around and go to *C'est La Vie.* They'll build their whole Christmas issue around these photos. We can't afford to give them such a competitive edge!"

For a moment Angela stood silently, thinking. "You're probably right, Hector. We can't afford to let that happen."

Hector smiled, sensing a victory. He knew Angela, and he certainly knew how to get her to do what he wanted.

"How much does Marco want?" Angela suddenly asked.

"He says thirty thousand, but I know he'll let us have them for twenty-five. He likes you."

"He loathes me, Hector, because he respects me. And that has nothing to do with anything at all. This is business, period! Give him fifty."

"Fifty?" Hector shouted. "Why?"

"Because, my dear, when he takes fifty he'll never dare complain when we fail to use his layout."

"Angela!" Hector responded in shock, his face reflecting his genuine disbelief. "You *can't* be serious! Marco would never forgive us! He's got too much pride. He'll—"

"He'll take the money," Angela continued softly, "blow it all on coke, and be back here next week trying to sell us the outtakes. Now, make the arrangements for me, will you, please? It's our maid's day off, and I've got to get home."

"Have you talked to Nelson yet?" Hector suddenly asked, changing the subject.

Angela looked quickly at him. "No . . . no, I haven't."

"Angela, if what I have learned is—"

"Hector, those rumors are simply that. Rumors. They can't be true. Nelson would never do that to me."

"Well, it doesn't seem like him, I admit, but Leggit is something else again."

"That's true, Hector. But Nelson runs this corporation, and he's very protective of his position, not to mention his power. No, I think we'd better trust him until I can learn what he has actually done. After all, he *is* my husband, you know."

"Yes," Hector replied, looking away. "He is that."

"And, Hector," Angela continued, "I'll find out tonight. I'm going home early so that I can fix up something special."

"Ah-hah," Hector sighed, grinning knowingly. "No wonder you're in such a hurry."

Angela shook her hair back, dropped her head slightly, smiled demurely, and looked up at Hector through her long, dark lashes.

"Oui, mon cheri," she whispered throatily. "Je me rejouis de rentrer a la maison. Je suis tres excitée!"

Hector laughed outright. "For shame!" he declared, grinning. "And you think those photos are too sexy."

Then, growing suddenly serious, Hector took Angela's arm and looked directly into her eyes. "Angela," he stated sincerely. "I really admire your sense of right. I'm happy to do whatever you suggest. But we're close, you and I, and that's why I want you to understand that I know something's wrong, something besides the rumors. I'm not prying, but if you need to talk about it, then—"

"Hector, nothing's wrong."

Hector looked carefully at this woman who meant so much to him, gazing deeply into her eyes. "Honest Injun?"

"Honest Injun."

"Then I believe you. But Angela, when you're ready to talk about it, I'll be here. Remember that. And remember that I'm insanely jealous of Nelson. He married way over his head."

Angela, taken back by Hector's unexpected insight, tried to smile. When she couldn't, when her eyes started filling with tears, she turned quickly away.

"Thank you, Hector," she replied quietly, hoping that her deception was still at least partially effective. "You're very sweet."

Then, continuing her little charade, Angela attempted to joke with the man who had so wanted to marry her. "Besides, Hector," she continued, "you've no reason to be jealous. I only married Nelson for his money."

Turning back then, she gently squeezed Hector's hands and looked up at him. "I'll see you Monday. And Hector, you're forgiven for shouting at me."

Hastily then, to cover her lies as well as her surfacing tears, Angela turned and made her way back to the elevator. As it descended she opened her purse, reached in to get her compact, and—

Oh, no! With a startled gasp Angela looked down, fearing—knowing! And she was right. *It was there!* The packet, the small package that had vanished from her desk, was there, in her purse!

And then it came again, the warm, pulsing, frightening feeling of being watched, of being . . . loved. Spinning, Angela turned about in the elevator, confronting the walls of her tiny prison, as alone as she had ever been in her life, not alone at all, and very, very frightened!

4

As the elevator moved upward, Nelson stepped away from his secretary, looked down into her lovely green eyes, and smiled.

"Nelson," she said softly, calling him by his first name, "you were wonderful. I'm always amazed at how firmly and how sensitively you deal with those around you."

"Why, thank you, Joyce," Nelson answered sincerely. "I appreciate the compliment. However, in spite of how things looked, handling Dick Leggit is never an easy proposition. His mind is frighteningly fast. I'm just glad that he's a good man. In fact, after that little encounter, I think I could do with a shot of Perrier. Care to join me while I sign the statements?"

Joyce looked up, cocked one eyebrow, and spoke seductively. "Now, that," she purred, "is the kind of invitation I like."

Moments later the two stood in Nelson's office, facing each other with the desk between them, a positioning Nelson had carefully contrived. Now, though, as he looked at his secretary,

Nelson realized once again how beautiful, how desirable, and how available the woman was. But as he considered the obvious possibilities before him, his grandfather's words echoed in his mind.

"Son," the old man had said, "if a man doesn't have integrity in his marriage, you can bet there won't be much integrity in his business dealings. Why? Because that man is out of control!"

Now, as Nelson recalled those words, he began to wonder, for the first time, if maybe the old man had been wrong. After all, his grandfather had not been married to a woman like Angie; he had not been lonely; he had not had to deal with someone who was suddenly, for no justifiable reason, demanding a divorce.

Then Joyce began moving around the desk toward him, a smile playing across the beautiful features of her face. As she moved, her hair glistened delightfully in the early afternoon light, and Nelson realized that his resolutions were wavering. She was beautiful, she was desirable, and above all else, she wanted him. She—

But then, as always happened, Joyce's face suddenly became Angie's, and the spell was broken. With a shake of his head, Nelson lifted his mineral water and forced a smile onto his face.

"Joyce," he said, his voice husky with emotion, "here's to the best secretary and supporter of her boss in all the world. No matter what either of us feels right now, for your sake, as well as for mine, let's keep it that way."

Joyce, stunned by the abrupt change, turned quickly away. She was momentarily disappointed, but she was by no means defeated. Never in her entire life had she wanted someone so badly. And he would be hers, she vowed. Somehow in the near future she would—

"Good grief," Nelson exclaimed, glancing down at his watch, "I think I was supposed to meet Angie at two o'clock."

Smiling to herself, Joyce nodded. "That's right, Mr. Armstrong," she said sweetly. "Your wife called, and said she would be expecting you promptly at two, down in Studio III. She was especially insistent that you not be late."

"Then I'd better hurry, hadn't I?" Nelson said, smiling. "Joyce, be an angel and see that everything's locked up before you go to the bank. And remember, even though it's Saturday tomorrow, we still go to Houston. Someone will let you know the time."

Reaching out then, Nelson lightly touched Joyce's cheek. "You're a sweetheart," he said quietly. "I'm very grateful for all you do. Without you, this whole place would disintegrate."

Quickly, before his secretary could reply, Nelson left the room, entered the elevator, and descended toward the studio level, his mind whirling with emotions and his heart troubled with a dread he did not know how to deal with. In that frame of mind he encountered Hector, but Angela was nowhere to be found.

"I'm telling you, Nelson, your wife left well over an hour ago."

Hector tapped his pen impatiently against the desk, wondering what was going on. When Nelson didn't respond, Hector spoke again.

"She told me that the repairs on her Mercedes were still not complete, it was the chauffeur's day off, and that she was taking the El Dorado."

Without answering, Nelson stood staring at the wall, his insides churning with anger and frustration.

"Why?" he finally murmured. "Why is she doing this to me?" Then, speaking once more so that Hector could hear, he continued. "If you ever figure that woman out, Hector, tell me about it, will you? Of course, something may have come up, and . . ."

Briefly he paused, and then, smiling, he continued. "Yes, that's it. Something's come up. Angie always has good reasons for what she does. She's a remarkable woman. I'll see you Monday, my friend."

Without waiting for a reply from the surprised Hector, Nelson turned and walked quickly out of the door.

Moments later he sat silently in his Lamborghini, waiting while the parking attendant cleaned the windscreen. Still upset, he drummed his fingers on the steering wheel, impatient to get home and to confront his wife.

Finally, as he pulled away from the parking terrace, Nelson noticed a man, a lone gardener, spading the earth beneath some shrubs. He debated about whether or not he should take a minute for some small talk, for Angela had certainly soured his mood. But with an effort he forced his mind away from her, braked to a stop, rolled down his window, and waved the man over.

"Floyd," he said, offering a handshake, "how are you getting along?"

"Great, Nelson," the man replied, grinning. "How're things with you and Mrs. Armstrong?"

"Oh, you know—never a dull moment. Say, I've been meaning to ask you about that hunting trip next fall. Do you have me scheduled in?"

"You bet, Nelson. Roy Jacklin and I were talking about it the other night. By the way, that mulie you shot? Down in the Henries? The taxidermist called and the mount will be ready next week."

"Great! But Floyd, *I* didn't shoot him, and you know it. You did. You've got to stop giving me credit. We both know who the real hunter is."

Both men grinned, and Floyd shuffled his feet uncomfortably.

"By the way," Nelson suddenly asked, "are you still moonlighting in that carpet business?"

"Yeah—Roy and I are still doing it. Funny thing about that, too. Bad as the economy's been, Roy and I can't lay the stuff fast enough."

"You know why, don't you? It's because you're honest. People know that you're not going to burn them. Say, not to change the subject, but how's Kathy doing? Has she had that new baby yet?"

"Any day, Nelson. She sure hopes so, anyway. She's so big that when she stands sideways she causes a total eclipse, and she's mighty uncomfortable."

"I'll bet she is," Nelson responded, chuckling. "What's it going to be?"

"Are you kidding? It's a boy, Nelson. Period!"

"Right. I'm with you, Floyd. I'm betting on a boy." Then, reaching into his wallet, Nelson pulled out a hundred-dollar bill.

"Floyd, I know how those eighty percent insurance policies work, and even though it's a little early, please accept this as a baby gift from Angie and me. We wish you both the very best."

"But Nelson, I can't—"

"What do you mean you can't? Just you remember that carpet deal you gave me. See you next week, Floyd. Give Kathy a hug for me."

As he drove away, Nelson thought of Floyd Bird, and of the numerous others who worked for him. All of them, he knew, were great people. And happy, too. Sure, they were struggling with one thing or another, but that didn't change anything. They were still happy. And Floyd and Kathy were even going to have another baby. He was thrilled for them, of course, but he couldn't help but think of his and Angie's own childlessness. What was wrong? he asked himself again. What had happened to his marriage, to his happiness? What had come over Angie, that she had turned so cold, so distant? And why on earth was she suddenly demanding a divorce?

He didn't know the answer, but he was determined to find out. In fact, as soon as he got all of his reports out of the way, and as soon as he got the next couple of out-of-town trips behind him, he was going to get Angie away for a weekend so he could find out. One way or another, Nelson determined that he was going to restore happiness to his marriage.

5

Angela, seated at her dressing table, was surrounded by a myriad of imported perfumes, eye-pencil sticks, lipsticks, sable-bristle brushes, designer scarves, and fashion magazines that she studied intently and that were the sum of her professional competition. As the radio played a soft, contemporary song, however, she ignored them, mechanically brushing her luxurious dark hair, thinking.

She had lied to Hector. She had lied to him when she *never* lied to anyone, and she felt terrible about it. And strangely, though she had lied about the rumors, she had not really lied about them at all. The *real* lie had been about the failure of her marriage. If she had admitted to Hector that what he suspected was true, then he would know. And that was what she had been trying to avoid. It hurt to admit that she had not been able to cope with Nelson's control of her life, and it hurt especially to admit it to someone who was as close to her as Hector was. The lie was even more disconcerting to her because she knew that, by the first of the week, Hector would know anyway. He would know when she and her attorney announced the divorce to the press.

Angela thought then of the strange sense of presence she had felt, and of the terrible fear it had engendered. There was just no reason for it, no reason at all.

As she considered it, she found herself wondering, almost, if she might be losing her sanity, approaching a nervous breakdown. Could it be the result of the tremendous stress she was under? That would be enough, she was certain, to drive anyone crazy, for from the things she had read, the same types of stress had done so to plenty of others.

But *no,* she *wasn't* crazy, and she knew it. The strange feelings of warmth and of being watched were real, not simply figments of her imagination. The small packet in her purse was enough to convince her of that. And though she didn't know what was bringing her fears on, she was certainly going to find out.

Now, though, as she worked the base for her makeup onto her face, Angela forced herself to relax, to empty her mind until she could see only herself before her.

She was pleased, of course, with the image in the mirror. In fact, she smiled at her reflection with pride, knowing that she was attractive, stylish, poised, and that she had somehow achieved a certain amount of class and perfection, characteristics that took effort, invention, and hours of intense study.

Her eyes were a brilliant blue—penetrating bold, and veiled with thick, dark lashes. She also had luxuriant dark hair, which she usually wore smartly up off her neck, gracing her face with stunning sophistication. She had a perfect nose which made her look well-bred, and that, plus her widow's peak, were gifts for which she would thank her mother forever. Of course there were other things her mother had given her as well, things such as her temper and her insecurity, which were nowhere near so becoming. Still, she was working on them, and usually they were safely out of sight.

Obviously pleased with her appearance, Angela smiled. The smile lasted only briefly, however, for she began to reflect upon the irony of her beauty. Sometimes, she felt, it was more a curse than anything else. She had the capacity, she knew, to transform herself through the artistic use of makeup and clothing from an ordinary creature into a stunningly beautiful woman. But the process of doing so seemed at times overwhelming. Every night, no matter how late the hour, there was the almost ritualistic cleansing process. The emulsions, the moisturizers, the creams, and in the morning the hot and cold packs and the hand massage, being careful to always rub upward instead of down, lest untimely aging should occur. It all took so much time.

Briefly Angela wondered how much these rituals had impaired the closeness she had once felt with her husband. To a certain extent, she knew, they had, for Nelson had hinted as much on one or two occasions. Yet Angela realized that, in spite of their differences, he was too much of a gentleman, too much in control, to mock her or persecute her because of her efforts to maintain her beauty.

And then Angela thought of something else, something Nelson had said one morning as he watched her putting on her face. "Too much concentrating on outer beauty," he had said, "leaves a person with too little time to develop inner beauty."

At the time Angela had simply become angry and defensive, but now she found herself wondering, worrying. Had she indeed become a shell, a beautiful, artificial shell? And in fact, had her selfish concerns also helped turn her marriage into a shell, a shell that was now breaking like an empty egg?

But no! That had nothing to do with it at all! The problem, primarily at least, was Nelson's. He was the one who had begun excluding her. He was the one who wouldn't talk, who wouldn't share. It was his control, his total control of all things, including herself, that so infuriated her. In spite of his gentle kindness, which she had come to believe was a facade, he had no respect for her as a person, as an equal. The latest example was his attempted sell-off of her magazine. Why, he had not only not discussed it, he had never even had the decency to mention that he was thinking of it. And *that* was why the marriage was over!

For a moment Angela's mind drifted aimlessly, angrily, and suddenly she thought again of the day when she had first seen her husband. What a contrast, she thought, between that day and this. And yet they had been much the same—days of momentous decision, with her entire future hanging in the balance. The difference was that then she had been giving control to another, while now she was taking it back. And that alone made all the difference in the world.

Once more her mind went back to the weekend at the ski lodge, and she felt again the thrill and excitement that had been hers when first she and Nelson had touched, had embraced, had kissed. She had been in ecstasy, and she had known almost immediately that Nelson was feeling the same. They were both falling—or growing—into love.

Yet strangely, that kiss had ended it. When they parted she had not seen him again, and there had been no further contact for several months. In fact, Angela had almost put Nelson Armstrong out of her mind. Almost.

Of course she had been busy with her struggling new magazine, *Fashion 1*, and had had little time to think of anything else. It was a good magazine, she knew, and she and Hector, her best friend and erstwhile suitor, by scrimping and cajoling and manipulating and pushing, had finally lasted beyond the difficult second year and could see success glowing in the future.

Then had come the offer to buy, an offer from a nameless, soulless communications conglomerate, an offer that she had ignored. That offer had been followed by another, still another, and yet a fourth, each one more insistent and each a little more difficult to turn down.

Yet Angela had continued to ignore them, and for weeks nothing else had occurred. Finally, just when she and Hector had decided that the threat was past, her door had opened one day, and into her life again had walked Nelson Thurgood Armstrong III. He, it turned out, was president of the nameless, soulless communications conglomerate she had been ignoring.

Angela was certain that the expression on her face must have shown as much shock as his, for neither had realized that they were dealing with the other.

For a few moments they had simply visited, and both had felt the old chemistry building between them. At length, though, Nelson had brought up the offers he had made for

Fashion 1, explained them, and they had both laughed over the fact that Angela had ignored them. Then Nelson had improved his most recent offer even more.

Angela was momentarily stunned, but finally stammered out her response. "I have to admit, Nel—uh—Mr. Armstrong, that your offer is very tempting . . ."

"*Nelson*, Angie."

Angela smiled. "Of course. Nelson. But you must understand that *Fashion 1* is simply not for sale."

"Well," Nelson responded, "make me a counteroffer."

"Nelson, it isn't a question of money. This magazine is me. All of my life has been a preparation to create it, and I finally have. It's more than a business—it's my baby."

Nelson gazed silently into Angela's eyes for such a long time that she became very uncomfortable, and at last she looked away. Only then did Nelson respond.

"I understand what you're saying, Angie, and I'm very much taken with what you have done. But listen, even babies need to grow. Yours is no exception. I have the distribution and marketing network already established that would permit you to go national, even international, within a year at the very outside. Think of it, Angie. You'd be influencing the fashion consciousness of women from Acapulco to Cairo, from Anchorage to the Riviera."

For a long moment Nelson paused, watching as his words tumbled around in her mind. Then he continued. "Angie, I do my best to buy talent, not properties. All of our market analyses indicate that you are the top young fashion expert in the country. I personally accept that opinion without question. If you come with us, you keep your entire organization, you remain publisher, and I guarantee that you will retain total editorial control. Now, what do you say?"

Again the two gazed into each other's eyes, and Angela found herself thinking, crazily, more about the soft blueness of his eyes than about his more than generous offer. But—but . . .

"I'm sorry, Nelson," she declared, her mind suddenly firm. "I'm very flattered by your offer, but I can't sell."

"Final word?"

"Absolutely!"

"Well," Nelson drawled, "you can't blame a guy for trying. If you ever change your mind . . . ?"

"I'll call," Angela replied, standing.

Nelson then stood and extended his hand in finality. At that moment Angela thought about mentioning skiing, didn't, and then he was out the door and gone, leaving her feeling more lonely than she had ever felt, more empty than she would ever have dared to admit.

Why had she said no? she anguished to herself. The offer was incredible, but even more important than that was the chance such a position would give her of being near him, even *with* him. But—

"Excuse me!" The door had opened slightly, and Nelson was standing with his head poked crookedly inside, grinning.

"If you won't sell," he drawled, "I have a better idea. Let's get married and merge."

Even now, after all this time, Angela smiled when she recalled the suddenness of the proposal, and the thrill that had surged through her as she had almost instantly accepted it. The marriage, which came several months later, had been storybook-like, the honeymoon to Nassau in the Bahamas had been beyond belief, and for the first year so had their marriage. They were the perfect couple, and everyone who came near them could recognize as much.

But then something changed, something subtle, and she and Nelson began to drift silently apart. They spent longer and longer hours in their separate offices, and the business trips for each of them became more frequent and of longer duration. In addition, their conversations with each other grew shorter, less frequent, and of only a surface nature, and suddenly, just a few weeks ago, Angela had realized that it was over.

Of course, Nelson had been aghast when she had first mentioned divorce, for in his opinion there was nothing wrong. And to this point in time, no matter what she said, he still refused to discuss it. As far as he was concerned they were married, had made a commitment to each other, and that was that!

Then had come the rumors concerning the secret sale of *Fashion 1*, along with a half-dozen other properties under the Armstrong Communications umbrella. At first she had tried to ignore them, but things, little things really, had started adding up, and soon she could no longer close her eyes.

In a strange way it all made sense, too. It was part of Nelson's mania about winning. If she left, taking her magazine with her, then he would lose control. It was apparent that he felt he could not let that happen. Thus the sale. And thus too her decision that she and her magazine, in its entirety, were taking a walk.

But Nelson refused to discuss it, and . . . and . . . well, the sense of being watched had come within hours of her decision, long before she had spoken of it with anyone. Therefore, what could it be? What could possibly be giving her such eerie feelings? She didn't know, but one way or another, she had to find out!

Her face at last was perfect, so the next thing to determine was what she should wear for dinner and the confrontation with Nelson. There were hundreds of possibilities in her wardrobe, but as Angela mentally sorted through her clothes, only two or three specific outfits came to mind.

Quickly she considered the effect each would have on Nelson, and in short order two had been eliminated. The third, a dress, was perfect for what she wanted it to do. It was an innocent pale blue, and with a short string of tiny pearls and lapis, she would create the effect she wanted—innocent, childlike, almost down-home, and most definitely not contrived. Now, if she could only find it in the maze of her wardrobe.

Reaching over, Angela turned up the radio slightly. Then, with a final toss of her hair, she stood and turned to go into her wardrobe, the fears and memories of the past hours and days now well behind her, the resolutions concerning her future solidly made.

But then she stopped, staring, while her eyes bulged and the bile of fear choked off her throat! At last came the scream, a hopelessly lost, crescendoing tremor of sound, filled with all the loneliness and terror that had built up within her, filled too with the horror of the present unknown.

For there, hanging neatly on her dressing stand, looking for all the world like she had put it there herself, hung the blue dress she had only seconds before decided that she would wear. On the dress, draped over it exactly as she would have placed it, was her pearl and lapis necklace. And too, on the floor before the dress, lay the little packet, the packet that somehow kept appearing in all the wrong places, the packet that somehow would not leave her alone.

And then again she knew that somewhere behind her, beside her, beneath her, or above her, someone watched, someone cared.

Angela screamed, long and loud, and in the midst of her scream merciful blackness came and wrapped her in its soft gentle arms and quietly carried her away.

6

Nelson T. Armstrong, his body and mind tense with frustration, held to the inside lane of the freeway. In exasperation he flashed his lights once again, quietly denouncing those who seemed to always poke along, claiming ownership of the passing lanes. His grip on the wheel tightened as finally he depressed the horn. Then deliberately he pulled his Lamborghini to within just a few feet of the slower car in front of him. That vehicle, an old Chevy, at last moved over, and in an instant Nelson's accelerator was pushed to the floor and the Countach S screamed forward.

Ahead the freeway was relatively clear, and so Nelson kept the pedal depressed as he watched the tachometer needle climb through six-six, six-seven, six-eight. The thrust was incredible, and as he thrilled to the pressure of his body against the seat he thought of how many times he had done this and of how even now he was not used to it.

Now he was in fourth, the tach was climbing again, the V-12 behind his head was snarling like a thing alive, and his speed was well above 120 miles per hour. There was a long curve ahead, a gentle curve to the left that was about thirty degrees. It was a curve that might normally give one pause, but he did not slow down at all. Rather, he shifted into fifth and watched again as the tach began its new ascent—six-nine, seven, seven-one—

And then he was into the curve with two cars flashing behind him almost as if they were driving in reverse. His hands rolled the wheel a few inches to the left, the nose changed course instantly, flatly, and the loading on his body switched to immense lateral pressure. His rib cage was pressed against the side of the seat, and he could feel the car body tugging against its tires. Still the tach climbed, and with the throttle wide open he came out of the curve at 7500 RPM, a flat 184 miles per hour.

For a moment he held his speed, feeling the exhilaration and sense of power, savoring the excitement of gambling with fate, and even enjoying the fear that was a hollow emptiness in the pit of his stomach. The dotted line stretching before him had become a steady ribbon of white, undulating and slithering past; the guardrails were a constant featureless blur, and the grass in the median, new and green before the onslaught of summer heat, was a solid, verdurous river to his left.

Nelson's palms were slippery with perspiration and his breathing was shallow, yet his control of the machine was gentle, very nearly perfect, and he was grinning. He wondered at that, wondered at the almost sensual pleasure he found in such a dangerous situation. But then he laughed softly, knowing that it had always been so.

As he considered that, he wondered if that, in fact, had been the reason for his becoming attracted to Angie. Of all the women he had known, she was the most exceptional, the most unusual, the most difficult to control, the most potentially dangerous. She was also the only woman he had ever wanted to marry, the only woman he had ever grown to love.

So why, he asked himself angrily, was she asking for a divorce? What was wrong with the woman? Sure, they had grown a little distant. That was because they had both become so immersed in their respective businesses. But that was no reason for her to toss in the towel. And now she was getting so petty that she had made an appointment with him and then had purposely broken it. Such a course was silly, it was childish, and it was definitely not like Angie!

In frustration Nelson pushed again on the accelerator, angry, demanding more from the machine than it was already giving him. Then—then a sensation that was entirely new came to him, an eerie feeling that brought a slight chill to his body. Drawing in his breath he held it for an instant, then quickly he glanced to his right, almost expecting to see someone seated there, almost anticipating the look of kindly patience in the eyes that he could feel boring into him.

The seat of course was empty, and as Nelson realized that, as he realized what he had just done, as the breath wheezed out of his body, the fear in the pit of his stomach raced through his every nerve. He was totally shaken, more frightened than he had been in years. Not of the feeling, not of the unknown sense of presence he had felt. That was normal. He knew of gremlins, mental hiccups that occurred under stress. That he understood. That he accepted. What bothered him was that he, Nelson Armstrong, had, for a moment, lost control. For an instant he had allowed his foolish fears to dictate his actions. No one paid attention to gremlins, and most especially he didn't. Yet he had, and therein was a weakness in his emotional fiber, a weakness in what, to the best of his memory, Freud had called his id, his subconscious mind. And that weakness, that unexpected loss of control, was what had really terrified Nelson Thurgood Armstrong.

Filled with inner turmoil, he eased off the gas, drifting for a moment as his heart and breathing and racing mind slowed to a pace more nearly normal. Then, forcing a smile onto his face, he began shifting down, slowing to the sixty-mile-per-hour crawl of the traffic ahead of him.

For a moment or two he held even alongside a silver Audi 5000, flashed his radiant and well-practiced smile at the gorgeous blonde who was sitting alone at the wheel, and watched her reaction, first to him, then to his incredible car, and then to him again. And she was like all the others. By the third glance her face was reflecting, even magnifying, his own smile, so that he knew he had not lost the old charm. He and the Countach were obviously a winning combination.

In his mind he thought of what the woman was seeing, and as he surged on past her and sped forward through the traffic he couldn't help but wonder. "Angie," he said aloud, "why can't I do that to you? What on earth have I done that has so alienated you? I'm no different than I've always been! I've been faithful, and I've tried to be thoughtful. So why are you trying to destroy what we have? You know, woman, that you almost make me want to . . ."

Ahead of him Nelson could see a new fire-mist-colored Toronado, and from the back it looked like another beautiful woman was behind the wheel. He was not certain that she was beautiful, of course, but it had been his experience that gorgeous women almost always drove gorgeous cars.

As he moved forward to get a better view of the woman in the Toronado, Nelson thought for a moment of his wife and of the growing distance between them. His thoughts then leaped to Joyce, his secretary, and in his mind he could see her face, her figure, and he could hear her low, throaty voice as she proclaimed her obvious desires for him.

For a moment he felt bitterness that he had never taken advantage of the unmistakable opportunities she had presented. If his marriage to Angie was over, and she at least was certain that it was, then Joyce was right, and he had been all kinds of a fool. In the name of integrity he had avoided Joyce and all the other women who had made themselves available to him, and all along it had actually been done in the name of stupidity!

Again he glanced at the woman in the Toro, which was still ahead of him. Perhaps, he thought, she was the answer. Perhaps the best thing he could do would be to find an unknown woman. Or three, or maybe even ten. What could it possibly hurt?

Nelson's mind went again to his car, to the metal symbol of power that was wrapped around him. For just an instant then he accelerated, not heavily, but smoothly, feeling the power of the engine beside him.

The Pirelli P-7 tires gripped the surface of the freeway easily —there was no spinning and no rear-end drifting—and as he felt for a few seconds the zero-to-one-hundred-mph-in-twelve-seconds acceleration of the Countach, all other thoughts left his mind.

The ride of the Lamborghini was firm, knobbly and jiggling and constantly giving him a feeling of intense communication with the road. Some who had ridden with him did not enjoy the tightness of the ride, but they were after ease and convenience. He was after control, which the Countach offered plenty of.

Of course the Lamborghini had cost him, there was no doubt of that. By the time it had been shipped over from Italy and had been finished to meet U.S. specifications, the cost had run a little over $140,000. And that was a bundle to pay for any car! Still, it was an incredible vehicle, and so with the speed and power he was a winner in all ways. Besides, as his grandfather had always said, it was better to buy the best and only cry once. And that he had obviously done.

With a start he realized that he had pulled alongside the woman in the Toro, and before he had even glanced her way he knew she was giving him the once-over. She had obviously seen him coming up in her rearview mirror, for she was already smiling, her dark eyes sparkling with intrigue that was as easy for him to see as was the sparkle in the fire-mist paint of her Toro.

Again he flashed his smile, and as the woman responded even further, he was struck by her dusky beauty. Spanish, he thought. She had to be at least partially Spanish.

For a moment he held even with her, and as he did so he felt his pulse quickening. She was indeed gorgeous, as he had known she would be. In a way her smile was like Angie's, more expressive and breathtaking than—

Blast! Angie again! Always he thought of Angie. But no more! At least no more today. If she wanted to make a fool of him in front of Hector and the others, that was fine. He was about to turn the tables, to show her that he was no longer wrapped up in a tiny package and dangling from her fingers. Angela, it seemed, was bent on ruining his life, and now he was ready to start throwing a few wrenches into hers. And the first wrench was sitting in the Toro just a few feet away, smiling at him.

Nelson smiled again and was just ready to make a signal to the woman indicating that he wanted to meet her, when a car pulled in front of him traveling just a little slower than he was.

He hit his brakes and cursed as he watched the woman pulling ahead. For a moment the slower traffic penned him in, dragging him down, and he grew even more anxious. But then a slight opening appeared in the lane to the right of him, and almost without thinking he checked over his shoulder, shifted down, snapped his foot from the clutch to the accelerator, and started to spin the wheel to the right. But at that moment the chills began racing up and down his spine again, and his reaction, instantaneous, was to tromp the accelerator as he sought with his eyes for some hidden danger.

Instantly there was a tremendous blast from an air horn, and as he glanced into his rearview mirror he was shocked to see, almost right on top of him, a diesel tractor-trailer. With a sickening sensation he realized that it was coming fast, too fast, and that there was no way, no way on earth, that a collision would be avoided. Instinctively he shrank, almost pulling into himself, his muscles tensing as he awaited the tearing shrieking sound of metal grinding on metal, of soul-wrenching pain as the metal and fiberglass fabric of his beloved Lamborghini tore him apart.

7

The phone was ringing. Somewhere the telephone was ringing—on and on and on and on. That miserable lazy maid! Where was she? Answering telephones was part of her responsibility.

And then memory returned, totally, and Angela opened her eyes in terror, not certain of what she would see, but positive that there would be something, someone . . .

But there was no one. The dressing room was empty, and except for the ringing of the telephone, all was silent. Struggling to her feet, Angela staggered toward the source of the incessant ringing. Just as she reached it, however, the clamor stopped and she found herself in the midst of a silence broken only by her ragged breathing. Even the radio was silent.

But wait! The radio couldn't be silent! She had left it on. She had even turned it louder so that she could enjoy the song it had been playing. Yet now it was off, and that was impossible.

For a moment Angela stood, holding her head in her hands,

wondering if the drink she had consumed had been drugged. Nelson might do that, she thought, but he hadn't been there.

The dress! What about the dress? Wheeling around, Angela stared at her dressing stand, her empty dressing stand, where a few moments before she had clearly seen her blue dress. Yet now the stand was empty, the packet was not on the floor, and she knew it could not be so.

Running, almost stumbling, Angela reached the door, unlocked it, and ran into the hall, yelling for either her maid or the butler. Yet the sound of her voice rang hollowly through the empty house, and Angela knew that she was alone. They had gone, at her instructions and with her permission, and she was alone in her terror-filled home.

Quickly she reentered her dressing room, and after a few moments of searching she found the dress, just where she had hung it nearly a year earlier when she had purchased it. The dress had not been moved, the tags were still in place, and now she knew.

It was drugs. It had to be! Nelson had somehow drugged her, and he was going to do something to her when he got home. That was it! That must be it!

"Well, let him try," she stormed. "If he thinks he can get away with that, he's in for one giant surprise!"

Quickly Angela removed the tags and slipped into the blue dress, noticing as she did that it was a little loose. Losing weight, she thought abstractedly, and not even trying to. Something strange was indeed going on.

Five minutes later, fully dressed, Angela glanced at the clock. Then, picking up the telephone, she dialed her maid's number.

"Helen," she said quickly, "I know I told you to take the rest of the afternoon off, and I'm sorry to do this, but is there any way you could come back for an hour or so and help me with dinner? You did? Oh dear. Well, do that then. By all means you go and do it. No, I'll be fine. I'll see you in the morning. 'Bye."

For a moment Angela stood silently, deep in thought. But then suddenly she smiled. She would cook the dinner herself, and let Nelson know that she had done so. If he was drugging her, he would surely realize that she could just as easily drug him. Such a thought would make him nervous, and that would just as surely show on his face and in his lack of appetite. Yes, the idea was perfect, and she was certain that it would work.

And so, with a firm step, she turned and entered the kitchen, determined to cook a meal that Nelson would never forget. After such a meal, she felt certain, he would be willing to rationally discuss the procedures for them to obtain a divorce.

8

For a moment Nelson wondered where he was. His hands, the primary objects in his field of vision, were lying in his lap, while directly above them a steering wheel was rolling gently to the left. The engine was roaring softly behind him, the guard-rails outside were slipping past in an even cadence, and—and then with startling clarity it all came back, Nelson instinctively braced for the impact with the diesel, and he grabbed the wheel as he did so.

Yet there was no impact, no horn, no squealing of tires, nothing except the subdued roar of the Lamborghini's engine.

Quickly Nelson glanced in his mirror, and the shock turned to a hollow feeling in the pit of his stomach as he saw, easily a full hundred yards behind him, the swiftly receding image of the huge truck.

But how, he wondered? How had he avoided the collision? How had he gotten so far ahead of the truck? Where was the woman in the Toro, and above all, what on earth was going on?

Suddenly he thought of how close he had come to dying, and as his mind grasped that idea his hands started to shake and he broke into a cold sweat. He had rarely in his life considered the possibility of death, and his sudden brush with it forced an entirely new galaxy of thoughts into his mind, thoughts that whirled around in chaotic disarray.

Thoroughly shaken, Nelson turned the wheel and braked to a stop on the shoulder of the freeway. As the car slowed and at last was still, he had the feeling that he was asleep and in the midst of a dream, a nightmare that had recurred through the years wherein he was floating somewhere, unable to touch anything and unable to gain control of himself. Yet this was no dream, no nightmare, at least it wasn't one that had occurred while he was asleep. For he wasn't. He was as awake as he had ever been, and as thoroughly frightened, as well.

For long moments he was utterly still, feeling the Lamborghini idling gently beneath him, and yet ignoring it as he gazed unseeing across the rolling hills and into the distance.

What had happened? he asked himself over and over again. What could possibly have happened? How could he have been so close to an accident, blacked out, and regained consciousness long moments later, completely unscathed and in an entirely different location? It did not make sense. It made no kind of sense at all!

As his rational mind slowly took control, Nelson found himself going back over the events of the past few moments, sifting them, analyzing them, doing his best to examine them in the cold clarity of emotional daylight. But no matter how he twisted and turned things, no matter what forms of mental gymnastics he forced his mind through, he could not avoid the inescapable conclusion that was staring him in the face.

No matter what he had been thinking concerning either Angie or the woman in the Toronado, no matter how well or how poorly he had been driving his own car, and no matter how real or unreal had been the sensation of another presence in his car, something else, something beyond his comprehension, had occurred. Something, or perhaps someone, totally outside of himself, had taken control of his car and had, very probably, saved his life!

He recalled then a particular psychology lecture at the university where the professor had delved at length into the unconscious, the psychoanalytic Freudian id, discussing its latent and repressed functions, and using as a portion of his proof the postulations of one Georg Gruddek, who taught that men were "lived" or controlled by forces outside of themselves.

How Nelson had battled against that nonsense, explaining to the instructor, as well as to the rest of the class, first that the idea of anything mental that was not also conscious was absurd and in defiance of logic, second that he and all others were masters of their own actions, and that through will power alone could a person control himself, his thoughts, feelings, actions, and emotions. Of course he had not convinced the professor, but he had won an "A" for his efforts, and he had, most definitely, convinced himself.

Now, for the first time in his adult life, he was wondering. He was really wondering if a man *was* always in control, and the very doubt in his mind frightened him. It was crazy! Maybe *he* was crazy. But he was also, despite that big diesel, alive!

As Nelson once again thought of that, he started to shake, a natural reaction to what he had just been through. Instantly his entire body was bathed in a cold sweat, and he chilled with the growing realization that there were things he did not know, situations that just might not be controllable or explainable in rational terms.

As he thought of that, Nelson suddenly thought of Angie, and instantly a warning flag fluttered across his mind. Was it possible? he asked himself. Could she have been behind what he had just been through? Obviously, the answer could be yes. She had set him up for the two o'clock appointment and goodness only knew what else. Somehow she could also have done this. She was certainly intelligent enough to have set it up. But no, she wouldn't have done it. She was capable of anger, and she had a wild temper, but she'd never do anything like that. No, it had to be someone else, something—

What if it was someone outside of either of them, someone who wanted them out of the way? Offhand he could think of no one, but over the years he had made some pretty shrewd deals, and the idea of revenge was a powerful force in some folks' minds. Such people might believe that if they could get him or Angie out of the—

Angie!

For an instant Nelson felt the stab of fear, not for himself but for his wife. If all this was true, then she might indeed be in danger, and have no knowledge of it at all.

Slamming his foot viciously against the clutch pedal, Nelson shifted the transmission into low, popped the clutch, and shoved the accelerator against the floor. The engine whined with wicked force, the tires spun wildly, and with a spraying of gravel and a terrible emptiness in his heart Nelson roared off down the freeway toward his home.

9

Angela, in the kitchen, heard her husband enter the house. Resisting an impulse to go to him, to greet him, to tell him of her fears, she turned to her hastily recalled houseboy, gave him further instructions for the table, and then continued with her own tasks.

Suddenly, however, she was aware of Nelson's presence in the room behind her. With all her heart she wanted to turn and face him, to confront him. She wanted to—

"Angie, are you okay?"

The voice was sincere, and she knew it. It always was. That was one of Nelson's greatest attributes. He was sincere; he cared. If only it had applied, ever, to her.

Slowly Angela turned around and faced her husband. "I'm fine," she said, smiling falsely. "Shouldn't I be?"

"Uh . . . yes," Nelson responded, a grin of relief spreading across his face. "You should be. But something strange happened to me a few minutes ago, and I got worried about you."

"Worried? You? About me? I can't believe it! You've *never* worried about me. But no, Nelson, nothing has happened to me. Nothing at all! I'm perfectly fine."

"There's an awful lot of sarcasm in your voice, Angie. I don't —"

"How perceptive!"

"Angie, what is the —"

"Come on, Nelson. Stop playing your games. I know what you're trying to do, and it isn't going to work."

"Good. I'm glad to hear that it won't. That should save me a lot of trouble. By the way, if you decide to tell me *what* it is that won't work, I'd be delighted to know."

Angela smiled again, sweetly, brightly. "I'll tell you, Nelson. When I'm ready. I'll also tell you what I'm going to do about it. Now dinner will be ready shortly, if you'd care to wait in the dining room."

Nelson looked carefully at his wife, decided that he would wait to pursue whatever it was she was talking about, turned, and left the room.

Angela, her smile gone from her face, turned again to the stove, where she viciously attacked the mashed potatoes, with visions of Nelson's grin filling her mind.

A little later, in their dining room, the couple sat silently ignoring each other as the houseboy served the meal Angela had prepared. Both were inordinately polite, thanking the boy for his services, and each ate carefully, appropriately, and very little.

Nelson broke the silence only once when he complimented Angela on the wonderful meal. Angela, watching her husband carefully, smiled in response but did not speak. Finally, though, when they were almost finished eating, she broke through the again-present wall of silence between them.

"Anything new on the Cable-X deal?" she asked, watching his eyes carefully.

"Possibly," Nelson replied quietly. "I should know more by next week."

Again the silence closed in around them, becoming strained

and intense. Angela, watching her husband through her thick lashes, wondered if she had detected any guilt, any sign of culpability. But she could not tell. True, he had eaten little, but that might mean anything, or it might mean nothing at all. She just did not know.

In fact, the only thing she did know for certain was that she felt silly, completely foolish, for suspecting her husband. He was literally the all-around Mister American Nice Guy. Doing something mean or underhanded was so out of character for him that she knew she had to be wrong. But, if she was, then what about the drugs, what about the sense of being watched, what about the secret sale of her magazine? Nelson was the only answer she could come up with, no matter how little sense it made.

"The salmon was fantastic," Nelson suddenly said, breaking the silence once more. Then he watched Angela's reaction covertly, hoping that he would see something in her eyes, some spark that might indicate a desire to communicate.

"Thank you," Angela responded stiffly as she watched him in return. "I think it turned out well myself."

Silence again, strained and dragging. Each watched the other, and each knew that the other was watching. Yet neither saw what they thought they might see, and so each simply waited, the one dreading, the other hoping, both watching.

Later, after the boy had removed the dishes, he complied with Angela's request for some cappucino.

"Angie?" Nelson's voice broke the silence. "Angie, I . . . uh . . . we need to talk." Stopping, he kept watching his wife, waiting. He was sure he knew how she was going to respond, and he had no solution ready. In fact, he had no idea how—

"I don't think we have much to say to each other, Nelson. I've told you what I want. What else is there to say?"

"What else? Angie, you're my wife. With what we've got going, it's crazy for you to demand a divorce!"

"Maybe, but I don't think so. I want it, and I want it *now*!"

Surprised by the intense anger in her voice, Nelson looked closely at his wife once again. "What's got into you?" he demanded softly.

"You," Angela snapped. "You, and deceit, and dishonor!"

"What? Angie, I don't know what on earth you're talking about. Those are pretty serious accusations, and I'd appreciate an explanation."

For a moment Angela didn't answer. In the silence she arose and, with Nelson following, moved into the sunken lounge where she sat down and removed her lipstick from her purse.

"What's that?" Nelson asked as he pointed toward the oil-cloth packet, which was still lying at the top of her purse.

Angela looked down at the small packet, wished for a moment that she had opened it before Nelson saw it, and then shrugged her shoulders. "Who knows?" she replied, doing her best to keep her voice calm. "Some weirdo barged into my office this afternoon and gave it to me. I haven't opened it yet. Does it feel warm in here to you?"

"Warm? Why yes, now that you mention it."

Nelson hesitated then, wondering why he almost ached to open the small package. In the worst way he wanted to, but the desire was foolish, and nowhere near so important as what they were discussing.

"Angie," he finally said, breaking his mind away, "what's happened to us?"

"Us!" Angela snapped. "Nothing happened to *us*. It's happened to *me*. My eyes are opened, and I can see clearly for the first time in years. I'm me, Nelson. Me! And *me* is through with *you*. Finished. I control myself, you don't!"

Surprised at his wife's reaction, Nelson mentally backed away, wondering.

Suddenly the silence was shattered by the ringing of the telephone, and Nelson impulsively reached for it.

"Hello? Oh, hi, Max. No, don't worry about it. We just took the rest of the afternoon off. Listen, if it fits in with your schedule, I want to be airborne by seven-thirty. Okay? Good. Could I impose and ask you to let the others know of the change? Thanks. See you then."

"What was that all about?" Angela asked as Nelson replaced the phone.

"I'm flying to Houston in the morning to work on the cable deal."

"Tomorrow?" Angela blurted, her voice filled with shock.

"That's right. We need to iron out some of the wrinkles in the TV-X merger."

Angela was stunned! Her husband would be gone on Saturday, the day of all days when she needed him to be at home. What was wrong with him? Why . . . ?

"Nelson," she cried, "you can't go tomorrow! It's Saturday, remember? Saturday! Tomorrow is the *awards* banquet!"

"I know," Nelson responded easily. "But that isn't until eight o'clock. I'll be back in plenty of time to escort you."

Angela gave him an icy look. "What if something happens? What if there is a storm, what if you crashed, or—"

"Oh, come on, Angie. We live with what-ifs all the time. They don't happen. Please don't make such a big deal out of this. I'll be back in plenty of time, and—"

"Nelson," Angela shouted, slamming herself down onto the divan. "It *is* a big deal! I'm being honored by some very important people, and I need your support! You've known about this presentation for weeks. Why couldn't you plan your Houston trip for Monday?"

"Because I *must* go tomorrow, Angie. I have no choice!"

"Wait a minute!" Angela now was seething, her eyes flashing with her anger. "You don't *have* to do anything! You're Nelson Armstrong, remember? You're the man who turned his grandfather's struggling newspaper into a billion-dollar media empire! Isn't that what *Time* reported?"

"Angie, don't start in on that again. Please. I'm in no mood for your theatrics."

"My *theatrics!* Just because I show some emotion and feel some pain, then suddenly I'm an actress. You should try it some time!"

For a moment there was heavy silence, and then Angela spoke again, her voice low and flat. "Nelson, we need to work out the details of the divorce."

For an instant Nelson stared at his wife, his expression

revealing volumes. "I'm going to pretend that I didn't hear that," he finally said, his own voice sounding very tired. "I just can't believe you're still pushing this thing. Angie, divorce isn't the answer, not for us. You know that as well as I do. What we need to do is sit down and work our way through our problems before we destroy everything we've worked for."

"Everything *we've* worked for?" Angela shouted, her anger rising again. "Nelson, you're blind. *We've* worked for *nothing!* It's been you working for one thing and me for another! It's never been we, only you and me. And *I'm* through. I'm filing for a divorce!"

Nelson, shaken as much by the tone of his wife's voice as he was by the force of her resoluteness, turned away. He had to stop her! For some reason the whole idea of divorce was *wrong!* He knew it, and somehow he had to get her mind off of it.

"Angie," he finally said, "don't be a quitter. You and I are survivors, not quitters. That's not our way. Remember? Sure we have some problems, maybe even some big problems. But so does every other married couple in America. So what? The smart ones don't quit, Angie. They just roll up their sleeves and work that much harder."

"But not me, Nelson," Angela seethed. "I want out, and you can take that to the bank! Frankly, I'm amazed that you have the unmitigated gall to stand there and ask me to work things out when for days you've been giving me drugs, and when for weeks you've been pushing negotiations to do away with *Fashion 1!* Yes, and without even discussing it with me. How can you do that? How can you speak out of both sides of your mouth at once? You *know* what *Fashion 1* means to me!"

Nelson's face clearly showed his shock. "Angie, I swear to you, I have no earthly idea what you're talking about!"

"Come on, Nelson! Don't try to con me with your little-boy innocence. It's too late for that. Just give me my freedom, and my magazine and I will be on our way."

Defensively Nelson picked up his briefcase and strode to the door. "Angie," he said, his voice quiet with controlled anger. "I'm through talking! There will be *no* divorce, and that's final!"

Angela, almost beyond control, grabbed up the closest thing to her hand, the small oilcloth packet. Viciously she hurled it at the closing door. Then, still shaking with anger, she rose to her feet, turned, and—and felt the eyes of someone boring into the back of her head, someone willing her to open the packet, to examine its contents. Suddenly her anger dissolved and she was filled with fear, fear so total and so thorough that she didn't know what to do.

"Cope, Angie," she whispered desperately to herself as she stood staring around her. "Cope with it! Nelson caused it. Remember that! *Nobody* is watching, and that package means *nothing*, nothing at all. Somehow Nelson is doing this to you, and it is up to you to deal with it. Find a way to take the offensive."

Smiling then with a sudden idea, Angela opened the door, moved into the hallway, and slid open the heavy oaken doors that led into the spacious library, her husband's inner sanctum. Walking quickly to the fireplace, she picked up a heavy poker, held it in her hands for a moment, took a deep breath, and, still watching Nelson, she walked to the far end of the room.

The stereo was playing softly. Bach, she thought. Nelson, still upset, was gazing into the cabinet where his priceless collection of American Indian artifacts was displayed. A history buff, her husband loved to gaze at his things, for somehow the pipe, the flute, the stone-tipped arrows and spear, the shield, the quiver, and all of the miscellaneous stone and bone implements seemed to give him a feeling of peace, of kinship with the original caretakers of the land. Often, Angela knew, especially when he was troubled with something, he would gaze into his cabinet, seemingly oblivious to the world around him.

Hurrying, giving herself no time to think, to consider the thoughts of her husband who was now, she was certain, watching her, Angela lifted the poker into the air. Then with both hands she swung it hard against the thick leaded glass that enclosed Nelson's treasure.

"Hey!" Nelson shouted, stunned. "Angie, what on earth are you doing?"

Ignoring him, and using the poker like a broom, Angela quickly swept the glass shelves with it, scraping the arrowheads, spearheads, axe heads, medicine bundles, and other artifacts into a trash basket which she held below. With a determined and satisfied smile she then lifted the wicker container, heavy with its priceless load, and made her way past her stunned and speechless husband.

For just an instant, then, Angela panicked. She knew that Nelson had left his chair and was behind her, following. What would he do? she quickly asked herself. How would he react when he saw what she was going to do? But then she smiled, for she knew that no matter how he responded, it would be better than the nonresponse he had displayed thus far.

Throwing the balcony doors open, she took up the basket and stepped out onto the spacious patio deck. There she stood gazing down at the red Lamborghini. With Nelson behind her, still speechless with surprise, she set herself, aimed, and let fly the contents of the basket much as one would empty a pail of dirty water.

For just an instant the ancient artifacts glittered in the afternoon light. Then, with a startling clatter, the stone, wood, and leather implements rained down upon the roof, hood, and windscreen of Nelson's expensive automobile, sustaining and doing irreparable damage as they fell.

Nelson, half out of the door, an expression of shocked disbelief still frozen on his face, stood aghast as he watched his invaluable medicine pipe shatter against the roof of his Countach, bounce once or twice, and then fall fragmented to the pavement. Lifting his eyes then he stared numbly at his ruined collection and at the gouges in the finish of his Lamborghini.

For long seconds he stared downward, but then at last he turned to face his wife. Bleakly he looked at her, his look filled with horror and pain and pity. At last he turned quietly away.

Angela, outraged beyond belief that he had not responded, shrieked in frustration and pushed past him back into his den. There, filled with an increasingly uncontrollable fury, she reached up, lifted Nelson's treasured McCarthy original western painting from the wall, and shattered it, frame and all, across his Remington bronze.

Nelson, watching horrified from the doorway, waited until Angela was finished. Only then did he speak.

"I'm sorry, Angie," he said quietly. "I'm sorry I—"

"Sorry!" she screamed. "I don't want you to be sorry! I want you to get mad, to lose your temper, to *do* something! I want you to grant me a divorce!"

Nelson turned slowly away. "No, Angie, I won't. My grandfather once said that—"

"Your grandfather? Your *grandfather!* Don't you ever think, act, by—by yourself? Can't you do *anything* that he didn't tell you to do? What is he? Sacred or something?"

"He's just my grandfather, Angie. He was a man I loved and respected very much. You surely must feel that way about your ancestors."

"Oh, you bet I do! I love and respect them all. My mother was a selfish social climber, my father was a gentle man who, rather than face her, drank himself into a hospital and a divorce. I never knew my grandparents, any of them, because they were smart enough to die before I came along, and all I know about my great-grandparents is that one of them abandoned his family. You bet I love and respect them!"

"Hey, Angie, I didn't know. I'm sorry that—"

"Sorry! Sorry! Sorry! I *hate* that word! Can't you say anything else? Can't you do anything but stand there looking . . . looking *sorry?* Oh, how I hate that!"

And then Angela, totally beside herself with rage and frustration, turned and fled to her bedroom. Nelson, following her, sat slowly on the bed, reached to put his hand on hers, thought better of it, and remained silent.

Finally Angela struggled to her feet, cleaned herself up, and turned to face her husband. "How much does it take," she asked, her voice trembling, "to make you angry?"

"Is it important to you that I get angry?"

"Yes, it is. Or at least it's important that you show *some* weakness. Do you know, you can't even profane!"

"I don't understand you, Angie. I don't understand what you have against strength. Anybody can swear. I just decided one day that I was smarter than that. I decided that I could control—"

"That's just it, Nelson. Your whole life is one big bundle of strength, one huge pile of control! And I can't stand it!

"But I'll tell you something that you don't control. Me! Never again. Furthermore, after Monday you won't control my business, you won't be able to play your little games of buy and sell with a concern that I happen to have given heart and soul to create!"

Astounded at his wife's accusations, Nelson rose to his feet and reached out to her. "You honestly believe that I'm doing that, don't you?"

"So completely, Nelson, that I have retained the legal firm of Gathman and Deb to see that it doesn't happen. They'll be at my side Monday morning when I announce to the press that I'm filing for divorce in order to protect what's rightfully mine."

Nelson, stunned, stared dumbfounded at his wife. After a moment of stark silence he sat back down and covered his face with his hands. Finally, barely audibly, he spoke. "You've made up your mind?"

"Yes, I have."

"Have you thought about how such an action will affect—"

"Nelson," Angela interrupted angrily, "don't come on to me like that. I'm not falling for it."

Nelson lifted his face and gazed upward. "Let me finish, Angie. I'm not talking about us, about you and me. I'm talking about the hundreds of people who have their livelihoods wrapped up in us."

"Nobody will lose his job, Nelson."

"You still aren't hearing me, Angie. I'm talking about the people who'll be hurt when the rival presses and magazines and news services start their field day. And there'll be a field day, you can bet on it. Do you think, Angie, that they'll just talk about us, about you and me? You know very well they won't. They're hungry for our success, and our divorce'll be prime stuff."

"I don't care, Nelson. I don't want to hurt anyone, but I *do* want out, and this is the only way—"

"No, it isn't. If you're this serious, I won't stand in your way. Not anymore. But I am suggesting that we do it quickly and quietly, without a media splash, and damage as few people as possible."

"What about my magazine?"

"It's yours."

"Will you put that in writing?"

Nelson chuckled lightly and without mirth. "Yes, if you'd like. I'll even call Dick and have him do it, if that will help."

Now Angela laughed without humor. "No way. I wouldn't trust that man as far as I could throw him. Your signature will do. Now what about the divorce?"

"How soon do you want it?"

"The sooner the better."

"How about tonight?"

"What? You can't . . ."

"Angie, I read the other day that divorces could be obtained in Mexico, day or night, within an hour or so of applying. We can go there."

"Mexico," she said, surprised. "But how—"

"The Lear, Angie. You've never been to see it, but it *is* real, and it's very very fast. If we left now, then we'd be home—I mean back, by morning. No fuss, no noise, and you'd have both your magazine and your freedom."

"Why this sudden change of heart?"

Nelson stood again and walked toward the door. Once there, he turned again and spoke.

"You probably won't believe this, but I love you, Angie. As much as anything in this world, I want you to be happy. It's pretty obvious that I've not been able to provide that for you through marriage. If this will do it, then I'm reluctantly willing.

"Now, change your clothes and put on something warm. The Lear sometimes is cold. I'll call Max, and we should be ready to go within ten minutes."

"You're still in control, aren't you, Nelson?"

Smiling thinly, Nelson responded. "I suppose so. But enjoy it, because I promise you, it will be the last time. You've won." Turning then, he started through the door.

"Nelson?"

"Yes," he replied quietly, turning back.

Slowly Angela moved toward him, her hands out, her heart pleading, her eyes now filling with tears. "I'm . . . I'm sorry, Nelson. Really I am. I didn't want it to end this way."

"Hey," he replied, smiling through his own emotions, "I know you didn't. I guess these things happen to everyone. Friends?"

"Friends."

"Good. I'll see you in ten minutes."

10

As Angela entered Nelson's wrecked den, she saw him standing with his back to her, the phone at his ear, waiting. Drying the tears that had started with her husband's departure from the room and that somehow wouldn't stop, Angela stepped around to where she could see her husband's face, trying to read what she had always been able to find written there.

The Regulator clock above the mantel ticked loudly, filling the silence of the room with a measured rhythm which Angela found herself trying to breathe to. For an absurd moment she thought of another clock, the one hanging in her mother's kitchen, the one whose rhythm her life had been measured by when she had been a small girl.

Forcing her thoughts back to the present, Angela wiped angrily at her continuous tears, resisting the fleeting sense of desperation, of loneliness, of helplessness that had been such a large part of her young life. But it wouldn't go, and she felt herself falling into a void.

"Max?" Nelson asked, his voice calm and controlled. "Yeah, it's me again. Sorry to bother you, but is the Lear operable tonight? Fine. Do you want to take a trip, a little jaunt to Mexico?"

Angela, listening, suddenly realized that she was methodically cleaning up pieces of broken glass from the floor and cupboard. Angrily she pushed them from her and strode from the room, listening as she left.

"Is that right? With your kids, huh? Sounds fun. Well, do you know anyone else qualified for a right or left seat in a Lear? Joe Eggett? He's the best, is he? Great! Can I get . . . ?"

And then Angela, out in the hall, could hear no more. For a few moments more she busied herself with her face, and then, gathering up her purse, she returned to the den.

Nelson had pulled open the top drawer of the desk and had taken out a packet of high-level flight charts. He had also cleared his desk of painting fragments, and now the charts were spread out on the desk before him. Only when he had found what he was looking for did he glance up at Angela.

"Are you ready?"

"Whenever you are."

"Is this as painful for you as it is for me?"

"I don't know, but I suppose so. I do wish that there was another way."

"Isn't there?"

"No, Nelson, there isn't. Not anymore."

Nelson dropped his gaze again to the charts. "We'd better take the El Dorado," he said quietly. "I'll be out in five minutes."

Five minutes later, when Nelson Armstrong climbed into his wife's El Dorado, he found Angela in the car waiting for him. Pulling the door shut, he stared appreciatively at her. In spite of it all, she was still the most beautiful woman he had ever known. If only . . . if only . . . !

As he started the car, Angela opened her old Gucci to take out her lipstick. For an instant she felt a slight tremor of shock as she encountered once again, within her purse, the thin brown oilcloth packet that had been given to her by the man from

Goodwill. As her fingers fumbled past it she wondered once more how the packet had gotten into her purse, for she distinctly remembered throwing it at Nelson's retreating form only a little while before. It was as if, as if . . .

And then for a moment it came again, the feeling of being alone with someone else watching, making her not alone at all. As the chills started she turned to her husband, instinctively seeking help. Yet as she saw the tight look on his face, her resolve strengthened and she casually looked away, determined that no matter what happened, she would handle it alone.

PART TWO

11

"Hey, Jim! How does she look today?"

For a moment the shouted question hung suspended in the high empty air of the giant hangar, almost echoing. But then there was a slight scuffling sound, and a finely shaped head, mounted on wide shoulders that tapered quickly to thin waist and hips, appeared through the cabin door of the Lear jet.

Jim Spaulding, thought Max Smith, *looks no more like a top-flight Lear mechanic than . . . well . . . than I look like a Lear pilot. How on earth could a man that good-looking, with a face so full of easygoing kindness, ever become so thoroughly proficient in the mechanical and electronic intricacies of a Lear? He looks more like a model than a mechanic. It makes no sense. But then neither did it when I—*

"Hi ya, Max!" Jim's deep voice boomed through the cavernous room. "You were right, as usual. And as usual you were pretty darn lucky, too. Both starter generators were gone —icing in the brushes, and that burned 'em good. You brought this bird in last night on no power, didn't you."

It was a statement, not a question, but Max nodded anyway. Then, because he knew the mechanic, and because he understood how much the Lear was a part of his life, Max told him, briefly, the details.

"What went first after the warning lights?" Jim asked when Max had finished speaking.

"The radios started dying, so I turned them all off except the transponder. Then I shut down the lights and all the auxiliary stuff. By then the DME showed forty-two miles to home, and then it died. The transponder faded, the VOR needles started wandering, the altimeter stopped at twelve thousand feet, and I was in a sweat."

"Did the boss know?"

"Yeah, he knew, all right. Not much gets past him. I'd have told him anyway, though, if he hadn't noticed. He's a steady man. I enjoy having him beside me, either seat."

"Was he scared?"

"Are you kidding? Nelson Armstrong is scared of nothing! Ever! In fact, he acted excited. And that worries me. He's the kind to take chances in this baby, and you just don't do that. You start messing around in a Lear, you better figure on kissing this old life good-bye. Follow the rules and there're usually no problems. Usually. Don't follow them and it's deadly. And he doesn't like rules. I think he's a little crazy."

"Maybe. But look where it's got him. *He* doesn't work for *us,* you notice."

"That's a point, Jim. It surely is."

"So without power, Max, in all those clouds, how did you bring her in?"

"Used my watch. You know, timed us. Then when I was close the boss found a hole, we dropped through, leveled at about five hundred feet, and followed the highway straight to the airport. Then we got the gear down, and there you are."

"Well, as usual you make it sound easy."

"No, no more than you do, repairing it. Which, by the way, is why I can fly this lady—because you keep her smiling. Is she all set for tomorrow?"

"You bet, Max. Generators are both in and functioning. I still need to fuel her, but she'll be ready. In fact, fuel is next on the list."

"Good. And leave the caps off, will you?"

Jim nodded, smiling. "You bet, Max. I will. Just like always. Oh, I just remembered something. Keith Hooker brought that big sack of survival stuff over today."

"Yeah, he told me he was going to. Nelson told me he was coming too. The Doc's a real believer in being prepared. He calls that bag his "possibles." Takes it whenever he flies. He picked up the habit when he was in Alaska, bush-doctoring. I guess he went down a few times, and learned the hard way. Did you notice what-all he brought?"

"Well, I didn't look in the plastic bag, but he had two or three of those wool army blankets and a couple of Arctic Air Force parkas. There was more, but I didn't pay a whole lot of attention. I guess Nelson told him what he wanted, and Doc Hooker picked it up for him."

"Well, that's good, Jim. I've never needed anything like that, but it never hurts to be prepared. If Nelson feels better, that's what counts."

Both men smiled, and then, as Max turned to go, Jim spoke again. "Hey Max, let's grab our wives and get together tonight, maybe after the kids are in bed. Annette and I just got a new Monopoly set, and we're just itching to become plutocrats."

"Jim, I'd love to, but Marilynn and I promised the kids we'd take them to the movies and it'll be late when we get home. How about next week?"

"Sounds good. Friday?"

"You bet. Friday it is."

Max, just before he stepped out through the door, looked back at Jim, and he wondered again how the man had ever learned enough to repair that delicate metal lady. The thing was, he did, and Max knew it. That was why he never worried when he had the Lear in the air. Jim always had it in top form. He was the best mechanic in the business, and he was Max's security.

"You're a good man, Jim," Max shouted. "See you tomorrow."

"Yeah. See you later!"

12

Meanwhile, several hundred miles to the south, the air seemed to hesitate, to pause. But then, because it was a hot day, because it was afternoon, and because it was high in the San Juan Mountains of southern Colorado, the breeze picked up once more, freshened, and moved up the boulder-strewn slopes with renewed strength.

Down in the valley of the Rio Grande it had been an excessively hot, dry spring. Farmers and ranchers, concerned for their crops and livestock, were soaking the burning earth with all available water. But the heat was intense, and before the thirsty soil could absorb the water an amazing volume was vaporized, rising in an invisible mass on the thermal created by the super-heated ground.

The thermal of warm, moist air, lifting upward, was boosted along by the super-heated southern slopes of the La Garita Mountains, part of the San Juans, which were creating massive thermals of their own. Quickly the speed of the air movement increased. What had been just a valley breeze drifting up the lower slopes, shifting the long grass before it, turned quickly into a wind of such power and force that it twisted trees higher on the ridges in the Rio Grande National Forest, and tossed their branches about like toothpicks.

The moisture from the valley, thrust upward by the orographic effect, expanded and cooled quickly in the thinner air. At about fourteen thousand feet, having cooled 3.5 degrees for each thousand feet of ascent, the moisture reached its condensation level and puffy cumulus clouds suddenly appeared, heaving and churning and drifting to the leeward of the jagged peaks.

It was so almost every afternoon, and yet it was not so, for this day it was different. This day there was more moisture in the air, a great deal more than was usual, and the winds were stronger than they normally were. In addition, during the previous week, thermals rising from the valleys below had spawned hundreds of dust devils—small, tight, spiraling winds that had sucked up great clouds of dust during their few minutes of existence. Most of the dust, of course, had settled back to earth. But some, microscopic in size, had been carried upward on the lifting air currents to finally hang suspended in the upper atmosphere, joining electrically charged ions that were already there.

This day, then, as the huge mass of cooling water vapor was shoved into the upper atmosphere, it encountered the unusual amount of dust and ions, foreign bodies, already suspended there. These quickly acted as condensation nuclei, growth seeds, to spawn water droplets in the clouds.

At that point the cumulus clouds changed form again, climbing and boiling in ever-maddening fury as the vapor within them condensed, froze, and was thrust constantly higher by the vicious winds from below. The cumulus clouds, relatively peaceful, had now become violent cumulonimbus, the feared thunderheads. In a short time these towering masses of destruction had thrust against the stratosphere, twelve miles in the air, were generating updrafts and downdrafts with speeds of up to two hundred miles an hour, and were filled with tempest winds, rain, pelting hail, and lightning. And worst of all, they had formed across jet route 13, Denver to Delicias, Mexico, and were sweeping down the San Luis Valley toward the Alamosa airport, sparing nothing in their path.

13

"Hello, Denver Center? Is Orval Skousen handy? Yeah, I'll hold.

"Hey Orv, this is Floyd Thomas from the Flight Service Center here in Trinidad. Yeah. How's it going? Me too. Just like the old dog said. Rufff!

"Say, did you fellers get into that storm up your way? You didn't? Well, I'll tell you something. You didn't miss anything! It's a real lulapalooza down here.

"Listen, Orv, we've got a problem down at Alamosa that you need to alert your flyboys to. The VOR down there is on the fritz. We think it's lightning, though we aren't certain of anything yet.

"Yeah, I know it's never happened. Right. I also know it's grounded. What? Sure we have. We've tried dialing up everything there, both VORTAC units and both TACAM units, too. Nothing works, though apparently the emergency generators are functioning.

"I agree. That's why we think it's lightning. A direct hit to the steeple, or even a nearby hit, could conceivably shift courses slightly on the monitoring antenna, completely shutting down all functions. Remember last winter when that blasted owl kept shutting us down trying to warm its feet on the antenna heaters? Those antennae are sensitive, and the owl's weight and body heat were just enough to shift courses slightly.

"You don't remember? Brother, I wish I didn't. It was a real pain in the neck. Yeah, the FAA boys couldn't figure it out, either. Then a new girl here, trying to dial the stuff back up and get everything working again, flipped the wrong switch, the warning horn out at the site came on, and the owl got scared off. Right away the equipment came back on, and droppings at the site told us who the culprit was.

"Very funny, Orv. Of course we've tried the horn again. Ha-ha-ha. Anyway, we think the shock of the lightning, or a charge, or maybe even the heat, has moved the antenna a bit. Whatever, we're shut down good, the FAA people have been notified, and since the facility is only six miles south-southeast of the Alamosa airport, right in the river bottom, we don't expect too much trouble.

"What? Oh, sure. Thirty minutes at the outside, maybe even twenty. Meantime, old buddy, keep your pilots away from Alamosa.

"Oh, really? You're kidding. Alamosa has their power out, too? That poor little airport's really getting socked today. No runway lights, clouds right to the ground, and now there's no VOR. Brother! Times are rough, all right. I'd hate to get in a spot and have no place but Alamosa left to go to.

"What? Yeah, me too. Well, keep 'em flying, Orv. I'll let you know when things change. See you later."

PART THREE

14

In the spacious hangar the Lear jet looked smaller than Angela had ever imagined it to be. The craft had been delivered to Nelson's company only nine months before, and from the way her husband had described it since, Angela had developed a mental image of a plane more nearly the size of a 747. But this jet seemed so tiny that it almost frightened her. It was less than fifty feet long, and except for the tail—a T-tail, as Nelson called it—it was so low that she felt that with a small jump she could see right over the top of it.

But what surprised Angela most of all were the wings. At 39½ feet total wingspan they looked awfully short and stubby. The rocketlike things at the wing tips didn't help any, and for a moment she actually found herself wondering, as she viewed the jet, if Nelson wasn't somehow playing some sort of cruel joke on her. After all, she had consistently refused to come to the airport to see it or to go for a ride in it, and so he might very well be getting back at her for that.

As she turned to question him, however, she found that he had already gone into the office. Somehow relieved, Angela followed him.

In the tiny office Nelson was busy poring over the same kind of maps she had seen him studying before they left home. Now, however, he was using them to fill out a small form. At her questioning glance he tersely told her that the maps were high-altitude flight charts and that the form was an IFR flight plan.

"Where's Max?" she asked innocently.

"He couldn't come."

"You mean you're going to fly it alone?"

"Sure. I've got over three hundred hours in this and the one we had before, you know. Besides, I can use you in the right seat."

Angela was astounded. "Me? But I don't know—"

"Hey," Nelson assured her, "relax. I'll tell you everything you need to do. In fact, if you'd like I'll start right now, by explaining what I'm doing."

"Fine, if it won't slow us down."

"Hardly at all."

"Very well, teach me."

For a long moment Nelson gazed at his wife, wondering if she was beginning to warm to him. With all his heart he hoped so, but she was so good at acting that he couldn't tell. Still, his grandfather had told him once that if he treated people the way he wanted them to become, they would ultimately become that way. How long it took he had no idea, but it was certainly worth a try with Angie.

"First of all," he began, "this is the flight plan. I have to file one of these every time I take off. The Lear is numbered NTA111, or November Tango Alpha One One One. The capital N, November, is the letter of all U.S. aircraft. The other letters and numerals, the balance of my initials, you will notice, were assigned by the FAA."

"By chance?"

"Hardly. I requested them and paid for them. Plenty! They're out of sequence for normal aircraft numerals, but I got them."

"Was it worth it, Nelson?"

"Who knows? At the time I did it, it seemed like it was."

"One of your famous instant executive decisions."

Nelson looked again at his wife, surprised once more at the anger, the content of pain, in her voice. "Angie," he finally said, "do you remember how we used to discuss the classics?"

Angela looked up at Nelson, but didn't answer. When she turned away, Nelson went on with his thought. "If you recall, Angie, Socrates in his *Protagoras* and Plato in his *Sophist* argue that each thing of issue in the universe can only have one opposite. Tonight, until we get to Mexico, let's consider the operation of the Lear to be our only opposition, rather than our divergent personalities and attitudes. How about it? Friends again?"

Angela remained silent for several seconds, and Nelson was about to pursue it further when she suddenly agreed. "All right," she replied quietly. "But I *would* like you to tell me what you are doing."

"I'll be happy to. Let's finish this form. The craft is a Lear 35A, true air speed is 440 knots, which is 506 miles per hour. Departure point, of course, is here. Departure time is in Greenwich, our time plus seven hours, which makes it 0230 hours. Our altitude is flight level four-one-zero, or forty-one thousand feet. The best route for us to take, I believe, will be jet route 17, or J17 to Denver. From there we'll take J13 to Delicias, Mexico, for a total of, let's see . . . nine hundred and eighty-nine miles. And that figures to two hours twenty-five minutes air time. We carry five hours thirty minutes of fuel, our alternate airport is Chihuahua, there are two aboard, and the Lear is blue on white. Now if you'll wait out by the plane, I'll deliver this to the tower and we'll be airborne."

Walking away, Nelson wondered momentarily if he could in fact pull it off. Thus far he'd convinced Angie, but that was only the beginning. Now he had to fly the jet alone. Of course it was illegal, and that bothered him a little, though he had certainly tried to live the letter of the law when he had called Max. The real problem, however, was one of practicality, not illegality. If trouble should develop, then it was imperative that two qualified pilots be present. Of course, the chances of that happening were slim, but still—

"Blast it, Max," he said, thinking aloud. "It kills me to do this. Why did you have to be busy? I hate to use your name on the flight plan, but I have no choice."

A little later, back at the aircraft, Nelson quickly made his walkaround preflight inspection. He could tell that Angie was getting anxious, and so he hurried faster than he should have. Removing the covers from the engines and Pitot tubes, Nelson then eased his head and shoulders up into the hell-hole in the bottom of the jet, where he checked the lines and gauges. Satisfied, he walked to the front and kicked the nose-wheel back in, grinning slightly as he recalled the story of the man who forgot to do that to his Sabreliner after a tow, and who ended up with a jet that wouldn't ground-steer.

For a moment Nelson stood looking at the Lear, a fear of having left something undone nagging at his mind. But finally, with a shrug, he climbed aboard, directed Angela into the right crew seat, closed and locked the clamshell door, and then strapped himself into the captain's seat.

While Nelson went quickly over the printed check list, Angela continued her visual inspection of the plane. Despite her misgivings, she was impressed with the interior of the jet. It had obviously been designed by someone who knew the proper utilization of space, and who knew it well. The interior, done in blues and dark wood grains, was as posh and sumptuous as even she could have wished for. Besides the rear divan seat and a front seat that faced sideways and covered a toilet, there were four swivel seats facing either forward or aft. In addition, there were two folding tables, a refreshment cabinet and ice chest, a coffee warmer, a water dispenser, a telephone, and a great deal of storage space. And all of that was in about seventeen feet of space that could not be more than five feet wide. It was, she admitted to herself, beautiful.

"What are you doing now?" she asked.

"This little book is the aircraft check list. When I do everything in here, then the whole operation works. The check list is broken down into prestart, start, taxi, pretakeoff, after takeoff, climb, cruise, descent, before landing and after landing."

"All of that?"

"Yes, ma'am. *All* of *that*. These two pages must be worked through before we even start the engines. I'm checking things like antiskid, flaps, fuel pumps, fuel quantity and counter, and so on. Everything checks, so what do you say we get going?"

For a few seconds Nelson hesitated, trying to come to grips with something—something—but there was nothing there, and he knew he was ready.

All right, he said to himself. *Show the lady what this baby's got.*

Nelson flipped the start switch for the right engine to the down position and pointed out the right tachometer to Angela as the turbine began to wind up. He then brought the right thrust lever around the horn, saw that the fuel-flow meter was registering, heard the snapping of the igniters, and showed Angela how the tail-pipe temperature was beginning to climb. Then the deep roar of the light-off became audible, and with obvious satisfaction he spoke.

"We have a light," he said quietly.

Once the turbine had stabilized at idle he flipped the starter switch to "generator" and eased the jet out onto the ramp.

"Ground control," Nelson said, speaking into the microphone he held in his right hand. He had set the transceiver to one-two-one point niner megahertz, and now he was broadcasting.

"Lear Tango Alpha one one one taxi for takeoff. Request permission to switch to clearance delivery."

"One one one approved," barked the overhead speaker. "Taxi to three-four right, call back when you are on this frequency."

"Roger," agreed Nelson, instantly resetting the transceiver to one-one-eight point seven. "Clearance, Lear Tango Alpha one one one IFR Delicias."

"One one one cleared as filed to Delicias. Maintain one zero thousand. Expect flight level one-niner-zero five-zero miles south of airport. Squawk zero-one-six-six, departure control one-one-niner point five."

Nelson repeated the clearance, switched back to ground control, and continued his taxi toward runway three-four right.

"Nelson," Angela quietly interjected, her interest sincere, "how on earth do you understand that gibberish?"

"I don't know, Angie. Practice, I suppose. One learns to anticipate the messages, and they become more clear."

"Another question, Nelson. Am I wrong, or did you only start one engine?"

"No, you're right. This bird is beautiful and she goes like crazy, but she has an insatiable appetite. She never seems to get enough. Each engine uses about six hundred pounds of fuel an hour just idling, which translates to a little over eighty-nine and a half gallons. We are loaded to maximum fuel capacity, about sixty-two hundred pounds, which will get us to Delicias and back and still maintain our forty-five-minute fuel reserve. But the reserve will be maintained just barely, so we conserve where we can, rolling on one engine and lighting the other just prior to takeoff."

"That makes sense. By the way, where are the gas tanks?"

"Uh . . . there aren't any."

"What? But you just said—"

Nelson grinned. "I'm sorry, Angie. I couldn't resist that. I said there were no gas tanks, and there aren't. We burn kerosene, and the fuel pods for that are located on the wing tips."

Angela groaned, knowing she'd fallen for an old joke. "You mean those rocket-looking things out there hold fuel?"

"Sure do."

"Might they not fall off?"

"I hope not. They never have yet. Of course, there is always the possibility. . . ."

Ahead of them a small Mooney was stopped short of the runway. Nelson braked behind it, fired his left engine, let it stabilize, then rechecked the freedom of the controls.

"Lear one one one is ready on three-four right in sequence," he said into the microphone.

"One one one hold short of the runway."

"Roger."

"Tower," a voice boomed out of the speaker, "Mooney four-five-niner Papa is first for three-four right."

"Four-five-niner Papa," the tower responded quickly, "hold short number two for departure."

"Hey!" Nelson shouted gleefully. "The Mooney got bumped. We're first!"

"Why?" Angela asked, a little surprised at his boyish enthusiasm.

"I don't know. The Mooney was doing his run-up, I guess. Anyway, get ready, lady. We're going to roll."

"One one one," the tower called, "are you at the intersection?"

"One one one affirmative."

"One one one cleared for takeoff, three-four right, no delay."

"Tower," the other voice boomed complainingly, "four-five-niner Papa is ahead of Lear one one one."

"Four-five-niner Papa, the Lear called first. Hold short number two. Delta three-four-niner turn at the next intersection, contact ground point zero. . . ."

As the speaker continued to blare instructions to other aircraft, Nelson moved the thrust levers forward smoothly but quickly, released the brakes, and the Lear, pushed by the seven-thousand-pound thrust of the two Airesearch Turbofan engines, leaped forward.

Angela, shocked, was pushed back hard in her seat, and for a moment she felt pure terror. She was going to die! She had allowed Nelson to take total control of her life, and now . . .

Unconsciously Angela twisted her head to the side, looking out of the window at the hangar as it flashed behind her, wishing with all her heart that she were still there, still—and then she saw, for the fleeting instant that he was visible, the figure of a man, a man wearing a tweed coat, who was standing beside the open door of the hangar.

And suddenly they were there again, the warm, gentle shiverings that told her she was being watched. Horrified, she closed her eyes and held on, trying to drown her fear in the terrible roarings of the twin jet engines that were so persistently and so rapidly pushing her forward into the late afternoon sky.

15

After rolling just over fifteen hundred feet Nelson drew back the yoke and snapped the landing gear switch to up. As the airspeed indicator moved through one hundred fifty knots, he raised the flaps and lifted the nose of the aircraft thirty degrees above the horizon. The rate-of-climb indicator showed six thousand feet per minute, and the altimeter was winding like a clock gone crazy.

Less than sixty seconds after takeoff Nelson eased the nose over at one zero thousand and held it, casually glancing at Angela as he did so. With great satisfaction he noticed the expression on her face, an expression he had not seen since . . . since they were first married.

"Well, lady, what do you think?"

"What?"

"What do you think? Do you like it?"

"*Like* it? I *hate* it! I'm scared to death!"

"Yeah, I know what you mean. This baby really moves out, doesn't she?"

"I'll say! It's more like a rocket than a plane. How long has it taken you to learn to fly it?"

As she asked her question, Angela realized for perhaps the first time how very little she knew about her husband's life. She knew him, of course, and yet she hardly knew him at all. She had no idea what he spent most of each day doing.

Was he the same way with her, she wondered? How much did Nelson actually know about her? For instance, his favorite color was blue, his favorite food was . . . Surprised that she did not know, Angela next thought of women. What color of hair did Nelson like best? Her own hair was dark, but was that his preference? He was always noticing blondes, she had observed, and he seemed quite attracted to women with dark red or auburn hair, women such as his secretary. Nelson was always flirting with her, and—

"Well, of course I've been flying since Nam," Nelson was saying, "but in jets I've been active for just over three years. Excuse me a minute.

"Denver Center, Lear one one one requesting clearance to cruise altitude."

Approval was shortly given, the Lear leveled finally at four-one-zero, Nelson punched the auto-pilot engage button, then the heading mode, and finally the altitude hold. He then reduced the power to ninety percent, sat back, and began once again to read the check list.

"Nelson?" Angela asked. "What about all these dials and things? Do you really understand them?"

"Of course. There are four groups here. This is the pilot's group, these are radio and radar, or avionics, these are engine instruments, and this bunch in front of you is the copilot group."

"What is this one?"

"That's called the HSI, or horizontal situation indicator. It shows—"

Nelson was interrupted by a voice on the loudspeaker above his head identifying itself as Denver Center. Nelson responded, and was told to maintain his present altitude crossing Denver. Then he switched frequencies and a recorded message from Automatic Terminal Information Service came on, giving local airport and weather conditions. At its conclusion Angela noticed for the first time a slight crease on her husband's forehead.

"What is it, Nelson? You look worried. What did he say?"

"Nothing, really. It's just that some thunderheads have built up over the San Juans and the La Garita Mountains south of here. It should be no problem, though. We'll go right over them."

Breathing a sigh of relief, Angela leaned back, relaxed, and did her best to blot out her thoughts. Her heart, she had discovered, wanted to think about Nelson, about the reasons why they had drifted apart. But her brain didn't want to think about those things at all. Her mind told her that it didn't matter anymore. It was over. Her marriage was finished, she needed to part company in a friendly manner, she needed to retain her magazine and her financial independence, and so on. But no matter what else, she needed her marriage to be over. That was the main thing.

As they flew, the constant roar of the engines worked their magic on Angela, allowing her to feel more at ease than she had felt in some time. And as the tension eased from her muscles, she began again, without even realizing what she was doing, to think of the man seated next to her, the man with whom she had once been so deeply in love.

As her thoughts about Nelson continued to bounce around in her mind, Angela glanced casually in his direction. The late afternoon sun, slanting through the plexiglass windscreen, cast a golden hue across his face, and Angela remembered once more the way it first had been. Her mind reached back again to the afternoon they had met, and to the strange longing she had experienced to touch him, to have him hold her in his arms. But he hadn't. He had gently refused to do so until he was ready, until he was certain that he was in love.

Quickly that love had come, she recalled, and yet just as quickly it seemed to have faded away. As she considered the emptiness and bitterness she now felt deep within the pit of her stomach, Angela wondered again how it had all happened. How could something that had been so beautiful and so good have become such a terrible burden of frustration and despair, a thing of such empty loneliness? Of course she did not have the complete answer, but—

"Angie?"

Startled, Angela glanced again at her husband, and for the first time was aware that he had been watching her.

"Yes?"

"Angie, driving home today I was nearly killed on the freeway."

"Oh, Nelson, I—"

"Don't, Angie. Not until I'm finished. The reason I was nearly killed was because something strange happened, something strange that caused my mind to wander, forcing me into a situation where—"

Suddenly, thoroughly frightened, Angela turned toward her husband. "Nelson, I—"

Nelson, ignoring Angela's startled expression, forged ahead with his thoughts. "I want to know, Angie, if you had anything to do with what happened to me."

For a full moment Angela stared incredulously, and then she burst into laughter. "Nelson," she gasped as she tried to catch her breath, "coming from you that is really humorous."

"What's that supposed to mean?"

"Come on, Nelson. Don't play ignorant. It doesn't suit you. I don't know how you've done it—drugs, or something. But for the past four days *I've* had the strange feelings. I'd like to know what *you* were trying to do to *me*!"

For a long moment there was again silence between them, the only sound the constant howl of the twin engines.

Far below them the cultivated valleys of the Rocky Mountains drifted past, obscured only occasionally by thin tufts of white clouds. The fields now were green with new growth, for the grain had been planted and summer was well on its way. It was a beautiful sight, but neither of the occupants of the Lear seemed to notice. Instead they were each intent upon the other, and the tension between them was almost electric.

At last, realizing for perhaps the first time the enormity of the almost-accusations each of them was making toward the other, Nelson reached out and took hold of his wife's hand.

"Angie," he said gently, "to the best of my knowledge, at least until today, you've never attempted to deceive me. I—"

"Now hold on, Nelson. You said *today.* How did I try to deceive you today?"

"Angie, you know very well what you did. You had Joyce tell me to pick you up at the studio at two o'clock. Then you purposely left before I got there. Actually, that's an awfully petty thing to—"

"Nelson," Angela interrupted, her voice rising with her emotions, "I did no such thing! I told Joyce to tell you that I was leaving, and that you *needn't* meet me."

"But . . . then why . . . ?" Nelson paused, his mind questioning, groping. "Ah," he exclaimed, a look of understanding spreading across his face. "Then it was *Joyce.* Of course! And I'll lay odds that this isn't the first time, either."

"But why, Nelson? What do you mean?"

"Well, it's really no big deal, Angie. It's just that Joyce's hormones have been quite active lately, if you know what I mean. But that isn't important. I'm just relieved to know you didn't set me up. But—well, if it wasn't you, then what caused those strange feelings today?"

"Nelson, let me tell you of *my* strange feelings, because frankly I'm beginning to wonder if you actually had nothing to do with them. Before I do, though, I want to know if you really are working toward the sale of *Fashion 1,* like everyone says."

Nelson looked carefully at his wife, almost as if he were measuring her, trying to analyze her question. At last, though, he spoke. "I did receive an offer on it, Angie—a *good* offer. Dick was all for it, feeling that you could do your fashion news on a special TV show instead of in a magazine, and probably do it better. However, I have consistently told both Dick and the buyers that we are not interested. *Fashion 1* has never been for sale."

"But why didn't you tell me that?"

For a moment Nelson remaining silent, thinking. "I don't know," he finally replied. "It just didn't seem that important to me, I guess. Besides, I've had this perverse and obviously erroneous notion that you were my wife, and that you ought to trust me a little."

Again there was an uncomfortable silence, which Angela finally broke. "Nelson, four days ago, shortly after I made my final decision regarding a divorce, I had the first of several strange and very terrifying experiences that have almost ruined me. I had the most eerie feeling of being in the presence of . . . of someone who was watching me. But Nelson, there was *no one there!*"

"Angie, you've explained exactly what I felt in my Countach today."

"What is it?" Angela breathed, gazing fearfully ahead. "What *is* it?"

"I don't know," Nelson responded quietly. "Has there been anything else, any other strange event or experience that you can think of?"

"No, not that I—wait! Today I thought of a dress that I wanted to wear, and when I turned around, it was out of the closet, along with my shoes and jewelry and everything, laid out perfectly on my dressing stand. I literally fainted when I saw it, and when I regained consciousness a moment or so later, it was all back in my closet, as though it had never been touched. That really terrified me, because I *know* it happened."

"I'm sure it did. Why didn't you call me, or—"

"Nelson, we're getting a divorce. Remember? You're the *last* person I'd turn to. Besides, I thought that it was all happening because of drugs you had given me.

"There was also the man from Goodwill Industries, Nelson! He was the strangest man I've ever met, and his eyes . . . they seemed to go right through me!"

"Wasn't he the one who gave you that little package?"

"Yes, he was the one. And that was weird as well. The minute I picked it up I had chills, and this has happened every time I have touched it since then."

"Did you bring it with you, Angie?"

"Yes, I did. And that's another thing. I have no memory of putting it back in my purse. Ever! But every time I open my purse, whenever I go somewhere, there it is!"

Nelson glanced again at his wife, grinning. "Lady, you do have strange problems. Frankly, I think it's a good thing we're going to Mexico. The longer I'm around you the more nervous I get."

"You're so sweet!"

"Hey, Angie, you know I'm kidding. Why don't you get the package out, and let's see what's in it."

"I think I will. But I wonder if—"

Angela was interrupted by her husband, who with an exclamation of concern was staring ahead through the windscreen. With a sense of foreboding Angela looked up too, and as she did so, the familiar chills started marching along her spine, terrifying her, turning her blood to ice in her veins. Suddenly she was terribly certain that she and Nelson were no longer alone in the plane. There was something—someone behind her, watching, waiting . . . expecting . . .

16

Cursing, Nelson stared ahead. "Angie, what're *they* doing there?"

Angela, still frightened by her strange feelings, leaned forward to better see through the windscreen. Ahead of them the sun glinted obliquely off a mountainous mass of clouds that towered far above even the plane's altitude.

"They're just clouds, Nelson. Aren't there always clouds?"

"What? Oh, sure there are always clouds. But not this kind. And not this high, either. Angie, we may be in trouble. Those hummers are too high to go over, and there's no way that we can go around them. It's too late. So we go through, and I hope you're saying your prayers."

"Nelson, what on earth are you talking about! What's wrong with those clouds?"

"Angie, those are cumulonimbus—thunderheads. Within those clouds is enough power to destroy a hundred jets like ours."

"Buy why . . . how . . . ?"

"Winds, rain, hail, updrafts, downdrafts, lightning, and so on. Is your belt on tight?"

"Yes, and so is my shoulder harness. But Nelson, I—"

"Then prepare for some turbulence. Keep your mouth closed, hang on to that handle, and trust me. This is a tight little craft, and we'll make it just fine."

An instant later the light dimmed and the Lear plowed into the first bank of clouds. Angela, tense with fear, was surprised when there was no other change. The Lear continued its smooth, even flight.

"Nelson," Angela finally spoke, trying to understand. "I thought there was—"

And then with a sickening lurch the plane rushed into an updraft and shot skyward, the altimeter spinning like a top as the pressure of the climb pushed Angela down into her seat. Then, just as suddenly, there was a slight jolt, a sustained pause, and Angela's stomach turned over as she was pressed upward against the straps that held her bound. The altimeter spun in the opposite direction, and she was aware that Nelson was fighting the yoke with both hands, trying to maintain control of the buffeted Lear.

Suddenly the pressure eased, the plane leveled out, and Angela was just breathing a sigh of relief when Nelson spoke.

"Blast!" was all he said. But as Angela quickly looked at him, she saw a red rectangle of light illuminated on the dash. Nelson was violently tapping the light with his finger, over and over. And, he was sweating. Nelson, cool, collected Nelson, intent upon the light, was sweating. And suddenly, so was Angela.

"Blast!" he repeated. "Blast it all . . ."

Angela sat up, now thoroughly alarmed. "Nelson, what is it!"

"Well," he responded, reducing the sound of fear in his voice as much as he could. "It's just this low fuel indicator light. Must be a short or something, because we can't be low on fuel."

"Are you sure, Nelson?"

"Of course I'm sure. Max told me it was full, and the gauge showed 'full' when we took off. We've only been airborne forty-five minutes, so if the light is on, there has to be a short.

"Besides," he continued, searching along the console at his side, "we had some electrical problems last night coming in from Minneapolis. Max told me that Jim had them fixed, but it looks like he missed something."

For a moment the plane was tossed about by more turbulence, and neither spoke. Angela simply held to her seat while Nelson maneuvered the yoke and thrust levers. After one particularly violent jolt, though, Angela suddenly thought of the wings, wondering how they could possibly stay attached with so much pressure being exerted upon them.

"Nelson," she whispered when the turbulence finally eased, "do wings ever come off?"

"No. Not that I've heard of. Of course, I suppose anything is possible if things get bad enough.

"Angie," he continued, his thoughts shifting, "this light frustrates me. Tapping doesn't seem to break the short, and I'm not certain what—"

"What about the fuel gauge, Nelson? What does it show?"

"It'll show us nearly full. It's just a short, and—"

"Nelson, will you please check the fuel gauge?"

"All right," he replied with frustration. "Let's see here . . . hmmm. Must be on the same circuit as this light. According to this, there's a little less than nine hundred pounds . . ."

The fading light in the cabin suddenly brightened and Angela was startled to discover that they had temporarily broken free of the clouds. Now she could see that all around and beneath them were churning thunderheads, completely obscuring the ground below.

Wiping his forehead on the sleeve of his jacket, Nelson continued tapping the light, softly cursing as he tried to make it go off. Anxiously Angela glanced back at the right wing.

There she saw, hanging in the air above the right fuel pod, seemingly suspended there, a small, round object. For a moment she watched in amazement, surprised that whatever it was could keep up an exact pace with the Lear. Turning then she looked at the left pod, and was somehow not surprised to see the same thing suspended there. In addition, she could see a light haze streaking backward from the left pod.

Frightened now in a way that was difficult to explain, Angela tugged at her husband's arm and tried to explain what she had seen. He turned to look, but at that instant they entered another cloud, the wing tips were obscured, and impatiently he turned back to the dash.

"Nelson," Angela pleaded, "I'm telling you that there is something out there! I saw—"

"Look, woman!" Nelson growled impatiently. "What you're describing just isn't possible! Do you hear me? You're seeing gremlins, brought on by fear! They show up for people all the time, and are only figments of overactive imaginations. Now be still and leave me alone while I figure this thing out!"

For another moment Nelson tapped the console. He knew it had to be a short, especially after the problem of the day before, but it was strange how even the fuel gauge was registering low. In fact, as he watched the needle he could actually see it dropping. They were below eight hundred pounds already—*if* it was right. Of course it couldn't be, but if it was, they had less than sixteen minutes of flying time left!

"See!" Angela shouted triumphantly, grabbing Nelson's arm.

Nelson turned to look, and then his breath was being sucked out by a huge hand of fear that knotted quickly around his chest, and he found that he could not will any of his muscles to move. He was frozen!

The gauges *were* right! They had been right all along. That was what he had forgotten in the preflight walkaround. Somehow he had forgotten to tighten down the fuel caps! They were both off now, floating at the end of their retaining lines, and the air pressure generated by the jet's speed had very nearly sucked the tanks dry.

Nelson had heard of such a thing happening before, but try as he might, he couldn't remember the proper procedure for dealing with it. Still, there were certain obvious things . . .

With his right hand he pulled back both thrust levers, while with his left he punched off auto pilot and began maneuvering the yoke. He then pulled free his charts and spread them out, instructing Angela to flip on the chart light.

"Denver Center," he barked into the microphone, doing his

best to keep the fear from his voice, "Denver Center, this is Lear Tango Alpha one one one. Do you have my position?"

"Affirmative, Lear one one one."

The plane, as Nelson waited for the response, was dropping now with the reduced speed, and Angela watched almost hypnotized as the altimeter rapidly unwound. The air-speed indicator read less than two hundred knots, and already they were dropping through twenty-five thousand feet.

The voice at Denver Center suddenly broke the silence, giving Nelson his position vectors. Quickly he plotted their location on the charts, drew an imaginary circle with his finger, and spoke back into the microphone. "At one-eight-zero knots, Denver, how many minutes to Alamosa?"

"Eight minutes, Lear one one one. But Alamosa is below IFR minimums, and—"

"Listen, buddy!" Nelson shouted. "I've got a serious problem and I can't worry about IFR minimums. I'm already below two-three-zero and descending. Get me cleared into Alamosa!"

"Negative, one one one," the tower responded, the voice emotionless. "Alamosa is socked in with zero visibility and no power. Also, their VOR is temporarily out of service. It took a direct lightning hit about six minutes ago, and we just got confirmation. Say your intentions."

"Where is the closest alternate airport?"

"Farmington, one one one."

"Uh . . . we'll try there. Request a vector direct to Farmington."

"Fly heading two one zero, Lear one one one. Farmington is clear. Descend and maintain one five thousand."

"Roger."

Angela watched Nelson's face as he maneuvered the jet. He had always been so calm, so in control. Now the muscles of his jaw were knotted, and beads of perspiration dotted his furrowed forehead. But his voice was what had surprised her the most. She had never before heard fear in it. Nelson had always laughed at fear, defying everything to prove his courage. Now it was there, controlled, of course, but still there. She looked at him again and knew that somehow she had to help him. Perhaps if she asked another question—got his mind working—

"Nelson," she whispered tentatively, "what does VOR mean?"

Tersely, Nelson answered her. He was about to explain further when the Lear shuddered slightly. There followed a change in the engine roar, and very quickly the air-speed indicator dropped through one hundred fifty knots.

"Denver Center," Nelson shouted into the microphone, "we have a flame-out on one engine! We have a flame-out—we have a . . ."

Nelson mentally shook himself, telling his mind to get control of things. And then suddenly it was there once more, the sense of presence, the sense of some unknown. For an instant he fought it, but then, because there was no more time, he shoved the feeling, insofar as he was able, aside. Then he spoke again.

"Angie," he said, sounding strangely calm, surprising both of them. "In the closet at the back of the jet should be some survival things. I want you to go back and get all the blankets you can find, and get two of those Air Force parkas. Get them for us, please. Right now!"

"Nelson!" she screamed. "What are you going to do? What about Farming—"

Roughly Nelson reached over and shook her arm. "Angie, get hold of yourself and do what I ask!"

Numbly Angela opened her belt and strap, pulled herself to her feet, and made her way to the rear of the cabin. In the closet she found four woolen blankets and two parkas. There was also a large plastic bag, but it was tied and she didn't even consider taking the time to open it. Taking the blankets and parkas, she made her way back to her husband.

"Good!" Nelson exclaimed when he saw what she had. "Now put on one of the coats, do it up, and hold this yoke while I put on the other."

Angela did as she was told, and then sat back down in her seat, her mind still numb. This could not be happening! It could not possibly be happening.

"Angie, do up your straps, put a couple of those blankets up in front of your face, and then start looking for a hole in the clouds. We'll never get to Farmington. We've got to find a way down while we still have one engine. If we don't, we'll . . ."

Desperately Angela strained her eyes, trying to see through the cloud cover. Her entire body was tense, and she realized with a start that she was holding her breath and biting nearly through her lower lip. For an instant she wondered how a swollen lip would look at the awards banquet the next evening. But then she realized what she was thinking—that she would never get to that banquet—and her fear returned.

"Nelson!" she cried out suddenly. "Over there! There's a gap in the clouds over there!"

Quickly Nelson responded, turning the yoke gently, bringing the craft around, further reducing the thrust and finally spiraling down into the rapidly closing hole. And while he did that he spoke, his voice sounding distant, coming almost from outside himself.

"We're going down, Angie. But don't worry. It'll be all right. Max and I just did this yesterday. It's a piece of cake! Now keep your eyes open for a soft mountain."

Suddenly they were below the cloud cover, in heavy rain, and Nelson brought the jet level barely five hundred feet above the mountain, pushing forward the thrust lever to give the craft additional power. For a few seconds there was a responding roar, but then there was a brief sputter followed only by silence, the eerie silence of whistling wind one hears only in a glider.

Angela, her face petrified in an expression of horror, stared numbly at the swiftly rising mountain. Both of her hands were on the cockpit handle, and all her knuckles were white from the intensity of her grip. Nelson, noticing this, let go of the dead yoke for an instant and reached over, gently caressing the side of his wife's face with his fingers. Bleakly she looked at him, but when he tried to smile she turned away, suddenly convinced that she was about to die.

"Why!" she screamed. "Why, oh why . . . ?" And then, finally, she closed her eyes, waiting.

As the Lear dropped further, Nelson, glancing down, realized that they were in luck, of a sort. The plane was heading up a narrow mountain valley that appeared, from his altitude, to be relatively flat.

"Well, Angie," he whispered tentatively, "I've never dead-sticked one before, but this looks like as good a place as any to learn how. Are you ready?"

"I'm scared, Nelson," she breathed hoarsely. "I—I'm scared to death!"

For an instant Nelson regarded his wife closely. "I'm sorry, Angie. I didn't mean for this to happen, I really didn't. And Angie, I'm scared too. But don't lose hope. I've got a feeling that we'll make it."

"Denver Center," he then said calmly into the microphone, "Lear one one one has lost both engines. We're going down."

"Roger, Lear one one one," the speaker blared after a brief hesitation. "Notation made." Then, almost as an afterthought, the voice added, more softly, "Good luck, fella. May God go with you. And wait for us, because once this storm lets up we'll be there to pick you up!"

"Thanks," Nelson muttered as he switched off the transceiver. Now his whole being was concentrated on getting the Lear down as gently as he could. His left hand was on the control yoke, his right still clutching the useless thrust levers. His eyes moved methodically as he scanned and rescanned his flight instruments. Pitch attitude good, wings level, air speed one hundred five, rate of descent eight hundred feet per minute and beyond his control, radar altimeter falling through two hundred feet.

Quickly Nelson touched the electric trim on the left horn of the control yoke, trying to bring the nose up slightly. It responded, but sluggishly, and Nelson knew they were very near stall speed, not that it would make much difference now.

"Angie," he spoke urgently, "why don't you get into that left rear-facing seat back there."

"Uh-uh! I'm staying right where I am."

"Angie . . ."

"Nelson, I mean it. Besides, there isn't time. Can you land on . . . that?"

"Sure. We'll leave the gear up and belly in. Those bushes look pretty soft, but we'll try to get beyond them to that snow-field. I think we can. Shouldn't be too much danger of fire, with the rain and all the fuel gone and—cover your head with those blankets. *Now!*"

For an instant before they hit, Nelson thought of the ELT, the emergency locating transmitter, and wondered if they had one on board. Max had told him that the FAA had pulled them from all planes because of exploding batteries, and he hadn't heard whether they had solved the problem or not. Then he thought of the son he'd never had, would never—

Angela, in that same instant, had an almost uncontrollable urge to take out her compact and check her face and hair. She wondered then that her habits were so strong, that she was—

And then they hit.

At first there was only a slight jar and a tiny scraping sound. Then for an instant there was nothing, and suddenly there was a terrible jolting and screeching, and both Nelson and Angela found themselves, despite their seatbelts and shoulder harnesses, being tossed violently back and forth. That seemed to go on forever, and then the Lear shot up the side of a low hummock of snow, twisted slightly to the side, bounced for an instant into the air, shuddered, and smashed down into some willows which were protruding up through the snow. The left wing, lower now, dug into the hardened surface and briefly held. Then, with a terrible wrenching sound, the plane broke free from the wing, its forward momentum pushing it into a frightening spin.

Incredibly they were still moving forward, the air was filled with the sound of screaming, and Nelson was aware that the screams were as much from himself and from Angela as they were from the plane. In an abstract way he began to calculate how much further they could slide, and then the willows parted ahead and he saw, rising directly before them a fifteen-foot embankment of white.

Instantly Nelson reached for Angela, trying to protect her from the impact. And then there was a terrible roar and all was blackness and he was going down, down, down into the soft, welcome silence of the dark.

PART FOUR

17

The silence that followed the wrenching crescendo of the crash was almost deafening in its totality, and Angela found herself struggling to comprehend the significance of it. Somehow she couldn't, and it bothered her. But there was something else too, something else that was troubling her, warning her, urging her.

Smoke! It was smoke! The acrid stench of kerosene and burning wires was engulfing her every breath, stifling her.

With a start, Angela lifted her face from the blanket. Cold terror gripped her heart as she realized that she was inside the plane, and that it was about to explode in flames. Smoke was everywhere, thick and dark, so dense that she could not even see her husband through it.

Choking and coughing, she reached out, felt Nelson's shoulder, and began shaking him with the little energy she had left.

"Nelson!" she gasped. "It's going to explode! We've got to get out of here!"

For a moment there was no movement, and so roughly, desperately, Angela shook her husband again, peering as she did through the wall of smoke, trying to see if he was conscious.

"Nelson," she pleaded tearfully. "Wake *up!* Please! Wake up!"

For an instant more there was nothing. But then, with a groan, Nelson slowly raised his head.

"A—Angie," he gasped, "where . . . where . . . ? Are you all right?"

"Yes," she replied, gasping with relief. "I'm fine, only the plane's going to burn and we've got to get out!"

Pulling himself groggily to his feet, Nelson staggered against the wall behind his seat. "My—my head, Angie. I must—I must have hit my . . . head. I don't know if I can—"

"Here!" Angie cried in desperation. "Put your arm around me. I'll help you out if you'll just tell me how to open this door!"

"The—the latch. The latch is in the . . . middle. Pull it down. And don't forget . . . the blankets. I feel like I'm frozen . . . already. We've got to have them!"

Even as Nelson spoke, Angela was gathering up the blankets and her purse in her one hand and tugging desperately at the handle of the door with the other. Suddenly it gave, the doors swung open, and Angela, supporting Nelson, staggered down the steps and onto the vast snow bank.

"Try to hurry, Nelson!" she pleaded, doing her best to clear her lungs and her eyes of the burning, stinging smoke. "We've got to hurry! There's a tree burning here, and it's all going to explode. Come on, it's only a little way to the edge of the snow! If we can get over the edge, we'll be safe."

"I'm—I'm trying, Angie," Nelson stammered drunkenly. "It's just that . . . I can't maintain . . . my balance . . . Legs feel like they're part of—of someone else . . ."

As Nelson's voice trailed off, Angela pulled them both forward across the crusted snow. Thank goodness it was hard, she thought. At least they weren't sinking in it. However, it *was* slippery, and she was finding it increasingly difficult to maintain her balance while she supported her husband's weight.

Behind them the Lear suddenly shifted position, making a grinding noise as it settled deeper into the snow. Angela, hearing the sound, screamed and dropped onto the surface of the glacier, anticipating an explosion, dragging her husband down with her. When nothing more happened, she crawled forward toward the edge of the snow-packed surface, reaching back constantly to drag Nelson forward with her.

"Hurry!" she pleaded, gasping for air. "We've got to get away!"

"I'm coming, Angie," he mumbled. "Don't . . . give up on me. These . . . these blankets. I keep losing the blankets."

"I can't carry them and pull you at the same time, Nelson. Now, hurry! We're almost to the edge. Just another few feet, and . . . Oh, *no!*"

"What—what is it, Angie?"

"Get back! Quick! It's a cliff! We're out over the edge of a cliff! I can feel it moving . . . !"

Suddenly, with a tremendous roar, the cornice onto which the two had blundered gave way, sending them plummeting hundreds of feet down the icy face of the glacier and the mountain.

18

Silence.

Silence and darkness.

Silence and darkness and—but wait! In the silence there was a sound, a faint sound from far off, a sound that was slow, rhythmical, and, she could now tell, coming closer.

Straining, Angela Westport Armstrong listened intently, trying to grasp with her mind the meaning of the unaccustomed noise. And then suddenly the sound was nearer, the uneven cadence of hooves being sucked out of mud as the animal walked slowly forward.

A horse!

Angela suddenly realized that the sound she was hearing was a horse, and it was coming directly toward her. Could there be a rider on it?

She strained to see through the misty darkness, trying to clear her blurry vision. There! There was something, someone . . . moving. But then the movement stopped, not more than a dozen feet away, and Angela, terrified that the man on the horse would leave, for she *knew* there had to be a man on the horse, cried out for help.

Then the pain came, a terrible crushing burning pain that made her feel as though the entire side of her chest had been ripped away.

Gasping, Angela clutched at the ribs beneath her arm, expecting she knew not what, but surprised to find no external damage. Holding herself tightly she took another deep breath and almost passed out with the intensity of the wracking agony. At the same time she began coughing, and quickly her mouth was filled with the salty taste of blood.

Holding herself tightly against the pain, breathing shallowly, and not allowing her mind to dwell on the possible extent of her injuries, Angela cried out once more, pleading with the unseen horseman. But there was nothing, no sound at all. Again she called out, again and again, her voice quickly becoming muffled in the silent drumming of the rain. For it was raining, she now realized, and it was cold.

Desperately, Angela rolled to her knees, trying to get up, to plead more forcefully with the shadowy rider. But the giant hand of pain gripped at her ribs once more, tearing at them, ripping, forcing her down . . . down . . .

"What was that?"

Angela, with her free hand, felt the still form beneath her, the still form that her exploring fingers quickly told her was her husband.

"Nelson," she sobbed in desperate anguish, "Nelson, can you hear me? I'm hurt! I hurt so badly, and the man won't answer! Nelson! Please . . . !"

But again there was no answer, no response. Momentarily terrified with the thought of her husband being dead and leaving her alone, Angela dropped her ear to his chest. At first she could hear nothing, nothing but the falling of the rain and the trickle of water somewhere nearby. But then, moving her ear higher, she caught the sound of Nelson's heart, beating lightly and rapidly, but nevertheless beating.

He was alive!

And suddenly the significance, the memory of the fall from the glacier, forced its way into her mind, and she knew.

They had crashed the Lear! They had crashed the plane on a glacier on the top of a mountain, somehow they had both survived, had fallen over the edge of a glacier, and now they were lying together on a muddy hillside in the middle of the night, it was raining, and they were freezing to death!

"Nelson," she sobbed, shaking him roughly. "Nelson, please wake up! We've got to find shelter. *Please!*"

But still there was nothing, no movement, no sound but the dripping of the rain and a quiet moaning she could barely hear, but which came with each ragged breath her husband took.

Sobbing uncontrollably, Angela buried her face once more in Nelson's rain-drenched parka, pleading quietly, desperately, for him to respond. Her chest ached violently, she was certain she had cracked or broken some ribs, and in addition she could now feel the burning sting where the glass must have cut her face. But why hadn't the blankets—

The blankets! Where were the blankets? They had been wrapped in Nelson's arms before they fell. They had to be somewhere nearby!

In the gray-black darkness Angela carefully groped around her, trying to locate them. But she could feel nothing, nothing but the wetness of the grass, the rocks and the earth. At last she grew still, trying to ease the throbbing pain in her side, her rational mind doing its best to take control of the situation, the impossible situation they were now in.

Her constant pleadings had failed to bring about any movement from the dark object on the horse before her. For some reason the man hadn't answered. But now, as her eyes gained even more their night vision, she became aware that there was no man, and no horse upon which he rode. The thing before her, the object from which she had been pleading for help, was nothing more than a tree, standing tall and silent in the darkness.

As she realized that, Angela's hope vanished. She was alone, alone with her fears and her unconscious husband, alone on the silent mountain. The sounds she had heard were not real, but were simply the effects of the crash, the fall, and her foggy and terror-filled mind.

The tears came then, the tears and the sobs, for she had never been so alone or so frightened. It wasn't fair that this had happened! It was like a punishment she didn't deserve. She didn't know the first thing about injuries, and she knew even less about . . . about living where no human being ought to ever live. How was she to get warm, or clean, or . . . and what about bathroom facilities? She suddenly realized that she had an urgent need to find a bathroom, only there wasn't one, it was dark, and —and she was so frightened that she could hardly stand it.

"Dear God," she sobbed aloud, "what am I going to do? Please, this isn't fair! I don't know what to do, and I've got to have some help. Please . . ."

Slowly Angela controlled her sobbing. At last, with most of it out of her system, she lifted her head and looked around, attempting to determine just where she was. Above her the dark gray of the sky was broken by the jagged black edges of some trees—pines, she assumed. To her right at some distance there appeared to be more trees, while below her in the blackness she could see something that looked shiny, a stream perhaps. To the left the hill sloped away indefinitely, finally vanishing into the darkness, and now she was fairly certain that she and Nelson had fallen onto the edge of a high mountain meadow.

Shivering violently, as much from shock as from the cold, Angela huddled in a ball, caressing her husband's now feverish forehead, and tried in vain to get warm. Around them the rain continued to fall, and for some time she sat thus, shaking, silent and unthinking. Only gradually did she become aware of the smells, the odor of pine, of crushed grass, and of wet soil. But besides that it was cold. She was chilled to the bone, perhaps more cold than she had ever been in her life. And if she was that cold, she reasoned, Nelson's body must be experiencing the same shock.

They *had* to have shelter, and Angela knew it. She also realized that if they were going to find it, it would be up to her to do so. Nelson was obviously unconscious, and perhaps should not be moved. Still, she reasoned, he could not remain where he was, exposed and in shock, and survive the long night. Somehow she would have to find shelter and take him to it. But it was so dark, so dark and so frightening, and she had no idea of what might be lurking out there, just waiting for her to make a move.

She could not do it! There was no way that she could go out alone into that darkness looking for . . . for goodness only knew what. She just could not do it! Not now, not—

Suddenly Nelson groaned, and Angela became aware for the first time of his shivering. He was shaking so hard that his teeth were literally rattling, and Angela knew then that no matter how difficult it would be, she had to move. For Nelson's sake she would need to find some sort of shelter. She had to do it, and that was all there was to it.

Slowly Angela forced herself to her feet, gasping in pain as she did so. Turning then, stooping over with the throbbing in her side, holding her chest tightly with her arm to ease the intensity of the agony, she stumbled off, moving down and away from where Nelson lay, staggering toward a nearby stand of trees where she might find some shelter.

Yet as she moved, Angela felt within her a growing sense of uneasiness. What if she got lost in the darkness? What would happen to Nelson if she couldn't find him when she returned? Yet, she reasoned, if she went back to him now, would she have the strength to drag him into the trees? She sincerely wondered, but the fear of being alone in the dark without him compelled her to turn back. Slowly she began the agonizing climb back to her husband.

Finally, sobbing with pain and fatigue, she reached his side, filled with such agony that she fell to her knees and thought for a moment that she would pass out.

Soon, however, the pain diminished, and gingerly she reached out, wrapped her one usable hand around her husband's pantleg, forced herself back up to her feet, and took a small step forward.

Again the pain blossomed up around her, washing behind her eyes in brilliant colored waves of darkness that she was certain would drown her. Steeling her mind against the nausea and the dizziness, however, she took another step, and then another, and to her amazement the still form of her husband slid after her.

She could do it!

Then his free leg suddenly caught on a bush, and she could go no further. With new pain driving against her mind she crawled around to Nelson's head, grasped the hood of his parka, and began pulling him headfirst down the slope, letting his arms and legs drag freely.

Down the hill at an angle she stumbled, pulling her husband behind her, striving to reach the stand of pines that stood black against the darkness below. There was no trail, yet the way seemed almost easy as Nelson's body slid across the wet grass and mud. There were also few rocks, and Angela felt thankful that she did not have to watch for them.

At one point she crossed a small ridge or lip of earth, and on the far side, which was steeper, her husband's body slid faster than she was moving, almost knocking her over as it came sliding into her legs.

Dropping the parka, Angela paused to catch her breath. These mountains were high, she knew, and she had heard how high altitudes caused shortness of breath. But this was ridiculous! She hadn't come much more than fifty or sixty feet, and she was gasping as though she had just run a mile.

For a moment then she coughed, and as she tasted again the salty tang of blood she almost laughed. In fact, if the pain hadn't been so bad, she probably would have. But honestly, she wondered, what else could possibly go wrong? A broken marriage, a crashed jet, a fall over a glacier, broken ribs, very likely a punctured lung, high altitude, a rainstorm, cold, no shelter, and above all else, a helpless husband who wasn't supposed to have been a husband any longer. It was enough to drive a sane person crazy.

Once more Angela grasped her husband's clothing, and again she moved off, slowly, dragging him behind her. A wind had picked up somewhere, a brisk breeze that drove the rain before it, lashing at the short grass and whipping the trees above. Angela, even while she was moving, found herself shivering once more as the wind pushed her wet clothing against her skin. She was so cold! She was so miserable and cold! Why? Why? Why had this happened to her? How could she cope with it?

And then Angela's rational mind reasserted itself, and she realized again that she had to find shelter. Somewhere there had to be a cave, a tree, or—

Close ahead, just below her, the huge form of a pine loomed out of the darkness, shapeless except for its jagged edges. Maybe she could crawl under that. Perhaps under its boughs there would be shelter. If she could just get Nelson down to it and get him in under the limbs with her.

Turning then, tugging at his body, trying to change the direction of his slide, Angela suddenly slipped in the mud and fell backward. Instinctively she threw out her arm, the one she had been using to hold her side, to catch herself.

The wrenching pain in her ribs was almost unbearable, and she literally screamed with agony. Slowly, though, the pain subsided, and as she pulled herself back to her feet she felt her hand, the one she had partially caught herself with, and then she knew another ludicrous agony.

"Nelson," she laughed hysterically, pulling herself close to the still form of her husband. "Now look at what I've done. Three years' worth of work and effort down the drain. See? Two nails! I've broken two nails! Can you believe it? That's almost as bad as crashing! Now come on! Slide easily! We're almost to the tree. I'll go under it first, and then pull you in. And Nelson, do your best to cooperate. Please?"

With determination born of despair, Angela turned and fought her way against the boughs of the pine, doing her best to get in near the trunk. But the limbs, covered with pitch and prickly needles, lashed at her injured ribs and tore at her face.

Finally, sobbing as much from frustration as from agony, she turned and backed down into the tree, pushing herself through the lower limbs and back against the trunk. For a moment or two she squirmed back and forth, getting as comfortable as she could. Then at last she was still, for the first time out of the rain, and for the first time totally aware of how really cold, wet, and miserable she had been. Being out of the rain was wonderful.

Thinking suddenly of Nelson, she reached out, caught the hood of his parka again, and with a strength she didn't know she possessed, dragged him beneath the spreading boughs of the large spruce. Desperately, fearing that what little strength she had would soon be gone, Angela maneuvered the dead weight of her husband so that he was lying across her lap, his face turned into the warmth of her body. Recalling some long-past lesson in elementary first aid, she made certain that his head was still lower than his feet, in case he was in shock, and then for a moment she relaxed.

Even though Nelson was unconscious, his body was shaking uncontrollably. And so, fighting the pain that was burning her ribs, she moved once more, loosening the buttons on her parka. She then wrapped it as well as she could around both of them, and almost immediately she felt the warmth of his body seeping into her own.

Knowing that the process of heat transfer was also operating in reverse, Angela finally allowed her mind to relax, letting it wander while she pressed herself even more closely to the unconscious man she held in her arms.

Holding her husband close, Angela rocked gently back and forth, her eyes closed against the pain in her side, her mind doing its best to close itself as well against the agony and the loneliness and the fear of the entire experience. She was so tired, so cold . . . and so tired. If only she could—

But suddenly into her consciousness, her reluctant consciousness, crashed the sound of horse's hooves being sucked out of the mud. And Angela, terrified, knew once more that the horse was moving, somewhere close the horse was walking, climbing the hill, gradually moving away.

19

For long moments there would be no sound, no sound but the sighing of the wind through the pine needles around her. Then, off in the darkness a tree would creak, and Angela would hold her breath in fear as she strained to see what might have made the noise. But that noise was never followed exactly by another, and holding her breath caused her ribs to ache and brought dizziness as well, so Angela would slowly let out her breath, certain that the hoofbeats she had heard were now coming back.

But then for a time there would be nothing, Angela would start to relax, and suddenly she would realize how cold she was. Never in all her life had she been so cold and so miserable, and as she thought of it she would start to shake and tremble. Her hands, buried beneath her arms, were so cold that her fingers were curling up, her wet clothing burned and felt like dry ice against her skin, and the wind, shifting constantly, seemed always, no matter which way she turned, to be blowing the misty rain directly into her face. And besides all that, her ribs throbbed with an agonizing violence that was relentless and horrible.

She would grit her teeth against the pain, steeling her mind as she tried to ignore it, as she tried to think of other things. But it would be too much, too great an obstacle, and at last, when she could stand it no longer, she would open her mouth to cry out, to scream forth her rage and her agony.

And then a tree would creak, again, off in another direction, Angela would suck in her breath in fear, and the whole painful, terrorizing process would begin once more. Never would Angela have guessed that a night could be so eternally long.

Somewhere in the crash or the fall from the glacier she had lost her watch. Nelson had also lost his, and so she had no way of knowing what time it was. But after what seemed to be dozens of hours it was still as dark as ever, and she had about given up hope of ever again seeing daylight.

Several times she experienced coughing spells, and after each of them she would be faint with pain. There was also the fear, for each fit of coughing brought the bitter, salty taste of blood to her mouth, blood that she was certain was coming from a punctured lung. If that was so, then she must be dying, and there was nothing she could do about it.

There was a fear too of the mountain, of the darkness, of the unknown. In her entire life Angela had never been camping, had never spent a night alone in the mountains. How did one do it? When people went camping, how did they keep warm? What did they eat, or drink? She had known people who loved to go out camping, and she could not understand their enthusiasm. The mountains were so vast, so foreign, so unbelievably empty and lonely. And there were animals, too, dangerous animals that would destroy her if they discovered her. They were all around her, everywhere. She could hear them constantly, making slight shuffling sounds as they moved from one place to another. Of course she had seen nothing, but that meant very little. They were still there, watching, waiting.

Oh, if only Nelson would regain consciousness. If only she could talk to him, lean on him, gain strength from his own seemingly endless supply. Wasn't it funny, she thought, how one moment she wanted to get away from him, be independent and free from him. Then, in a matter of moments, everything had changed, and she was wishing with all of her soul that she could talk to him, be part of him once more.

Was that love? she wondered. Did she still carry feelings of love for Nelson? Or was it simply the need, the overpowering need of the moment? Oh, how her side ached—her side and her head. Never had she felt such pain . . . such pain, such agony, such loneliness.

"Oh, God," she pleaded softly. "God, if you are there, you can't let us die! We're both too young, and we have too many things to do. We're just getting started. We *can't* die! You just can't let us! Please send help. Please . . . I won't die, I won't, I won't . . ." And Angela sobbed softly into the darkness and the haunting silence of the mountain.

Much later, exhausted and sick with pain, she drifted off into a troubled sleep, a sleep where she dreamed of darkness, blackness—

But it was suddenly a different kind of darkness, an empty, floating space where Angela could catch onto nothing, could take hold of nothing with which to gain control. Terrified, she reached out wildly, grasping, groping, crying out—

And then the noise started, a distant thunder that quickly drew nearer. Turning in the darkness, trying desperately to see, Angela cringed as the drumming, pounding, reverberating boom of thunder drew nearer, ever nearer. Still she floated, back and forth, back and forth, as though she were on the end of a long swing, each cycle taking her in longer and longer swoops. Desperately she reached out, flailing her arms, trying to slow down, trying to get off. But the noise of the thunder was deafening, and somehow she understood that the overpowering sound was the drumming of horses' hooves, many of them, coming from all directions, coming closer, closer, about to run over her, about to—

"Angie?"

Startled, Angela jerked her head upward, bumping solidly against a tree limb. At the same time she gasped deeply, and the excruciating pain in her ribs made her cry out. Through that, however, came the realization that she had been asleep, that she had been asleep and dreaming, for even yet the sound of thunder was rumbling off into the distance of the mountains. Yet what else was it? What was the other thing, the other sound that—

"Angie . . . ?"

"Nelson!" she cried out. "Oh, Nelson, thank God you're alive! Talk to me, please!"

"Angie . . . Angie, are you all right?"

"I—I don't think so, Nelson. Something's wrong with my ribs, and—and I'm coughing blood. What about you?"

"I don't know, Angie. I—I think I'm all right except for my head. How far did we fall?"

"I don't know, Nelson. A long way. And we lost our blankets. But I've felt your head, and I can't find any sign of a wound."

"I must have really knocked it in the crash, Angie. Thank goodness for the blankets. I'm sure it's only a concussion, but it's really crazy. I get all dizzy, and when I close my eyes I'm back in the Lear, strapped into the seat, trying to get out. But I can't, and the smoke is so bad I can't see anything, and . . .

"Hey," he continued softly, changing the subject, "I'm sorry, really I am. I should never have brought you; I should never have tried flying the Lear alone. Here, let me get up. I . . . Angie, I'm sorry you're hurting. I . . . something's wrong. . . . Oh, no. . . . I'm going again . . . I can smell the smoke. I—"

"Nelson!" Angela called out. "Nelson, answer me!"

But there was no answer, no response, no sound but the whispering of the wind as it drove the rain down the barren slope, sifting the grass before it and moaning, softly moaning, through the pine boughs above them.

20

They were coming!

From far off she could hear them coming, getting closer—closer beyond the ridge, riding up the slope, crossing the top, coming down, yelling, shouting—

"Nelson, wake up! Nelson, they're here, they're . . ."

Angela, jerking her head around, stared uncomprehendingly at the gray light filtering down through the pine needles. It was daylight, she could understand that, but where were the people, the men on the horses who were yelling excitedly because they had found the two survivors? Where had they gone? Why had she . . .

Crawling from beneath the tree, Angela painfully staggered into the light. She ached all over, and was so stiff she could hardly move. Her side once again was throbbing and so she held it, breathed as lightly as she could, and looked carefully around.

It was early morning, and though the rain had stopped, the clouds still hung low, obscuring the hillsides around her. Angela felt certain that the weather was not improving, but that there was simply a lull in the storm. Besides that, it was cold, so cold that when she breathed the mist hung like small clouds in the early morning air.

Her immediate impression was that it was getting ready to snow. But she knew that was not possible, for it was late spring and summer was nearly upon them.

She understood now that the sound of hoofbeats had been a dream, yet still she listened carefully, unwilling to give up even the smallest shred of hope. However, except for the twittering of some small birds nearby, there was no sound. The hillside was totally silent.

Thoroughly discouraged, shaking with cold, and more frightened than ever, Angela sank down onto the trunk of a long-dead pine. And then the sobbing began again. Why were they not there? Why was it taking so long for the search party to arrive?

"Nelson," she cried out into the silence of the morning, "Nelson, talk to me! I can't stand being alone! Nelson—I mean it! Please!" And Angela, still weeping, finally crawled back in under the tree, where she pressed herself against the still form of her husband.

"Nelson," she pleaded, now quietly, "don't die. *Please* don't die. I can't stand the loneliness, the silence! Oh, please . . . Nelson, please *wake up!*"

For a long time Angela sat, numb and unfeeling, doing her best to shut the clamoring silence of the mountain out of her life. How she hated the stillness, the deathlike quiet that surrounded her. All her life she had enjoyed the interaction of other people, their conversations, even their movements and actions. She loved to watch people on the street, the endless variety of them; she enjoyed listening in on their conversations, and she loved being a part of their busy world.

But now she was alone, and she could hardly stand it. There were no conversations going on around her, there was no one to watch but herself and her unconscious husband, and the only human voice she could hear was her own. It was terrible, and she hated every minute of the loneliness of it.

Even worse, though, was the lack of music. Angela could not

remember when music had first entered her life, nor could she remember when she had been without a radio. In fact, she had been told that she was singing entire songs before she was two. She had also been told that after her father had gone away and her mother had been forced to go to work, her mother had placed a radio in her room to keep her company and to help her feel that she was not alone. Interestingly, it had worked.

Her love of music had grown and matured as she herself had done, from her mother's choices to rock to country swing, and now she enjoyed classical music and concerts as much if not more than any of the rest of it.

Now, suddenly, there was no music anywhere, and she found herself wondering if she wouldn't go crazy with the quiet! It was more than she could bear. Of course there were sounds: wind, trees, water, birds, wild animals, and so on. But those were horrid sounds, filled with menace, and she hated them. There were also songs in her mind, but for some reason she could not bring herself to dwell upon them, let alone sing them. They were absolutely foreign to this awful mountain.

And so Angela, alone with her unconscious husband, suffered horribly, as much from what wasn't happening to her as from what was. And no matter how she twisted all of it in her mind, no matter how she rationalized or fought with herself, she could not come to grips with it, she could not cope. She was very lonely and very afraid, and that was that!

At last, realizing that she had to move, that she had to find a better shelter for herself and Nelson, Angela crawled again from under the tree.

As she stood up, she suddenly remembered the blankets, lost somewhere above her. She realized that they had to be at the foot of the glacier, near the point where she and Nelson had stopped falling, and she knew that she had only to climb the hill and the blankets would be hers. Carefully then, and with a quick glance to determine that Nelson would be safe until her return, she set off slowly up the hill.

The trail she had made dragging Nelson was very apparent, and she followed that, oblivious to the lowering sky. Once a jay screeched near her, frightening her terribly. But when she had determined that it was only a bird she shrugged, ignored its humorous antics, and continued climbing the hill.

As she climbed she was surprised to see how far she had dragged Nelson. She'd had no idea they had traveled so far. Twice in her climb she was forced to rest. Both times she endured spells of coughing that tore at her side with burning fury, and yet neither time did she cough up blood. Weakly she smiled, thankful at least that a few things were going her way.

Finally, after what seemed to her to be hours, she reached the point where they had fallen the night before. Rocks and snow littered the ground, and she could see her footprints in the mud where she had started walking. Looking upward, she was shocked to see how far she and Nelson had fallen. Although not perpendicular, the hill was extremely steep, and she could see that they had fallen and rolled for several hundred feet. For a moment she sank to the ground with dizziness, her chest heaving with pain and her mind reeling with the enormity of the ordeal she and her husband had survived. In fact, as she looked up at the hillside, she could not even imagine that they had done so. It was incredible that they were in as good shape as they were.

Finally, after resting for a few moments, Angela once again dragged herself to her feet and looked around. She had come for the blankets, for she and Nelson needed them in the worst way. The trouble was, they were nowhere in sight.

Totally confused, Angela turned and looked once again at the ground behind her. No, there was no mistake. The deep gouges in the hill made by Nelson's dragging body were there. And they led directly to where she was standing. If that was so, and it was, then where were the blankets?

Suddenly, out of the corner of her eye, Angela saw something that seemed out of place, something that she had not noticed before and yet that most definitely didn't belong. Slowly she turned her head, cautiously, wondering, wondering—

Yes, there in that little dip in the hillside, not more than thirty or forty feet away, were the blankets. But as she made her way toward them, she found herself wondering that they had fallen so far from where she and Nelson had stopped.

Quickly she pulled them free from the ice and snow that had

fallen upon them, and was pleased to find all of them together, dirty but intact. One of the blankets had quite a bit of dried blood on it, which surprised her. But then, as she thought about it, she realized that the cut on her face had probably bled into it.

Gingerly she felt the long gash with her finger, and she was not surprised to find it all puffy and tender. Strange, but it had been hours since she'd noticed the pain of the cut. Yet as she thought of it, she concluded that she hadn't felt it simply because she had been so busy feeling everything else.

For a moment she considered the scar she would have on her face, a scar that would grow worse the longer she stayed away from a good plastic surgeon. But then she forced that thought from her mind, knowing that worrying about it did absolutely no good. Besides, it was time to stop feeling sorry for herself, time to get busy helping both herself and her husband to survive.

Stooping, she gathered together the blankets, stood up, and was just turning away when she saw, lying on the ground beneath where the blankets had been, her expensive golden-hued purse.

Startled with the realization that she had been without it all night and had not even missed it, Angela reached down and picked it up. Instinctively she opened it, and as she examined its contents, she was immediately aware that the packet, the brown oilcloth packet given her by the man in the tweed coat, was gone.

Quickly she looked around, knowing that it had to be somewhere near. But it wasn't, and after a hasty but careful search she gave up. Frustrated, she turned to look up the hill again, and then it started, the creeping feeling that sent chills racing up and down her spine.

She was being watched! For the fifth day in a row someone was watching her. Again she felt no menace, but still she was terrified by the element of an unknown presence. Whirling around, she looked everywhere, but there was nothing, no one—

"Listen!" she screamed, her voice filled with fear and anger. "I don't know who you are, and I don't care! I'm sick and tired of being stared at! I won't stand for it anymore! Now get away, whoever or whatever you are! Get away from me and stay away! I mean it! *Now!*"

Angela stopped, and as she did so the last echoes of her voice reverberated from the high-up peaks, bouncing back at her again and again, gently and more gently, fading finally into silence, leaving her alone once more on the mountain.

21

"Angie? Angie, where are you?"

Faintly, Nelson's voice drifted up the hill. Angela, lifted and thrilled by the sound, scrambled to her feet. Thrusting her fears, her unnerving terror into the back of her mind, she took the blankets and her purse and started running down the hill. She had not gone many steps, however, before she was forced by the pain to slow down. That was a surprise, for she had not anticipated the jarring caused by walking downhill, and it was as painful as the heavy breathing brought about by climbing had been.

Angela also found herself filled with apprehension about how she looked, and that too surprised her. It had been a long time since she had cared about what Nelson thought of her appearance, yet now she found herself struggling to get a hand free so that she could adjust her straggly hair. She was also worrying about how badly her tears and the rain had streaked her makeup, and she found herself wanting mightily to stop and use the compact that was in her purse. How strange, she thought, that she would feel such things when simply walking toward Nelson, toward the man who, by today, should have been her ex-husband.

Once again Angela was surprised by the distance she had dragged Nelson, and as before it took longer to get back than she would ever have expected. By the time she reached him, she was perspiring freely, and she was certain, from the way she felt, that the sweat was caused more by pain and fever than it was by her walking.

Yet Nelson, who was doing his best to raise his head into the air, looked far worse than she felt, and she was shocked to see how swollen his face had become. Still he tried to smile, and as she squatted near him, he weakly raised a hand to touch her face.

"Are you all right?" he asked, his voice little more than a whisper.

Angela nodded, fighting back her tears.

"Thank God! Angie, I'm sorry that I got us into this mess. I really am. Still, I guess it's about over, now that all those men are here. By the way, why are they spending so much time at the plane?"

Angela stared at her husband, unable to comprehend what he was talking about. For a moment she thought he was joking, but the look on his face said otherwise. He was serious, she could tell that immediately. Yet he couldn't be! He hadn't heard anything. He had been unconscious. It had been her that had imagined the hoofbeats, had dreamed them.

"What men?" she finally asked, afraid already of what his answer would be.

"Why, those men on horses. The ones we heard yelling and screaming just when you awoke this morning."

Angela, now thoroughly shaken, gripped Nelson's hand. "Nelson, that was a dream. *My* dream! You didn't hear anything—you *couldn't* have heard anything!"

"Yes, I did, Angie. They were on the hill up here, coming over the ridge. The memory of it is becoming more clear all the time. I even remember you jumping up at the sound."

"No . . . I—"

"Yes you did, Angie. You even shouted out and told me. I remember it, very well."

Nelson stopped talking, too weak to continue, and Angela stared at him in horror-filled silence. Behind them somewhere a squirrel chattered angrily, and above them a hawk drifted noiselessly across the cloud-shrouded sky. Other than that there was no movement, no sound but the soft, distant murmur of the stream.

"Nelson," Angela whispered, her throat tight with fear. "There *are* no people, but what is it? *What* is going on?"

"I don't know. I really don't know! But whatever it is, we can't dwell on it. Not if we're going to survive. We've got to plan out our course; we've got to decide what to do, and then we've got to get on with it."

"You're right, Nelson . . . I know that. And I'm trying to handle it, I really am. How far away is the stream?"

"Uh . . . I'd guess seventy-five to a hundred yards. Why?"

"Well, before we go anywhere, we've got to have water. I know I have a fever, and you've had one since last night. We both need water badly."

"You're right, Angie. We do. And after we get some, we can start moving down the canyon—"

"*Down* the canyon?" Angela echoed with surprise. "Aren't we going to try to climb back up to the plane?"

"Are you kidding? Angie, look at that cliff! There's no way that we could make a climb like that. I agree with you that the Lear would be the best place to wait for our rescue, but I really don't know how we'd get there."

"Well, how about if we try to go around? Couldn't we cross the canyon and try a different route to the top? One that was less steep?"

For a moment Nelson thought about her question, and then slowly he answered. "We could try it, Angie, but with this storm and our injuries, I don't think we'd make it."

"But why, Nelson? I—I want to get back to the plane, to get rescued! I—"

"Hey, lady. I want to get up there as badly as you do. But first off, it would be an easy matter to get lost, especially in weather as thick as this is going to be. And weather is the second problem, too. You can bet that there won't be any search planes out looking for us until this storm lifts. I'm convinced that our best chance for a quick rescue is to go down the mountain until we hit a road, and then follow it until we come to a house. In this country there's bound to be ranches and farms around. From there we can call for help. Okay?"

With a sigh Angela agreed. At last she rose carefully to her feet, assisted Nelson to his, pushed her pain into the back of her mind, and looked down toward the stream.

The canyon where they were was small, never more than three or four hundred yards wide, and at this point it was grass-filled and relatively flat. In the valley's approximate center, yet meandering back and forth from one side to the other, was the stream. Or at least Angela assumed that it was there, for the willows were so thick that she could not actually see the water.

As her eyes moved down the canyon, she was startled to notice, for the first time, the amazing distance she could see. The canyon continued almost level for perhaps a half mile before it seemed to end in a wall of trees. Above that distant hillside was another range of mountains, gray in color because of the storm. Beyond that was another, and yet another, each more faint in color and form. Finally, way off in the distance, where the earth and the sky came together, was a last range of mountains, so faint and dim that they seemed to be almost one with the sky. Of course she had no way of guessing accurately, but Angela was certain that she was looking across a distance of at least a hundred miles.

For an instant she stood staring, awed and even frightened by what she could see. But then Nelson squeezed her hand, smiled his encouragement, and together they moved carefully down the hill toward the stream.

The willows, when they reached them, were not as tall as they had expected, but they were a great deal more thick. For a moment or so they tried to push their way through, but Nelson was too weak and dizzy, and Angela could not support him and fight the willows at the same time.

At last, realizing that they could go no further together, Angela left Nelson seated on a stump while she searched alone for a pathway or trail. Finally, fifty yards or so upstream, she found what she was looking for. Carefully she began picking her way forward, doing her best to stay out of the oozy mud.

The ground, soggy and wet, was covered with the footprints of all sorts of animals. When Angela finally became aware of this, realizing that she was on a game trail of some sort, she came to an abrupt halt. She had never thought much of animals, one way or another, before last night. But now, alone and in the wilderness, and knowing nothing of their ways, Angela was suddenly terrified by the thought of a wolf, a bear, or even a lion, possibly crouched behind the willows just ahead, ready to pounce if she moved just a single step nearer to where it was hidden.

Angela's fear was in an instant a terrible thing, wild and uncontrolled. Her heart, beating rapidly, felt like it would come right out of her chest, and her breathing was rapid and shallow. She stood very still, peering forward, doing her best to see around and through the brush. But she could see nothing, nothing at all. Nor was there any sound, any noise. There was nothing but the constant murmuring and gurgling of the unseen stream.

Angela stood silently, shaking with fear, not moving at all until at last her muscles began to cramp and ache. Then, very slowly, she began to inch her way forward. There was a sudden, slight rustling in the brush to her right, and Angela's heart leaped to her throat as she spun toward the sound. But . . . there was nothing there! Cautiously she took another step, and then another, hoping, almost praying that—and then, beneath her foot, Angela felt the twisting movement of a small snake.

With a scream of terror she turned and fled back along the trail, paying no attention at all to where she was going. She was simply fleeing, twisting her way through the rocks and incredibly deformed shapes of the dead trees, trying to escape from her fears. But they would not go away.

Finally, out of breath and weak from pain, Angela stopped running and collapsed onto the top of a large rock. Then for a time she just sat, collecting her thoughts, calming her fears, waiting for her heart to stop pounding so wildly.

How could she do it? she asked herself over and over again. How could she force herself back into the willows? And why was she so filled with fear? It was like that strange feeling she had experienced back in the office, or in her home, or back up at the foot of the hill. What had caused it? Why had the thoughts of an animal in the willows so terrified her? Why, she didn't even know if there was one there. And if there was, it would probably be more afraid of her than she was of it. Somewhere she had heard that, and she was certain that it was true. At least her rational mind told her that it was. But, if it was true, why was she so afraid?

There was also the matter of water. She had to have some, and so did Nelson. Why was it that she was suddenly responsible for both of them? And that in such a—a foreign place. For this mountain was indeed foreign to her, as foreign as if it had been on another earth. She knew nothing of the wilds, hated them in fact, and certainly she knew nothing of survival.

She thought then of one of her friends, a woman who had purposely taken a survival course. The woman had spent an incredible thirty days in the desert with an instructor and a few others, and she had come back a different person. Angela couldn't explain exactly what the differences were, except that the woman seemed less, well, silly. Or giddy. She had become much more quiet, and she seemed so much more self-assured. In fact, Angela had even considered taking the course herself, but had quickly discarded the idea when he had learned that her friend had, for one three-day period of time, subsisted on *bugs.* She had also gone the full thirty days without a *bath!* Now, as she thought about it, Angela found herself wishing that she *had* taken the course, dirt and bugs or not.

"Well," she said aloud, doing her best to motivate herself, "I didn't, and it doesn't change anything. I still have to get water!"

Reaching over, Angela picked up a long limb that lay on the ground before her. Holding it in her hand, she realized that it would make a fairly effective weapon, should one be needed. Then, taking a deep breath, she stood and resolutely made her way back down into the willows.

Again there was a rustling in the brush beside her, first on one side and then the other. But now Angela tried to ignore the sounds, steeling her mind against the fear of what might be there.

At last, perspiring freely despite the cold, Angela reached the bank of the small stream. Then, kneeling on a rock, she considered what would be the best way of getting water up into her mouth. She tried leaning way down but almost slid into the water, and so gave up on that. She recalled having heard once that cowboys had given their horses water in their hats, but she had no hat. Finally she made a cup out of her hands, and then she scooped handful after handful of water into her parched mouth. The water was a little muddy, and she wondered as she drank that she was doing so, yet it tasted so wonderfully good that she didn't even care. In fact, for the first time she really understood how her friend had been able to eat bugs, and she realized that under present conditions she might even be forced to do the same. What really surprised her, though, was that the thought of it did not seem very revolting at all.

Once her own thirst was satisfied, Angela began to consider how she would get water back to her husband. She had nothing to carry it in, nothing except—

Suddenly her face broke into a grin, and stooping down she unzipped her boot, removed it, zipped it back up, rinsed it in the stream, filled it again with the cleanest water she could find, and then began the cold but triumphant march back to her husband.

"But your boot, Angie?" Nelson said as she handed it to him.

"Hey," she said easily, "don't be such a baby. I've washed my feet at least once this week. Whatever's left is bound to be as good for you as pure protein. Besides, you once drank wine out of one of my shoes, and you seemed to like it then."

"Yuck!"

"Oh come on, Nelson. Drink up. Then maybe you can get my feet warm again. There was a time, you know, when you were pretty good at that. You haven't forgotten how, I hope."

For a moment their eyes met. Then Nelson winked, lifted the boot to his lips, and began drinking.

The two of them spent the remainder of the afternoon working their way slowly and tediously down the canyon. For most of the distance they were forced to make their way across the fallen timber of the steep hillsides, which greatly reduced their speed of travel. They did this because the bottom was either so choked with brush as to render it impassable, or else it was filled with swamps that had been caused by innumerable beaver dams.

Toward evening, thoroughly exhausted, the two sank onto a log to rest. It was then that the first snowflakes, drifting down out of the darkening sky, brushed against their haggard faces.

"Oh no," Angela groaned in fear. "It's snow! Nelson, what else could possibly happen to us?"

"Don't ask," Nelson gasped, suddenly coughing. "If you mention something, it's bound to happen. I'll tell you something else, Angie. We've got to have a shelter, and we've got to have it fast!"

"But where, Nelson? I don't—"

"Angie, we'll use the blankets. There's nothing else that we can do. Help me find a couple of short sticks with forks in them. We'll also need a long limb to serve as a ridgepole. Then, if we can set it up between these two trees—no, let's set it up there, between those pines." Nelson pointed up the slope, perhaps thirty yards above where they were sitting. "That'll get us out of the main thrust of the canyon winds.

"In addition," he went on, suddenly aware that Angela was watching him intently, "we need to level the ground so that the lean-to will face down the canyon but not downhill."

"But why?" Angela questioned. "Why go to all that trouble and work, when—"

"Angie, listen to me. A canyon, in the morning and the evening, acts as a sort of barometric wind tunnel. As temperatures rise during the day, the winds blow up a canyon. As they drop at night, the winds blow downward. We need to situate our shelter so that we will at least minimize the effect of the cold night wind. This snow tonight is going to make it a real doozer."

"Well," Angie replied slowly, "I'm impressed! Where did you learn all of that?"

"It was a part of my flight training." Nelson now grinned at his wife. "I may not be able to fly too well, but once in a while I remember *something* worthwhile."

Both grinned, and an hour later the blanket was in place, the sides were protected by closely placed pine boughs, and a small fire, lighted with Angela's cigarette lighter, was struggling to consume the wet wood they had placed upon it.

However, the snow was falling more heavily, and with no dry wood anywhere, both sensed that they were in for a long, cold night.

22

"Nelson," Angela whispered as her body shook uncontrollably, "Nelson, are you cold?"

There was no answer, no sound but the blanket snapping in the wind above them.

Angela curled herself more tightly into a ball, trying to stop her teeth from chattering as she did her best to get warm. What on earth was wrong with her coat? she wondered. How could it possibly keep men warm in the Arctic if it couldn't even keep her warm there? Of course it was wet, but it had dried a lot, and should be doing a better job of keeping her warm than it was.

What a miserable wind, she thought. And it was blowing down the canyon, exactly as Nelson had said it would. She was indeed impressed, and she knew it.

Longingly she looked up at the blackness that was the blanket, hanging suspended above. Oh, how she ached to take it down and wrap herself in it. But she couldn't, not now. The snow was falling heavily, was weighing the blanket down anyway, and it had become their only protection from its icy grip. But why did—

Thud!

"Nelson," she gasped, "did you hear that? Something's out there! Close!"

"Angie," her husband replied groggily, "I hope you aren't as cold as I am."

"Nelson," she repeated, more frantic than ever. "Nelson, there's something out there in the trees! I—"

Thud! Thud!

"There," she whispered, her voice filled with terror. "Did you hear it?"

"Angie, I—I can't hear anything. But we've got to get closer to each other. We've got to, or we'll never keep warm. I—"

Screeech!

"Nelson! You surely heard that, didn't you?"

"It's just a tree creaking in the wind, Angie. Trees do it all the time."

"But those other sounds weren't trees, Nelson. They were footsteps! I know they were footsteps!"

"Probably just snow. It builds up on the trees, and then falls all at once. Now come on. Lie down and let's at least try to keep each other warm."

Angela complied, and for a few moments she was silent, thinking. "Nelson?" she suddenly asked, her voice filled with fear. "Could we freeze, do you think?"

"No," he replied after a minute. "Not as long as it's snowing. The temperature moderates when it snows, Angie. Now stop worrying so much, relax, and let my body heat go to work on you. That's it, close. That way both of us can keep warm."

Already feeling a little warmer, Angela thankfully closed her eyes and did her best to relax. Unfortunately, directly beneath her hip was a rock, a giant boulder by the feel of it. There were also two or three others beneath her shoulder, another poking her in the ribs, and a branch from the shelter that was constantly brushing across her face.

Twisting and turning, Angela maneuvered her body, trying to find a comfortable position. Reaching under her she dug with her fingernails and finally pulled out four or five rocks. Then she settled back down.

But now there were new ones, jagged boulders in places where before there had been none. Rolling, turning, she dug at them, tearing her nails, getting her hands filthy, and still suffering from the hard and uneven ground.

"Angie," Nelson groaned after a few more minutes, "what's the matter? Why can't you sleep?"

"It's this awful ground," she replied. "Every rock on this mountain is under me."

"Here," Nelson growled. "Sit up, and let's trade places."

Quickly they did so, Angela grinned with delicious guilt as she thought of Nelson's coming discomfiture and of her own luxury, and soon she settled down. Oh, it felt so good, so—

And then she noticed that a sharp rock was digging into her, into her spine. Twisting about, she was doing her best to move her body to the side of it when she heard soft sounds, sounds of snoring, coming from her husband.

Astounded and hurt that he could be so comfortable, Angela slammed her body against her husband. Then she dug at another rock, feeling great satisfaction as she heard Nelson groan and roll over. If she was going to be miserable, she decided, then so was he!

"Oh," she wailed with self-pity, "I hate these rocks!"

"Yeah," Nelson agreed ruefully, "I can tell. However, I'll agree with you. This certainly isn't the most comfortable bed we've ever slept on. Do you remember that bed in the hotel down in Nassau? I've never seen a—"

"Nelson!" Angela cried, interrupting her husband. "Do you realize that right now my banquet is going on? Even worse, it's going on without me—without us."

"That's right," Nelson replied sadly. "It is. Honey, I'm sorry that you've missed it. I really am. I know how important it was to you. But I'll tell you what. Since it was my fault, I'm going to do something about it."

Angela, still wondering at the tingle she had felt when her husband had called her honey, stammered and finally didn't answer. But Nelson, not seeming to notice, continued.

Struggling onto his elbows he groped around in the darkness until he found what he was looking for. Then, rolling onto his side, he lay facing his wife.

"Angela Westport Armstrong," he said stiffly, "in honor of your being the most beautiful woman I've ever known, and in honor of your being the only wife I've ever been about to reluctantly lose, please accept this magnificent award as a token of my admiration and esteem."

Thoroughly shaken by her husband's words, Angela reached out into the darkness, took the award, realized that it was a soggy pine cone, and burst into laughter.

Without speaking further the two snuggled more closely together, closed their eyes, and each thought of the fact that as quickly as they were rescued, their divorce would take place. It was not a pleasant thought upon which to fall asleep, yet both did, and quickly.

In the hours that followed, the snow continued to fall, softly and silently, drifting across the ridges and filling in the hollows behind them. Each flake was not much, but added together the white blanket soon covered everything to a depth of at least a foot, and sometimes a great deal more. It was certainly not conducive to an easy survival experience for either of them.

A long time later, in the darkest hour before the dawn, and far up on the hill, sound suddenly seemed to hesitate. Then, for a moment, there was absolute silence.

Angela, sleeping lightly, opened her eyes and lay still, listening. In her mind there was the echo of hoofbeats, a faint drumming of sound, accompanied by voices, voices that she could not quite hear. Had she been dreaming, she wondered? Had she—

And then something else was there, a silent something on the mountain that gave her chills of fear and made her think of death. Nor was it the same as the eerie feeling that she had so recently experienced. That feeling, though spooky, had never been deathlike. This *was*, and in respect of it, or perhaps in fear of it, even the wind seemed to pause.

Angela cringed against Nelson's body, her breath still and her eyes wide and staring as she searched fruitlessly into the darkness of the mountain.

Their struggling fire had gone out, and yet the night, which was moonless, was not entirely without light. The snow, which covered the ground, cast a pale glow that gave the trees a spectral presence, turning the mountainside into a ghostly vista of strange forms and unearthly shapes.

Each of these shapes Angela watched closely, and each of them seemed, just as she looked away, to move. Catching her breath she would then stare once more, watching until her eyes ached from the strain and she would be forced to look away. And so it continued, the sense of death, the strain of suspense.

The scream, when it came, jarred against Angela's raw nerve endings like a rasp, and her body so leaped with fear that for an instant there was no part of her in contact with the earth.

But the scream, the long, unearthly, pathetic protest against all that was horrid and evil, persisted. At first it was almost silent, but then it grew louder, a tormented pleading, demanding, wrenching lamentation, filled with agony and with pent-up rage that death should thus be made manifest. And worst of all, the source of it was near, down the slope somewhere, near the willows, perhaps even in them.

And then, just as suddenly as it had begun, the scream was over, and the only sounds in the night were the sounds of wind and water, and an occasional slight cracking noise, as of bones being broken.

Totally unnerved, with chills of fear racing up and down her spine, Angela shook Nelson awake and did her best to explain to him what had occurred. Yet no matter how she tried, she was unable to explain to him the terror of that horrified scream, that cry of death.

Nelson, groggy with sleep, mumbled something about the

law of the jungle, and of the strong living by preying upon the weak. Then he was asleep again and Angela was alone once more.

For some time she lay silent, deep in thought. Over and over in her mind she played that scream, that terrible scream, and no matter how she twisted things around, she could not find a way to justify it. Of course Nelson was right. It was the law of the jungle, the law of the wild. The strong did prey upon the weak —even among people it was true. But still, that did not make it right. It could not be right, not when that scream had been filled with such injustice, such anger, and such helpless fear.

For the remainder of the long night Angela shivered in the cold, wrapped in the blanket next to her husband but hardly keeping warm. Nor did she sleep. She could not, not when her mind was reeling with so many questions.

Additionally, she was beginning to experience intense pains in her stomach, pains of hunger. And no matter how hard she tried, she could not will them away. It was as though—

Suddenly, from out in the trees, out in the darkness, a low and mournful howling assailed her ears! Angela, terrified, reached over to shake Nelson awake, but as she started to whisper his name he took her arm and placed his hand over her mouth. They waited then together, in the darkness of the night, for the frighteningly lonely sound to repeat itself. Angela's throat was dry with fear, and she found herself shaking again, trembling with fear, clinging to Nelson, wondering—

And then it came again, chilling, long and low, haunting, rising both in power and pitch until it seemed deafening, overpowering in its strength.

"Wolves," Nelson whispered. "That's what you heard a little earlier, I'm sure. A wolf killed a rabbit or something. The wind's blowing from them to us, though, so maybe if we're still they won't scent us."

Angela nodded in silent agreement, and then both waited tensely, listening . . .

The howling, when it came again, was definitely farther away, up the canyon and higher on the slope. A little later it came from even farther off, and after that they heard it no more.

"Wolves," Nelson repeated, speaking quietly. "Probably two of them — mates most likely, hunting together."

"Do they actually hunt together?" Angela asked, surprised.

"Sure they do. Their teamwork is amazing and, I've been told, very effective. Many animals actually work as teams."

"Oh, come on, Nelson. How can —"

"Angie, almost all birds work together. That's just one example."

"Well, yes. But —"

"Hey, let's forget it. Okay? Forget I said anything. My head feels like it'll split open any minute, and I just don't want to argue. Not now!"

Angela turned away, upset that she had been arguing and even more upset that Nelson had so effectively cast the blame for their disagreement upon her. It wasn't fair! It wasn't right! Why was it that, in a confrontation, she was always wrong?

Now, as her thoughts drifted once again to the impending divorce, she realized anew that for both of them it was the only sensible alternative. They had simply grown too far apart to ever be happy living together.

A little later, after an eternally long night, darkness at last began to fade. The light was increasing, and the black, featureless shapes of the dark were gradually turning into trees and stumps and rocks, snow-covered but still there. Angela, up on her elbows, gazed out through the still-falling snow, momentarily enthralled with the misty beauty of the canyon.

But then her mind went again to her husband, and she found herself wondering if it might be best for both of them if she were to leave him in the camp and go on ahead, find help, and send it back for him.

Such a move would accomplish several things, she knew. It would eliminate the conflict that was always between them, it would allow her to travel much faster alone, thus speeding up their rescue, and it would allow —

"Angie?"

Spinning, Angela looked guiltily down into her husband's eyes.

"Oh," she stammered, "I—I didn't know that you were awake."

"Have been . . . for quite a while . . . now. Since we heard the wolves. My head hurts too much to . . . sleep. Angie, I was just thinking, or at least I was trying to, though with this head of mine, thinking's a pretty rough proposition."

Nelson did his best to grin, and Angela looked quickly away.

"Angie, we may have many . . . irreconcilable differences between us, as they say. If we do, I'm sorry about them, and wish they weren't there. But in spite of them, I want you to . . . know, lady, that I'll be forever grateful for the way you . . . you've helped me the past two days. Without your help I'd never have made it."

For a long moment Angela stared bleakly out into the snow. Absently she picked up the pine cone Nelson had given her the night before, and with all her strength she hurled it away. Then, without answering, she dragged herself to her feet, shook the snow from the blankets, helped Nelson to his feet, and began preparations for leaving.

23

For all of that day Angela and Nelson struggled slowly down the canyon. Early on their going was easy, for the ground sloped gradually and the snow was not yet really deep. As the day wore on, however, the canyon steepened, and by afternoon they were in an area of cliffs and steep terrain. In addition, the snow continued to fall, wet and heavy, and soon the couple were encountering two- and three-foot drifts.

Frequently they fell, and in their starved and weakened condition they found it increasingly difficult to continue. Yet they did, for they had no choice, stumbling and falling and helping each other as best they could.

There was little conversation, for not only was there nothing to talk about, but neither of them had enough energy left to speak. Once, though, early in the afternoon, when a sudden fall had jarred Angela's side in a particularly bad way, she found herself in such pain that she was unable to get back up.

Nelson hurried quickly to her side, but even then she didn't move, didn't rise. She simply lay in the snow, her tears flowing freely. "Nelson," she finally sobbed, "I can't go on! I hurt too badly, and I just can't take anymore!"

For a moment Nelson looked helplessly at his wife. Then, taking her chilled hands into his own in a feeble attempt to warm them, he quietly spoke. "I know it's pretty hard on you, Angie. It's never fun to be cold and wet and in pain. But lady, we've got to keep going. If we don't, we'll never get out alive. Now come on. You can do it! I know you can!"

"But Nelson," Angela sobbed, "where are the planes? Where are the people who are going to rescue us? It's been nearly two full days now, and I haven't even *heard* a plane!"

Nelson gazed down at his wife, aching for her and wishing that he could somehow take her pain upon himself. Yet he couldn't, and he knew it. He knew also that she was right, that she could take little more. She had never been prepared for such an ordeal as they were going through; they were both suffering from exposure, and despite the fact that he was no more prepared than she, he knew that, of the two of them, his wife was suffering most.

Of course he was in pretty bad shape, too. His head was throbbing as though it were about to explode, and twice in the past hour he had fallen and had lapsed into momentary unconsciousness, finding himself again in the cold, dark cockpit of the Lear, trying to break free. He was also more thoroughly exhausted than he had ever been, and with each step he wondered where he would find the energy for the next one.

Additionally, there was another problem — the cold. Both of them had been cold and wet for so long that they were literally dying from exposure. Their core heat was being drained rapidly, and they were doing nothing to replace it. They had no food, and they had no shelter or dry clothing, things that were absolutely essential to the preservation of body heat.

Rubbing his hand across his face, Nelson felt his whiskers, and as he scanned the hillside below him, he tried to remember the last time he had gone two days without shaving. Or eating, for that matter, he thought ruefully. His stomach was now twisted into knots, and more and more he could feel the dizziness that came with hunger.

Once more he looked down at his wife, wondering, but then he decided that it was best to tell her. After all, she had as much right as he to know.

"Angie," he said quietly, "there won't be any search planes, at least before tomorrow, and even then there might not be any."

"What?" Angela shouted, struggling to sit up. "But why not? Denver knows that we went down! They must have notified—"

"You're right, Angie. They know. But when they investigate, they'll find that I filed a false flight plan, at least so far as the names on it are concerned. They might then conclude that the whole thing was a hoax, someone involved in criminal activity trying to cover his tracks, and never send out a search group at all. And even if they do, there will be no chance of anything going up before this storm lifts, and that will be tomorrow at the earliest."

"But why, Nelson? Why on earth did you . . . ?"

"I don't know, Angie. Pride, I guess. Or anger. I was so angry that I decided to get you to Mexico no matter what I had to do. I used Max's name because there had to be two pilots listed. I was only one, and you certainly weren't another. Whatever my reasons for doing it, it was pretty stupid of me. I—"

"I can't believe it!" Angela stormed. "The great and moral Nelson Armstrong, lying and—"

"Wait a minute, Angie! Remember, it was *you* who pushed me into that insane rage. You were the one who dumped my Indian things onto the Countach."

For a moment Angela was silent, staring at the ground. He was right, she knew that. She had pushed Nelson way too far. But how was one to know? How could one tell that—

"What about a ground party?" she suddenly asked. "Why can't a ground rescue party come after us?"

"There's a good chance that several groups are out already,

Angie. I hope so. The trouble with any search at all is that we must have flown several miles after we dropped below Denver Center's radar. They probably have no clear idea of where we actually are. Even in good weather a ground party would find looking for us to be like looking for the proverbial needle in the haystack. No, Angie-baby, if we're going to get out at all, we're going to have to do it ourselves."

"Don't you Angie-baby me," she snarled, more angry with herself than she was with him. "Now get out of my way! I can't wait to get out of here!"

Struggling to her feet, Angela stomped past her husband and began sliding down the steep slope, growing more angry by the minute. *Why,* she thought, *of all the incompetent—*

Suddenly, as she was crossing a large rock, she lost her footing and seemed about to fall. Nelson, horrified, reached out to catch her, to steady her. As he did so his own foot slipped, and as he thrust Angela back, he himself plunged headlong over the rocky precipice that he had just saved his wife from going over.

Angela, more surprised than anything else, simply stared at the place where he had vanished. Then, horrified, she made her way to the edge.

Twice she called Nelson's name, and when there was no answer she leaned out and, in the gathering darkness of early evening, saw the body of her husband lying still and silent about ten feet below.

Filled with intense anguish, she made her way slowly and carefully down to where he lay. There was a little blood on the snow beneath him, and a quick examination showed Angela that her husband had once again injured his head.

For a few moments she rubbed snow onto the wound and then onto his face, stopping the bleeding and trying to arouse him. When that didn't work she began shaking him roughly, pleading with him as she did so.

"Nelson!" she shouted. "Wake up! You've got to wake up before you freeze to death. Please, Nelson. Please wake up . . ."

And then Angela, totally exhausted and discouraged, sank back into the cold snow and commenced to sob, crying like she hadn't cried since she had been a little girl. She was so cold, so cold and so miserable, and now Nelson was gone, she was alone, and she was never going to get off the mountain alive.

For some time she did nothing but cry, her mind oblivious to all else. But finally, when there were no tears left within her, she struggled to her feet and looked around. Her will to survive was strong, and she was looking for a shelter, some place where she could drag Nelson where they would be out of the snow and the wind, some place where they might once more spend the long, lonely night.

Angela cringed at the thought of dragging Nelson, for her side throbbed angrily, and she knew she could not do much with it. Yet she had to, for there was no one else who would. If Nelson's life was saved, it would be her who would save it.

Carefully then she stepped downward, moving off the small shelf of rock, working her way down the steep slope, groping through the darkness of the trees, looking for a level spot of ground, searching for—

At first Angela thought that her eyes were deceiving her, much as her ears had done earlier with the sounds of hoofbeats. But no matter how hard she rubbed them or blinked them, she couldn't make the sight go away. There, down through the trees, glowing brightly, was the cheerful light of a small fire.

PART FIVE

24

The fire, when Angela finally reached it, was in the center of a small cove. The ground there was nearly level, and it formed a sort of shelf or bench, dropping off at the front and rising sharply behind. On three sides grew thick stands of timber, while the soil was fertile and covered, beneath the snow, with tall grass. To the left of the clearing some long-forgotten wind had ripped out literally dozens of trees, and they were now stacked helter-skelter along the slope. On the bench itself were three large boulders, ancient castoffs from the cliff above, and these formed a nearly perfect triangle. It was within this triangle, beneath a tautly stretched canvas covering, that the fire burned.

After catching her breath, Angela slowly looked around the camp. It was neat and well situated. Besides the fire beneath the shelter, she could also see some fur robes, and behind those were two or three packs, with some traps lying on the ground in front of them. Additionally, off near the edge of the clearing, almost out of the circle of firelight, grazed at least two animals, probably horses.

Fur robes? Packs? Traps? Horses?

For a wild instant Angela wondered if she had somehow chanced onto the location for the filming of some movie. That, of course, would explain all of the strange props that were scattered around.

A movie! That would mean actors, a crew, and so on. It would also mean rescue.

Turning slowly in a circle Angela called out into the darkness, pleading for help. But there was no answer, no sound but the wind and the whispering of falling snow. Suddenly she was lonely again, lonely and frightened almost to death by the terrifying emptiness of the mountain.

And then it came once more, the sense of being watched, of eyes behind her, boring into her back, willing her to—

Spinning, she looked wildly around, and then slowly she backed toward the center of the clearing, her eyes darting back and forth in a desperate effort to learn who was near. Her mouth felt suddenly dry, but when she tried to lick her lips she found that her tongue had stuck to the roof of her mouth. Working it loose and moistening her lips she backed toward one of the large rocks, her hand held out behind her feeling her way, her eyes bulging with fear.

"Who is it?" she pleaded in a hoarse whisper. "Where are you? Please don't—"

Click!

With her heart in her throat Angela spun toward the sound, and found herself staring directly down the muzzle of a huge rifle. Behind the rifle, his face obscured mostly by darkness, was the outlined form of a bearded man.

Angela screamed, long and loud, over and over again. But the man never wavered, never moved, and at last her voice grew still and she sank to the ground, shaking with fear and despair.

For long seconds there was intense silence, and Angela, her breath caught in her throat, thought she was going to suffocate.

But then, in a language that seemed almost foreign, the strange man spoke, and his voice was quiet, deep, and strangely gentle.

"Weel, ol' hos," the man said, apparently speaking to himself, "hyar's damp powder and no fire to dry it. As sartin as ol' Fetch-um Under hyar has hindsights, this afore us be a female critter. Aye, and a white one at thet, I says. Moreso, she's got the worst mess of flutterin' fantods this child ever seed, and all over nothin' a'tall."

"Please, mister," Angela pleaded, her words flowing out in a torrent, "my husband and I crashed our jet up on the mountain two days ago! We've eaten nothing since then, Nelson has hurt his head badly, he's unconscious up there in the snow, I can't move him anymore, and I've got to have help or we're both going to die! Please, don't shoot—"

"Whoa, marm," the man said, his rifle not wavering an inch. "Sech fofarraw words as thet don't shine with this child nohow. Now, get up off'n the ground and make yerself decent. It don't matter none thet yer some gaunt and look sort of undone in them-air men-clothes. Ye still won't pass inspection for arything but a woman under half a mile. Why, ye air showin' more underside right now than a gut-sick buffler calf. This ol' hos air plumb chagrined."

Angela, embarrassed in spite of the fact that she was more than covered with her slacks and parka, did as she was told.

"Now," the man continued, "be ye jabbering of yer companyero, of yer husband?"

"Oh, yes!" Angela declared, breathing a sigh of relief that the man had understood. "He's hurt badly, and I don't know what to do for him. Can you help us, sir? Please? We'll pay you anything you ask, and—"

"Weel, ol' Fetch-um Under," the man declared, speaking to his rifle again. "Strikes this child as how I might have company this night after all."

And then, slowly, he lowered his rifle. "Marm," he asked, looking once more at Angela, "be thet-air scratch on yer face the result of a Yuta arror?"

"What?" Angela responded, her hand going instinctively to

her cheek. "I—I . . . don't think so. I'm not certain what you just said, but I got this in the crash."

"Now, marm," the man said gently, "this child sees thet ye be some teched in the head. Set yerself down by the fire thar, chew yerself down some of them venison boudins, and I'll be fetchin' yer man."

Surprised, Angela looked again at the man. "But—but how will you find him? It's dark, you don't know where he is, and—"

"Marm," the man said, his voice now filled with impatience, "ye white female critters be all alike, noisier'n six pickaninnies with a possum up a gum tree. Squaws, now, air different, speak around men only if thar be something worth sayin'.

"Now, ye came from him to hyar, didn't ye? And ye left a trail in the snow, didn't ye? Aye, ye did, and this child'd bet a season's catch of prime plew yer trail'll be wider'n a buffler bull's. Wagh! Marm, this ol' hos could foller a trail sech as ye left, blindfolded. Aye, and all thet with a Blackfoot arror in his hump ribs. Wagh! Now go on! Do as this ol' coon tells ye. Fetch yerself a mouthful of them boudins, and I'll be back directly."

Then he smiled, and suddenly, once Angela had seen that smile, she felt certain she would never feel quite the same about a smile again. It was wide, splitting the man's face from ear to ear, spreading to his eyes, squinting them, crinkling them, filling them with a dancing light that somehow made her think of laughter and music and gentleness and . . . and care! That was it! The man's smile, his open, radiant smile, flowed out from his face to envelope her, the clearing, the trees, the muddy ground where they stood, the animals, and everything else that she could think of. And even more amazing, his smile appreciated it all, telling it all, telling *her,* that he cared! With all his heart he cared, and somehow it didn't even matter who, or even *what,* she was!

Turning, and silent as the steadily falling snow, the bearded man took three or four steps, paused, looked back, smiled at her again, and then disappeared into the darkness.

Angela, embarrassed, amazed, relieved, and thoroughly confused all at once, opened her mouth to call the man back.

Then she hesitated, wondered at what she was feeling, turned, and walked slowly to the small fire.

Who was the man? she wondered. And what was he doing there, in a blizzard like they were in? Was he really going to help Nelson; where on earth had he learned to *talk* like that; and above all else, what or where or how or why, his smile? Why did his marvelous smile affect her in such a strange way? It was also somewhat familiar, that smile, but for the life of her she could not recall where she had seen it, or the man, before.

Slowly Angela warmed her hands, seeing before her only the man's radiant smile. But at last, disgusted with her silliness, she forced all thoughts of it from her mind, tentatively reached out, and quickly pulled a small section of roast meat from the fire. Brushing the ashes from it, she carefully examined it, wondering what it was. *Boudins,* the man had said, whatever that meant. It looked something like sausage, only it was longer, and to be honest, it smelled wonderful.

Tentatively she took a small bite, chewed it, liked the taste, and took another. It certainly didn't taste like sausage. Yet it was good, she was more hungry than she could have imagined, and a quantity of it was before her.

Ravenously then she ate, and as she did so her mind raced in circles, from the crash to Nelson to the strange man and his smile and back to Nelson again, wondering if he would live, wondering if the bearded man could help him, wondering if he could help her to get off the mountain.

Who was the man? she asked herself again and again. With his greasy buckskin shirt and his huge beard he looked terrible, and yet Angela did not feel threatened by him at all. She could not, having once seen his smile! Rather, she felt safe and secure. At the same time, however, he made her worry, for something about him was not normal, was not right.

But no matter about that. He had willingly shared his food, and had willingly gone out after Nelson. Surely she could give him the benefit of the doubt. Besides, the meat *was* good, the fire was working wonders with her frozen body, and she was feeling a deep sense of relief and gratitude.

Shortly the man was back, Nelson's still form gathered in his arms in such a way that Angela wondered if it had been any effort at all for the man to carry him. Easing the unconscious body slowly to the ground next to the fire, the bearded man knelt down and began to examine him.

"Wagh," he said to himself, totally ignoring Angela. "Fetched hisself onct or twice on the noggin', I be thinkin', and right smartly, at thet. Onct he wakes up he'll have a headache built more fer a hoss than a human.

"Marm," he said, turning then to Angela. "Fetch this-hyar child his possibles, would ye please?"

"What?" Angela asked, totally bewildered by the man's strange speech.

"Thet-air parfleche bag, directly behind yer elbow."

Turning, Angela obediently pulled out the large leather bag. Then, struggling with the weight of it, she handed it across the fire to the outstretched hand of the stranger.

Mumbling something that Angela could not understand, the man began to rummage through the bag. At last, apparently, he found what he was looking for, pulled it out, and went to work.

"Wagh," he said to himself, ignoring Angela again. "It be a pity I've no vinaigrette at hand. The smell of sech salts would fetch this-hyar pilgrim around right smart, I be thinkin'."

At length the man appeared satisfied with his examination, for he dipped a strip of cloth into a pot of water that was steaming by the fire. Then, with gentle movements, he cleaned the wound on Nelson's forehead. Next, working almost more quickly than Angela could imagine, the bearded stranger placed a compress of dry leaves over the wound and bound it with another strip of cloth, this one dry.

"Whar be yer possibles, marm?" the man suddenly asked, looking over at Angela. "And yer weapons and yer horses, too? Be they all gone?"

"Possibles?" Angela repeated without comprehension. "I . . . I don't know . . . er, what do you mean?"

"Yer gear, marm. The truck sech as keeps ye alive from day to day. Wagh! Ye be slower'n the eighth scab on the seven-year itch!"

"I told you," Angela repeated, growing somewhat upset herself, "we have nothing save what we are wearing. That and these blankets. All else was lost in the crash of our jet."

"Weel," the man replied, shaking his head with obvious understanding and compassion, "without hos and beaver altogether, be ye? Sech doings shine with this child, they do. Been there hisself he has, time to time. Now fetch yerself over hyar, marm, and let this ol' coon doctor up that scratch whet slices acrost yer face."

Hesitant, and yet wanting desperately to be helped, Angela worked her way around the fire to where he sat.

"Wagh," he said as he looked at her wound, "let's see what sort of doings thar be hyar, now. Why, ye poor little heifer, ye air so skinned up thet yer maw wouldn't know ye from a fresh-taken beaver plew."

As the man worked gently on the gash that had torn across her cheek, Angela took the opportunity of examining him more carefully. His eyes, she noticed, were a deep blue, and in the light from the fire they seemed almost, even when he was not smiling, to dance with excitement. His nose was narrow and straight, and his teeth, when he smiled his radiant smile again, were even and very white. In fact, they were so white, so straight, and so even that Angela found herself wondering where he had had his orthodontic work done.

The rest of the man's features were hidden behind his full beard, which was dark and only lightly touched with gray. His hair, which he wore shoulder-length, was of the same color as his beard, and despite the old felt hat that he wore, it appeared to be neatly groomed and well cared for.

His fingers, Angela observed as he worked on her, were long and slender, and reminded her of her own hands. In fact, his one little finger was curved in the same strange way as her own. He was also tall, though not quite so tall as Nelson. Yet still he seemed the larger of the two, which was something she did not understand.

"How is my husband?" she suddenly asked, forcing her thoughts to change direction.

"Weel," the man replied softly, "his noggin'll be sorer'n a scalp-lifted Mexican, I be thinkin'. But he'll live, he will."

Again there was silence, broken only by the wood popping in the fire. Beyond the light from the flames one of the horses stomped its hoof, and then the man, his task nearly completed, spoke again. "Without hos and possibles," he said, smiling secretively. "Wagh! And a shame it be, with all this other fofarraw ye both be wearin'. Why, this child's never seed the likes of sech finery. Ye both be so purty thet this ol' hos feels like he oughter take off his hat. Trouble air thet it be more ornamental than useful. Whet be yer handle, marm?"

"Handle?" Angela questioned.

"La, marm. Whar were ye raised, thet ye don't know good English? Yer name, marm. Whet be yer proper Christian name?"

"Oh," Angela replied, grinning now as she started to grasp his verbal antics. "It's Angela. Angela Armstrong. And I do know good English. It's yours that I don't understand!"

For a long moment she defiantly locked gazes with the stranger. At last, though, he grinned, widely and joyfully, she smiled too, and the tension was gone.

"And yer man, Miss Angela? How might he be called?"

"His name is Nelson. Nelson T. Armstrong III. But how about you? What is your name?"

"Weel," he answered slowly, "out in these-hyar hills a man's name don't count fer much, 'specially when he's alone. Back to Pennsylvania, whar I were a wee one, I were given a good Christian name which I never liked much nohow. Nowadays, when there be reason and the other party be friendly, this child generally be known as Port."

Again the man was silent, though his hands continued to work on Angela's face, applying a compress similar to the one he had used on Nelson.

"What are the leaves you are using?" Angela asked quietly. "What are they supposed to do?"

"Yarror, marm. Grows wild hereabouts, and it be a narcotic of sorts. Aye, it be wonderful what yarror do to torn flesh."

Pausing then, the man who called himself Port examined his work, grunted with satisfaction, and then turned back toward the fire. Reaching in he pulled out a small strip of boudin, and without even cleaning off the ashes he began eating, chewing with great gusto.

"Hos and beaver gone, eh?" he said to himself between bites. "This child recollects a time onct, a few seasons back, when he and Ol' Bill were fetchin' beaver up on the Belle Fourche. Makin' 'em come, too, we were, right regular. But thet be Blackfeet country, and no worse brownskins ever thrust a lance or let fly an arror than the Blackfeet.

"It were early spring, it were, the ice were thick one mornin', Ol' Bill and this hos had broken through, and two prime plews were a-comin' into hand. Sudden though a duck flew over, movin' fast and straight, and Ol' Bill he dropped his catch and headed directly fer the bank.

" 'Do'ee hyar, now?' Bill asks without lookin' back. 'This coon sees sign ahead, he does. He'll be afoot afore long if he don't keep his eyes skinned, he will. Injuns air all about, they air, Blackfoot at thet. Wagh! Watch yer top-knot, ol' hos,' he says to me, and jest then a Blackfoot arror sighs outa nowhere and fetches itself into Bill's leg.

"Surprised? Weel, this ol' hos should stand hyar and say he were. More surprised'n a hen whet's hatched a duck, he were.

" 'Wagh!' Ol' Bill shouts, 'and this child without a hos to hand.'

"Weel, this hos turns, and off through the willers he sees thet-air Blackfoot gettin' set to fly another arror. Wagh, marm! This coon ups with ol' Fetch-um Under hyar, lets fly a lead pill, and makes thet-air Blackfoot come in a hurry.

"Wagh, this child says, startin' in to grin, fer he reckons thet the battle be over. Sudden though about fifty more brownskins pops out of the willers, leapin' and hollerin' like a whole passel of so many devils, with howlin's thet'd drive a wolf to suicide. It were a sight to give pause, marm. It sartin were!

"Bill, he lets fly with his piece, and then the both of us raises dust, arror in the leg and all.

"La, marm, it were a tight run air a long'un, I'd tell a man. But we kept our top-knots. Trouble is, fer the rest of thet season this child were without hos and beaver. It were a longish season too, and hungry, says I. Afore it were o'er I were gaunt as a gutted snowbird.

"Ol' Bill, though, he air a mean one. He pulled thet-air arror out, turned him around a few days later, scouted up them same Blackfeet, and made a raise of his outfit, he did. Throwed seven of the brownskins under, too, and sent the rest of 'em packin'. Thet Ol' Bill Williams air a wonder, he air."

Angela, totally captivated by this strange man's even stranger yarn, as well as by his unique way of expressing himself, was nevertheless troubled by the story. "Excuse me," she asked carefully, "but did you say that you were in a fight with *Indians?*"

"Aye, marm. Blackfeet. And more'n one fight too, I be thinkin', if the truth be known."

Angela laughed then, not sure what she should say next. Why, the man was either a liar or else he obviously had a problem of some sort. But she didn't want to confront him. Not now, not after all he'd done. Still, from what Nelson had once told her, the last Indian fight in the United States had been fifty or a hundred years before. This man couldn't have been involved in that. He was too young.

"Well," she finally said, almost imitating him. "You tell wonderful stories, Port. You really do. But I didn't know we still fought Indians in this country."

"Wagh, Miss Angela," the man said slowly, "this child don't know which country thet be which ye air speakin' of. As fer brownskin fights, this ol' hos has seed more'n he ever wants to see. I reckon thet Ol' Bill, were we to catch up with him, would tell ye the same, only more so.

"Howsomever, fer this night it's never no mind. Git outa them-air wet clothes, help me git yer husband outa his, and we'll set 'em to dryin'. Then—"

"You must be joking," Angela interrupted. "There's no way that I'll take off my clothes. I'm already cold, and—"

"Marm, it be the clothes what be makin' ye cold. Howsomever, ye do what ye will. This ol' hos been asked to patch holes in ye, not pontificate on no highbrowed principles of survival. Whichever ye decide, wrap them-air blankets about ye and yer man, and get ye onto thet-air side of 'im. Onct this ol' hos fetches Miss Clementine and ol' Flop-ears over thar some vittles —I'll . . .

"Miss Clementine," Angela interrupted again, laughing delightedly. "You have a woman here too?"

The mountain man looked at her with a quizzical expression on his face. "How ye do jabber on, marm. Miss Clementine be my hoss, and a fine critter she be. Flop-ears be my mule, and no finer critter ever packed beaver plew. Now turn ye in over yonder, and this child'll bed down hyar. Betwixt us and the fire, marm, we'll keep that man o' yourn warm until first light."

Angela, exhausted, nevertheless felt a sense of compassion for this good man who had to be at least partially insane. Yet, she thought as she snuggled down next to her husband, she was thankful for him, too. And intrigued. What on earth could he be doing . . . ?

Suddenly, out in the trees, sounding very close, an eerie howl rose into the still night air. Angela, terrified, sat straight up, her eyes staring out into the darkness.

"What . . . what was that?" she asked, her voice a whisper of fear.

"Marm?" the man questioned.

"That—that noise. What made that terrible howling?"

"Why, Miss Angela, thet-air were jest a varmint, a wolf-critter."

"But . . . aren't you worried that it will attack us?"

Slowly the mountain man turned his face toward Angela, smiling again as he did so.

"Marm," he replied gently, "thar were times when this child welcomed the company of sech critters. They be curious, aye, and they be hungry. Oftimes they even be friendly. But rarely, marm, rarely be they dangerous."

"Well . . ." she questioned, confused, "what about other animals? Surely some of them are dangerous!"

"Wagh!" the man said, stirring the fire with a stick. "Thar were a grizz onct, over on Embargo Creek, thet were a mite dangerous. She were an ol' sow grizz, one the mountain men called Bad Foot, and the night this-hyar pilgrim had his run-in with her, she were comin' on fast."

As the mountain man spoke, Angela sat transfixed, and the man's words carried such power that she could literally envision in her mind the experience as it had occurred.

"Thet-air grizz were in the berries, stowin' away vittles like her tapeworm were hollerin' fer fodder. She were a big'n, she were, and about as sociable as an ulcerated back tooth. Thet were on account of her bad foot, this ol' hos be thinkin'.

"Weel, this child were hardly more'n a youngster then, so green the other fellers had to tie up one of his legs afore they could clip his locks. I were happy, too—happier'n a lark on a sunny spring morning, fer I'd jest raised a stream whet were plumb filled with beaver lodges.

"*Wagh*, I said to myself thet day as I swung down the hill with ol' Fetch-um Under in my hand. *Fifty plews thar in thet-air creek if thar be a-one. Sech doins shine with this ol' hos. It surely do. Wagh!*

"Thet be the trouble with berries, marm. They do distract a man. This child had his mouth plumb full of 'em hisself, and were a grabbin' fer more, when thar were a commotion in the bushes dead ahead of him.

"Afore this ol' coon had a chance to more'n look up, thet-air grizz heaved up onto her hind paws, let out a wonderous fearful grunt, and throwed out her paw.

"Weel, this ol' hos caught thet-air saucer-sized hoof comin' in, and it hit me like a ten-pound maul. Them claws were filthy, covered with mud, and they took this child in the shoulder and cut diagonally down acrost my back, hurtin' like fire and leavin' a six-inch wide trail acrost my ribs and spine. La, marm, but it must've bin a sight to see."

Angela, her eyes wide with shock and her own growing fear, could not speak. She nodded only to indicate her understanding, and waited for the man to continue.

Port, though, was stirring the fire, not paying any attention to her, apparently finished with his story. Finally, unable to wait any longer, Angela asked him what had happened next. But her voice was filled with frustration and anxiety, and doubtless the mountain man noticed this.

"La, marm," he replied gently, "ye be wonderful curious—more'n ary woman I ever met in all my pershinations. Howsomever, if thet be the way yer stick floats, I'll oblige ye.

"This child," he continued, "were throwed some twenty feet down the slope into more bushes, and thar I lay, quieter'n a throwed-out feather duster. I reckoned thet the ol' grizz were about to hang out my hide, but when it didn't happen I lifted my head to see why.

"*Wagh!* says I when I seed thet-air sow grizz. *This day'll shine yet, it will.* Why? La, marm, thet ol' bar were movin' away, goin' up the hill. In a bit she were gone, and soon it were so quiet thet ye could hear evenin' fallin'."

"And that happened to *you?*" Angela questioned incredulously when the man called Port had stopped speaking.

"Aye," he said quietly, "thet it did."

"But—but what happened next?" Angela demanded. "How did you survive?"

"Weel, Uncle Dick Wooten, who were this child's partner thet-air season, patched me up. He used the yarror, same as I used on ye, and this pilgrim were up'n about in no time a'tall."

"Is the bear, is Old Bad Foot, still alive? Is it still . . . still around here?"

"Reckon so, marm. Reckon so."

Finished speaking, the mountain man stood and slipped into the darkness, leaving Angela with nothing but silence to contend with, silence and her visions of the angry grizzly. At last, though, even with those thoughts bouncing around in her mind, Angela succumbed to the warmth of the fire and to her own exhaustion, and fell asleep.

Some time later, back from moving the picket pins of his animals, the man who called himself Port smiled down at the sleeping couple. Then, quietly, he seated himself by the fire, opened his possibles, extracted a small leather Bible, and for several moments read in silence, his lips forming the words as he read.

That task completed, he pulled out another bundle, untied it, and removed a small journal. Then, working laboriously, he recorded the day's events. Only when he was finished did he ease himself into the shelter where, within minutes, he was also asleep.

25

Angela opened her eyes with a start and stared up into the darkness. For a few seconds she lay still, wondering where she was. But then she remembered, and instantly she knew that something, some sound, had awakened her.

Sitting up, she looked out into the darkness. She had apparently been asleep for hours, for the fire had burned down, and only a few red coals remained, winking in the night. In the blackness of the shelter she could see her husband's form lying next to her. Beyond him, where the mountain man should have been sleeping, there was nothing. The man called Port was gone!

Suddenly it came again, the noise that she was certain had awakened her. It was not much, just a slight sound of movement through the snow behind the shelter, but instantly Angela knew she was hearing the movement of a bear!

There would be nothing for a few seconds, and then a brief scraping sound, as of dead twigs or bushes being moved, and then there would be nothing again.

In the dim light from the coals, Angela looked around, searching for a way out. Her palms were wet with perspiration, her heart was beating rapidly, and in her mind she could clearly see the giant grizzly called Bad Foot.

Twisting, Angela reached to shake Nelson. As she did, she bumped the side of the shelter, making a terrible racket. Freezing, she listened for the bear to react. At first she heard nothing, and she was almost ready to breathe with relief when the shuffling sound came again, much closer and definitely coming toward her.

For a moment Angela could not move, and in the silence the sound of the animal seemed amplified a thousand times. It was very large, she could tell, and it was moving slowly, snooting around with its nose, looking for something to eat.

Suddenly she remembered reading about how a grizzly bear had attacked some campers in Glacier National Park a few years before. What had *they* done? she asked herself. How had they handled it? That's it! she remembered. They had kept still and had played dead. But—but one of them had been killed, and the other had spent months in the hospital. That wouldn't work!

Into her mind then came a scene from a movie, *Man in the Wilderness*, in which the lead actor, Richard Harris, had been clawed nearly to death by a giant grizzly bear. *For heaven's sake,* she said to herself, *stop thinking about it! You're just making things worse!* But she couldn't, and things couldn't get much worse anyway. When she closed her eyes all she could see were horribly mangled bodies. When she opened them, all she could see were the dim coals from the fire—

Fire! Weren't animals supposed to be afraid of fire? Yes! But how could she get to the fire to build it up? How could she—

Thump!

Angela was immediately still, her breath frozen within her chest. Listening intently, she felt her fear rising in waves around her as the bear nosed against the rear of the shelter. Slowly then it began moving to the side, coming around the canvas covering, a thin membrane that was all that remained between her and the giant grizzly.

There was no way that she could fight it off, no way at all. Yet it had to be done. If she and Nelson were to survive, she had to do it. The mountain man was gone, Nelson was still unconscious, and she was the only one left.

Groping around in the darkness, Angela's frantic hands suddenly grasped a round limb, a long limb that had somehow escaped the fate of the rest of the firewood. Holding it before her, pointed toward the entrance of the shelter, Angela wiped her sweaty palms on the blanket and waited. Her muscles were tense and rigid, her breathing was shallow, and she was absolutely *not* ready to fight a bear!

Oh, she groaned within herself, *if only—*

And then, suddenly, it was there! Where before there had been nothing, a huge black shape loomed menacingly out of the darkness. With a scream that was more to give herself courage than it was to frighten anything away, Angela thrust out with the nearly useless branch.

For an agonizingly long instant the makeshift spear touched nothing, and Angela was certain that she had missed. But how could she have done so? How could—and then, with a shoulder-jarring thud, the stick struck into flesh and bone. There was a low grunt, a quick movement backward, and then Angela, sobbing loudly, withdrew her spear and struck again. Once more it impacted, and suddenly the shape seemed to grow in size as it moved forward, coming toward her.

Screaming in fear and in defiance, Angela herself crawled forward, thrusting again and again, shoving the point forward as hard as she could. Once, as she struck out, a substance she *knew* was warm blood splattered across her face, nauseating her; several times she missed with her thrusts altogether. But she connected often enough that the huge bear stopped and began backing off.

"Oh, thank God," Angela sobbed with relief. "I *got* him! I did it!" And Angela watched triumphantly as the creature slowly backed away into the darkness.

For a few seconds there was the sound of movement—retreating, moving farther away.

And then the realization, the reaction to what she had done, began. First she shook violently, shivering so that she could hardly remain on her knees. Then tears came, copiously, and her body was wracked with sobs, long, choking sobs.

Putting her hands to her face, Angela felt the blood, now sticky, that had splattered there, and instantly she was nauseous. Crawling from the shelter she retched violently into the snow nearby, gasping and choking in the darkness until she was exhausted, wishing with all her heart that—

"Miss Angela," the voice called gently out of the darkness. "Air ye all right?"

Spinning in terror, Angela looked up, swallowed, and sighed with relief. It was the mountain man. It was Port.

"Port," she gasped, collapsing into his arms. "It was the bear! It was Bad Foot, you weren't here, Nelson is still unconscious, and—"

"Marm," Port said soothingly, "let this-hyar child help ye to the fire. Thar now. Set yerself down whilst I stoke up the coals."

As the flames began to lick at the fresh pile of wood, Port apologized for being absent, explaining that he had been off stripping bark from some cottonwoods to feed his animals.

"And ye fought thet-air critter alone?" he questioned wonderingly. "Thet were powerful courageous, Miss Angela. Ye'll do, ye will.

"Marm," he continued, seating himself across the fire from her, "the most wonderous act of courage thar be is to fight the unknown, to fight fear. Tonight, thet be whet ye did. And ye won, Miss Angela. Ye came out on top."

"Thank you, Port. To tell you the truth, I was scared to death!"

"Ye should have been, marm, fer to ye it were the bar. And it could've been, too. Fact thet it weren't makes no difference a'tall. In yer heart, marm, a grizz is whet ye fought. And the courage to fight a grizz be whet ye have."

"*Could have been?*" Angela questioned. "But wasn't it?"

"No, Miss Angela," the man said, smiling his radiant smile. "It weren't. Fact is, it were a porcupine—a big'un, says I, but still a porcupine. Its sign be right thar in the snow."

Angela stared at the man incredulously. "But—but—I thought . . . did I kill it?"

"No, marm. Wounded it, though, ye did. Them-air wolf critters thet we heard earlier? They be eatin' thet-air porcupine fer supper, I be thinkin'. Fact is, if ye air quiet, ye can hear 'em. If they could, they'd be a thankin' ye fer yer help."

Looking silently at each other, both suddenly began to laugh. Long and loud they laughed together, the hills around them echoing back their mirth.

At last, though, when the laughter had died, the two simply sat and looked at each other. Angela, more impressed and touched by the man's gentleness than she could say, found herself longing to touch him, to hold—

"Marm, what is it ye be thinkin'?"

Angela thought about the question, and sensed in it the fact that the man was vastly lonely, and wanting badly to talk. Of a sudden, so was she.

"Port," she requested softly, "sit down and say something sweet to me. I'm so scared and so lonesome that I could cry."

For a moment the man hesitated. But then he smiled, lowered himself to her side, and gently took one of her hands in his. "Miss Angela," he said quietly, "ye've no need to hear sweet nothin's from sech as me. Ye be a mighty fine woman, and thet ol' hos thar on the ground'll be the one to whisper sech words into yer ear. He'll do it, too, soon's he gits a little meat back on his ribs.

"Now, as to bein' skeered and lonely, I reckon I know the feelin'. I know it like ye can only know somethin' ye've lived with all yer life. This ol' hos be skeered and lonesome too. And a mountain sometimes can be the most lonesomest and most wonderously frightful place in all the world. Thet-air be true 'specially in the night."

"But Port, not you! Why, you've no reason to be scared!"

"La, marm. Thar be a whole passel of things whet skeer this child. First and foremost, thar be my own human frailities, of which I carry a sight, I'd tell a man. Thar be also the human nature of others, Miss Angela, which oftimes be lower'n skunk stink and every bit as putrefactin'. Sech dogged meanness be plumb discouragin', 'specially when this ol' hos has him a pretty fair idea of whet sech low-down action fetches. I worry about those folks, I do. I'm skeered fer 'em. And if'n the fat of folks sech as thet weren't already well done by the simple fact of thar onerous natures, why most of 'em'll go ahead and throw it into the fire and burn it to a chittlin' crisp simply because they persist in tryin' to destroy others along with tharselves. Them-air be some of the things sech as skeer me.

"Now, marm, I've bin rattlin' my jaws long enough. It be your turn. What skeers ye?"

"Everything, Port. I'm scared by everything. This mountain, the storm, my husband, his health, my health, the quiet, you name it. But especially I'm scared of the quiet! Two days ago everything was going so well, and now . . . this! It just isn't fair!"

Port laughed quietly, delightedly. "Wagh, Miss Angela, but thet air the truth. Thar be justice, all right, but it do seem a long time in comin'. Most always life air like the Camptown Races. Some ol' hos bets on the bobtailed nag, another bets on the bay. And then dogged if the black don't get up in the last furlong and wins it goin' away. If only we could take the long shots all over agin. But ye know, marm, a man gambles ever time he fetches hisself outa bed. If'n he aren't careful he'll stub his toe, fall and break his leg, and have to be shot. Still, that's no call to stay in bed fer the rest of yer life, is it? Aye, justice be a hard understood thing, sartin-sure as it be."

Now Angela laughed. "Port," she sighed, "I don't know who you are, but you're a tonic to my soul. Thank you."

"La, Miss Angela, I've done nothin'. Ye air a fine woman. Ye feel better because thar be better inside of ye, jest a-bustin' to git out. Now yer husband thar be shiverin' agin. What say we warm 'im up and git some shut-eye ourselves?"

Angela nodded, and they crawled into the shelter, lay down on opposite sides of the unconscious Nelson, and went quickly, peacefully, to sleep.

26

"Nelson," Angela whispered the next morning when the man called Port was out of hearing, "I agree with you completely. He's as looney as they come. But he's also one of the finest men I've ever known. Besides, we've no choice that I can see. If we're going to survive, we've got to stay with him."

Beside them the small fire burned brightly. It was sheltered by the rocks from the snow, which had almost stopped falling. That was a good sign, for both of them fervently hoped that the weather would clear. Another problem had arisen, however, that could very possibly delay any rescue attempt. The wind had started to blow, and in the early morning light Nelson and Angela could see icy fingers of snow drifting across the ground, already obscuring low-lying rocks and bushes. If such a wind got worse, they knew, it would not only hide them from sight of search planes, but it would make it impossible for such planes, or even helicopters, to land. Still, both felt good that morning, and each found it difficult to be pessimistic.

For Angela the night had seemed particularly wonderful. At least the final hours that had followed her encounter with the porcupine had felt good. It had grown bitterly cold, but she had hardly noticed it at all. The rocks and the shelter had contained and reflected the heat from the fire, and she had slept soundly and warmly for the first time since the crash.

Nelson too was well rested. He had regained consciousness shortly after Angela's fight with the "bear," which she had jokingly told him about already that morning. He had quickly realized that he had been rescued and that he and his wife were being taken care of, and so he had almost immediately thereafter fallen into a deep and restful sleep.

With daylight, however, had come the realization that, though they had indeed been rescued, the situation was not quite as he had expected it to be. First, the man who had rescued them was alone, and seemed to have no intention of joining others in the near future. Second, he was going up the mountain, not down. Additionally, he flatly informed both Nelson and Angela, in his unique speech pattern, that to do otherwise in such a winter would be "plumb foolish."

The final problem, and the one most potentially serious, was that the man had lost touch with reality and was likely insane, for he seriously considered himself to be a nineteenth-century mountain man.

Angela, when she could, had told Nelson of most of the man's statements of the night before. Those, coupled with things he had said that morning, were enough to convince Nelson that the fellow needed help.

Yet in spite of that the man called Port was quick and filled with savvy, and he seemed to have an instinctive ability to discern their needs and occasionally even their thoughts. To Nelson especially that was disconcerting, though Angela declared that it was comforting in a way to know that a man cared enough to worry about what she was thinking.

The man was also well armed, and though his rifle and knife were old-fashioned they were in amazingly good condition, and apparently had seen much use. He had also spoken once or twice of "raisin' hair," and from such statements Nelson concluded that the man was not averse to violence. Yet in contrast to that, his speech was never loud, his movements were always gentle, not only with them but with his animals and belongings, and he had a warmth about him, a humanness to his personality, which neither Nelson nor Angela was able to resist. In short, the man was an absolute enigma.

"Port," Nelson had finally asked that morning in an effort to draw the man out, "who exactly are you, and what are you doing here?"

"Wagh!" the man had replied, stirring at the fire with a stick. "I air a mountain man, pilgrim. This child be a cross betwixt a buffler bull and a painter; too strong to quit and too quick to fetch under. Sech folks as be less than thet don't shine with this ol' hos, nohow. Thar be nitro in these-hyar veins of mine, and these-hyar bones be forged of the same sech iron as forged ol' Fetch-um Under hyar. Ol' hos, this coon air a mountain man!"

Nelson had looked at Angela then, and in spite of themselves both were grinning.

"Uh . . . are there others—other mountain men than you?" Nelson had finally asked.

"Wagh! Course thar be others," the man had snorted. "We be on the trail of one or two right now. Ol' Bill be right up thar on thet mountain, as be Alexis Godey, Josh Ferguson, Henry Wise and Tom Breckenridge. Good men they be, and true. Thar be others, too, but not so many as when beaver were thick and Ashley were payin' eight dollars fer prime plew."

"And are all mountain men like you?" Angela had questioned.

"Weel . . ." Port had replied slowly, "not reg'larly speakin'. Most mountain men air plumb tough, meaner'n a catamount and sorer'n a scalped Blackfoot. This child air a greenhorn next to the likes o' them."

"Then I'm not certain," Angela had expressed, smiling, "that I'd want to meet any of those others. But Port, what *really* are you doing here, right now, today?"

At Angela's question the man's eyes had twinkled, and his

dazzling smile had worked its way across his face. "Wagh, Miss Angela," he had replied softly, looking down into the fire, "this ol' hos be on his way to the valley of the Salt Lake. We talked of lonesomeness last night, ye and me? Weel, hyar's why. Thar be a woman waitin' in thet valley, a woman whet puts me in mind somewhat of you. Why, thet-air woman be purty as a sunset over a mountain lake, and when she smiles it be like the sun breakin' through a bank o' storm clouds above a high mountain meadow. She and a little one, a son whet I hyar be even handsomer than his Pa, be a waitin' fer me. They be my family."

"Your *family*?" Angela had asked, surprised. "You have a family—I mean—uh—how long has it been since you saw them?"

Again the man had spoken slowly, and his voice had suddenly filled with loneliness and sorrow. "It be nigh onto two years since I seed my Sarah, marm. And this ol' hos's never seed the child a'tall."

"Two *years*!" Nelson had exlaimed. "Good grief, man, why not? Where on earth have you been?"

"Hyar. This ol' hos's been hyar these two years, huntin' and trappin' these hills, doin' his best to build up a stake fer them whet wait."

"But man," Nelson had continued, "two years? That's a long time. Why didn't you fly over, or drive, or take a bus or something? How could you ever stay away for so long?"

For a moment the mountain man had peered closely at Nelson, apparently concerned. "Wagh," he had responded finally. "This ol' hos be worried about ye, pilgrim. Ye speak funny, and this child don't savvy what ye be sayin'. How could I drive o'er when I have no livestock to drive? Whet air a bus I sartin don't know. And as fer flyin', thet don't shine neither. This child air no angel, I'd tell a man! Thar be no way he's earned his wings. Jest ask my Sarah.

"Now," he had declared, looking from Angela to Nelson and back again, apparently finished with the conversation, "I don't like to rush ye, but I've a notion we'd best get to movin'. Pack yer gear, wrap yer blankets about yerselves, and foller me."

"Very well," Nelson had replied. "But where exactly are you taking us?"

"We be goin' up this-hyar mountain," the man had declared laconically.

"*Up* the mountain!" Angela had exclaimed. "Port, we've just *come* from up there! We've got to get to a phone so we can notify the authorities. They'll be out searching, and—"

"Miss Angela," Port had stated, interrupting her. "You air usin' words sech as don't shine with this child nohow. But thar'll be no goin' down, not with this ol' coon. Should ye go it alone and foller this ol' hos's backtrail, it be nineteen days hard winter travel to Hardscrabble. It be nearly that to Taos, and no trail whatsomever to foller. Thar be no white settlements ary closer!"

"But what about farms or ranches?" Nelson had asked, suddenly wary. "I know this is agricultural country. And for that matter, what about all the small communities in this part of Colorado?"

"Pilgrim," the man had answered, exasperated, "thar ye go again. Ye be speakin' the King's English weel enough, but whet ye be sayin' makes no sense whatsomever. Now farms thar be near the Pueblo and at the abandoned Mormon town on the mouth of Fountain Creek. Thet-air be one day beyond Hardscrabble. Farms thar be as weel at Rio Hondo, one day this side of Taos. But they be Mexican, and oftimes not friendly to whites. As fer the Colorado, thet-air be whet the Spaniards call the Grande River, sech as flows off thetaway. Thar be no communities whatsomever along thet-air river, 'cept fer a few Yutas, who air friendly or not, as fits their fancy."

Nelson and Angela had looked again at each other, and each had seen the concern and wariness in the other's eyes. More and more the man was showing how far off the beaten path his mind had wandered, and more and more they were wondering just how much they could rely upon him.

"Wagh," the man called Port had continued. "With the snow this deep and more a'comin', this child reckons ye'd best stick with me. It be only the fourteenth, and this December be the worst fer snow and cold thet this child ever seed. Howsomever,

Ol' Bill be two days up the mountain from hyar, and if we foller him, we'll make it sartin."

With that final statement the man had arisen and, without looking back, had proceeded to his animals. These he had commenced saddling and packing, whistling a nameless tune as he worked.

"I'm telling you, Angie," Nelson now whispered, "he scares me to death!"

"He is a little spooky, isn't he," Angela replied. "Can you believe that he thinks this is December?"

"Well, it *does* look like it."

"Maybe so, Nelson. But that doesn't make it so."

"Another thing, Angie. He actually believes that we're following Old Bill Williams. Good grief! Bill Williams has been dead for way over a hundred years. He was killed by Indians . . . I think. Somehow this guy's lost a screw and fallen off the shelf, and somewhere in the fall he's also lost a hundred and thirty years. So you're right. The man's cracked, and it's kind of scary trusting ourselves to him."

"Still, Nelson, we really have no choice. He's the one who knows these mountains, not us."

"That's true, Angie. But we don't have to stay with him. We can go on our own, just like we were doing before we ran into him."

"Oh sure, Nelson. And we were doing great, weren't we?"

"Hey, what is this, Angie? Is there something going on between you and him that I don't know about?"

Angela's face flushed slightly, but she did not drop her gaze. "Frankly, no, though I can't say that I wouldn't enjoy it. No, Nelson, my sole reason for wanting to remain with him is that, crazy or not, he at least knows what he's doing out here. Neither of us knows anything about survival. Until we're rescued, I really think we should stay with him."

"Well, there *is* another thing to consider."

"What's that?"

"The weather and the Lear. The storm looks like it's lifting, and if we go with Port, I'm sure that we can get him to take us to the plane. Of course you know that the site of the crash will be the first place where the search party will look for us."

"I know, Nelson. Actually, there is only one thing about going with Port that bothers me. I'm not at all sure that I can make it back up that mountain. I really don't know if I have the strength to do it."

"Well, that's a valid point, Angie. But if we take our time and go slow, and if I help you, then I'm sure you can do it. Besides, it's coming on summer. The snow's bound to melt, and the climb won't be that difficult. By the way, how do your ribs feel?"

"They still hurt, but Port wrapped them while you were off in the bushes, and they already feel better."

"Well, my dear, you *have* gotten to know him!"

"Nelson, that was uncalled for."

For a moment the man looked at his wife, watching her eyes, wondering. "Yeah," he said at last. "You're right. It was. I sincerely apologize."

"Accepted. And you must admit that he *is* good at some things."

"Yes, but he's also about as different as a three-dollar bill."

There was another significant pause, and then Nelson, choosing his words carefully, spoke again. "Angie, that's another reason why we ought to go with him. We're indebted to him. He's saved our lives, you know. When we're rescued I'd like to take him with us. Then, after we've joined him with his family, we can take all three of them home and give him a good job and a little security."

"Are you really serious?"

"You bet I am! Wouldn't you like to do that too?"

Angela smiled. "Of course I would. But there's something else, too."

"What's that?"

"Well, you can't forget to throw in a few visits to a good psychiatrist. Maybe you could even set him up with Doctor Thomas."

Nelson laughed. "You're right again, lady. We'll get him an appointment with the Doc. Then he'll really be taken care of."

They both laughed then, sobered quickly, and sat looking at each other. Finally Angela broke the silence. "Nelson," she said quietly, "whatever you do after our divorce, don't stop liking people. You really care about them, more perhaps than anyone else I've ever known. That's probably your greatest quality."

"Angie," Nelson responded, "I—"

"Wait a minute," Angela declared, quickly interrupting him. "Don't say it. It won't work, and it isn't smart to think otherwise. Besides, I don't—"

"Hyar, you two," the mountain man called from the edge of the clearing. "Air ye holdin' a debate? If so, yer motion's carried and the floor's closed, cause thar's no time left fer further palaverin'. Whet I'm sayin' is thet ye'd best be hurryin'. Thar be a poudrie blowin' yonder, and a body freezes quick in sech a mess. Get a move on now, ye hyar?"

Again Nelson and Angela looked at each other. Then both smiled, wrapped their woolen blankets about themselves more tightly, and pushed forward through the snow toward the edge of the clearing, following resolutely in the tracks of a horse, a mule, and the strangest man either of them had ever met.

27

By the time Angela and Nelson had reached the bank of the rushing stream, about a hundred yards below their camp, they knew two things. First, the storm that they had blundered into, which had not seemed so bad while they had been in camp, was no ordinary spring storm. The snow, even where it had not drifted, was above their waists, and where it had drifted they had no idea *how* deep it was.

The second thing they knew, after that first hundred yards, was that they might be in very serious trouble. They were both completely out of breath, both were cold and very wet, and both realized that they had only just begun.

"Port?" Nelson gasped as they all paused to rest their laboring lungs. "What day did you say this was?"

"Wagh," the mountain man replied after he had cleared the phlegm from his throat. "It air the fourteenth of December. This child made away from the Pueblo the twenty-third of November, and has been battling the cold and the snow these twenty-two days. This-hyar be Thursday, accordin' to my reckonin', and it be the fourteenth of December. It be also," and the man added this for emphasis, "the *worst* winter this ol' coon has ever seed. And he's seed a heap, he air thinkin', from the Bitterroots to the Gila, and whetsomever in betwixt."

Nelson wondered for a moment whether or not he should ask the next question. But then he looked at Angela, realized that she was silently encouraging him, and so he went ahead.

"And what year is it?" he asked innocently.

"Wagh, pilgrim. Thet-air bump on yer noggin caused ye to be a mite fergetful, didn't it? It be the year of grace 1848, sartin as can be."

"And one more question, Port," Nelson continued seriously, hiding his concern. "Where exactly did you say we were?"

"Other than saying we were on Ol' Bill's backtrail, ol' hos," the man avowed, "this child didn't rightly say."

Turning then, the man called Port began adjusting the mule's pack, retying the knots and making the wooden bows of the saddle more secure.

The snow at last had stopped falling, and the clouds were beginning to thin. It was cold, however, bitterly cold, and the wind, which was quickly picking up strength, made the cold even worse.

Despite the blankets that Angela and Nelson had wrapped around themselves over their parkas, both were shivering violently, and Angela was certain she could go no farther. "Nelson," she whispered hurriedly while the mountain man's back was turned, "he's totally insane. Even if he's a good man, I'm starting to have second thoughts about following him."

Nelson nodded understandingly. "Maybe you're right. But Angie, the storm is lifting, and within another hour or so we should be seeing search planes. Frankly, I'd like to get up on that glacier where the Lear is. Our best chance of a quick rescue is there. And you were right a little while ago. Crazy or not, I'm sure this Port fellow can take us there."

"I don't care if he can, Nelson. I'd rather stay here!"

For a moment Nelson stomped his feet into the snow, trying

to restore circulation. His shoes seemed to provide no protection at all, and already he could feel a numbness setting in.

"Well, you've surely changed sides in a hurry, lady. Of course, I suppose we could stay. But if the search party doesn't find us for two or three days, what would we eat?"

"Oh, I'm sure Port will share his food with us, Nelson. He was generous with those boudin things last night and this morning, and—"

Suddenly the mountain man turned around and pushed through the snow toward them. "Weel, ol' hos," he said, speaking directly to Nelson. "Thet-air were the easy part, I be thinkin'. From here on it be steeper'n the price of calico goods in Santa Fe, and no good footin' either. Wagh!"

Slowly he reached up, pulled a pine needle from a bough above his head, and placed it carefully between his teeth. Then he spoke again. "Be ye thinkin' of stayin' behind?"

Startled by the man's perception, both Nelson and Angela started to deny their intentions.

"Wagh!" the man said disgustedly, cutting them off. "The two of ye lie like lame mules in full gallop. Ye deal out a whole passel of spurrous incinerations, and then when the chips air down ye won't back 'em up. Ye know, this ol' hos air comin' onto thirty years of age. I got one arm stiff with a Yuta arror down on the La Trinchera, a ball from a Comanch rifle took a hunk outa my ribs down near Santa Fe, and I air all gimped up with arthritis. But folks, this child'll be a suck-egg coon if'n I can't tie my one good arm behind me, stand on my bad leg only, and still whup me the livin' daylights out of sech as the two of ye be, either on the behind or stand up face to face, dependin' on which of ye wants to go at it. Now stay behind if'n ye've a mind to. But whichever, be a little more kindly with yer speech."

The man stopped speaking, and Nelson and Angela simply stared at him, too surprised to respond. When they didn't, Port continued. "As to yer earlier question about whar we be," he said gently, "these be the La Garita hills, which be a part of the Saint John Mountains. And, though I wish it weren't so, I swear thet this hyar creek be Alder Creek. I raised thet-air camp back thar afore, and know it weel."

"What's wrong with Alder Creek?" Angela quickly asked. "Why do you wish it wasn't so?"

"Nothin's wrong with it. Trouble is, marm, if thar be a pass up this-hyar creek, as thar needs to be, then it's been weel hid. Course, Ol' Bill knows him a heap, he do, and he be all'ays pulling up surprises. This ol' hos reckons as how Bill's cached more in his noggin in one year, and then fergot it, than most folks ever raise in a lifetime. Hurraw, says I, fer Ol' Bill. I air a-bettin' on him!"

"Are you trying to say," Angela demanded, shocked, "that you might be lost?"

The mountain man looked at her, smiled, and remained silent.

"Well, that does it," Angela snapped. "I'm not going another step! Port, we'd like to buy some food from you, enough to last for at least three days. You may name your price, and—"

"Wagh," the bearded man muttered, spitting out his pine needle. "Thet-air be impossible, marm. It be poor bull in these parts now, and hungry doin's, I be thinkin'. Them boudins whet we fetched down this mornin' air plumb gone, and with 'em went the last of our vittles."

"Oh, no!" Angela groaned. "Do you mean that—that you have no more food?"

"Thet be plumb-center true, Miss Angela. 'Course, ol' Fetch-um Under hyar be primed and ready, and most any critter whet moves'll be made meat right quick. Now, this-hyar trail be Ol' Bill's sign, and this hos don't like the feel of this-hyar wind. Marm, fetch yerself up on Miss Clementine thar, whilst yer man and I be breakin' trail. We air in fer a bad'n, I be thinkin'."

Without further ado or discussion the man turned his back upon Nelson and Angela and moved to his horse, where he waited. Nelson looked helplessly at his wife, shrugged, and spoke. "Angie, this guy may well be lost. But we aren't! We *know* that the Lear is up on that mountain. All we have to do is reach it, and we're home free. I say, let's go for it."

Angela gave Nelson a bleak look, shrugged her shoulders, and pushed past him toward the horse where the man called Port was waiting. "I'm ready," she said with resignation. "Would you mind helping me to mount?"

The man helped her up, and then turned to Nelson. "Ol' hos," he stated, "Flop-ears and I be goin' first, breakin' trail. You foller close, leadin' Miss Clementine and yer woman. And mind yer step, this child says. This-hyar trail be slicker'n a Blackfoot brave. Wagh!"

Slowly then the mountain man led out, beating down a trail with his body so that his animals would not be forced to buck-jump through the deep snow. And so began what was to become the most miserable day that either Angela or Nelson had ever spent.

Ol' Bill, or whoever it was who had gone ahead, had climbed the west side of the narrow canyon. He had traveled in a north-northwest direction, making a definite trail that was now almost filled in with new snow. And whoever it was had also chosen his route well, for the other side of the canyon was mostly jagged cliffs and deep gorges. In addition, there were a great many trees on the side they were on, both quaking aspen and yellow pine, and these served well for handholds and footholds.

A fire had burned through the canyon some time before, however, and the dead trees, most of which had fallen, made climbing and leading the animals very treacherous. The trees lay beneath the snow where they could not be seen, and constantly both men and animals were tripping over them, the men falling and the animals hesitating to move at all.

For some distance the trail wound like a snake up the steep hillside, and this they followed slowly, feeling their way carefully lest a misplaced foot send man or animal plunging toward the bottom. At first Angela feared riding the horse. But soon she realized how much easier it was than walking, and she began to appreciate it.

At one point, though, where the narrow trail pressed against the edge of a deep chasm, the horse slipped and very nearly went over the edge. Angela immediately dismounted, and no amount of persuasion could induce her to ride either of the animals again. If she was to fall, she insisted, she would do it on her own.

At length the trail came to the base of a high cliff. There it turned abruptly, descended to the bottom of the narrow canyon, crossed the churning and snow-covered stream, and continued up the other side. When Nelson and Angela reached the stream, leading the horse, the mountain man was already at its frozen edge, attempting futilely to force the mule to cross.

"Hyar, ye mangy ol' flop-eared mule critter!" he shouted. "Get on acrost thar!"

But the animal, bellowing with fright, was running up and down the bank, smelling at the ice, feeling it with its forefeet, and in general making a great deal of commotion.

Finally the mountain man, reduced to total exasperation, took up a pole that was lying nearby. Then, shaking it threateningly at the mule, he began smashing the thin ice that covered the edge of the creek, opening a watery pathway for himself, the mule, and the rest of the party.

Finished, he commenced taking off his outer clothing, paying no attention to Nelson and Angela at all. Surprised, they simply stared as he peeled right down to his long-handled red flannel winter drawers, complete with buttoned front and drop seat.

"Wagh!" he stated as he turned and picked up the lead rope of the mule. "Thet-air water looks colder'n the kiss o' death. Howsomever . . ."

And then both Nelson and Angela started to laugh. They did not want to laugh, they did not plan on laughing, but they could not help it. They laughed anyway, because they had never seen anything so funny. They had never seen long underwear before, and they had certainly never seen a scrawny-looking mountain man in red long johns, a big floppy hat, and bare feet, hopping about on the cold snow trying to keep his toes and heels from freezing.

"He—he looks like a dancing scarecrow," Nelson gasped.

"Or a red rooster," Angela added, holding her sides against her laughter. "I—I wonder how long he's practiced?"

As he saw that neither Nelson nor Angela was doing anything but laughing at his expense, the mountain man snorted again. "Weel, tinklin' hot brass shades of Hades!" he growled disgustedly. "It be a nachural misery travelin' in the company of sech wonderously unmiscerated comedians. Whet be ye pilgrims laughin' at? Have ye never seed no long johns afore? Git along thar! Climb on out of them-air fofarraw'n duds, the both of ye, and let's git on acrost this-hyar creek!"

With that he wrapped the rope two or three times around his hand, stepped into some willows, and peeled off even his long johns.

"Now wait just a minute!" Angela shouted, suddenly aghast at the prospects of what the mountain man had demanded. "Port, you can't be serious. You surely can't expect me—us, to strip down and wade naked across this river! Why, that's crazy!"

"Maybe so, marm," Port replied, grinning across the tops of the willows at her. "Howsomever, it's either strip now and keep these-hyar clothes dry, or strip over thar and put on other dry clothes then. If'n ye do thet, whar will ye git the dry clothes?"

"I—I—I'll wear these, and I'll stand by a fire until they dry."

"Miss Angela, thet's plumb onreasonable. It'll take far too much time. Now, if'n it be yer pride thet's holdin' ye up, git shut of it. If it be yer modesty, why, step on behind Miss Clementine thar, and stay behind her whilst ye cross. She makes a wonderous fine curtain.

"Howsomever, whetever ye decide to do, do it quick! Yer husband's peelin' off, and this ol' hos's about through chin flappin'. I be as bare as a Mexican baby's backside, and in this breeze I be startin' to turn solid. Come on, Flop-ears, let's git along!"

With that, Port lifted his clothing, his rifle, and his powder horn high into the air, and leading the mule he stepped boldly into the frigid water. Nelson and Angela, staring in amazement, watched breathlessly as the man worked his way through the chest-deep stream to the far shore, a distance of perhaps twenty feet.

Once on the bank he hastily wrapped a blanket about himself and commenced to dry off. "Weel," he called back through chattering teeth, "it be cold, and it be wet, but it be a good crossin'. Take yer woman by the hand, ol' hos, and lead her and Miss Clementine acrost."

"I can't do it!" Angela shouted. "I can't wade across that river! I'll die of pneumonia!"

"Thar were a time," the mountain man called out over the gurgling of the stream, "when this child had a mule sech as wouldn't cross cold water. Came to the day when I were in a hurry, trying to avoid some Rapahos whet were out to lift my hair. Left thet-air mule critter behind, I did, and felt mighty sorrowful about it. Year or so later this ol' hos passed thet same spot. *Hyar,* says I. *Thar be my mule!* And so she were, 'cept that she weren't. Only bones were left, fer wolves had feasted on the rest.

"Now, marm, ye stay behind if'n ye want, but I and the critters, and I be thinkin' yer man, air goin' on. I reckon I'll be back in about a year, should ye care to wait."

With that the man turned his back upon them and began leading his mule on up the trail.

"That isn't fair!" Angela shouted. "Port, that's playing dirty!"

Nelson, doing his best to hide his grin, spoke. "Come on, Angie. Get your clothes off, and let's go."

"No way! I'll cross because I'm too scared not to. But I won't take off my clothing."

"Don't be such a prude. There's no one but us around, and—"

Angrily Angela interrupted her husband. "I'm no prude, and you know it! I'm just freezing, and it's insane to stand here in the snow, already cold, and strip nude. I told Port how I was going to do it, and I meant it!"

"You sure?"

"Absolutely positive!"

"Okay, lady. Suit yourself. Let's go!"

Nelson reached out for Angela's hand, squeezed it, and plunged bravely and very nakedly into the freezing water, pulling his wife and the horse behind him with one hand, holding his bundle of clothes above his head with the other.

Angela, envisioning wolves chomping at her bones, reluctantly allowed herself to be led into the ice-filled stream.

For the first couple of steps she felt only the coolness of the water through her leather boots, and she was glad that she had left them on. But then the streambed dropped off, the water was immediately above her waist, and Angela's chest caved totally inward, her breath locked tightly into her lungs!

Nelson, seemingly unaffected, kept pushing forward, but she couldn't breathe, couldn't move. She tried to cry out but couldn't, and Nelson's insistent tugging dragged her even deeper into the stream.

Frantically she beat at the water with her free hand, trying desperately to maintain her footing. Yet the rocks beneath her feet were slippery, chunks of broken ice pounded mercilessly against her, and still she could not breathe!

The water was now nearly up to her neck, and her whole body was clutched in its icy, deathlike grasp. Fervently she prayed for the strength to breathe, for the stamina to reach the far bank.

Suddenly, though, she saw Nelson look back beyond her, his eyes showing a startled concern. Angela, twisting her head, was horrified to see the huge form of the horse almost directly above her. The animal's eyes were wide with fright, its nostrils were flared, and at that instant it was lunging forward, its entire frame bearing down upon her!

With a scream Angela pushed herself to the side, her pantleg caught on a sunken tree limb, she lost her footing, and she was instantly submerged. Then, for what seemed to be forever, she remained suspended in the icy blackness of the water, hooked to the tree. She knew that she was dying, and she found herself wondering that there was no pain, no deathlike agony, associated with it.

Suddenly, however, an arm was around her waist, she was pulled to the surface—and as she gulped in the cold, wet air, she realized that her husband had saved her life!

Immediately other arms were around her, taking over, and

she found herself being carried out of the stream by the mountain man, who had plunged back in, clothes and all, to help.

"Breathe, marm," the man repeated over and over. "Ye must breathe deeply, fer the cold has driven the air from yer lungs."

Then, while Angela sat huddled against her husband, her breath coming in ragged gasps and her teeth chattering incessantly with the cold, the man struck a spark and soon had a warm fire blazing before them.

While Nelson helped his wife remove her already stiffening clothing, Port hung out his own homespun trousers and shirt over the fire. Then, wrapped tightly in his blanket, he commenced drying and rubbing down the animals.

"Wh—why are you doing that?" Angela asked through chattering teeth.

"Animals git cold same as people," the mountain man replied quietly. "They'll freeze to death too, if'n we aren't careful.

For some time there was silence in the makeshift camp. The wind blew, and logs popped in the fire, but other than that there was no sound, none at all. Finally Angela spoke.

"Are my clothes dry yet?"

"No," Nelson responded quietly, "no more dry than you are sorry."

"Sorry!" Angela snapped. "Why should *I* be sorry?"

"For nearly getting us all killed," Nelson answered hotly.

"Coming from you, mister ace pilot, that's quite a speech."

"Whoa thar, pilgrims," Port interjected, doing his best to stop what was happening. "It be past now, and—"

"Past?" Angela spat. "Past? What's past? Nothing, that's what! I've crashed in an airplane, thanks to my dear husband, I've staggered over half the Rocky Mountains in a raging blizzard, nearly freezing to death, and finally I've nearly drowned in that miserable river, thanks to you. And now I'm supposed to be sorry. Well, I'm not! I'm mad, clear through!"

"La," Port replied, grinning at Nelson. "Thet woman of your'n has more brass than Grandma's bedstead, like a woman oughta have. Fact is, she kinda reminds me o' my own Sarah."

Scornfully Angela turned away, and Port, stirring the fire, looked up and winked once more at Nelson. For some time no one spoke, and then Port, after watching Angela reveling in her hurt pride and anger, finally spoke.

"Wagh," he said slowly. "The quiet be so thick around hyar thet I reckon we could slice it up and serve it."

When that brought no response, he spoke again.

"Point of actual fact, Miss Angela, ye did right fine crossing thet-air creek, considerin' thet it were yer first time and thet ye had yer clothes on and all. And *ye* did good as weel, ol' hos. Thet water were almighty cold!

" 'Course, this child recollects a time, six or seven winters past, when I were with two fellers, names of Black Harris and Scotty McKnight, up on the Yellerstone. We run into fearsome cold water, much worse'n this. It were deathly cold, so cold thet even the birds had froze with their songs stuck in their throats. Boys, says this ol' hos to them other fellers, thar be beaver hyar, and thet a'plenty.

"Trouble is, them-air lodges be acrost the Yellerstone, over yonder. To raise them plews, I says, we've got to wade the river. And with thet I strips off and plunges in.

"It were cold, I'd tell a man! Colder'n the kiss of death. This child's breath left him with one whoosh, and he never breathed again 'til he were on the other side.

"Black Harris, he were right with me, hurryin' and feelin' the same. Scotty McKnight, though, declared he'd rather die'n take off his clothes. Weel, he waded in with us but soon dropped behind on account of he were weighted down somethin' fierce with all them wet duds, and afore Black and I knowed whet had happened, Ol' Scotty were froze solid, plumb in the middle of the stream.

"Black and I looked at each other, and both of us knowed that Scotty were gone under. We also knowed it were Blackfeet country, and ary a brownskin but whet wanted to lift our hair. That meant we had to raise them-air beaver plews quick, if we were goin' to do it a'tall.

"Without sayin' a word then the two of us turned our backs on the froze remains o' Scotty, went to work, and in a few days we'd raised a sight of fine beaver.

"It were near a week, marm, afore we finally finished. Then we fetched Ol' Scotty out, built a fire, and thawed him down fer burial. Black and I were right sorrowful, too, watchin' him thaw, fer we'd lost sech a fine companyero. We were gettin' set to plant him deep, though, in spite of it bein' winter in the middle of Blackfeet country.

"Funny thing, though. When thet-air fire had melted the ice down to Scotty's chest, he whooshed out with a sudden breath of air, give a loud holler, and said, Hurraw, boys! Thet-air river took my breath away. It be nice to be pulled out so quick. Now bring on the beaver. I air fit to be a mountain man again!"

For a moment no one spoke, and then, almost simultaneously, both Nelson and Angela burst out laughing. Finally Angela threw up her hands. "All right," she gasped, "I'll stop fighting. I can tell when I'm beat. Besides, crossing naked *can't* be any colder than this is."

After another silence while the three of them watched their clothing steam above the fire, Nelson asked the mountain man a question. "Port, you are always talking about killing Indians or nearly being killed by them. I don't mean to be critical, but haven't you ever heard of racial tolerance, of all men being brothers, and so on? In your work, don't you ever work in cooperation with them?"

"Ol' hos," the man answered, "thar be many brownskins as trap the beaver with us. I've knowed a few, but I'll tell ye of one sech as would do ary a man proud to know.

"This past spring a feller name of Bill Sharp and I decided to head fer the Salt Lake country to join with my Sarah, pickin' up a few plew on the way to make the trip worthwhile. We left early, crossed the Wet Mountains and the Sangre de Christos, and came into the La Garitas near hyar. We picked up a stream whet had plenty of beaver lodges, set up camp, and Bill went one way to set out a line whilst I went the other.

"I had mine set, and were on my way to help Bill when I

seed his hoss a-comin' down the draw, all lonesome like. Weel, something were mighty wrong, so I fetched myself back into the trees and out of sight. The hoss came nigh the bottom and stopped, and then out of the trees up above come four Rapaho braves, and I knowed Bill had gone under.

"Fer some time I studied on how I could get to my own critters, whet were acrost the canyon. Thar weren't no good way, but each time the brownskins were out of sight in the trees I raised a little dust my ownself, movin' down and acrost the canyon.

"I were about to the bottom when I reckon they heard my hoss, fer of a sudden they come straight down the mountain toward me, and I were sartin I were goin' under too. I did have ol' Fetch-um Under but hated to shoot because of whet Sarah'd bin tellin' me about lovin' my enemies. So I lay low, and each time the Rapahos went into the trees I made another move, changin' directions, hopin' to get acrost the ridge with my hair.

"This child were about a hundred yards short of the ridge when the brownskins stopped and looked off down the canyon. Whet they were a seein' were a puzzlement to me, so I hunkered down and skittered out a mite to see fer my ownself. And thet were a shock, says I. Eight Yutas, and I were sartin I would lose my top-knot now.

"Weel, with a whoopin' and a hollerin' them brownskins went at each other, and it were a grand and bloody sight to see. Howsomever, the Rapahos were no match fer the Yutas thet day, and all but one went under quick. Thet one, though, fought long and fierce, and downed all the Yutas but one. They went at it again, and both went down, I thought to stay. But the Rapaho pulled hisself to his feet, staggered to his hoss, and went down onct more.

"This ol' coon waited about an hour afore makin' a move, and then I went on down to see what I might see. Weel, all the brownskins were dead but thet one Rapaho, and he were about done in. As I stood lookin' down at him I could see thet he'd bin hit purty hard, and would sartin need help if he were to live.

"The thought crossed my mind thet a year or two past and

this ol' hos would've let him die. But betwixt Sarah and the Lord I were a changed man. I gathered whet of the hosses together thet I could, and with the Rapaho on one of 'em I crossed back over to my camp.

"Weel, I cleaned up his wound and then went to look fer Bill Sharp. Couldn't find him, so I figured he'd made it out without his hoss. When I got back the Rapaho were still thar, so I reckoned he liked my help.

"Thet-air brownskin had learned him some English, and we soon got to palaverin' about this and thet. I were some surprised to learn thet he were a peaceable man with a family and sech. Thar were differences betwixt us, but we agreed on a great deal.

"After a few days thet-air wound were healing wonderous fine, so we packed all the hosses and lit out o' thet Yuta country, me and the brownskin travelin' together. 'Course we went slowly, and on the way we kept on palaverin', about his ways and mine, and about his feelin's of peace and mine. I were tryin' to love all people, and he already loved practically the whole blamed earth, includin' all the critters whet were alive on it. I could see thet I had some to go. 'Course fightin' to him were not an act of anger or hatred, but of honor. So ye see he had some way to go as weel.

"When we rode into his village some weeks later, I were a hero. I were invited to share his lodge, and thet were a new experience fer me. His folks were wonderous fine, howsomever, and give me all of whet they had, and would've got more had I asked fer it.

"The Rapaho were a big man in the village, so in no time I were adopted into the tribe, given a medicine bag and a new name. I can't tell it to ye, pilgrims, for it be sacred. But the name means something like Brother-Beyond-Years.

"This ol' hos reckons the main thing he got thar in thet village, though, were a clearer understandin' of some other folks thet the Good Lord had placed on his earth. And pilgrims, even missin' out on the chance to get to Sarah this past spring were worth it considerin' the friend whet I made."

"So you actually are good friends with an Indian?" Nelson questioned again.

"Aye, ol' hos, thet I be. And he be my friend, too."

"Well," Angela replied, her voice sounding unintentionally sarcastic, "at least you don't scalp them *all* the time."

But then, after seeing the hurt look on Port's face, she realized what she had said and quickly apologized. After all, they were in a pretty tough spot, and Port was a good man to have around when the going was rough and one was stuck without "possibles" on a desolate mountain in the middle of a late spring storm.

It turned out that the ice-filled stream had to be crossed eight separate times that day, and each time the experience was more terrible. Never from that first plunge were the three able to really get warm. Although their clothing remained basically dry, for even Angela stripped after the first crossing, they walked with stiff and frozen limbs, and their body heat slowly dissipated.

Finally, late in the afternoon, with the frigid wind whipping the snow into a frenzy around them, the three chilled and exhausted travelers stumbled around a rocky point on the steep hillside and entered a small grove of trees.

"Wagh!" Port muttered as he paused to look around.

Angela, grateful for any kind of rest, no matter where it was, sank into the snow at her back and closed her eyes.

"Weel," the mountain man said after a minute. "Thar be little enough hyar, says I. Still, thar be no doubt about it. This wonderous spot on the mountain be Ol' Bill's camp, and thet be a sartin-sure fact!"

"Camp?" Nelson echoed in surprise. "You've got to be kidding! Who'd ever camp in a place like this?"

"I would," Angela groaned resolutely. "In fact, I'd camp in the middle of that frozen creek back there if I thought I could sleep for an hour or so."

"Port," Nelson uttered, ignoring his wife, "I'm serious. This is a steep hillside! How could anybody sleep in a place like this?

One false move, one roll in your sleep, and it would be the last good-bye—down the mountain you'd go!"

The mountain man looked around again, pushed his way up the hill three or four feet, and then began to kick the deep snow aside with his foot. "Ol' hos," he said finally to Nelson, "come hyar and take ye a look-see. This be a side-hill bed, sure as ol' Fetch-um Under has hindsights. This-hyar bed were fine lodgin's fer two men."

Nelson looked more closely, and saw two newly cut logs lying one on top of the other, both horizontal to the slope. Against those logs, on the uphill side, snow had been packed until the narrow spot behind them had become almost level. Finally, on top of the snow, pine boughs had been laid, and that constituted Old Bill's side-hill bed.

"Wagh," Port said then, smiling brightly at Nelson and then at Angela. "This be the spot, and this be the time to do it. Set ye both down and take a breather, and in no time a'tall this child'll have us a camp what'd put a Yuta brave to shame. Wagh!"

28

Working quickly but with great difficulty, the man called Port led his animals into the trees, picketed them, removed their saddles, and brushed them down. When he had finished he threw his packs over his shoulders and made his way back through the deepening snow to the shivering forms of Angela and Nelson.

Then, as he spread his canvas shelter over some quickly placed limbs, he apologized for taking care of his animals first. "It air my way," he explained forthrightly. "The good Lord gave man the sense to use hisself and care fer hisself. Animals, though, be dumb, and when man uses 'em, he ought to care fer 'em as weel. Besides, them critters has done a heap of work fer this child today. I'm beholden to 'em."

While the mountain man was finishing the shelter, Nelson dragged himself onto his feet and began foraging through the snow for firewood. However, there was not much readily available, the snow was deep, and in Nelson's weakened condition the task was anything but easy. Still, after a great deal of effort, he managed to accumulate a substantial pile.

Port, rummaging through his possibles sack, removed his flint, steel, and small bag of punk. To his disgust, however, he discovered that the punk, or tinder, was sopping wet.

Hurriedly he trampled through the snow to the nearest pine, where he scraped around near its base, searching for dry needles or bark. Gathering what he could find, he made his way back to the shelter and began his futile efforts toward starting a fire.

The wind by then was howling fiercely around them, driving the snow before it, slamming the icy particles into their already numbed bodies, chilling them more than ever. In its fury there was no chance for Port to strike a light.

As Angela watched Port work, her clothing, where it was wet, began to freeze to her body. Her feet had long since lost any feeling, and she was certain that she had suffered at least some degree of frostbite.

Nelson was in no better condition, but he was standing rather than sitting, and so was able to move about, thus aiding his circulation.

"Miss Angela," the mountain man said as he struggled with his wet tinder, "ye'd best stand and move about some, afore ye freeze to death whar ye sit."

"I—c . . . c . . . can't," Angela articulated through chattering teeth. "I ca . . . can't move. Please hurry . . . with the fire!"

"Here, Angie," Nelson said, doing his best to blank his own misery from his mind, "I'll h . . . help you."

Gently then Nelson assisted his wife to her feet, and together they paced back and forth in the trodden-down area before the shelter.

"I air plumb ashamed," Port at last admitted as he held his chilled hands up to his face so that he could blow warm air upon them. "Cain't recollect the last time this child couldn't strike fire."

"Nelson!" Angela exclaimed. "My purse! G—get my purse! It's in—in the pack . . . over there. We can use the lighter that Hector gave me last Christmas."

"That's right! You do have it with you."

Port, looking thoroughly puzzled, at last spoke. "Listenin' to the two of ye," he muttered, "air about as understandable as eavesdroppin' on a couple of wooden cigar-store Indians. Ye might as weel be sayin' nothin' a'tall."

Both Nelson and Angela ignored him, and so Port said nothing more, but watched silently as Nelson pulled the small Gucci bag from the possibles sack. Nor did his expression change as Nelson finally located the small gold lighter. "Here," he said excitedly, holding it out to the mountain man, "use this."

Port, his eyes reflecting his total bewilderment, took the small object and, turning it this way and that, did his best with his frozen fingers to examine it. Finally, unable to solve the puzzle, he spoke.

"Whet be this-hyar fofarraw, pilgrim?"

"Oh, come on," Angela replied impatiently, rolling her eyes at Nelson. "You know as well as we do what it is. Now please hurry and start the fire."

For a long moment the mountain man sat quietly, looking first at Angela and then at the lighter. "Marm," he said finally as he turned the lighter over and over, "ye've got the best of this ol' coon. If this-hyar fofarraw be goin' to strike fire, then one of ye'll have to do it."

Nelson, muttering his disgust, reached out, took the lighter, and flicked it into flame.

"Wagh," Port exclaimed, falling backward, his voice filled with surprise and fear. "Now if thet-air arn't enough to take the gristle off'n a painter's tail. Ol' hos, this child never seed sech fancy doin's! Give this ol' coon another look at thet-air striker."

Nelson, now feeling honestly sorry for Port's illness and childish ignorance, looked at Angela, shrugged his shoulders, handed the lighter to the man and showed him how to work it.

"Wagh!" Port whispered in awe. "Don't thet-air beat all? This child never seed sech flint 'n steel. Ol' Bill'd give a prime plew to see this, I be thinkin'. Wisht he were here, I do."

Beaming then with the pure pleasure of his discovery, and yet obviously sorrowful because his friend could not share it with him, Port flicked the lighter a few times, knelt down, and in no time at all had a warm fire blazing before the shelter.

As the welcome heat began to thaw their outer clothing, Port showed Nelson and Angela how to slowly peel each article off, lest they injure themselves or the clothing that remained beneath. Draping the wet clothes over a makeshift drying rack, they wrapped themselves in the almost-dry blankets, and then they huddled before the fire, fighting the smoke and the freezing wind that was howling down off the peaks above them.

"Them-air be fancy boots ye be wearin'," Port said, pointing at Nelson's and Angela's recently removed footwear. "They be fair trade-goods, more'n likely, but poor doin's in weather sech as this. Now, thar be extry moccasins in my possibles whet ye ought'er wear. And Miss Angela, though they be a mite out-sized, we'll wrap yer feet in extry blanket strips, and ye'll be fine."

Such footwear, he went on to explain, made of moccasins and two or three layers of wrapped blanket strips, was warmer than most other kinds of boot, for it allowed greater circulation in the legs and feet. Additionally, such shoes dried easier and more quickly when they were wet, and did not disintegrate from constant exposure to water.

"Now," Port continued, his smile once again lighting his face, "yer socks be finally thawin', and thet-air be a good sign. Don't ye peel 'em off, though, 'till yer feet be throbbin', and then do it slow-like. Otherwise, ye'll lift yer skin off too."

Doing as they were told, Nelson and Angela carefully peeled themselves down to their underwear, using blankets for privacy and warmth as well. Then, standing on the buffalo-skin robe, they moved back and forth, keeping their circulation going while their clothing warmed and dried.

Finally dressed again, Angela moved off into the trees alone. Port, watching her go, turned at last to Nelson. "Miss Angela be a fine woman, ol' hos, and purtier'n a new red wagon."

Nelson, leaning back from the fire, looked at the man and responded, at last, with a question. "Port, how do you know her beauty isn't just skin deep?"

"Weel, ol' hos," the mountain man drawled, "thar be many things whet tell me thet. Now ye take her gait, fer instance. She moves loose and easy, with plenty of reach and swing. Her fetlocks air trim, her cannons slim, her hips—"

"Wait a minute, Port. She's not a horse."

"Wagh, and thet-air be the truth, pilgrim. Miss Angela air a woman, a fine woman, and it'd be a nachural sin if'n ye were to let her git away from ye."

"But Port," Nelson groaned, "you don't understand! She—"

"Pilgrim," Port snorted, "this ol' coon understands plenty. Ye've both bin about as cheerful as a couple of fly-bit buffler bulls, and thet tells me a whole lot. Now unlock yer brain-wheels! Ye air burnin' brakeshoe leather faster'n ye can strap it on. Thet woman be the catch of a lifetime, and ye air lettin' yer marriage come unraveled. Don't let it happen!"

With that, Port pushed himself slowly to his feet and, without speaking further, removed a small, blackened cooking pot from his possibles. This he filled with snow and placed carefully on top of two green logs that had been laid parallel across the fire.

Later, after Angela had returned, and while the snow in the pot was melting, Port rummaged again through his possibles sack, which seemed to Nelson and Angela to be filled with everything a person might ever need. Soon he extracted a hardened, tightly wrapped ball. This, he explained as he pulled back the outer layer, was rawhide, the uncured hide of an elk that he had killed the winter before.

With his long hunting knife, which he called a "Green River" blade on account of its trademark, Port cut from the roll two small sections. These he placed in the already boiling water.

"T'arn't much," he said ruefully, "and it be poor bull at thet. Still, it be hot, and fer three starvin' pilgrims it be as good as fat cow."

Angela, aghast at the prospects of such a meal, watched with revulsion as the pot boiled and steamed. That was worse than bugs! It had to be! Still . . .

At last, when the first hot cup of this rawhide stew was

handed to her, she gulped down her feeling of nausea and looked pleadingly at her husband, somehow hoping that he would help.

Nelson, however, simply grinned and spoke. "Bottoms up, Angie-baby. It's a whole lot better than nothing, and that's the only other item on the menu."

Tentatively, and holding her breath, Angela pressed the steaming cup to her lips and tasted the foul-smelling brew, fully expecting to lose whatever might be left in her churning stomach. To her surprise, however, and though she was terribly reluctant to admit it, Port's "poor-bull stew," as he called it, was not at all bad. In fact, the more she drank of it, and the more she realized how hungry she had been, the better it tasted.

Later, after all had drunk their fill, and while Port was out watering the animals and helping them to find forage, Nelson and Angela hurriedly made up the bed within the shelter. Then, already shivering from their brief exposure to the cold, they scampered quickly inside and buried themselves beneath their blankets and Port's heavy buffalo-skin robes.

Suddenly Angela, surprising herself with her spontaneous concern, rolled over, and with her body she warmed the spot where Port, that strange yet gentle and compassionate man, would sleep.

Within a few moments he was back, stomping his feet, clapping his arms about himself in an effort to restore his circulation, and vocally worrying about the starving condition of his animals. Then, using what appeared to be a large clavical bone from some animal, which he had also pulled from his incredible possibles sack, Port banked the snow high around the fire and around the shelter, protecting all of them even further from the raging wind.

Finished at last, he piled the fire high with all but a few of the remaining limbs that Nelson had gathered, and then he crawled quickly into the shelter.

"Ahhhh," he said as he snuggled into the blankets, "it be warm! Thet-air be what my Sarah did of an evenin', marm. Thar be no better bed-warmer than my Sarah, I'll tell a man. Howsomever, ye'll run a close second. Thank'ee, Miss Angela. Thet were mighty kind."

For a time then no one said a word. Each seemed content to simply gaze into the warmth of the fire before them, thinking, dreaming. . . . At last, though, Angela sighed and spoke.

"I don't know why exactly, but mountains really do *frighten* me. . . ."

Her words seemed to float out into the darkness, hanging suspended in the air. For a moment neither of the men responded. But at last Port, apparently stirred by Angela's statement, took a deep breath and replied.

"Why, Miss Angela," he said kindly, "I air surprised at ye. Mountains be God's country. Up hyar be whar He lives. How can ye be afeered of thet?"

"Maybe that's why they frighten me," Angela replied, laughing lightly. "But seriously, I don't understand them at all. There is so much that is unknown, so much that is dangerous, so much that is foreign to everything I understand."

"Marm," Port asserted, his voice filled with his own smile, "mountains be jest flat country, which the good Lord fer some reason left standin' on thar ends."

They all laughed then, and finally Angela, anxious that Port should understand her feelings, spoke again. "I know what you're trying to say, Port, and I appreciate it. But it still doesn't change the stillness up here. Of all the things I find uncomfortable about mountains, the quiet is the worst of all. I can't tell you how much I miss my music."

Suddenly Port grew serious, and in the darkness he began once more to speak, to paint a scene with his words which Angela and Nelson could almost see.

"It were early mornin', Miss Angela, and as this ol' hos crawled from beneath my bedding I saw the most beauteous golden sunrise a feller ever saw creeping down the craggy peaks above me. As I looked up, a flock of honkers winged past, their 'V' movin' on south, seekin' some warmer place to spend the winter.

"The mountains, the Saint Johns, these-hyar very ones, in

fact, have fourteen peaks that rise above fourteen thousand feet. When it rained whar I were, as it oftimes did, it were usually snowin' on those peaks. Winter comes early to the high country, and a man in these hills had best be ready fer it if he's to survive. Even in the summer the nights be cold, for the air be thin and heat escapes the ground easy.

"The creek whar I were trappin' were in a small park, located at about ten thousand feet. It were an October mornin', and as this ol' coon stood and stretched, I watched my breath drift off into the frosty air. Then agin I glanced upward.

"The rock walls above me looked sheer, pilgrims, but I knew they were broken enough so that I could have climbed them. In fact, I'd done so afore. The cliff above me were crowned with a thick forest of pine and fir, and beyond that lay some of the most wonderously beautiful parks in all the world. I knowed thet herds of elk and deer fed in them parks. From the ridges above them, this ol' hos'd seen all the way south to Taos, and I'd gazed into that misty distance often.

"Movin' quiet in the silent dawn I headed off toward the creek, plannin' to wash and take my mornin' drink. Sudden though, as I topped a small rise, I come on three deer, a doe and her two fawns. The deer were browsin', nibblin' at the brush along the stream.

"For a moment they stepped along unawares. But then a mornin' breeze carried this coon's scent to 'em, their heads come up alert, long ears pointin' forward, they looked at me, and then with a bounce they were gone into the trees. Miss Angela, I'd never seen anythin' so graceful, so god-like.

"The stream, comin' down from the high-up peaks, chuckled and sang as it danced over the rocks beneath it. The water, crystal clear, chilled by the meltin' snow, shaded by the pines, the aspen and the willows, caught the color of the sky and bounced it back at me, tellin' me that everthin' I saw were pure and clean, makin' me feel the same.

"Below me a family of beaver had built a dam, spreadin' the creek into a mirror of a pond, broke only by the widenin' 'V' of an old beaver swimmin'. There were also the spreadin' circle where a rainbow trout had just leaped up fer breakfast. The water showed the trunks of the ghost-like aspen and the gold of their leaves a-dancin' in the first rays of the sun. It were a beautiful sight, pilgrims, one I wish always to remember.

Port paused for a moment, gazing into the darkness of the canvas stretched above him. Then, after a long sigh, he continued.

"Miss Angela, this child don't know whet it be thet ye want out of life. But if I were ye, I'd pray thet the good Lord would one day let ye walk alone through a high meadow filled with wild flowers, and let ye listen to the music of a summer wind singin' in the pines. I tell ye, ye've never heard sech a hymn, sech a wonderous fine symphony, as thet. Music? Why, thar be no finer music in all the world than thar be right hyar.

"And Miss Angela, until ye've sat a horse on a rocky cliff somewhar above timberline, with naught but the strong bare peaks about ye, and seed the great black thunderheads, swollen heavy with rain, gather about ye, with lightnin' flashin' and thunder boomin' and bouncin' back and forth amongst the cliffs —until ye've bin thar and heard thet, Miss Angela, ye've never heard a real sermon.

"And finally, until ye've looked upon vast distance, until ye've stood on a high narror ridge at twilight, above whar yer trail dips down, disappearin' into a deep canyon whet be brimful of darkness and shadows, the mountain about ye as quiet as the day after the earth were born, until ye've stood thar in air so clear that the distance dies and ye can see peaks risin' through the purple haze hundreds of miles away—until then, Miss Angela, ye can never understand how glorious God be, and how magnificent be His handiworks. Talk about a prayer! Thar be no better prayer than a mountain, risin' high to be near the feet of God. Thet be whet mountains air like, and thet be also why I love 'em."

Angela, as she lay in the silence that followed, realized that this man, this strange man who uttered such powerful words, had been speaking to her soul. For he had calmed it. In some inexplicable way he had soothed her spirit, so that, in spite of her pain and her agony, she felt better inside than she had felt in years. And then she wondered, as sleep overtook her, whether or not Nelson was feeling the same.

29

Angela awoke with a start. Sitting up, she quickly pulled the blankets around her neck and then stared out through her steaming breath. Nelson was already up and sitting alone by the fire, seeming almost to be pulled tightly back into himself, shutting himself off from the unbelievable cold. His hands were stretched toward the flames, and even as close to the fire as he was his breath was visible for long seconds after he expelled it. It was cold, bitterly cold, and Angela could not bring herself to leave the warmth of the bed.

"Good morning," she said brightly as she pulled the blankets even more tightly around her neck. "Aren't you cold?"

Nelson looked up, did his best to smile, and nodded.

"Well, why don't you wrap yourself . . ." Angela had started to ask why he wasn't using one of the blankets, but had suddenly realized that he wasn't because *she* was. Nelson had left her his blanket so that she would be more comfortable!

Scrambling quickly, she wiggled into her parka and crawled from the shelter, bringing the blankets with her. Two, which had been closest to her body, she gave to Nelson. Then, feeling already nearly frozen, she pulled the others quickly around her shoulders.

"Wh—where's Port?" she asked, her teeth starting to chatter.

Nelson, still shaking with cold, nodded his head toward the grove of trees where the animals had been bedded down the night before.

"Over there," he answered slowly, "moving more snow so the animals can find something to eat. He's worried about them, Angie. Says they're in pretty rough shape."

"Does he think they might die?"

"I don't know," Nelson replied, looking at his wife. "How are you feeling?"

"Cold. But my ribs don't hurt at all. And I'm also *starving!*"

"Yeah," Nelson said, grinning again. "Not to worry, though. Port's fixed us a whole new pot of poor-bull stew."

"*New?*" Angela questioned.

"Well, sort of. New water, anyway."

Angela forced her cracked lips into a smile and, reaching up, adjusted the blanket more securely around her husband's shoulders.

"Thanks, Angie," Nelson said as he moved closer to her. Then, after a moment of silence, he spoke again. "Wind's stopped, but there are six inches of new snow. It's almost five feet deep. I measured."

"I just can't believe it, Nelson. Five feet of snow, and it's supposed to be summer! I'll bet the ski resorts are going crazy."

"Probably. You know, Angie," he said, changing the subject, "this may sound foolish, but sometimes I almost wonder if Port isn't right and it *is* December. . . ."

"Come on, Nelson," Angela scoffed, "you can't be serious?"

"No, not really. But I've never seen anyone look so lost as he did last night when I handed him your lighter. Either he has honestly never seen one before, or else he's the best actor I've ever seen."

"I don't think he's acting, Nelson. I really believe he's a hermit, and has fantasized himself into believing that he is an honest-to-goodness nineteenth-century mountain man. The insane, you know, seem the most plausible to themselves. Port has somehow adopted his own time period, he has imagined the reality of having a family, and it is so very real to him that he actually believes he is on his way to Salt Lake City so that he can be with them."

"I've read where that has happened, Angie, and I think you're probably right. Did you notice the expression on his face when you unzipped your parka last night?"

"Uh-uh," she replied, shaking her head.

"Well, Angie, if you'd been looking, you would have seen the same puzzled look on his face that we saw when he first took your lighter. I really don't believe Port knows he has seen a zipper before last night. In fact, twice while your coat was drying I saw him examining the zipper, working it up and down."

"That *is* fascinating," she answered.

"I'll say it is. What else do you have in your purse that is a twentieth-century invention?"

"I don't know. Let's open it up and see."

Quickly Angela and Nelson looked through her purse, bringing out lipstick, a ball-point pen, a fingernail clipper, a plastic comb, and a fifty-cent piece that carried John F. Kennedy's portrait and had been minted in 1977.

"Show him everything but the money, Angie. We need to be sensitive to his mind, and that date on the coin might be too much for him."

"I think you're right, Nelson. But I agree with you that we ought to show him the rest of these items. Then we can play the coin thing by ear."

"Angie," Nelson said thoughtfully, "there's something else going on that I find strange."

"Oh? What's that?"

"It's the trail, Angie. Someone with a lot of horses or mules is moving ahead of us up this mountain. I saw the droppings and the hoofprints over in those trees last night. They were all over the place."

"I believe that. It explains the hoofbeats and the voices we heard a couple of days ago, when we both thought we were dreaming."

"That's right, Angie. But it *doesn't* explain who they are and why they're climbing the mountain in a storm like this."

"Maybe someone's rounded up a herd of wild horses—or maybe we're actually following a bunch of horse thieves."

Nelson laughed. "Maybe we are. But even if it—"

"Mornin', pilgrims!" Port called as he hove into sight, making his way toward them through the deep snow. "Air ye ready fer another climb?"

"I suppose we are," Nelson answered, "though to be honest, I think we'd both rather sit right here, drink your stew, and enjoy the fire until the storm lifts and the search planes spot us."

When Port's face displayed its look of incomprehension, Angela poked Nelson lightly and motioned toward the articles she had taken from her purse.

"Port," Nelson said, handing the several items to the man, "you've been in the mountains for quite a while. Have you ever seen things like these before?"

"Wagh," Port replied quietly as he fingered the articles. "My wife, Sarah, wore a comb sech as this in her hair the day she set out fer the valley of the Salt Lake. But hers were tortoise shell, and this ol' hos don't rightly know whet this'n be made of. As fer these other pieces of fofarraw, whet air they?"

As Angela described the items one by one, both she and Nelson watched Port's face. And never, they both declared to each other later, did they see anything but an almost childish delight as he learned the use of each article. To both of them it was apparent that Port honestly believed that he had never seen such fofarraw, as he called them, in his entire life.

"Wagh!" he said finally, his voice filled with wonder as he flicked the ball-point pen up and down. "These-hyar trade-goods be the most matritooshunal albilooshinizin' fofarraw . . ."

Angela laughed outright. "Port," she giggled, "you don't make any sense!"

"La, marm," the mountain man replied, grinning himself. "Ye air throwin' fancy senseless words around this mornin' yerself, and it shines with this ol' hos, it do. Now leave me show off my own doggon eroodification, lest ye think yer travelin' with an unedyecated idjit."

All three laughed then, and finally Port, still grinning his wonderful grin, began dishing up their breakfast.

They ate the liquid meal in silence, with Port constantly putting down his cup to finger the items Angela had shown him. At last, deep in thought, he stood and led his animals to the fire where he loaded the packs onto the already secured saddles.

Angela, when she first saw the horse and the mule, was shocked at the appearance of them. "Oh, Nelson," she cried, "look at the poor things!"

Both animals, having eaten nothing for nearly two days, were skeletal creatures made of heavy flanks and yellow teeth. Both had large globs of mucus frozen around their eyes and nostrils, and there were frozen scabs of sores hanging from their coats. Additionally, during the night the starving mule had eaten nearly all of the horse's tail, chewing it off clear to the flesh, which was now covered with a bloody scab.

"They air in bad shape," the mountain man agreed sadly. "Trouble is, thar be nothin' else this child can do fer 'em."

As the three people began their lonely trek, leading the weakened animals back onto the barely discernible trail, Port turned and again spoke. "This child," he said, obviously still thinking of the things he had been shown by Nelson and Angela, "has seen a heap in his day, of strange and wonderful goods. But none held a candle to whet ye showed me last night and today. This ol' hos still can't decide whet to make of it."

Then, with another shake of his head, he turned and plunged forward into the morning—the morning and the rapidly worsening ground storm.

All day long the wind howled into the faces of the weakened and staggering party. The mountain man, fully aware of the dangers of freezing, did his best to set an easy pace. There were things a man learned about the cold, he explained to Nelson and Angela during their first rest. The first was to never work up a sweat. When a sweating man slowed down or stopped, he explained, the sweat froze inside his clothing, forming a thin layer of ice near the skin. After that, unless the man found shelter quickly, it was only a matter of time. He had also learned, he said, not to dress too heavily, and to wear his clothing loose so that it formed a cushion of warm air next to his body.

Following their instructional rest, the three set out again, traveling even more slowly than before. For the next two hours there was no talking at all, and the only sounds, other than the constant moaning of the wind, were the groans of the laboring animals and people.

Shortly before noon, according to Nelson's reckoning, they came to the mouth of the narrow draw they had been following. Before them a small valley opened up, white and desolate. Their trail crossed it diagonally before beginning the ascent of a steep and totally barren mountain that rose abruptly on the far side.

Where the party stopped, there was almost no wind. Yet on the slope across from them it was blowing wildly, scattering the snow before it in huge, billowing clouds.

As Angela gazed at the enormous hill, she shuddered at the thoughts of climbing it. Leaning back gratefully into the wall of snow at her back, she closed her eyes. Then she did her best to slow her labored breathing while she tried to temporarily release her mind from the ordeal she was experiencing.

Angela was soon joined by the mountain man and her husband, and for some time the three silently regarded the hill that rose before them. Angela, deep in thought, was aware of the exhausted condition of the animals, and she found herself wondering not how long it would take the party to climb the hill, but whether they could climb it at all.

Port, gazing toward the summit, which was perhaps three hundred yards above them, suddenly spoke. "It were on a hill sech as thet one be," he drawled slowly, "whar ol' Bill saved this-hyar child's life."

Angela, expecting another yarn, looked at her husband, grinned in spite of the pain to her face, and turned expectantly back toward the mountain man.

Speaking quietly, and not looking at his listeners at all, Port began his brief narration.

"It were winter, this pilgrim were a greenhorn, fresh from the east, and thar were no one who could show him aye or nay. He reckoned he knowed it all, and could show the others a thing or two hisself.

"Aginst considerable advice, he pushed off alone, a blizzard a-comin', fer his first shot at raisin' beaver plew.

"On a hill sech as this-hyar, his animals give out and went under, and he were stranded with a gimped-up leg and no food nor fuel, nor any way of raisin' any.

"Fer two days this ol' hos fought thet-air blizzard, and had near lost the battle when outer the churnin' wall of snow come a mountain man. Wagh! His hair were red, and his face were browner'n a berry and yet covered hairline to chin with freckles. Altogether he were near the ugliest and yet the purtiest sight this child had ever seed. His name, he told me, were William Sherley Williams.

"Well, thet-air mountain man warmed me up, fed me, fixed up my leg, and hauled me off thet-air mountain, he did. And thet is how ol' Bill saved this-hyar pilgrim's life."

Angela, deeply touched by the man's brief story, found that she could not help comparing it to her own. Yet even more than that, she was touched by the things Port had left unsaid, and by the deep emotion that she had detected in his voice.

"You think a lot of Old Bill, don't you?" she heard herself saying.

The man looked at her for the first time since he had begun his story, and again he spoke. "Of mortal folks," he said with feeling, "Ol' Bill be my third closest friend. He be a man I love with all my heart!"

"Your *third* closest friend?" Angela repeated, not understanding.

"Aye. My wife, Sarah, be my closest. Wagh! And she be the one this child'll spend ferever with, I be thinkin'. The Rapaho be my second."

"The Indian?" Nelson asked, surprised.

"Aye."

There was a prolonged silence, and then Nelson spoke again.

"And this Bill Williams who saved you, is that the same Old Bill that we're following?"

"Aye, thet it be."

"Then . . . if you're so close to him," Nelson continued, "why aren't you with him now, instead of following him? It's pretty obvious that you aren't really trying to catch him."

"Weel . . ." the mountain man responded slowly as he turned his face away from them. "It were his wish."

For another moment no one spoke, but then Port turned back and, his wonderful smile lighting his face, pushed himself out of the snow. "Wagh," he said, doing his best to cover his recently exposed emotions, "thet-air hill yonder be goin' nowhar fast. If it's to be climbed a'tall, then we'd best git about doin' it. Air ye game fer a little run to the top, ol' hos?"

"I don't know," Nelson responded, his face serious. "Are you?"

"Game but a little gut-shrunk at the prospects," the mountain man answered, grinning. "Fact is, I be shakin' like a duck in the desert, I air so nervous. Miss Angela?"

"I guess I'm ready," she replied, laughing. "But Port, I'd like to know where you get all of those sayings?"

"Whet sayin's be thet, marm?" he responded seriously.

"Why, all those . . . those . . . oh, never mind. Just don't stop. That's half of what keeps me going."

"Whetever ye say, marm," Port responded, winking at Nelson as he did so. "Whetever ye say.

"Hyar, ol' Flop-ears," he shouted then, turning to his mule. "Get along thar! And ye as weel, Miss Clementine. Hyar! Get on with ye!"

And so, with Angela and Nelson struggling to keep up, the man who called himself Port pushed off down the slope, working his way toward the opposite hill.

30

The mountain, once the party reached its base, looked incredibly high, incredibly steep. Already cold from crossing the stream at its base, the five frozen forms began inching up the treacherous slope.

Port, who was leading the way, beat out the trail ahead of him with a wooden maul. This he had fashioned the night before from a large misshapen pine bough, the base of which had inexplicably grown into a heavy wooden ball. With this he pounded his way forward, winding back and forth up the slope, doing his best to follow Old Bill's filled-in trail.

The work was tedious and exhausting, and after an hour the small group had advanced less than a hundred yards up the hill, The snow, extremely deep, was never lower than their shoulders, and in places the drifts were over fifteen feet high. What made matters worse was that the animals, with their greater weight, sank repeatedly through the bottom of the packed-down trail, and digging them out proved to be a continuous process.

Finally, thoroughly exhausted and unable to lead the way any longer, the man called Port sank back into the snow. Nelson, without a word, pushed his way past Angela and the mule, took the maul from the mountain man's hand, and began beating the snow down ahead of him, leading the way for the first time.

The frigid wind, which bore mercilessly down upon them, swirled the snow before it in such heavy clouds that their visibility was reduced almost to zero. Angela, looking up, had no idea whether the sky had cleared or whether she and the others were in the midst of a terrible blizzard. She recalled how, the night before, Port had called this type of storm a *poudrie,* a French word that, to the best of her knowledge, meant a ground blizzard.

Endlessly the hill stretched above them, obscured by the fine particles of snow. Once Angela looked back, and was startled to see that the trail, just a few feet behind her, had already blown nearly full again.

A little later, when they paused long enough for the men to change places, Angela was horrified at their appearance. Their breath had frozen upon their faces, and their lips were so stiff from the ice that it was almost impossible for them to speak. Their eyelids, Angela saw, were in a similar condition from the freezing of the water that the cold wind had forced upon them, the ice standing out on their lashes almost like stalactites. Long icicles hung down from their nostrils, and Port's heavy beard and hair stood out white and stiff with the frost, each hair suspended by itself.

The aspects of the horse and mule were suited to those of the men; their eyelashes and the long beards about their mouths stood like icicles, and their breath, passing back, settled upon their chests and sides until they were perfectly white with frost. Also, the snow beneath them would clog upon their fetlocks and under their hooves until it formed clumps six inches long, making the animals appear as though they were walking on stilts.

As the day progressed, Angela found herself turning her back to the wind more and more often. Her face, numbed with cold, was becoming frostbitten, and Port, noticing this, fashioned a hood for her out of a blanket. He did this by draping it over her head, cutting holes for her eyes and mouth, and putting her parka back on over it.

Nelson, following suit, did the same for himself, thus escaping the worst of the terrible wind-chill effect. Port, on the other hand, avoided the worst of the cold with his long hair and full beard, which he explained was why he grew them in that style.

After traveling nearly all afternoon the party at last reached the summit of the hill, only to discover that, after a short but steep descent, another hill of even greater proportions lay silently before them. Each would have liked nothing more than to stop there to rest, but the wind, which had been bad on the slope, blew now with almost hurricane force.

Unable even to breathe because of the wind's power, the party floundered across the drift-covered ridge, hit the down-slope, and slid and tumbled to the bottom, doing their best to keep out of the way of the sliding animals.

Struggling up out of the snow, they regrouped the horse and mule. Straightening the animals' packs then they pressed onward, sick and numb with cold, fighting their way forward through a continual fury of wind-driven snow.

Angela, barely able to move, had lost all sense of time or purpose. Nelson seemed no more than a walking skeleton. Even Port, who had seemed almost tireless, reached a point where he could hardly lift the wooden maul.

Finally, just as daylight was beginning to fade, a grove of pines loomed out of the obscurity of the storm. Angela watched numbly as Port turned to the side, and with a feeling of intense relief she followed the men and animals into the grove.

The wind still lashed at them there, but its fury was broken by the pines and the rocks. Angela felt, as her frozen body finally stopped moving, that she had never in her life seen a more beautiful place.

With numbed and bleeding fingers, Port and Nelson worked

together, untying the packs from the exhausted animals. Then, turning them loose, they allowed them to wander about and browse upon whatever shrubs or ends of twigs they might find.

Quickly, with all three working as one, they dug out the fallen limbs of the dead timber that lay buried beneath the snow. Once a large fire was burning, Port dragged out his pot and his rawhide, mixed up his soup, and set the concoction on the fire. Then all waited anxiously, their mouths watering with expectation, for it to boil.

Angela, realizing this, tried to smile. But she could not, for her frozen lips cracked and bled with the least movement, and she found that she could not even speak. Nelson and the mountain man, in the same condition, also remained silent, and so the only sound around the popping and snapping fire was the occasional groan or almost human sigh from the horse or the mule.

And there was also the wind, the ever-present, constantly howling, frozen wind.

Angela, exhausted and still cold even after she had eaten the soup, would have wrapped herself in her blanket and laid down to sleep in her wet clothing had not Nelson stopped her. Tenderly he helped her peel her soaking outer clothes from her body, encouraging her gently while he did so. She in turn helped him, and then they hung the clothes as close to the fire as they dared, hoping that by doing so they would dry more quickly.

Finally, still silent and yet still working together, the three scooped several feet of snow from an area between four trees, secured the canvas shelter between the trunks, propped it up with a limb in the center, and piled snow over the entire thing. Then, working as quickly as they could, they moved their packs, blankets, clothing, and bodies inside.

With the fire in front, which had melted into the snow to a depth of nearly five feet, the shelter quickly warmed. The three, huddled beneath their blankets, robes, and parkas, gradually relaxed. Then, while Nelson and Angela slept fitfully, the mountain man read briefly from his Bible, made a few hasty notes in his journal, smiled slightly, and went to sleep himself, feeling almost comfortable.

For the animals who stood outside, however, it was an altogether different matter. These, in their pitiable condition, roamed about all night, uncomfortable because of their extreme weakness, following partway back the path of the previous day, pawing in the snow three or four feet deep for some sign of vegetation to keep them alive. They fell down continuously, bellowing their distress, and then, when no one came to their aid, they struggled to their feet and began the process all over again. Finally they were reduced to eating the ropes and rawhide lariats with which they had been tied during the day. When those were gone they commenced again on each other's manes and tails, eating into the flesh once more.

Altogether it was a miserable night for anything that lived and moved upon the mountain.

31

"He's gone! Nelson, he's *gone!*"

Nelson coughed and rolled over, doing his best to wake up.

"What?" he gasped. "Who . . . ? Are—are you all right, Angie?"

"Nelson," Angela groaned, "I'm freezing to death! But that's not what I was talking about. I said that Port's gone. When I woke up there was no sign of him. I think he's left us, Nelson."

"Wh—why would he leave us, Angie? Where would he go?"

Without waiting for a reply, Nelson wrapped his blanket more closely around him, pulled on his parka, and crawled from the shelter. Once outside and standing up he was hit by the full force of the howling wind. Instantly he squatted back down, dropping below the level of the snow.

"Angie," he called out, coughing as he wiped the snow and the smoke from his eyes. "If anything, this storm is worse now than it was last night! If Port has left us, I wish him luck. But frankly, I don't think he's gone."

"But . . . where is he then, Nelson?"

"I don't know. Maybe he's just out in the bushes. Besides, take a look around. There's his elk hide, there's his buffalo robe, and there're his packs. His animals are probably still over in the trees, too. If the snow wasn't blowing so hard, I'm sure we could see them."

For a moment the couple fought the swirling pine smoke in silence, simply enduring the cold. Then Angela shuddered violently, drew her blanket more tightly about herself, and inched her way even closer to the fire.

"Nelson," she groaned, "I have never been so cold, so miserable, in my entire life!"

"Me either, Angie. I hardly slept at all last night. My teeth were so noisy they woke me up with their arguing."

"Nelson," Angela asked, ignoring her husband's attempt at humor, "do you really think we're going to get out of this alive?"

Shocked, Nelson looked at his wife. Overhead the wind screamed more fiercely than ever, whipping the pine trees back and forth violently. The smoke from the fire, whipped by the wind, spiraled around the hole that the fire had created, and no matter which way the two turned, they could not escape its acrid effects.

"Angie," he coughed, answering his wife's question, "of course we'll make it. We've *got* to. I know the storm is bad, worse than anything I've ever seen. But I have a feeling that at this very moment Port is out finding something for us to eat. Once we get some nourishment, we'll have no trouble waiting out the storm, hanging on until we're rescued."

"Well, I surely hope so," Angela responded sincerely. "But how on earth is a crazy mountain man supposed to find food in a blizzard like this?"

"I don't know, Angie. But I'll say this much: Crazy or not, he's never let us down yet!"

Again there was silence, and the two caught their breath and squinted their eyes tightly against the momentary denseness of the swirling smoke. Finally Angela, coughing and gasping, crawled back into the shelter.

"Well," she murmured, almost to herself, "I hope you're right, Nelson. If you're not, I don't think I can go on."

Nelson, quickly joining her in the relative stillness of the shelter, wiped the smoke-caused tears from his reddened eyes.

"Angie," he said, coughing deeply, "I've got an idea. When Port returns I'm going to . . . to try to help him. I'll ask him some leading questions. I'll confront him with some names and some dates, and gradually help him piece together the fact that this *isn't* 1848."

"Nelson, why bother with it? What does it matter what he believes, as long as he's happy and as long as we get out of here? I don't understand how you can worry about that when you're nearly dead, yourself."

"Well, Angie," Nelson replied, thinking carefully about his answer, "besides the fact that we owe him something, I really believe that he is lonely, that he is missing out on what life's all about. The best way to solve that is to bring him back in touch with the real world. As long as we're sitting here with nothing else to do, I'm going to see if I can do something for him. And frankly, Angie, I would really appreciate your help."

"Well, your heart's in the right place, Nelson. I'll admit that much. But isn't the whole thing quite academic? I mean, he's gone and here we sit, alone, starving, and freezing to death."

"You're right," Nelson said, nodding his head resolutely. "And since we're alone with absolutely nothing else to do, let's take advantage of it. Let's talk about us, Angie, about you and me."

Angela turned sadly away. "Nelson," she said carefully, "I . . . I just can't."

"Why not, Angie? Why can't you, just for a moment, deal with *us?*"

"I just can't, Nelson. The pain is too deep; the wounds are just too fresh."

"*What* wounds, Angie? Be specific . . . *please.*"

Angela raised her hands and then dropped them into her lap, showing with the gesture her total frustration and resignation. "No!" she said emphatically. "I can't *say it!* There is nothing for me to say! I don't have any specifics, I just have *feelings.* And how can I explain my feelings when I don't understand them myself?"

"Try, Angie. Will you please try . . . for *us?*"

"Nelson, that's just it. There isn't an *us.* For a thousand reasons that I can't even begin to name, the *us* is over with."

"Angie," Nelson pleaded earnestly, "look at me. Look into my eyes—"

"Oh, Nelson," she groaned, her voice filled with exasperation. "Please . . . I can't . . ."

"Lady," he said gently, lifting her chin toward him as he spoke, "someone once said that eyes are windows to the soul. You're looking into my soul, Angie, and now you're going to hear it speak.

"Angela Armstrong, *I love you!* I want you to be my wife forever, and I want to remain your husband!"

For an instant neither moved. And then Angela, her heart filled with a sense of total helplessness, spun away. She had to get away! She had to get away from Nelson. She had made up her mind, had already dealt with the emotional loneliness of the decision, and she was not about to go through the whole thing again.

But just as she was crawling from the shelter to get away, a distant voice floated out of the storm, and instantly Nelson was forgotten.

"Hyar the camp!"

"We're *here!*" Angela shouted, scrambling to her feet beside the fire. "Port, we're over here!"

Slowly the bleak form of a man emerged from the snowy whiteness of the blizzard, a man who was burdened with a heavy load.

"Wagh, pilgrims!" he gasped as he staggered to the edge of the fire pit. "Hyar be fat cow, and fancy doin's at thet. Stoke up thet-air fire, and let's warm up these vittles."

While Nelson, who had quickly followed his wife from the

shelter, helped Port lift the heavy pack down to the fire, Angela brushed the ice and snow from the man's face.

"Is it really food?" she asked, her voice trembling as much from excitement as from hunger and cold.

"Aye, marm. It be food, and prime hump-meat at thet. Wagh. And hyar be blankets, too. Plenty of 'em."

"But how . . . where?" Nelson asked as he struggled to take the pack from the mountain man.

"Hyar, ol' hos," Port replied, stomping his feet and beating his hands against his sides in an effort to restore circulation. "Dump them-air fleeces and boudins out and set 'em to roastin'. This child'll grain my animals and be back directly. Then I'll answer yer questions, by gum, every lock, stock, wipin' stick and willer-stretched beaver plew'n one of 'em."

Then, with a grunt, Port took the heavy pack away from Nelson, picked it up, turned it over, and emptied its bloody and gruesome contents into the snow.

"Miss Angela," he directed, smiling widely, "throw this-hyar fat cow onto the coals. It be time fer breakfast!"

Without another word he turned, clambered up out of the fire pit, and disappeared once more into the blizzard.

"Yuck!" Angela whispered as she stared at the grizzly pile laying on the ground before her. "Nelson, what *is* it?"

"Uh . . . food, Angie. Fat cow, according to Port."

"But what is it, *really?*"

"Well . . ." Nelson replied tentatively. "There's a little meat here, I think. Most of it, though, looks like the intestines from some animal."

"Oh, gross!"

"Now, now, lady. Remember how hungry you are. We'll all eat it and be glad for it. Trouble is, I'm not sure how to go about cooking it. I . . . hey, you've told me often enough how much you enjoy cooking. How do we cook this stuff?"

"You've got to be kidding! I wouldn't know—"

"Jest lay 'em on the coals, pilgrim," Port answered as he worked his way through the snow back toward the camp. "Jest stretch 'em out even-like, and let 'em sizzle."

"Oh, no!" Angela exlaimed, her voice filled with shock. "You can't really expect us to eat *intestines*!"

"Intestines, marm? La, don't call 'em thet! Them be boudins. Ye ate 'em afore. Seemed to think highly of 'em, too, as I recollect."

"*Boudins*? Boudins are . . . are . . . ?"

"And whet else might they be, Miss Angela? 'Course, thesehyar aren't buffler boudins, but they be mule! And according to the 'Pache's, mule meat be the best eatin' of all."

"Mule? This isn't . . . isn't old Flop-ears!" Angela exclaimed.

"Wagh, no, marm. This-hyar mule were Alexis Godey's. It were in the trail, near fifty yards up the slope from hyar. It were froze plumb solid, still standin', and were chewed some by wolves. But the fleeces were left, by which I mean the high rib meat, and so were the boudins.

"Weel, ol' hos, says I to myself when I found it. Hyar be fat cow, and thet fer sartin. The three of us'll be feastin' fer today, says I. More luck still—thet mule were packin' near ten pounds of shelled corn, which Godey unaccounterbly left with it, and a whole passel of blankets. It be fat cow fer my critters and all of us, says I. Truly, the good Lord air bein' kind today."

"I can't believe it," Angela whispered as she stared at the sizzling intestines. "I just can't believe that those are boudins, and that I *ate* them."

"Weel, marm," Port replied, still smiling warmly, "thet they be! Course, given my druthers, this-hyar child would've preferred buffler, 'er even better, painter meat. Why, there ain't no finer vittles this side of Saint Louey than the meat of a mountain lion. Season or two back this ol' hos were sittin' in Taos, jawin' with Ol' Bill, Kit Carson, and Dick Owens. Hyar, says I to them-air pilgrims, be roast painter meat, and no finer doin's anywhere. 'Wagh,' says Carson. 'It be good alright. But this child likes it fried.' Owens sided with me, but Ol' Bill put us to silence by remindin' us of the tastiness of raw painter liver, sprinkled liberally with gall juice. 'Thar aren't a finer meal on God's green earth than thet-air,' says Ol' Bill, and this child's inclined to agree."

"*Gall* juice!" Angela whispered, horrified. "Do you mean to tell me—"

"I think he does, Angie," Nelson answered, interrupting her. "And take my advice. If you want to be able to eat, don't pursue this conversation any further."

Puzzled, Port glanced from Nelson to Angela. When neither of them said anymore, he turned back to the fire and waited patiently for the mule meat to cook.

"Wagh," he murmured to himself. "White-skin greenhorns be stranger'n a peaceable Blackfoot brave. Thar be no understandin' 'em, a'tall! Me, now, I'm hongryer'n a wolf whet's smelled a first-fresh buffler cow with a wet calf. Bring on the vittles, says I. Bring on the vittles!"

32

"P—Port," Nelson stammered as he shivered with cold, "W—were any of your ancestors involved in the Civil War?"

The three had eaten their fill of roast boudins and fleeces, and were now huddled together in the shelter, listening to the bansheelike screaming of the unrelenting wind.

"How much, pilgrim?" Port responded, looking quizzically at Nelson.

"Were your family northerners or southerners in the war?"

"La, ol' hos," the man replied, spitting out into the fire. "I heered thar were troubles 'twixt the north and the south. But I hain't heered 'til now thet it had come to war. Would it be ol' Zack Taylor who started it, I wonder, or would it be thet blamed democrat Cass. Have ye heered yet as who won the election?"

Nelson, sensing that the time for quizzing the mountain man was perfect, glanced at Angela and continued. "Well, yes. From what I remember of my history, the Whig candidate, Taylor, won the election. He died in office, I think, and his vice-president, Millard Fillmore, took over. Fillmore was ousted by Pierce, in 1856 James Buchanan was elected, and in 1860 Abraham Lincoln took office. Port, it was during *his* administration that the Civil War was fought."

Angela, amazed as always by her husband's almost encyclopedic knowledge of history, and curious as to the outcome of the conversation, decided at that moment to support him.

"Port," she said kindly and sincerely, "all of that happened well over a hundred years ago. We are now living in the 1980s, we not only drive around in cars and fly through the air in planes and jets and rockets, but in July of 1969 a man named Neil Armstrong became the first man to stand on the moon. Port, you deserve to know this."

"Wagh," the man said, shaking his head. "This ol' coon air sartin-sure speechless. If it all be true, then I feel somewhat ignoorant, like I never got past the flyleaf of my first-grade primer."

"Port," Nelson continued, speaking softly and yet resolutely, "you don't need to feel that way. Being uneducated is no sin unless a man chooses to be. Now tell us about yourself. Where are you from?"

For a long moment the mountain man looked from Nelson to Angela and back again. "Weel," he said at last as he lifted his head and spat to windward, "cain't do no harm, I reckon. I were born on a dirt-poor farm in the high-up hill country of Pennsylvania, whar our main crop year after year were Pennsylvania boulders. I were the eldest of eleven. The day I raised sixteen I told my pap I could do a whole lot better most anywhar else than I could thar a-pickin' up them rocks daylight 'til dark. Thet were the last I heerd of my family."

"But—but," Angela stammered, "you mean you left? At age sixteen? Didn't you miss them? Didn't they come after you? Haven't you at least called them?"

"Call, marm?" Port questioned slowly, not understanding. "It would be plumb foolish to stay near enough to call back and forth. Even if'n there'd been land I'd not have stayed. I were a man full growed, and were an extry mouth fer my pap to feed. He surely wouldn't want to come after me. No, marm, it were best fer all thet I were gone, so I took off from thar like a tail-burnt bat lookin' fer a bucket of sittin' grease, and I've not gone back since.

"In Saint Louey," he continued, looking now into the fire before them, "this child took up the wagon and harness-makin' trade. Did right weel, too. But marm, it weren't to my likin'. Since I were knee high to a short stump I had me a hankerin' to see the far blue mountains. My chance came the day a feller name of George Perkins walked into my wagon shop, draggin' a harness whet needed fixin!"

For the next hour or so Nelson and Angela sat spellbound as the man who called himself Port entertained them with the story of his life.

"Weel, pilgrims," he said, finally concluding, "thet-air be it. Last time this child were in Saint Louey were on account of a willer post, which I run through my leg whilst fleein' a passel of Blackfeet. It wouldn't heal, so I took my leg to Saint Louey to get it fixed. Thet were three year back, in the summer of forty-five. These-hyar hills've been my home since then."

"What year were you born?" Nelson asked casually, tossing a new log down onto the fire as he spoke.

"Either twenty or twenty-one, don't rightly know which."

"And if this is 1848," Nelson continued, "that makes you about twenty-eight years old."

"La, ol' hos," Port replied, his contagious grin working across his face. "And hyar I thought I were nearer thirty. Why, I air still a spring chicken!"

"Oh no you aren't," Angela asserted. "If you actually *were* born in 1820, you are over one hundred and sixty years old."

"Wagh!" the mountain man replied disgustedly, spitting again into the fire. "Talk sech as thet don't shine with this ol' hos, Miss Angela. Why, my hair aren't even gray."

"Did you serve in Nam?" Nelson asked suddenly.

Once again the man's face was blank. "Nam?" he asked sincerely.

"Oh, come on, Port!" Nelson snapped. "Stop being so blasted phoney. We're not idiots, you know. You *must* have heard some news while you were living out here. Now stop playing these games and start leveling with us!"

For a long moment the mountain man gazed easily into Nelson's eyes. When he didn't waver, Port spoke. "Ye know, ol' hos," he said softly, "ye've got all the endearin' charms and overwhelmin' good humor of a hung-over undertaker. I've enjoyed about all of this-hyar conversation thet I'm willin' to enjoy!"

In the instant of tense silence that followed, a log popped on the fire and one of the animals coughed out in the trees. Then Angela, unable to stop herself, burst out laughing. She was soon joined by both men, and quickly the tension was gone.

"I'm sorry, Port," Nelson said sincerely. "Forget that question. I've read a lot about Old Bill Williams, and he's intrigued me. Could you describe him to us?"

"Weel, ol' hos," Port replied, his eyes immediately taking on a new sparkle, "thet-air be a question sech as this child can answer, and willingly, too. Bill, thet long-legged, short-stirrupped, mean-tempered son-of-a-gun, be a legend, sure as ol' Fetch-um Under has hindsights, and I'll tell ye of 'im.

"From whet he onct told me, he first came west as a sort of missionary to the Osages, but purty quick he laid aside his Christianity in favor of his rifle. He liked to go off into the mountains alone, which he usually did, fer months at a time, campin' near to hostile savages. But he was as sly as them brownskins, and tho' he bore the marks of balls and arrors, he was a terror to 'em. He also spoke many of thar tongues, but he liked thet-thar to be a secret. He were a dead shot with a rifle, and shot with a double wabble, pullin' the trigger whenever his sights crossed paths with his target. He never could hold his gun still, though the ball always went where he directed it. He did plenty of walkin', but like his gun he never could hold to a straight line with his feet.

"Thet ol' coon," the man continued, enjoying his telling immensely, "sits a hoss leaning forward on the pommel of his saddle, with his rifle afore him, his stirrups set at high water, his breeches rubbed up to his knees, and his legs ferever rubbed bare.

"As ye'll see, pilgrims, when we fetch up to 'em, his hair'll be red, speckled with gray, his clothing'll be buckskin even in bad weather sech as this, and his cap be an ol' wool blanket tied up in two corners. He air a perfect specimin of our kind. Thar be nothing about him thet be like another soul, which air the way mountain men like to be. He loves excitement, he craves danger, and the only reason he works hard is to give him powder and lead, and off'n on a big spree. I heered onct thet in Taos on one spree he went through six thousand American dollars and left the place in debt. Sech air Bill Williams, the man whose trail we be tryin' to foller.

"Now, pilgrims," he continued, suddenly rising to his feet, "afore we do any more chin flappin', thet-air fire be near as gut-shrunk as we be. It air wood we be needin', and thet a-plenty, says I, fer it be cold'n gettin' colder right along!"

And without another word the man called Port climbed out of the hole and disappeared toward the trees.

Nelson, shrugging his shoulders in response to Angela's questioning glance, forced his cracked lips into a smile, and then quickly followed Port out into the blizzard.

When she was alone, Angela sat quietly, deep in thought. She should have been thinking of Port, of his problem, and she knew that. The trouble was, somehow she couldn't. All her mind seemed to focus on was Nelson. All she could see were his eyes, boring into hers. All she could feel was the touch of his hand on her chin, and all she could hear, over and over again, were the words, *I love you.*

Groaning with an agony that was as much mental as physical, she dragged herself to her feet. "Why did he say that?" she asked herself aloud. "Blast it! Why did he *have* to say *that*? And above all, why does it need to affect me like this? Nelson and I are past! I'm over him! *Finis*! The end! Forever! What's wrong with me that those stupid, phoney words would so scramble my mind after all this time?

"Dear God," she cried as she crawled out of the hole and into the blizzard, "if you can hear me above this miserable wind, please let the rescuers find us. I've got to get off this mountain before I lose my mind! Please . . ."

33

For the remainder of that endless day, while the blizzard raked the mountains around them, Nelson and Angela shivered and did their best to listen while the man who called himself a mountain man and a trapper wove together more of the fabric of his life. His speech was earthy and simple, yet gradually the couple realized how very eloquent the man actually was. In addition, he was also knowledgeable, but in a distinctly unique way. His knowledge only went up to a point. And that point was, Nelson finally admitted to Angela late in the day, the point of 1848. Beyond that single year in time, the man called Port revealed absolutely nothing.

But oh, the things he knew from before, things that pertained especially to the trappers and to the mountains. He spoke with intimacy of other trappers, famous men such as Carson, who could neither read nor write, Sublette, who became wealthy trading with other trappers, Jed Smith, who never lost his deep faith in Christianity, and John Colter, who, naked, outran a hostile tribe of Blackfeet and who then died in bed of jaundice.

But other names came as readily to Port's tongue, names that meant nothing to either Nelson or Angela. He spoke of Louis Ambrose and of his death at the hands of the Cheyenne; he spoke of Michel Cerre, who retired from trapping to raise buffalo in St. Louis; Mariano Medina, who bought his Flathead wife from his partner, P. D. Papin; and Robert Newell, one of the few free trappers who could both read and write, and who did plenty of both. And of course he spoke always of Old Bill Williams, the one whom he considered his best friend among the trappers.

Port described in detail the possibles a trapper carried with him. For an entire winter's work, he explained, a trapper would have the clothes he wore, usually made of buckskin or homespun, with one extra set of leggings. He carried several knives, a pipe, tobacco, and perhaps, if he could read, a Bible or some other book. He also kept spare locks and flints for his rifle, some twenty-five pounds of powder, and a hundred pounds of lead. The rifle most trappers preferred was the heavy .40 to .60 caliber weapon manufactured by the Hawken Brothers of St. Louis, and thus called The Hawken.

Additionally, except for a little flour, coffee, salt, tea, and sugar, he carried no food at all. He lived almost exclusively off the land. And, when reduced to it, he ate whatever he could lay hand to, roots, bark, moccasins, his shirt, anything. Still he preferred good red meat, and would eat whatever moved before the sights of his rifle.

Finally, the trapper's most important possessions beyond his rifle, Port explained, were his beaver traps, of which he usually carried five or six, each weighing four or five pounds.

Trapping, he said, was done in two seasons—both cold enough to make cows give icicles. Plews were taken in late fall and early spring, when the fur was prime and could be reached. At both times it was a cold and miserable task at best.

The standard procedure was to wade into the freezing muck of a beaver pond and set the trap underwater in such a way that the animal would be held under and drowned. The trap was baited with either a bit of greenery or a dab of scent, called castoreum, for which each trapper had his own secret recipe. The baited trap was then marked with a floating stick. Finally, all that remained was to check the trap every day or so, haul a forty-pound carcass out of the mud and cold water, skin it, stretch the skin on a circular willow frame, and "grain it out," or scrape it free of all unwanted flesh.

Port then described the Indians he had known, lived with, and fought with. He spoke with authority of the Sioux, the Cheyenne, the Arapaho, the Utah, and especially the Blackfeet, those scourges of the primest beaver streams in the world. In addition, he mentioned briefly the Apache, the Kiowa, the Paiute, the Crow, the Gros Ventre, and several others.

He next told Nelson and Angela of the personalities of the Indians, or brownskins, as he called them. He talked of their almost childish pride and their great humility, their supreme confidence and tremendous faith, their ignorance of "white man" thinking and their strangely superstitious ways, and lastly he told of their keen intelligence as they adapted their lives to the world around them.

With the couple totally caught up in his words, Port then taught them a little of the Indian sign language, a sweep of the brow for the sign "white man," the handshake sign and finger moving up from the lips, both of which meant "friend," the two-fingered sign for "double tongued" or "lying," and the two clenched hands held at the chest and then swept apart and downward, which meant "I am finished," or "that is all."

He spoke of the Indian custom of selling their women, and explained that the price might be as little as a jug of whiskey or a horse, or as high as $2,000 in prime beaver plews. And, in response to Angela's almost indignant question, he replied that he had never taken an Indian wife primarily because the opportunity had never presented itself.

In another vein, the trapper spoke of the economy of 1848, especially as it existed near the headwaters of the Arkansas. Beaver had again gone up in price, he told them. Buffalo robes were more valuable than previously, almost all of the forts on the Platte and the Arkansas had been abandoned, and most Indian nations were in the mood for serious trading with the whites. For instance, he explained, Sioux villages were spread out for eighty miles along the Platte, and the Cheyennes and Arapahos camped in Big Timber had more robes to trade than ever before. In other words, 1848 had been a prime year for the free trapper, and Port confessed that he himself had done "tolerable well."

He spoke freely of his white neighbors, too, and seemed to know them well. He mentioned Bill New and Calvin Jones at Greenhorn, John Brown and his family, Charlie White, Jim Waters and Rube Herring, all of whom were farming at the trail crossing of the St. Charles, and Calvin Briggs and John Burroughs, who had grown the most recent crop of corn at Hardscrabble. He also spoke of some real bargaining he had done with Lancaster Lupton, who was getting set to close Hardscrabble's last store. He concluded by saying that he had spent a few nights in the jacal of Marcelmo Baca and his Pawnee wife, who "were a sight better cooker than she were a looker," and who had encouraged him to begin his present journey.

When Port at last had concluded his narrative and had gone once more to check on his animals, Nelson and Angela realized that the frigid day had ended. For some time then they sat in silence, staring into the fire. Finally Angela spoke.

"Well," she asked quietly, "what do you think?"

Nelson pulled the fur trim of his parka a little tighter around his face, scooped up a handful of twigs, and tossed them onto the red coals of the fire. "I don't know, Angie. I really don't. Port is either the greatest liar I've ever met, or he has the strangest mental disorder I've ever heard of. So far as I could tell, he didn't make a single slip. Do you realize, Angie, that we kept him talking nearly all day, questioning him about some pretty trivial things, and not once did he mention anything, or anyone, that was modern? At least he didn't so far as I could tell."

"I know, Nelson. I even listened for speech patterns, because

I studied them once. His are pretty unusual, as you know. But to the best of my knowledge, which admittedly isn't great, there were none that were out of place."

"I didn't hear any either, Angie, though to be honest, I was usually too busy laughing to pay much attention. I mean, when he tells us that he's colder than a banker's heart, how can you help but laugh. I've known too many bankers not to think that's funny.

"Another thing I noticed, though, is that he didn't make any obvious historical mistakes. Of course my knowledge of western American history is only a hobby, and he was way over my head a great deal of the time. Still . . ."

"Nelson?"

"Yes?"

"Can I ask you a really screwy question?"

"Sure, if you want to."

For a moment Angela squirmed uncomfortably, not sure how to say what she wanted to say. But then, after a deep breath, she simply plunged ahead. "All right, how did you feel while you were listening to him?"

"I—uh—what do you mean?"

"Down here, Nelson, right in the middle of you. Did you feel good, bad, comfortable, uncomfortable, entwined, put off, or what? You know—how did you *feel*?"

"Same as I do now," Nelson answered, grinning. "Very very cold!"

"Come on. Be serious about this."

Nelson, before he replied, took a long look at his wife. "Well," he said carefully, "it *is* interesting that you should ask that. To be as honest as you've asked me to be, I don't know if I've ever felt so many feelings. In fact, I spent a great deal of my thinking time today just trying to sort them out. It was . . . well, it was almost like Port was *giving* me feelings to experience."

"Ah—hah! He got to you too, then! Nelson, when he describes something, it's almost like I'm *there*. I feel the situation; I see it clearly in my mind; I can almost smell it!"

"That's about how I'd put it, Angie."

"But Nelson, there's something else. Have you noticed how you feel about the people he describes?"

"Well, no . . . but—"

"Nelson, think about it. Are there any of them you don't know, don't *like*?"

For a moment the man sat quietly, staring into the crackling flames. "Do you know," he replied quietly, "there aren't. I feel like those people he described are my friends as well as his."

"There you are," Angela said, smiling triumphantly. "And that, my dear Nelson, is what I'm getting at! Somehow, Port has the ability to make us feel good. He literally *likes* everyone, including us. In fact, I'm not certain that anyone has ever liked me as much as he does. And strangely, that makes me like myself, him, you, and everyone else. It's like a contagious disease."

"Well, this is getting pretty deep, Angie. Are you certain that you want to pursue it any further?"

"What do you mean?"

"I mean, if you are going to pursue it, you've got to face the issue straight on."

"Nelson, I don't understand—"

"It's the word-usage, Angie. I think, instead of *like,* that I'd use the word *love* if I were you."

"Oh, no you don't, Nelson," Angela stated flatly. "I never—"

"Hey, Angie, don't be so defensive. You don't have to take all this personally. I feel the same as you do about him. But a little while ago, while he was telling us of that storekeeper in Hardscrabble, and of how he had bargained with him, I realized that Port actually loved that man, in exactly the same way that he loves Bill Williams or that Indian he saved. Port's concern was for Lipton, or whatever the man's name was, not for himself.

"It was then, Angie, that I began sensing that he loved us, too. He *cares,* and isn't that the same as loving?"

Slowly Angela nodded. "I suppose it is," she said at last, looking away. "I suppose it is."

And then, strangely, Angela found herself thinking about

herself again, not Port, wondering bleakly why she somehow lacked the ability to care, to love. What was it about her, about her past, that prevented it? Why could she not be more like Nelson, like Port? What was it that made her shy away from it? Why couldn't she accept Nelson's devotion, his affection? What was it about Port's spontaneous acceptance of her that made her feel so low, so discouraged? And finally, why, oh, why had Nelson's touch and his statement done such damage to the great wall of her resolution? What was happening to her?

Nelson, unaware of his wife's sudden somberness, continued. "And I'll tell you something else that's ironic, Angie. Do you know that all afternoon I've been sitting here liking Port, feeling sorry for him, actually wishing that this was 1848?"

"That's interesting," Angela replied, doing her best to bring her mind back into focus, "because I've found myself wishing the same thing."

For a moment Angela got a faraway look in her eyes, seeing beyond Nelson, beyond the fire, even beyond the mountain. "Wouldn't it be funny," she suddenly said, speaking more to herself than to her husband, "if somehow it turned out that he was right, that it actually was 1848, and that we had in some way slipped back in time. Wouldn't it be nice if we could start all over, if all of our past had become our future?"

"With us too?"

"Especially with us."

"I'd like that, Angie. I wish it were true."

Angela paused, deep in thought. But then, standing up, she spoke with finality. "But it isn't, and we can't. Nobody ever goes back! Now, come on, let's go help the mountain man find more wood."

"Right," Nelson responded, scampering in exaggerated eagerness to his feet. "I'm coming."

Angela, ready to climb out of the firepit, almost tripped over the pack Port had carried the meat in.

"Nelson," she said, "let me move this ghastly pack Port brought back this morning, and . . . no! Oh, *no*!"

"Angie, what is it! What?"

Angela, quickly dropping to her knees next to the pack, moved it slightly, and began brushing away the snow.

Nelson, mystified, stared silently as his wife stopped, gazed at something on the leather pack, and then looked up at him.

"Good grief, Angie, what is it? You're white as a sheet!"

"Nelson," she whispered, her voice shaking, "does this pack look old to you?"

"I don't know . . . a year or two, maybe. No more than that. Why?"

"Nelson, this is either well over a hundred years old, or . . . or . . . Nelson, look at *this*!"

And Nelson, dropping to his knees in the snow next to his wife, was dumbfounded to read, engraven into the leather on the underside of the pack, the inscription:

U.S. Army Topographical Corps
St. Louis, MO.
1846

34

It was still dark the next morning when Angela felt someone softly shaking her arm.

"Miss Angela," Port's voice called quietly out of the darkness, "it be nearly dawn, the wind be stopped, and we'd best be movin'."

Angela groaned, rolled over, sat up, and quickly pulled her blanket tightly around her neck. Nelson was already up, kneeling by the fire, doing his best to blow the coals into flame. Yet it was a futile effort, and all he was getting was faceful after faceful of ash and smoke.

Grinning in spite of the pain it caused, Angela crawled from the shelter and stood up. The horse and the mule were standing just outside the fire circle, up to their bellies in the snow, and looking even worse than they had the day before. Port was doing his best to tie the packs to the animals, and the sight of the packs brought the inscription to mind.

Angela had lain awake for some time the night before, considering that inscription, and no matter how she twisted it about in her mind, no matter how much she worried it, she could find no sense to it. She had also gone over all of Port's stories, troubled by the fact that something seemed to be missing. Yet it had not been until she was nearly asleep that it had come to her, the missing element in Port's narration. In all of his stories, at least yesterday, he had never once mentioned his wife or her people.

She was certain that Nelson had asked about the woman, but somehow the man had avoided the question and had moved on, doing so in such a way that neither she nor Nelson had noticed. Now, as she thought about it, Angela wondered if the man's omission was significant. Could it mean, perhaps, that she had been right? Could it mean that Port's family was not real, except in his mind? If it did, then such an omission would also say a lot concerning his other claims and beliefs.

But what about the inscription? What about the stamped date of 1846 on a fairly new piece of leather equipment? There was no answer, no way that she could come to grips with all of it at once. Yet she had to do it, she had to find a way of rationalizing what she was experiencing, or . . .

At that moment Nelson rose to his feet and turned to face her, and Port came around the back of the horse, also facing her. And the instant became, for Angela, a vital moment of realization. Whatever the solution of the riddle concerning the date, both in time and on the pack saddle, it really didn't matter. They were actually in trouble, she suddenly understood, and no matter the date, there was the definite chance that they might not make it. Both men, now that Angela was really seeing them, looked awful.

She supposed that she looked as terrible, but though she hastily began combing her hair, she did not do it by looking in a mirror. Of course, now that she thought of it, she recalled that she had lost the mirror at the same time that she had lost the packet. But that was probably a good thing, for she knew that she was not emotionally prepared for the shock she was certain such a look would give her.

The blanket over her face each day had helped, but there was still a great deal of pain there, and she was sure that the causes of it would be very evident. Her hands also were raw and sore, as were her feet, and she was afraid that she was getting to look as old as she suddenly felt.

Nelson, on the other hand, seemed almost to be growing younger, more rugged. His beard was now out to almost a quarter of an inch, and seemed to itch him terribly, for he was constantly rubbing at it. Yet at least it hid the gauntness in his face, that and the sores where his cheeks had been frostbitten. The whiskers also, Angela found herself admitting, gave him a rugged look that she found very appealing.

Port, on the other hand, had grown more appealing to her in a vastly different way, not at all physical. Though his hands and face were cracked and bleeding, and though by his movements she could tell that he ached in every muscle, he never complained. In fact, he did the opposite. He was constantly inquiring about either hers or Nelson's well-being, he smiled continuously, and she was sure that he would have whistled if his lips had been able to do so.

He was, in short, happy. Incredibly and yet genuinely happy. And it was that happiness, that constantly radiating joy, which made Angela almost fear him and yet feel so strongly that she wanted to be near him. That was what she had been trying to say to Nelson the night before, and that was what Nelson had also been trying to say to her.

Angela knew that her husband had been thus affected by Port, for though he had said nothing more, she had never seen him work so hard or so consistently. Nor, save for an occasional sigh, did he complain. He seemed to be watching the mountain man constantly, and within seconds of whenever Port started some task, Nelson would be there beside him, assisting him in it. It was almost humorous, except that Angela had found herself doing exactly the same thing, completely without realizing it. In fact, she admitted to herself that morning, both she and her husband were becoming quite a bit like the strange mountain man. That alone, she knew, could turn out to be a good thing for both of them.

It was still not daylight when Port got the party moving, beating a way forward up what they were certain was the ridge that marked the Continental Divide. Their elevation was close to twelve thousand feet, and so they climbed slowly, fighting for every breath, taking their time, beating out an almost impossible trail with their maul.

There was no trail for them to follow, no indication that they were going in the right direction. The wind, which had diminished somewhat, had filled in Old Bill's path with drifted snow, leaving no sign for them to follow. Higher they climbed into the somber darkness of the forest, praying that they were going right, only occasionally able to see the stars above them.

Periodically Angela found herself thinking of rescue planes, wondering briefly why they had not yet seen or heard any, wondering even more that she had spent the entire previous day not even thinking of their rescue. As she thought of that, Angela considered the man called Port, thinking again of his unusual warmth and his tremendous capacity to love.

Where had he learned that? she wondered. Was he sincere? Did he have ulterior motives? And above all else, how could he possibly make her feel so strongly that he loved her, loved her without *any* restraints. He had never said he did. He had never even gone out of his way to be particularly kind to her. In fact, he frequently teased her. Still, in spite of all that, she *knew* that Port loved her.

And what about Nelson? she questioned as she inched her way up the slope behind her toiling husband. Did *he* love her? Had so much changed that finally nothing had changed, and they were back at the beginning?

Of course, even if that proved to be true, which she doubted, it changed nothing regarding her own feelings. Though in ways she did love him, she could not face the pain of remaining with him, of being dominated, controlled by his insufferable goodness. It was too much, and she would not do it!

But—what about when he touched her? Why had she felt so strange when he had touched her chin with his fingers? It was a difficult question, for as far as she could tell there was no satisfactory answer, none except that perhaps in their desperate life-and-death situation she was more vulnerable, more inclined to want to feel loved. Still, that touch, that touch . . .

In the predawn darkness it was terribly cold, and suddenly a gust of wind from off the high peaks lashed at the pines, moving them restlessly, making violins of the pine needles, moaning low among the rocks and across the waste-spaces above timberline. It was a ghostly sound, and even more than the chilling cold, it made Angela shiver.

For hours they continued to climb, staggering a step backwards for every two steps they took forward, their minds and bodies growing continuously more numb. It was a terrible ordeal, and Angela wondered, when she was able to wonder at all, that it was actually *her* who was experiencing it.

She had never been involved in such a nightmare, had never in her life even imagined that she might be. Yet now she was, and she was actually holding up under it. In fact, if she could just last until they reached the top of the ridge they were climbing, she was positive that they could easily make it to the downed jet. Once there, she reasoned, they would find food and warmth, for surely the search parties would have set up their base of operations nearby. And there too, she was certain, she would find answers, answers that would bring her the peace she was so desperately seeking.

At last the party emerged from the trees onto a vast slope, dotted here and there with ghostlike clumps of stunted pine. They continued to climb in silence, with only the angry wind for company and the ragged shadows of the wind-ravaged trees to watch them. It was a pain-filled and never-ending process, one of pounding down snow, tromping frozen feet into it, dragging animals forward through it, and keeping it out of eyes and nostrils and mouths. Hands and fingers were numb and long forgotten, toes and feet ceased to be anything but painful wooden stumps, dripping blood was not even noticed, and self-pity was killed by sheer exhaustion. It was an ordeal that Angela would never be able to remember, and yet one that she could not possibly forget.

At last, upon reaching the serrated edge of the ridge, they were dismayed to again discover, beyond them, yet another mountain, higher and more forbidding than ever.

"Oh, no!" Angela cried into the wind. "I—I thought . . . this was the last one!"

"Weel," Port shouted back, wiping the build-up of frost from around his mouth, "this-hyar child thought as what he'd seed this-hyar hill afore. Ol' Bill has surely follered the wrong hunch this time. Why, the divide air twenty mile thetaway, if it be a mile!"

"So, what do we do?" Nelson shouted, wiping the blood and frost from around his mouth as he did so.

"Wagh, ol' hos! It be time to stop follerin' and start ketchin'. Ol' Bill needs to know thet he's raised the wrong route fer his pass. Have ye got it in ye to go on?"

"Aye," Nelson shouted, forcing his cracked lips into a grin, "thet this child do, he be thinkin'."

Port, hearing, winked, and across his face spread his sunburst of a smile. Then, handing the lead ropes of the animals to Angela, who was also grinning crookedly, he picked up the maul and, facing into the bitter teeth of the wind, attacked the high drift that loomed before him.

For the better part of an hour the men tried to beat a path across the ridge. With blood flowing freely from their nostrils as well as from the cracks in their flesh they fought the awesome gale, doing battle even when their noses, ears, faces, fingers, and feet were frozen, trying to continue even after Port's eyelids had frozen shut.

At length, however, exhausted to the point of unconsciousness, they were driven back by the fury of the cold, the wind, and the snow. No matter how hard they tried, they simply could not advance against the forces of nature that had conspired against them.

In the lee of a fifteen-foot snowdrift the small group huddled together—all of them, even the animals, trembling from exhaustion.

"Wagh," Port gasped, looking back along the ridge. "It be more'n a man can do, fer the hurricane winds be too much. This child says we ought to raise our backtrail, I . . . reckon . . . fetch back into camp . . . dig in proper thar to wait out the storm. Thet-air be our only chanct to not go under."

"But Port," Angela groaned, "we can't go clear back down the mountain. I'll never make it. And look! Our trail is almost gone as it is!"

"She's right, Port," Nelson interjected. "I don't think that's the answer. None of us have the strength to go clear back to our camp."

"Weel, ol' hos," Port replied slowly, "Thet-air weren't whet I were thinkin'. Around the brow of this-hyar ridge and down the slope a mite, thar be a stand of fir. This child cached hisself thar onct afore. It be a wonderous fine camp with water and fuel a-plenty. This pilgrim says we do our best to raise thet-air camp. Whet say ye?"

"Well," Nelson said, taking his wife's hand in his, "it's a whole lot better than a snowdrift in our backs or a blizzard in our teeth. I say we go for it. How about it, Angie? Can you make it?"

"I guess so," she groaned. "At least I—I think I can."

Leading out once more, Port pounded his way forward through the blowing and drifting snow, doing his best to concentrate on the seemingly endless and impossible task before him.

35

With painstaking care, the small and desperate party crawled forward through the incredibly deep snow, keeping below the crest of the hill and thus avoiding the worst of the terrible blasts of wind. Often they fell, and just as often they dragged themselves slowly to their feet, somehow able to continue their forward struggle.

When more than an hour had passed, Port paused, utterly exhausted, and closed his eyes in silence.

Nelson and Angela, watching him from behind, were each aware that the mountain man was praying, pouring out his soul in a plea for help. When at last he lifted his head, he looked for a moment at them, did his best to smile, turned, and peered carefully down the steep slope.

"Ol' hos," he called back to Nelson, "this child be seein' things, he air a-thinkin'. Fetch yerself up hyar and tell me whet ye see."

Nelson, stumbling forward, pushed his way past Angela and the animals to where the man stood.

"Wha . . . what?" he asked. "What do you want me to—"

"Down thar, friend," the mountain man replied, pointing down the slope before him. "Whet see ye?"

Nelson, squinting his eyes against the glare and the wind-blown snow, could see nothing. The slope dropped away quickly, its pure whiteness broken only by the protrusion of an occasional clump of brush.

"I don't know, Port," he at last said, "I don't see anything but snow."

"Thar, ol' hos," Port said, "them-air two points of black. Unless this child be dreamin', they be the flop-eared top-knot of a mule. Aye, and them mounds thar could be other mules."

"They *could be*!" Nelson replied excitedly. "You could be right. It's worth checking out, don't you think?"

"Weel, this ol' coon reckons so. I've raised a sight of prime beaver in my day, pilgrim. But no sign ever shined brighter'n those ears, says I. Wagh, thar be fat cow fer the fire tonight, I be thinkin'."

Without another word they plunged down the slope, making their way with desperate haste toward the frozen mule—for such it proved to be.

When they reached the animal, it was actually still standing beneath the snow. It had died, but had never fallen over, and had been left as it was by the party that had gone before them.

With numb and fumbling fingers, Port drew out his knife and cut free the wooden packsaddle. Then, heaving it to one side, he began immediately to butcher the gaunt and scab-covered animal.

While Nelson assisted the mountain man, Angela tried to keep her mind away from the packsaddle. She tried, but it was no use. Her thoughts and her eyes were riveted to the imprinted date on its side, which she could see, but could not make out.

Finally, thoroughly frightened by what she was certain she

would find, and yet unable to keep away from it, she crawled forward on her hands and knees until at last she reached the saddle. And there, as she had known it would be, was the U.S. Army Topographical Corps logo, and the engraved date of 1846.

Frightened and confused, Angela slumped down and buried her face in her blanket-wrapped and all but frozen hands, doing her best to blank the implications of that date from her mind. It was not possible, she knew. What had to be true simply could not be so. It was . . . it was . . . Could she be going crazy, she wondered? Was it not Port so much as it was her? Why couldn't she—?

"Thar!" Port grunted with satisfaction. "Thet be as much as air worth gettin'."

While Angela watched numbly, her heart sick with worry and confusion, Port and Nelson loaded the meat onto the back of Flop-ears, Port's mule. Then, taking the reins of his horse in his hands, Port patted Nelson on the back, thanked him for his assistance, and pushed his way forward into the never-ending drifts of snow.

He had not traveled more than fifty feet, however, when something startled Miss Clementine, the starving horse he was leading. With a squeal of fright the animal reared backward and to the side, lost its balance, and tumbled headlong down the hill and out of sight over some rocks. Port, the reins wrapped tightly around his hand and wrist, was dragged over the steep precipice with his horse, and Nelson and Angela watched in horror as the two vanished into the snow below.

In the eerie silence that followed, the couple, standing very close together, could not yell, could not cry out. It was not possible! It was not—

"Hyar!" a voice called weakly from below. "Be ye thar, pilgrims?"

"Port!" Angela screamed with relief, as she and Nelson peered into the desolate whiteness below.

There was a sudden muffled rifle explosion, the snow heaved upward, and at last the mountain man appeared. As he dragged himself slowly up the hill toward them, both Nelson and Angela realized that he had been injured.

Now, as quickly as he could, Nelson worked his way down to where the mountain man lay in the snow. Then, taking the man's rifle, Nelson reached down to help him to his feet.

"Wagh, ol' hos," Port said, his eyes filling with tears, "hold up a minute." Wincing in pain, he swiped at his eyes with his blanketed hand. "It air no good, pilgrim," he finally said. "This-hyar be poor doin's. Miss Clementine busted her back, and I had to shoot her. Wagh! And it weren't her fault a'tall, I'd tell a man. No siree, it weren't. Don't seem right, somehow, to shoot one o' my best friends."

"How about *you*?" Nelson asked anxiously, hardly understanding Port's concern with his horse. "Are you hurt?"

"Weel . . ." the man slowly replied, "this child aren't gone under, and it be a lucky thing it were me and not one of ye. But aye, this-hyar leg be broke. If we weren't in over our hocks afore, we sure as skunk juice stinks air up to our bellies now. Maybe ye'd oughta shoot me too, ol' hos."

"Here," Nelson urged gently, "don't talk like that. Let me get my arm . . ."

Then, without finishing his sentence, Nelson gathered what little strength he had and lifted Port to his feet.

"Angie!" he called urgently. "Can you get the mule down here? Port's leg is broken!"

Without a word Angela took the lead rope of the mule and inched her way down to the narrow rock shelf. There, using every ounce of energy she had, she assisted Nelson in helping the injured mountain man onto the back of the mule.

Taking up the maul, Nelson led out, and together they made their way forward and down until at last they reached the stand of fir.

"Angie," Nelson gasped once they were in the comparative shelter of the trees, "help me get him off the mule. We've got to set his leg before—"

"Ol' hos," Port said feebly, interrupting Nelson as he spoke, "this-hyar leg be goin' nowhar. Aye, and the storm be gettin' worse. Fetch me down off'n the mule, prop me against thet-air tree, and this child'll instruct ye in the fine art of buildin' a permanent shelter whet'll be tighter'n the bung in a green oak barrel."

"Permanent?" Angela cried, "But I—"

"Now, Miss Angela, don't ye get to frettin'! It be permanent only so long as the storm lasts. Now, fetch yer man thet-air shoulder-bone shovel out of my possibles, and while he be diggin', ye commence to gatherin' firewood."

Like a kindly general, the mountain man directed Nelson and Angela in their tasks. While Angela was digging out and dragging into the camp large quantities of dead limbs, Nelson was busy digging into the face of a huge drift of snow. Under Port's direction he shoveled out a cave that was six feet deep and perhaps four feet high at the top of the domed roof. Still following instructions, he created a bed out of a large bench of snow. This he covered with pine boughs. Then he dug a trench to one side that angled down and out of the cave, a trench that would carry out the cold air.

Once Nelson had placed all of the packs safely inside the cave, he used small blocks of snow to wall in the opening until only a small entranceway remained.

Angela, meanwhile, had succeeded in lighting a fire, and this was now burning briskly, radiating heat to the freezing figures.

"Okay, Port," Nelson said, once some mule was roasting on the fire before them, "let's take a look at your leg."

"Wagh, ol' hos," the mountain man said, shaking his head, "not yet. Ol' Flop-ears, thar, be thirsty, and more critters die in winter of thirst than most ary other thing. Thar be a stream off yonder through them-air trees. Lead her to it and she'll do the rest."

Sensing the futility of arguing, Nelson took the mule's rope and led the animal off into the trees. Only when he had finally returned, and when the mule was picketed near the warmth of the fire, did the man called Port allow Nelson to examine his leg.

36

"Hyar, ol' hos," Port said, wincing in pain as he handed Nelson his knife. "Take this . . . and slice up through thet-air homespun around my leg. Thet'll relieve it some, I be thinkin'."

Nelson took the knife and shaking his head, laid it to his side in the snow. "Port," he said, "I don't know much about this winter survival business, or about mountain men or trapping, but I did spend a year in Nam flying choppers, and along the way I managed to learn a little about injuries. Trust me, and let me see if I can help you."

Port stared without comprehension at Nelson, and at last he answered. "Ol' hos," he said, "these-hyar ears still don't comprehend yer lingo. Whet air choppers and Nam I sartin-sure don't know. But as fer trust, ye be a fine man, and ye have my life in yer hands."

"Nelson," Angela questioned, very concerned. "Are you sure you know what to do?"

"No, Angie, I'm not. But I've seen legs set plenty of times in Nam. If you'll help me, I think we can do it."

Gently, then, Nelson began probing the mountain man's leg.

"All right," he said after just a few seconds of investigation. "It's the femur. It's broken, no doubt about it, and though it isn't a compound fracture, there *is* a lot of swelling. That indicates internal bleeding. We've got to get a traction splint on it fast, set it, and then wrap his leg so we can keep him from going into shock.

"Angie, get me the thinnest blanket we have, and on your way back bring that long pole over there, the one with the fork in it."

A moment later Angela was back with the blanket and the pole, anxious and willing to help.

Nelson, taking the mountain man's knife, cut and tore the blanket into several long strips, none more than three inches wide. At the same time he explained to Port the need for a traction splint and for MAS trousers, which would act as a temporary transfusion, forcing the blood out of his legs and up to his heart and brain.

"Port," he concluded, "I know you're in a lot of pain, and this is going to hurt much more than it does now. But if we're going to save your life, I've got to do it."

"Wagh," the man said, catching his breath as Nelson moved his leg a little. "It air nothin' compared to the day I said goodbye to my Sarah. Do as ye need, and this child'll be uncommon grateful."

Quickly Nelson went to work, strapping the pole to Port's side with the fork beneath his arm.

Angela, seeing the mountain man's eyes glaze over with the agony of movement, stepped quietly to his side. There, with tears filling her own eyes, she took the man's hands in hers, rubbed them gently, and did her best to comfort him.

"Miss Angela," the mountain man said weakly, but with surprising sincerity, "tell this ol' coon about yerself, about yer folks, and about the things ye did as a young'un."

"Not right now, Port," she started to protest. "Not when—"

"Marm," Port said, "talk to me. Sech palaver will ease my pain mightily."

And so, while Nelson used traction to pull the broken bones apart until they slipped into their proper position, Angela spoke of her childhood.

She talked of her earliest memories, of her parents' divorce, and of the years she had spent being reared first by one of them and then by the other. And as she told the mountain man of her childhood poverty, she happened to notice the expression on Nelson's face. He was looking at her wonderingly, and she could see that he was very touched by what she had said.

She wondered at that for a moment, and suddenly realized that this was the first time she had allowed herself to speak with anyone, even Nelson, about her life as it really had been. And, although she felt awkward at first, revealing the hidden secrets of her past, the men's total acceptance of her, and their non-judgmental attitude, made it almost easy for her to continue.

As Angela's floodgate of memories opened and the hurt and agony of her childhood was released, Angela herself was even surprised by how much pain she had absorbed and had kept hidden. She described her father's constant drifting from one job to another. She spoke of her mother's endless years of sewing, sewing for the wealthy and socially prominent who lived above her.

Now, speaking as much to herself and to her husband as she was to the mountain man, Angela recalled the day she had attended her first teenage party. Her mother had sewn for her, out of expensive scraps, a new squaw dress which she had worn proudly to the outing. Once there, however, a couple of other girls had discovered that she had, horror of all horrors, put her dress on backwards, with the darts in the back. The other girls squealed with delight, pointed the error out to all of the boys in attendance, and then chanted mockingly as she fled from the party in tears.

"I vowed that day," Angela said through teeth firmly set with remembered pain and determination, "that I would never go to another party until I was better dressed than anyone else."

As she finished speaking, Angela felt rough hands squeezing hers, looked down, and was surprised to see the mountain man, his eyes filled with tears, gazing with compassion up into her own. But before the man could speak, she felt the touch from Nelson's hand too, and, spinning, was startled to see the same compassion on her husband's face.

"Angie," Nelson said slowly and gently, "I . . . I had no idea. I . . ."

"There's more, Nelson, much more. Would you like to hear it?"

Nelson nodded, and Angela, with a strange sense of eagerness, continued her story.

"Nelson," she said, speaking now only to her husband, "do you want to know why my magazine is so important to me? You've never understood that, so let me explain. It is the family I never had, the mother who never had time for me, the father who could never afford me. *Fashion 1*, Nelson, is the supportive companion I have never had.

"It is also," she continued, "my only child. Let me tell you of the labor pains that preceded its birth."

As both men listened silently, Angela described her years of loneliness through high school, her sense of hopelessness, her feeling of never being as beautiful, as intelligent, as successful as the girls around her.

She then told of the day she had finally quit her carhop job, packed her few belongings into a battered suitcase, emptied her meager savings account, left a note of farewell to her mother, and departed. Her destination had been a distant university, for there, she realized, lay not only an education, but also her ticket into a future she had always coveted.

She had attended college ravenously, she explained, working nights as a waitress to support herself. She had also avoided relationships with men, for college men, she felt, had not yet reached the point where they could give her what she so desperately needed.

Angela shared then how she had consciously forced her

mind to bypass the flamboyant and outrageous, both in appearance and in acquaintances, thinking only of things sensible, elite, and traditional. In this she had experienced satisfaction and success. She had gained confidence in her good taste, her understanding of the contemporary world of fashion, the antiques and the collectibles which had become so fascinating to the wealthy. This newfound confidence, in turn, had allowed her to repel mediocrity, and had carried her into knowledgeable battle against a world of tongue-in-cheek artists. She had learned to recognize and create design in fabric as though it were the emotional expression she would not trust to have surface in other areas of her life. She knew this to be her release, her emotional and intellectual resurrection, and she had reveled in her new sense of self.

As Angela continued, describing the ultimate creation of her own fashion magazine, Nelson listened attentively. Not only was he totally captivated by her story, but, for the first time in their relationship, he was beginning to understand the reasons behind his wife's attitudes, priorities, and yes, even her insecurities, which he had always regarded as foolish.

In fact, he found himself so engrossed in her narrative, and she was so completely immersed in the telling of it, that neither of them noticed the expression of relief, almost joy, that had settled onto the face of the injured mountain man. With an almost audible sigh, Port closed his eyes, settled back onto the buffalo robe, and willed his muscles to relax.

At last, when Angela had finished speaking, a subdued and definitely affected Nelson served his wife and the injured mountain man a supper of warm water and roast mule. Several times while they were eating Nelson seemed about to speak, about to tell his wife of his feelings. But for some reason he did not seem able to put them into words, at least not yet, and so he let it go.

Later, with the blizzard increasing even more in its intensity, Nelson and Angela maneuvered Port into the snugness of the snow cave. Once inside and settled, Angela was suddenly aware of how comfortable the shelter was.

"I can't believe how good this feels," she exclaimed. "It's really warm."

"Aye, marm," Port gasped, "thet it be. Snow air a fine protector from the cold."

"What do you think the temperature is in here?" Nelson asked.

"Weel, somewhars betwixt thirty-two and thirty-eight degrees, according to Ol' Bill."

"Thirty-two degrees?" Angela gasped. "That's freezing! It's got to be warmer than that."

"No, Miss Angela," Port replied. "It air jest that yer body be gettin' used to the cold. Ye air bein' conditioned to the mountain."

With that the conversation ceased, and the three, bundled together in their remaining blankets and furs, attempted to sleep.

Outside the wind howled relentlessly, sounding like screaming banshees as it tore mercilessly through the trees and down the canyon. The heavy snow, drifting before it, rattled against everything in its path, filling in the pockets of the earth, covering everything but the brightly burning fire.

Nelson, who could not sleep, listened in awe as snow slides continuously tore loose from the distant peaks, booming now close, now far away, thundering down the steep slopes, carrying trees and all else before them.

In addition to the noise of wind and snow, there was the constant braying of the starving mule, which had found its way into the fire pit before the shelter. Having eaten all the rope and rigging from its packsaddle, and having lost the horse upon which it had also gnawed, the mule was now floundering in the deepening slush by the fire, sticking its nose into the cook kettle and occasionally falling into the flames in its efforts to locate food and warmth. Three times, in fact, Nelson had to kick its nose out of the opening of their cave, where it was doing its best to devour the nearest of their much-needed blankets.

All in all, for the animal at least, it was another miserable night.

37

By morning the wind was blowing with near-hurricane force, swirling the pungent smoke from the fire into Nelson's and Angela's eyes, and freezing the two even as they huddled close to the flames, doing their best to prepare another meal.

All day long the icy snow rattled against the rocks and the branches of the pines above them, a blizzard so dense that visibility was limited to only a few feet.

The day also seemed to be one for silence and introspection. Port, his face ashen and white, spent most of the time sleeping. To Angela fell the duty of attending to the tourniquetlike wrappings on his legs, redoing them constantly so that his circulation would not be destroyed.

Nelson, on the other hand, spent the day foraging for wood, tender brush ends for the mule to eat, as well as the larger branches with which he fed the fire. He also cut down three small trees with Port's hand axe. These he leaned against the drift near where their cave was. Over the trees he tied Port's canvas covering, and then into that simple but effective shelter he led the mule, coaxing it with the tender branches he had found.

By night the only change for the party was that once again they were almost out of food. That, and the grim fact that the mountain man's condition had definitely worsened.

Angela, thoroughly concerned about Port's appearance, at last crawled from the shelter and quickly apprised her husband of the situation.

"Nelson," she said, her voice echoing her fear and concern, "I'm afraid for him. If he'd only eat. But he won't because he knows there's not much left, and he wants us to have it. What'll we do?"

Nelson, deep in thought, stared into the sporadic flames of the fire. At last, tossing on another log, he spoke.

"The only thing I can think of, Angie, is to lie to him. Could you do that?"

"What do you mean, Nelson?"

"Let's convince him that we have more mule meat than we actually have."

"But he'll see through it, Nelson. He knows how much is left."

"That's true. So if he asks, let's simply tell him that I climbed back up there, found another dead mule, and butchered it."

"But Nelson, I can't bear to tell him—"

"Angie, can you bear the thoughts of watching him slowly starve to death?"

"Well, no . . . but . . ."

"I feel the same as you do about integrity, lady, but this man means an awful lot to me, and I know he means as much to you. Besides, I'm sure that I can actually find another mule up there tomorrow. Port pointed out to me several mounds in the snow that he thought were mules. Come first light, I'll try to get to them."

"But you *can't*, Nelson! You'll never make it back!"

"Angie," he answered, his voice thick with emotion, "if it was me lying in there with a broken leg, Port would never give such a suggestion a second thought. He'd just go and get it done."

For a long moment Angela looked up into her husband's eyes. "You know something," she said softly, "you've changed. You really have."

"Well," Nelson replied, drawling it out, "this-hyar ol' hos hopes so, Miss Angie. He most sartinly do. After all, he needed to change somethin' frightful."

Then, smiling down at his wife, who for some strange reason could not keep the tears from filling her eyes, Nelson squeezed her hand, bent down, and picked up the last of the roasted mule.

"Angie," he whispered as he started toward the shelter, "forget the lying. If we work together we can do it honestly. I'll get him talking, and you feed him."

"Port," Nelson said, once they had crawled inside the shelter, "You're something else! I had a broken leg once, and I know how badly such an injury can hurt."

"Wagh," the man replied, doing his best to smile, "it be a little thing, ol' hos."

Angela, sensing that the gaunt and emaciated man's mind was occupied with a memory, broke off a piece of meat and fed it to him, bit by tiny bit, talking as she did so.

"You look like you're remembering something," she said softly. "What is it?"

Port, seemingly unaware that he was being wheedled into eating the last of the meat, spoke while he chewed, giving both Nelson and Angela another opportunity to listen to his delightful storytelling.

"It were down on the Cimmeron," he said slowly, "and though I were not much more'n a greenhorn, I found myself with a trappin' party a-fightin' the Comanch.

"We beat 'em, but the last brownskin to ride off turned and fired his piece. The ball smashed into this child's elbow, blowin' a fair to middlin' chunk of it away.

"Weel," the man continued, speaking around the bits of meat Angela was feeding him, "the wound weren't cleaned proper, and afore long it were filled with gangrene. The other fellers were beside tharselves with worry o'er whet to do, fer on the one hand I were set to go under any moment, whilst on the other the Comanch were considerin' another raid aginst us. Thar were only one course of action to take, and so the trappers took it.

"Givin' this child a solid belt of Mexican firewater, they hauled out a Green River blade, wetted it clean, and commenced the surgery. When the flesh had been bared away and peeled back, a wood saw were used to sever the bone. Then a big bolt, which had been heated to a gray-red color in the fire, were slapped aginst the open wound. In a matter of seconds the whole stump were seared over, bandages were applied, and this child and the entire party were on our way."

"Good grief!" Angela cried, shocked. "You lived through *that*?"

"Weel, no, marm," the man said, grinning feebly, "actually I didn't. Besides losin' this-hyar arm, I died thet very night."

"What? But . . . but . . ."

Nelson suddenly broke into a loud laugh, and Angela, realizing how effectively the mountain man had sponged her, also grinned. "Well!" she said, chidingly. "See if I ever feel sorry for *you* again!"

There was more quiet laughter, and then the mountain man reached up and took Angela's hand. "Marm," he said, gently but seriously, "ye've now fed this ol' hos all the meat thet were left. Whet will the two of ye do?"

"Well, I—uh—" Angela stammered.

"Port," Nelson said, interrupting his wife, "we're both fine. You're the one who needed nourishment tonight. When it's daylight I'm going to take old Flop-ears and work my way back up to the dead mule. I can get a little more off that animal, and like you said, there may be others frozen nearby."

"Weel," Port replied, "thet-air be mighty risky doin's, ol' hos. Be ye up to sech a jaunt?"

"Sure! I'll just pretend I'm back in jump school. Nothing could be worse than that was."

"Jump school?" Port asked, confused. "Whet air thet?"

Nelson grinned and leaned back against the side of the cave, where he sat looking from the mountain man to his wife and back again.

The wind outside, if anything, had increased, and with the wind-chill, the temperature was way below zero. Yet in the snow cave the air was still and warm, and the three relaxed in comparative comfort.

"Port," Nelson said at last, "I think I'd like to tell you about me. And because I know that some of what I'll say will be difficult for you to comprehend, I'm going to show you something."

"Ol' hos," the man replied, "say whet ye will, and show whet ye will. I've come to know yer heart, and ye be a man of truth, I be thinkin'. Have yer say and this child'll be believin'."

"Angie," Nelson said, turning to his wife, "will you get that fifty-cent piece from your purse?"

Silently Angela opened her battered Gucci bag, extracted the coin, and handed it to her husband.

"Port," Nelson continued, handing the man the coin, "this is a United States of America half dollar, a fifty-cent piece. This "D" on it signifies that it was minted in Denver, which is a large city of several hundred thousand people, situated approximately one hundred and fifty miles northeast of here.

"The bust on the coin represents John F. Kennedy, a president of our country, who was assassinated in November of 1963, just six years after I was born. This date, Port, is the date this coin was minted. Can you read it in this light?"

The mountain man struggled to hold the coin so that the light from the fire outside reached it.

"Weel," he said as he slowly examined the coin, "this-hyar date be 1977. But how be thet possible?"

"Port," Nelson continued, "that's what we've been trying to tell you. This is *not* 1848. It's 1982."

Then, while the man called Port listened intently, doing his best to understand, Nelson told of his own youth in the sixties and seventies. He told of a mother who was obsessed with wealth and status, who never displayed affection, and of a father whom his mother considered weak and ineffectual. He also told of his crusty old grandfather, whose heart was gold, but whose voice was loud and often harsh and critical when speaking to his son, Nelson's father.

"A boy doesn't have to be very old," Nelson continued, "to see things and to understand them. And it didn't take me long, Port, to realize that my grandfather was not happy with Dad, who was not strong and did not believe in himself. I also watched Mother mocking Dad, and I knew that she also had no respect for him.

"Port, even at that young age I vowed that I would never be weak like my father. I wanted, for his sake, to be a winner. If I was strong, I felt, then Mother and Grandfather would cease their ridicule of him.

"Trouble is, Port, I never had a chance to show Dad *or* Mother how strong I planned on being. For, two days after my eighth birthday, my parents were killed in an automobile accident. From then until the day he died, my grandfather was my only parent."

Nelson then described his meteoric rise to power within his grandfather's firm, and his incredible luck in transforming the business into an international multi-million-dollar conglomerate.

"How many dollars be thet?" the mountain man questioned, sounding unsure.

"Several million, Port. I don't even know how many for sure."

"And ye be worth *thet*? All by yer lonesone?"

"Well," Nelson said, shrugging, "I guess so. At least Armstrong Communications is worth that much."

"Wagh," Port said, struggling to become more comfortable in his makeshift splint. "This child never knew a man yet who were worth more'n a pinch of powder onct he had extry cash money. Whet happened to *ye* that ye turned out so good?"

Nelson and Angela both laughed.

"Port," Angela said, growing serious, "something surely must have happened to him. I've never known anyone who was so anxious to give away money, or himself even, to total strangers. Nelson is a very generous man, and I mean that sincerely."

"Well," Nelson laughed uncomfortably, "I don't know if that's right or not, Angie. And maybe I overdo it, too. I don't know.

"But I'll tell you something, Port. Most of the time I feel like two people. One day I'm flying around in my Lear with a bunch of stuffed shirts, wheeling and dealing for every advantage I can get, putting together multi-million-dollar deals and manipulating the lives of people that I'll never even see, much less get to know.

"The rest of the time," Nelson continued, "whenever I have a leisure moment, I'm drawn to the common folks, usually the ones with less money, the ones who in my opinion are the *real* people.

"Port, you ought to meet my employees. They're the salt of the earth, almost every one of them! I'd a whole lot rather spend an afternoon with one of them than with most of the corporate executives I've known. Besides, the vast majority of wealthy people are totally amoral, and most of them act like they can walk on water nearly any day of the week."

"Ol' hos," the mountain man interrupted, "ye may be right. Howsomever, maybe ye and me have been lookin' fer the wrong things. Maybe we ought to concentrate more on lookin' fer the good in them what have acquired substantiable means."

"You know, Port," Nelson said, after a minute's thought, "maybe you're right. My grandfather once told me that if I spent my life looking for the good in others, then I'd have spent it wisely. It's funny that I would follow that counsel with those who are not my competitors, and yet totally overlook it with those who are. What's even more strange is that until this moment I had no idea about what I was doing."

"Nelson," Angela said, interrupting the conversation, "you shouldn't be so hard on yourself. I've never seen you be less than honorable and totally polite with your associates."

"Ah, Angie," Nelson said, glancing through the near darkness at his wife, "it's a good thing you can't read my thoughts."

For a moment there was silence, and then Angela, almost in a whisper, spoke. "Yes, perhaps it is," she said. "And I'm just as grateful, Nelson, that you've never been able to read mine. Now let's all of us go to sleep, and—"

"Now, wait jest a little minute hyar," the mountain man interjected. "This ol' coon has one more question. I'm jest itchin' to know . . . yer folks went under in an autermobile crash, or some sech thing. Ol' hos, whet air an autermobile?"

"My friend," Nelson said, suddenly grinning from ear to ear, "an automobile is a car. And I'm going to tell you about mine. Close your eyes, ol' hos, and let me tell you the wonderous story of *my* baby, my Lamborghini Countach S."

And so, with a smile, Nelson began.

38

It was dark when Angela awoke, and she knew immediately that the weather had changed. The wind had apparently stopped, for she could hear nothing. In addition, the temperature had dropped noticeably. In point of fact, she quickly realized, it was far too cold for her to sleep.

For some time she tossed and turned, curling one way and then another. But no matter what she did, she could not get warm. Finally, unable to endure the misery any longer, she crawled from beneath the blankets where Nelson and Port lay sleeping, and moved quickly out to the fire. Taking several large logs from the stack before her, she piled them onto the flames, and soon a roaring blaze was sharing its warmth with her.

For some time, perhaps an hour, Angela sat in silence, feeling the fire and simply enjoying at least one side of her body being warm. Nelson awakened once and suggested that she come back inside, curl up in a ball, and relax. She pointed out to him that it was difficult to relax when her teeth were having such a lively conversation. He grinned, shrugged his shoulders, and went promptly back to sleep, and Angela was alone once more with her thoughts.

For a time she dodged the smoke from the fire as she watched its light flickering on the blackness of the trees around her. Gazing upward, she noticed that the clouds had vanished, and that the trees seemed to be pointing inward, pointing toward the circle of star-shrouded sky directly over her head.

Angela had never really noticed the stars before. Large and luminous in the clean black depth of the sky, an incredible number of them looked down upon the far empty land and on the white dark wilderness of the mountain and upon Angela Armstrong who was looking back in awe at them. How could there be so many? she wondered. How could there *possibly* be so many? Why were they there, and how had God ever managed to put them in their order?

She had heard somewhere of the vastness of space, and as she thought of the estimated distances to the stars she was seeing, she suddenly realized, for the first time in her life, that the stars above, or the light given off by them which was striking her eyes, would have left the stars themselves some tens of millions of years earlier.

It was very probable that some of the tiny points of light above her no longer even existed. In actual fact they could have burned out or exploded eons before, and the messages of light just hadn't had time to arrive. Nor would those messages arrive, possibly, for millions of years yet to come. It was sad, Angela thought, for who would be around to record them? No one! Possibly by then even the earth would be gone, and there would be nothing left of anyone.

And suddenly, as Angela gazed upward, she realized that she was seeing time as much as she was seeing light. As she looked at stars that might not even be there, she was actually gazing back into time.

Was it therefore possible, she found herself wondering, that she and Nelson were doing more than just looking? Could it be that they had, in the process of the crash or the fall from the glacier, accidentally fallen through a hole in the fabric of time? The idea, she knew, was totally illogical. And yet, what about Port and his sincere belief? And even more disconcerting, what about those packs, those obviously new 1840 vintage packs and saddles?

"Oh," she groaned aloud, looking upward once more, "if only the rescuers would come. If only a search plane would see this fire, pick us up, and put this whole unbelievable experience to rest."

Later a sliver of moon came out, and Angela noted with amazement how much light it gave. The trees, of course, were still black, but the never-ending snow took on a soft silver hue. The mountains, where there were no trees, went from black to blue, and Angela wondered if she had ever seen anything more beautiful.

As the hours slipped away, her sense of loneliness continued to grow. She tried not to think about it, but her loneliness wasn't really based on thoughts so much as it was upon feelings. Her emotion was one of missing someone, missing someone so desperately that it left an ache deep within her soul. She tried to analyze who it was she was missing, but for a time the solution eluded her. It wasn't Nelson; it wasn't her mother or father. Nor was it anyone else she could think of. It was . . . it was . . .

And then Angela knew. She was missing herself, herself as she had once been, herself as the man called Port had again made her feel.

How long had it been, she wondered, since she had honestly liked herself? How many years had passed since she had been a little girl, pure and clean like the air around her, filled with innocence and wonder and the simple joy of being alive? It had been a long time, she knew, much longer than she cared to admit.

And yet, the more she considered it, the more she realized that she was actually beginning to feel that way again. Port, in some strange and fascinating way, had caused her to begin to like herself, to examine herself closely and to want to become what he seemed to think she already was. The remarkable thing about all of it was that Port, without any apparent effort, had seemed to bring about the same attitude in Nelson.

As Angela's thoughts turned to her husband, she remembered again the touch of his hand on her chin, the pressure of his arm on her shoulder, the warmth of his hands around hers. And she wondered at the feeling of joy she had experienced when he touched her. What was it? she asked herself over and over. Why was this happening *now*? Was it simply because they were alone together and forced to rely upon each other? Or was it something deeper, more significant?

Angela thought again of her impending divorce, and wondered for the thousandth time since the crash whether her decision had been hasty, ill-timed. She had never really known Nelson, she now realized. Or at least she had never really understood his motives. But now it all seemed so clear, so reasonable and so justifiable. What little boy, she wondered, seeing his father dominated by a forceful woman who could never see her own selfishness, would not want to achieve where his father had not been allowed to?

Actually, the more she thought about it, the more Angela realized how much she and her husband were alike. Both had been deprived of a happy childhood, both had felt great insecurity, and now both had become great achievers in order to compensate for what they had missed. The only difference between them was that somehow Nelson had learned to give, and she had not.

Anxiously Angela stomped her feet against the incessant cold, wondering why she could never get them warm. Actually, she could not even remember the last time her feet had felt comfortable.

As she inched even closer to the fire, Angela noticed a small rock that was lying on the outer edge of the ashes. Carefully she touched it, found it to be warm but not hot, and was seized with a sudden idea.

Picking the rock up, she carried it quickly into the snow cave. There she placed it beneath the bedding, on top of one robe but beneath the others. Then she hurriedly crawled under the blankets herself, snuggled her feet against it, and smiled with pure pleasure as the warmth seeped into her nearly frozen toes.

Closing her eyes then she offered a silent prayer of gratitude, relaxed, and knew nothing more until Nelson gently shook her awake a few hours later. Quietly he suggested that she attend to Port's leg, and then he crawled from the shelter to care for the mule.

In the gray light of dawn the mountain man looked much worse than he had looked the night before. His face was white and pinched, and the lines around his eyes were etched deeply with pain. Carefully Angela crawled from the cave, leaving the man to continue his restless sleep.

The clear sky of the night before was gone, and more clouds, already obscuring the peaks, brought with them the threat of new snow.

For a time the two stood silently, hands out to the fire, simply absorbing its warmth. And though their thoughts ran swiftly, neither seemed uncomfortable with the silence that was between them.

Angela, as she stood there, wondered at that, and mentioned it to her husband.

"I know," Nelson replied quietly. "I think it's because we're getting used to the quiet up here. Also, there's no longer any strain between us. Neither of us has reason to question the other's thoughts."

"But why don't we, Nelson? What has changed?"

"It's Port, Angie. Somehow he's shown us the need for change, and even the way *to* change. Weren't you thinking of him a moment ago?"

Angela nodded affirmatively without speaking, and Nelson continued.

"So was I. And that's how he has done it. Without even intending it, I'm sure, he has provided a need that only the two of us, working together, can satisfy. In other words, Angie, he has united us in working toward a common goal."

Quickly Angela looked up at her husband. "He's done something else, too. Do you still feel it? I wasn't certain of the word you used the other night, but I am now."

"You mean love?"

"Uh-huh, I do. That man literally radiates love, Nelson. I've never known anyone like him. And I've never known anyone I so wanted to be like."

Nelson looked down at his wife, met her gaze, held it momentarily, and then turned slowly away. "I think that's wonderful, Angie," he replied quietly. "I really do. He makes me feel the same way. With all my heart I wish . . . I wish we could love each other."

Neither said anymore, and moments later, with the mule saddled to the best of Nelson's limited ability, he turned once again to his wife.

"Angie, I don't think that dead mule is more than a mile from here. Trouble is, the snow is deep, and I'm not in the best of shape. What I'm saying is that it'll likely take me a good half a day, and maybe even a little more, to get there and then get back. Without doubt, though, I should be back before dark. If I'm not, then you and Port had better make other plans."

"Nelson," Angela cried, "don't say—"

"Angie, nothing's going to happen. It's just my old business mind, trying to cover all my bases before I even get up to the plate. I—oh, no!"

"What's wrong, Nelson?"

"It's snowing again. Blast it all! I . . . Angie, I'm not going to take the mule. It'll slow me down, and in the off-chance that you have to move Port without me, the mule is your only hope. Now, keep your chin up and I'll see you tonight." Again Nelson took his wife's hand in his, squeezed it, and turned to go.

"Nelson," Angela suddenly called, stepping toward him.

Nelson stopped, turned, and waited in silence, watching his wife. For a moment they stood together, each looking into the other's eyes, each waiting, each aching to . . . to . . . But then the moment passed, and Angela stepped backward.

"Good luck," she said quietly. "Good luck, Nelson. And hurry back, please."

Nelson grinned, winked, and moved off into the snowy wilderness. Angela watched him until he was out of sight, and then she entered the cave to ease the wrappings on Port's legs, all the while wondering at the feelings that were so consistently filling her heart.

39

Throughout the morning Angela cared for the injured mountain man, wrapping and loosening and rewrapping his legs, feeding him as much warm water as he could drink, and gently encouraging him to sleep.

While he slept, Angela busied herself around camp, reheating the rock and putting it next to Port's feet, talking to and comforting the mule, washing its sores, and doing everything she could to keep her mind from Nelson.

She shuddered anew each time she thought of him alone out there, somewhere in the terrifying and blinding silence of the snow-covered mountain. In her mind she could see him as he staggered through huge drifts of snow, struggling to move forward, falling back, and struggling to move forward again.

She could visualize the ice from his breath crusting on his face and whiskers. And in her mind she could see the blood on the snow, blood from the cracks and cuts in his torn and frozen hands. How could he stand it? she asked herself over and over.

How could Nelson bear the terror of going alone into the cold and desolate stillness of the mountain?

Angela thought then of the words of the man called Port, of his literal love for the wilderness. She wondered again how anyone could love such fearful solitude.

It was snowing heavily now, and Angela suddenly became aware that the wind, which had stopped during the night, was blowing sporadically again. Anxiously she looked off up the mountain, hoping to see some sign of her husband. But there was nothing there, nothing but the cold and drifting snow. From all the signs there was a new storm coming, and Angela was suddenly scared.

An unexpected munching sound almost in her ear caused Angela to spin, screaming in fright. But it was only the mule, which in its pitifully starved condition had attempted to take a bite of her hair. Angela, her heart going out to the poor animal, patted its cheek and softly spoke.

"Flop-ears," she said sincerely, "I'm sorry. I forgot all about your hunger. Here, drink the water in this pot, and I'll go and see if I can find some bushes or something for you to eat."

With great effort Angela pushed through the snow away from camp, angling slightly uphill so that her return, whether she found branches or not, would be downhill and therefore easier.

After traveling about fifty yards she arrived at a small stream that was surrounded by clumps of short willows, almost entirely buried in the snow. After her initial surprise and wonder that the stream was not frozen over, she brushed aside the snow and, kneeling down, began to saw off the exposed willows with Port's knife.

At first her mind was busy, preoccupied with thoughts of Nelson, Port, and the mule. But as she knelt in the intense silence of the afternoon, Angela suddenly realized that she was listening to music. She was actually hearing the music that Port had spoken of days earlier, the music of nature!

The initial sound she heard was a curious hollow chuckling sound coming from the narrow stream. Rising, Angela moved slowly to the bank, where she found that a small flow of the icy water was dropping down between two rocks, making the hollow sound as it fell into the tiny pool below. It was definitely rhythmical, decidedly musical.

A few feet further away the water was making an entirely different rhythm and sound. It was a deep sound, more like a bass fiddle and drum working in harmony. Still, though, it was there, just as Port had explained, a perfect blending of wonderfully musical sounds.

At another spot the pitch was high and rapid, and sounded like bells or chimes ringing out. In a different place the water and the rocks combined were making woodwind sounds, in another the music of brass instruments could be heard, and all along the stream Angela could hear music.

And then as she paused again to listen, thrilling with the very sense of it, she became aware for the first time that the wind made a different sound blowing through willows than it did blowing through pines. Inspired, she pushed out into the deep snow of what would likely be a meadow, paused, and listened again. There she heard yet another sound, a sound made as the wind whispered across the top of the snow. These sounds seemed to her to be all stringed instruments, different from the water, unique to themselves, but instruments nonetheless.

Growing more excited by the minute with her discoveries, Angela gradually became aware that even the falling snow made tiny sounds, whisperings like the wind only decidedly different. There were larger sounds as well, sounds of trees bumping against each other in the wind, and groaning and snapping from their own internal pressure and cold.

And suddenly, as she moved slowly back toward the stream, it all came together in her mind, and Angela knew. She was listening to a symphony! In fact, she was listening to the world's first symphony, one which was old as time itself, and probably more beautiful than any imitation that man had yet created: the tremendous orchestration of nature.

Throwing herself down in the snow, she stared up into the flake-filled air and opened herself to the music around her, listening not so much with her ears as with her whole being. And finally, as she absorbed the beauty of it, Angela realized that she was no longer an alien, listening to the menacing sounds of silence. For the first time in her life she was alone without fear, alone in the midst of silence that was not silent at all. Nor was the wilderness hostile as she had always thought it to be. It was not even a wilderness. In fact, it was exactly as Port had said it was. It was literally the home of God!

40

Much later, feeling strangely refreshed, Angela staggered into camp under a heavy load of willow branches. Nelson had still not returned, and as she fed the mule and rewrapped the sleeping mountain man's legs with the long strips of blanket, she grew more concerned than ever about her husband.

Hour after endless hour she watched for him, moving from the fire to the shelter and back again, comforting Port during his occasional brief periods of wakefulness while her own fears mounted.

And then, with the abruptness that characterizes the deserts and the mountains, it was dark. Night had fallen and there was still no sign of Nelson. Angela, thoroughly terrified at the prospects of what might have happened to her husband, and hoping in some small measure to help him, heaped much of the remaining wood onto the fire.

Within minutes flames were leaping ten feet into the air, and Angela, standing away from the intense heat, stared expectantly out into the darkness. Over and over she cried out Nelson's name, screaming with all of the force of her soul. But the only answer was the lonesome whine of the wind, a wind that was no longer making beautiful music.

When the fire at last had burned to a heaping mass of coals, a grief-stricken Angela turned back to the shelter. It was no use, she now realized. Something terrible had happened up on the mountain, and Nelson was not coming back.

Doing her best to hide her fears and sorrow, Angela crawled slowly into the cave, where she silently worked into position the warm rock she had heated for Port.

"Air he back?" the man asked, his voice sounding surprisingly weak.

"No, Port . . . he's not. Something must have happened, and —and . . ." Angela's words trailed off as she dissolved into tears, burying her face against the mountain man's chest.

Gently the man wrapped his arms around her, and quietly he spoke. "Ye love him a powerful lot, don't ye, marm?"

"I don't know, Port. I just don't know. I did once, but so many things have happened, and—"

"Miss Angela, don't let yer yesterdays hold yer tomorrows captive. Let loose of yer heart and give it a chance to love. Without it, yer soul be in prison. With it, ye can make yer way into paradise. Do ye understand?"

Silently, and still crying, Angela nodded her head.

"Miss Angela, the good Lord taught us to love, even our enemies. Thet were the message of his life. Now, yer man were onct yer enemy, so to speak, but no more. Why, thet ol' hos has somethin' in him thet shines out like a ranch-window lamp on a stormy night. He's as fine a man as I've ever knowed!"

"Do you really mean that?" Angela asked, wiping at her eyes with her parka sleeve, doing her best to smile.

"Most indubitatingly sartin, Miss Angela. Thet husband of your'n air right as spring rain in sproutin' time. 'Bout as right as ye air, matter of fact."

Angela, hearing that, burst into new tears. "But he's gone," she wailed. "He's gone, and he won't be back!"

"Thar . . . thar, marm," the mountain man said soothingly. "Don't get to frettin'. Whar be yer faith? The good Lord loves yer man too, ye know, prob'ly a whole lot more'n ye do. He be takin' care of the ol' hos. Now, dry them-air tears, and fetch me my Bible outer thet possibles sack. Thar be comfort in thar, most 'specially fer troubled times. Hyar now. Read ye this psalm, and as ye read it, remember how the good Lord loves ye."

Angela, drying her eyes, haltingly began reading from the small leather-bound book, reading words that slowly brought a strange sense of comfort to her heart, words that had done the same for millions of others. And as she read, it was almost as though she was listening again to the music of the wilderness, almost as though her spirit were being calmed by—

"Hello the camp!"

Angela, suddenly sitting erect, sat still, unable to believe the faint call her ears told her she had heard. But when it came again, closer and louder, she spun from the bed, dropped into the trench, and crawled frantically out of the shelter. Nor did she see the smile, the smile of satisfaction that just briefly lit the haggard features of the injured mountain man.

41

"Nelson!" she screamed as she plunged into the snow outside. "Nelson, we're *here! We're here!*"

And, floundering wildly forward, the two forms at last came together, falling into each other's arms, laughing and crying and holding each other against the fear in their hearts, the terror of their combined loneliness.

Suddenly though, with a strange feeling of discomfort, Angela pulled back, looked up at Nelson, and then turned and made her way slowly back to the camp. Oh, how she ached! How she wished that she could follow her feelings! How she longed to know that it was all real, that she could trust what was happening, both to her and to her husband! But she couldn't! Not yet. Not until she knew and understood what was happening in her heart.

Nelson, confused and saddened, simply followed her in.

Later, as the three sat within the warmth of the shelter, chewing on the incredibly delicious mule, the mountain man smiled and held up the piece of meat he was eating.

"Wagh," he said cheerfully, "these vittles be better fare than whet's served even in New Orleans, says I. And the menu be the fofarrawinest menu this ol' hos could ask fer."

"Menu?" Nelson questioned. "Seems to me this meat's a pretty limited menu."

"Limited?" Port argued, his eyes sparkling. "Wagh, ol hos, it be a wonderous fine menu, with the main headin' naturally bein' mule. Fer soup thar be mule tail. Fer fish, thar be baked white mule and boiled gray mule. The meats air mule steak, fried mule, mule chops, broiled mule, stewed mule, boiled mule, scrambled mule, shirred mule, french-fried mule, and minced mule."

Winking then at Angela, and obviously enjoying finally getting at Nelson, the man went on. "Thar also be mule on toast . . . without the toast, and thar be short-ribs of mule with applesauce . . . without the applesauce. Fer relishes thar be black mule, brown mule, yeller mule, bay mule, roan mule, and mule fat, if ye can find any on these poor gaunt critters. Finally, fer beverages thar be snow, snow water, and creek water.

"All in all, pilgrims," he concluded, "it's a much better menu'n the one we had a day or two back, I'd tell a man."

The mountain man paused, took another bite of meat, chewed it, swallowed it, and then, looking at Nelson, spoke again. "Ol' hos," he said, suddenly growing serious, "ye've told me about yerself, and this child was plumb pleased to learn of ye.

"And marm," he continued, turning now to Angela, "ye've done the same. It be time, I air thinkin', ter hear about the two of ye, together."

For a moment there was an uncomfortable silence. Angela squirmed but remained silent, and so Nelson coughed and spoke, his words sounding quiet and empty.

"Port," he said, gazing down into the man's eyes, "you're in a bad way, and we've got to get you to some help. Storm or not, your leg needs medical attention badly. I think we ought to move out in the morning."

The mountain man glanced silently at Angela, whose eyes were downcast. Then, looking back at Nelson, he sighed.

"Whet destination be ye thinkin' of raisin', ol' hos?"

"I don't know, Port. Where's the closest medical help?"

"Weel," he drawled, "thar be a sawbones in Taos, and—wagh! Hold up thar, pilgrim! Thar be a doc with Ol' Bill, too. Feller by the name of Kern. He be a part of Fremont's party."

"Great! Then we can—wait a minute!" Nelson interrupted, suddenly very alert. "Who did you say Bill Williams was leading?"

"Wagh, it be Fremont, him as was—"

Nelson, suddenly, thoroughly shaken, moved closer to the weakened man. "*Colonel* Fremont?" he asked, his voice merely a whisper. "Colonel *John C. Fremont*?"

"Aye. Thet be him."

"And this is December, in the year 1848?"

"Aye," Port replied again, puzzlement showing on his face. "But whet . . . ?"

Suddenly Nelson sat back, a grin splitting his face from ear to ear. "Angie," he said, doing his best to keep from laughing, "I know where we are, and I also think I've lost my mind!"

"But, Nelson," she asked, her forehead creased with worry, "what on earth—?"

"Just a minute, Angie. I need to ask one more question.

"Port," he asked, turning toward the perplexed mountain man. "What day is this, exactly? Do you know?"

The man closed his eyes and concentrated. "According to the record in my journal, ol' hos, this hyar be December . . . uh . . . twenty-fourth. Wagh! Think of thet! It air Christmas Eve, and this ol' coon plumb fergot."

"Ah-hah!" Nelson exclaimed, ignoring the remark about Christmas. "That's great! Just great!"

"Nelson," Angela interrupted with growing frustration, "would you please explain?"

"You bet, Angie. Right now. And when I'm finished, you'll think I'm as looney as *I* think I am. Still, it might work. Stranger things have happened.

"Angie," he continued, his voice filled with excitement, "late in the fall of 1848, Colonel John C. Fremont, with a party of thirty-two other men and well over a hundred mules, made his way west out of Missouri into the heart of the Colorado Rockies, searching for a route through which the Central Pacific could run a railroad to the coast. That ill-fated party, Angie, was led by a mountain man known as Old Bill Williams."

"But . . . how do you know this?" she questioned, still unsure of where the conversation was heading.

"I did a paper on it in college! Grandfather actually flew me into the La Garita Mountains to examine the location where the party spent Christmas, the location they called Camp Hope."

Ignoring the questioning, almost frightened look that had spread across Port's face, Nelson plunged ahead. "Angie, that expedition ran head-on into the worst winter in Colorado history. Worse still, either Fremont or Bill Williams, whichever had assumed leadership at that point, became lost and led the men onto a mountain twenty miles east of the pass they had hoped to find.

"At the top of the La Garita Mountains," he continued, "at above twelve thousand feet, a fierce ground blizzard forced them to a stop. After fighting drifts as high as fifteen feet, and finding canyons filled with snow to depths of over one hundred feet, Fremont at last gave up."

"Wagh," the mountain man said softly, "I don't know how ye ken all this, ol' hos, but ye be right, nonetheless. The pass Ol' Bill calls the Wagon Wheel Pass air twenty miles due west. But Fremont quit? Thet-air be somethin' this ol' coon finds hard to believe."

"Well, believe it or not, Port, it happened. And before they made it back to Taos, ten men and well over a hundred mules had frozen to death or died of starvation and exposure."

"Ten?" Port asked, his voice suddenly very serious. "And do ye recollect the names of them poor fellers?"

"No, I don't. I do remember, though, that Old Bill got safely back to Taos, and so did Fremont. I also remember the names of some of the others on the expedition. There were three Kern brothers, a Preuss, a Vincenthaler, a man named Micajah McGehee, a Thomas Breckenridge, and . . . and a King fellow. I learned the names of all of them when I wrote that paper, but I guess that's all I can remember."

"Weel, ol' hos, thet be the party, but it beats all how ye knowed sech as thet."

"Yeah, Port, it does beat all. And the more a man thinks of it, the more stupefying it becomes. But what's really crazy is what I'm going to suggest next.

"Angie," he continued, "you told me this morning that you were looking at the stars last light. Did you happen to notice the North Star?"

"Yes," she replied after a moment's thought. "Yes, I did. It was that way, straight up the mountain."

"Okay," Nelson breathed, rubbing his whiskers vigorously as he concentrated. "The dead mules we've found have to be on Fremont's trail, and that can't be more than a half mile from here. Now, on the twenty-second of December, which we have to assume was the day before yesterday, Fremont began moving his camp two miles directly southeast of the position they called Camp Desolation, which was above Wannamaker Creek. His new camp, called Camp Hope, was established in a thick stand of pine on the top of the ridge separating Embargo Creek from Benino Creek. Fremont and his men will be there with the doctor in Camp Hope until day after tomorrow.

"Angie," Nelson continued, becoming even more excited, "I think I can find that camp. I really do! I believe we must still be in the Alder Creek drainage. If we are, and if we strike out almost directly northeast, we'll run straight into them. And if we do that, Port will have the help he needs."

"But, Nelson," Angela whispered, her face showing her shock and horror. "What's the matter with you? This *isn't* 1848!"

"I know, Angie. That's what my brain tells me. But then if it isn't 1848, then neither is that mule we've been eating a real mule. Nor are those Topographical Corps packsaddles real. Do you understand?"

"What . . . what do you mean?"

"Angie," Nelson said gently, "I found three mules today, all in the same condition, worn out and frozen to death. That's why it took me so long. I spent too much time looking for others. But the point, Angie, is this. The bridle on one of those mules bore a stamped date, the same as on the pack you showed me. And on the saddle of another had been carved one word. That word, Angie, was *Fremont*. Somehow, and don't ask me to explain it, we have landed in the winter of 1848, and we are on John C. Fremont's trail. In the morning we're going to try to catch him.

"Now, let's all do our best to get some sleep. Tomorrow, I think, is going to be a pretty big day."

42

With first light the party was ready to leave. Nelson, concerned about how bad the mountain man looked, asked him if he preferred leaving immediately or putting off the trip for another day.

Port, his face white and glistening with fever-induced perspiration, looked up at Nelson, did his best to smile, and spoke. "I reckon we'd best go now," he replied weakly.

"We'll get you out of here," Angela encouraged. "Don't worry. You'll be home with Sarah in no time."

"Home?" Port sighed weakly. "I've no home anymore. I left my Sarah to seek somethin' nowhar near so important, and the Lord won't let me see my home agin. I be like the Good Book says about Jesus. The foxes have holes, and the birds of the air have nests; but the Son of Man hath not whar to lay his head."

"What's that?" Nelson asked, surprised.

The mountain man paused, his face lined with fatigue, his wonderously blue eyes dark with the pain of the injury that had torn apart his leg.

"Matthew," he answered quietly. "Eight, twenty."

Nelson and Angela looked quickly at each other, turned away, and with no more discussion they were soon angling their way up the mountain, Nelson slowly pounding the way ahead with his maul. Immediately behind him struggled the scrawny mule, old Flop-ears. It was pulling a makeshift travois, upon which had been tied the silent and uncomplaining form of the mountain man. Behind him, coming last so that she might better insure Port's safety, toiled Angela.

The snow had stopped falling, but the wind was blowing constantly down the mountain, throwing up a seemingly solid wall of icy snow particles. It was into the ground blizzard's icy teeth that the group fought, hour after endless hour.

Late in the afternoon, at Port's insistence, Nelson halted in the lee of a great drift of snow. There he constructed another snow cave, as well as a lean-to for the mule, hastily made of Port's ragged canvas.

There was no fire that night because they could find no wood nearby. Yet the three ate cold meat and were basically contented, for the air in the cave was warm and still, and they were together, alive.

At last, just as they were about to drop off to sleep, Port spoke quietly into the darkness. "Friends," he said slowly, "I hope thet the birthday of our Savior were a merry one fer ye, and thet the year ahead be wonderous and bright. Thank ye, from the bottom of this ol' child's heart, fer yer generous help."

Neither Nelson nor Angela knew how to reply, so they remained silent, and gradually all three of them dropped off to sleep.

The next day the wind seemed to have let up a little. But the snow was, if anything, deeper, and so the party made no better time. Constantly they labored forward, sometimes directly up the slope, and sometimes, when the way grew too steep, zig-zagging back and forth. Yet always they climbed, never daring to consider the obvious insanity of what they were doing.

Angela's mind and body had long since grown numb, and for most of that second day of travel, which Port told them was

Tuesday, December twenty-sixth, she felt almost as though she were two people. One of her was lurching upward through the snow—falling, rising, staggering forward, falling, and rising once again. Her other self, the self who seemed to be the keeper of her mind, watched all of this—watched, wondered, and marveled that she was actually climbing the mountain. Yet that was all that the self which held her mind could think of. Thoughts of rescue were no longer a part of her consciousness, nor, strangely enough, were thoughts of warmth or of food. She thought only of the next step, the next two feet, the next dozen yards. And, she thought also of the men.

How could Nelson continue? she asked herself constantly. Watching him as he staggered upward through the blizzard, she wondered how he could possibly go on. Where, she wondered, did he find the strength to continue using his body to beat a pathway through the chest-deep snow?

And Port was another question in her frenzied mind. How much more could that poor man possibly endure? She watched the jolting he took as the mule lunged forever upward through the snow, dragging the bouncing travois behind it. The man's face was ashen with pain, and every jolt of the mule made it worse. Yet he never complained. He neither murmured nor cried out, and Angela marveled too at his courage.

There was also the mule—a poor skeletal creature of protruding bones, open sores, and hanging flesh. It was a creature that surely could not move another step, and yet it was a wonderful animal that somehow always managed to do so. Angela's heart ached for the mule at least as much as for the men, and she wondered at the strange twist of her compassion.

And so the day dragged slowly forward, one agonizing step following another, endlessly, endlessly . . .

Until, late in the afternoon of that Tuesday the twenty-sixth day of December in the year of 1848, if it actually was then, they suddenly crested the ridge.

Nelson, stumbling forward, stopped and gazed around him, so exhausted at first that he was unaware of what exactly had happened. His eyes were nearly closed with frozen snow, and he was unable, at first, to comprehend that they need climb no more.

"Angie," he finally croaked back, his voice hoarse with exhaustion. "We—we did it! I think we did it! I think we're on top!"

Angela staggered forward to the side of the travois, where she reached out and took Port's chapped and bleeding face into her hands.

"Port," she cried urgently, trying to awaken him. "Port? Can you hear me? Port, answer me, please!"

"Aye, marm," the man mumbled at last through his cracked and frozen lips. "I hear ye."

"Port, listen to me! We're *here*! We're on the top!"

"Weel . . ." the man sighed, doing his best to smile. "Fancy thet. Air we at Ol' Bill's camp, then?"

"Not yet, but—"

"Angie!" Nelson called, his voice filled with hope. "Those trees over there where I'm pointing? Yes, over there! Is that smoke? Can you see it from where you are?"

Angela, squinting to see through the swirling snow, could barely see the outline of the trees.

"I . . . I don't know, Nelson. I—"

"Angie, that's about where Fremont's camp was. I'm sure of it! There's even a forest service sign telling about it. We'll see it when we get there. Unless . . . well, there *will be* a sign, anyway. At least there will be, or was, when I was here in 1979. . . ."

Nelson stopped speaking and grinned painfully, realizing how absurd he sounded. "Good grief!" he scoffed aloud to himself. "This is crazy! What on earth have I done?

"Anyway, let's get moving. But be careful. This mountain top is covered with short, thick bushes that are hard to get through even in good weather. Be careful where you step. One broken leg between the three of us is plenty."

Carefully Nelson moved forward, and soon all of them were fighting the treacherous bushes that lay cunningly in wait just beneath the snow. Gradually they drew nearer to the trees, and at last Angela, squinting ahead, saw smoke.

"Nelson!" she screamed excitedly. "I see it! I see *smoke!*"

"I know, Angie," Nelson called back. "We've made it. We're here!"

Turning then, Nelson cupped his hands to his mouth and faced the trees. "*Helloooo the camp!*" he shouted. "Helloooo, Colonel Fremont!"

There was no echo, for the snow muffled his voice. Yet even so, the intense silence that greeted them was eerie, disconcerting. Nelson called again, and then again. When still there was no answer, he plunged forward once more, suddenly angry, tripping, sprawling, rising and lunging forward in a desperate bitter haste to reach the trees.

Angela, now leading the staggering mule, did her best to keep up, fearing as she ran what she would find, fearing equally what she might not find.

Soon she was standing next to her husband in the silent shadows of the forest, her heart aching with desperate helplessness. Before them, scattered haphazardly around, were deep pits in the snow, deep fire pits. From each of these pits trailed thin wisps of gray smoke. Other than that, and the swaying of the trees in the terrible and never-ending wind, there was no movement in the silent forest, no movement at all.

Fremont and his men were gone!

43

A red eye winked alone in the darkness. As the frigid wind, swirling into the pit, fanned the coal which was the red eye into life, the flickering light revealed three figures, huddled together and quietly shivering in the night.

Automatically Nelson reached out, picked up a limb, and laid it gently onto the small flame. Methodically he added another, then another, and soon the fire was once more roaring brightly.

"I can't believe it," Angela sighed, sounding totally discouraged. "I can't believe how close we came."

With a frustrated groan Nelson pushed himself to his feet, turned, and climbed out of the fire pit. "They were here," he said, speaking more to himself than to anyone else. "They were actually *here*! Look! Here's a couple of tin plates, here's a pot, and look at all of these trees, cut down in the past few days for firewood. When I was here in '79, these were old and dead, rotting and almost gone. Now the cuts are fresh, and this camp has only just now been abandoned.

"Do you know, Angie," he continued, speaking directly to his wife, "I keep thinking that if we had only arrived an hour or so sooner, we could have prevented what became one of the major disasters in western American history. And then of course, maybe we couldn't have. Maybe a person isn't allowed to interfere.

"Still, I can't get over how eerie this feels, actually being here, seeing what Fremont and his men went through. Look here, Angie. Here's a packsaddle, hanging here in this tree."

"It air a cache," Port explained, his voice weak and quiet. "One of the fellers cached it thar, figurin' to return one day and retrieve it. Point of fact, thet-air saddle looks like it be Tom Breckenridge's."

"Well," Nelson replied, stretching upward, "let's get it down and see." Straining, he shook the saddle loose from the branch upon which it had been hung. Catching it by its canvas wrappings and wooden crosses or bows, he carried it back to the fire.

"It's a packsaddle, Port, like I thought. Do you recognize it?"

"Aye. It be Tom's. I carved them-air bows fer him not more'n a year ago, down to Bent's Fort. Fact be, I did the black-smithin' on them-air rivets and rings, too. I were—"

"Well, look at *this*!" Nelson suddenly exclaimed. "There's a leather bag fastened beneath the bows here on the saddle. It's heavy, too. I wonder . . ."

Working quickly, Nelson untied the straps that bound the small bag to the saddle. Made of rawhide, the bag was approx-imately three inches wide and nine inches long, and pulled together at the neck by a long loop of leather which Port called a whang.

Carefully Nelson loosened the thong, grinning widely as he did so.

"Do you know what I think?" he asked softly as he lifted the bag into the air. "I think we've found ourselves a little cash in this cache. Let's just empty it out here, and . . . good grief! Look at this, Angie! It's *gold*!"

"Aye, ol' hos," Port said matter-of-factly. "It be gold, all right. Spanish doubloons. Thar be one thousand dollars thar, and it be Tom's. It air his life savings."

"Yeah," Nelson said, thinking deeply. "I remember now. Breckenridge was assigned to go with three others, including Bill Williams, for relief. From what I read, Breckenridge left his money for Fremont to bring out, and for some reason Fremont didn't do it. Breckenridge never saw his money again."

"Wagh," Port muttered quickly. "Thar ye go again, pilgrim, knowin' things whet ye can't know. Tom told me thet-air gold were meant fer his family, whet be back in St. Louey. Thet ol' hos'll be back fer it, sartin. Ye can lay yer mind to rest on thet account."

"Uh-huh," Nelson said, placing the Spanish doubloons back in the leather bag. "You're more than likely right. We'd better leave it here for him. Besides, I'd surely hate to foul up history."

Gathering up the saddle, Nelson pushed back through the snow to the base of the tree where it had hung. "Not much of a place to cache a thousand dollars," he said as he lifted the saddle back into the tree. "Still, nobody ever found it again that I know of, so it must have worked."

Then, returning to the fire, Nelson spoke to his wife. "You know, Angie? You're right. We *were* close. And we could have caught them, too, if poor old Flop-ears hadn't been so given out."

Instinctively Angela turned and looked behind her, gazing at the dark, shapeless mass that had been the—

"Port!" she cried, leaping to her feet and scrambling out of the fire pit. "Port, Flop-ears is down. Oh, no!"

Quickly she examined the fallen mule, caressing its neck while she felt for some sign of life. At last she rose slowly to her feet.

"Port, he . . . he's *dead*!"

Groping her way back into the fire pit, Angela wept unashamedly. She did not know exactly why she wept, except that the mule had become a vital part of her life, a part that had given its all for one of the men she had grown to love. As she wiped the tears from her eyes, Angela thought again of Port, and her heart went out to him. When she spoke again, her voice was filled with tenderness.

"Port, I . . . I'm so sorry. He was a beautiful animal. I never imagined that an animal could be so human, could give so much when he had so little left to give. I . . ."

And then Angela stopped, startled by the mountain man's expression.

"Port," she asked wonderingly, "didn't you hear me? Flop-ears is dead!"

"Aye, Miss Angela, I heered ye."

"But . . . but don't you even care? I mean,—you don't *look* like it even matters."

"Wagh," Port replied, hitching himself into a new position. "Miss Angela, listen to me. A woman cries like the rain, all on the outside. The fall be hard and over quickly. When things get real bad, then a man cries inside like a deep spring. It seems dry on top, but down deep underground the water never goes away."

Port then lifted his hand and placed it below his left breast. Then, humbly, he continued, "I cry fer ol' Flop-ears in hyar, marm, inside. And the mule were a good'un, thet-air be sartin. Miss Clementine were a fine horse, too. Seems a shame to lose 'em both all to onct. Leaves a man lonely and kind of empty inside, I be thinkin'."

"In the morning," Nelson stated firmly, purposely changing the subject, "I'll go after them. I'll get Doc Kern and bring him back."

"Aye, ol' hos," the mountain man replied, doing his best to smile. "Anything beats sittin' hyar like a rack of hump ribs smokin' over a roastin' pit. And if ye decide to go, then it's beholden to ye this ol' coon will be."

Angela looked down at the injured man, and she was suddenly terribly frightened by the lifeless look on his face. What could she do? she wondered. The man had given up, and she definitely had to find some way to help him regain his will to live.

"Port," she said, feeling suddenly inspired, "tell us about your wife. Tell us about Sarah, and about how you met her."

"Ah . . . Miss Angela," the man sighed, looking up at her, his eyes sparkling with sudden light. "Thet-air be a story now, I'd tell a man—"

"Well, then tell *us*," Nelson added, encouragingly. "We'd like to hear it."

"Weel, ol' hos," the man drawled weakly, clearing his throat as he spoke, "it goes back to late in the fall of '46, two years past. This child and a few others were two days out from Bent's Fort, headin' fer Taos, when we met up with a bunch of Mormons who were on their way to Santa Fe. They were part of whet they called the Mormon Battalion, and they'd been fixin' on fightin' fer the government in the Mexican War.

" 'Cept of course thet this-hyar outfit was made up of disabled men, thar teams were give out oxen, and whet wagons they had were sure enough castoffs. They were headed, they said, fer the Pueblo.

"Weel, feelin' natural sorry fer 'em as I did, them bein' so down and out, and knowin' thet the Yutas'd bin raisin' a mite of a fuss hyar and thar, and had commenced to chargin' the same price fer travelers to cross the mountains as Ol' Nick charges to let poor souls past the seven circles of the Styx, I left my companyeros and guided them Mormons into the Pueblo, fer I knew the place a-plenty.

"Winter were gettin' ready to set in, and after some of the Mormons started to feelin' better, they began throwin' up log houses, put together from the cottonwood trees whet lined the river. This child, anxious to help out those poor down-and-out pilgrims, offered my services as a carpenter. They were natural friendly, and I felt right to home with 'em.

"By February of last year," he continued, his voice seeming to pick up, "Mormon Town, as folks come to call it, held fifty-some houses, a blacksmith shop, and a large log meetin' house, whar they held worship services and dances. Thar were over three hundred souls thar, almost fifty women, and a whole passel of young'uns.

"The Mississippi Saints, as the first group to arrive called theirselves, had arrived thar the previous August, had cleared the land, and had planted turnips, corn, melons, and pumpkins. With thet-air, and with the fine huntin' in the mountains done by the Battalion members, thar were a-plenty to eat in their camp.

"One of the Mormons were a feller name of Nathan Thomas. He were a single man about the age of this child, and the two of us became fast friends. He were a religious sort, and this child were a heathen. But thet didn't seem to make no difference a'tall. When he could get leave from his officers, we hunted together in the mountains, and when he couldn't, we were together in Mormon Town. He were a fine man, and more and more this ol' hos found hisself wantin' to be like him.

"Nate of course told me somewhet of his religion, but I were a hard sort, and whet-air he said made little more than a dent. Strange thing, though, fer the first time in my natural-born life this child found myself wanting to get to know the Lord.

"One day I saddled up Miss Clementine, and rode over to Hardscrabble, whar I run smack into Ol' Bill. We cuffed each other a bit, palavered fer a spell, and I finally got around to raisin' my account of the Mormons and my interest in 'em.

"Ol' Bill were some shocked, and declared thet he thought he'd learnt me better'n thet. He'd been a preacher onct, ridin' the circuit so often he declared thet the chickens used to draw lots when they seed him comin', jest to decide which one would become dinner."

Nelson and Angela grinned, and Port continued.

"Weel, the more cussed upset Ol' Bill got, the more stubborn I got, fer my heart were sayin' to pay attention to Nate. When I told Ol' Bill thet, he commenced to read me from the Book, spoutin' scripture at this child wonderous fast. Strange thing, though, from thet-air day to this, Ol' Bill, who air wonderous good at preachin', but who no longer believes in it, has called *me* the Preacher. 'Course he don't say it to my face, 'cause he won't even speak to me. Nor does he seem to want me around.

"Now, Miss Angela, gettin' back to yer original question, I'll tell ye about the most wonderous and fearful night of this ol' coon's life.

"When I got back to Mormon Town from seein' Ol' Bill, Nate were waitin' with an invite fer me to come with him to the fandango whet the Mormons had set up.

"Now, marm," Port continued, suddenly speaking louder and with unusual enthusiasm, "this child were born with feet whet didn't match a'tall when it comes to dancin'. 'Sides, genteel white women were a rare commodity in the mountains, and jest the sight of sech a creature put the fear of death into my bones. All in all, howsomever, my curiosity got the best of me, and I went to thet-air dance.

"Well, I were sittin' by, doin' my best to hold up the wall, a-watchin' the gravel fly, and in general enjoyin' myself, when I spotted this-hyar little Mormon gal.

" 'My-oh-my,' says I to myself, of a sudden interested. 'My-oh-my yes! Thet-air be the purtiest little heifer this side of the Cimmeron,' I says. 'Oh my yes, and more'n likely then some.'

" 'Off'n yer feed, Port?' asked Nathan Thomas, who were holdin' up the wall next to me. 'Thought somehow you weren't up to these fandangos, but of a sudden I see a glint in yer eye.'

"Weel, I were givin' thet ol' coon a right witherin' look, lettin' him know whet I thought of his poor humor, when the caller yelled out fer a ladies' choice.

"About then I saw thet-air little gal head straight acrost the room, aimin' plumb fer me, and I'd like to've gone under. My heart started hammerin', and right thar I know'd I'd ten times rather take a Blackfeet arror in the hump ribs than stand up next to her. Only trouble is, thar were no choice. She were thar, hitched up and tethered in front of me, and I had to take her out fer a spin.

"Weel, her eyes were softer'n blackstrap molasses poured on a tin plate, and when she held out her hand and looked up at me, I near lost my breath.

"Miss Angela," Port continued, his voice suddenly soft, "thet-air little lady were jest about the purtiest thing I'd ever seed. Her hands were small and soft, and were a big difference from all the harness and beaver plews I'd bin workin' with. Her voice were soft and musical, like a swift-runnin' stream, and her hair? La, marm, it were somethin'!

"All in all, it took about everything I had to even get my breath, let alone move my feet. And when the dance were o'er, I decided it were a good thing I'd wore my moc's, fer with boots on I'd have worn the tops of her toes plumb off.

"Weel, thet were how I met my Sarah, purtiest and most wonderous fine little gal east or west of the mighty Mississippi, not even to mention the Cimmeron."

"So when did you get married?" Angela quickly asked.

"Shortly thereafter, marm, on the twenty-seventh day of March. 'Course her Pa were somewhet concerned about his only daughter marryin' a heathen, a man whet he called a Gentile. But after a fine and special day in the mountains between my-ownself and the Lord, thet-air were taken care of. I were a heathen no longer, and the weddin' were held."

"What did she look like that day?" Angela then asked, her voice filled with excitement. "What did she wear? How did she have her hair fixed?"

"La, Miss Angela!" the mountain man exclaimed, laughing and coughing all at once. "Ye all think alike, don't ye. Don't women ever change, fussin' fit to be tied over how other women look?"

Both Angela and Nelson smiled knowingly, and Port continued.

"She were purty as a picture, marm, bright as a summer morn, and sweet-smellin' as a whole mountain of wild flowers. She wore a dress o' white, and her soft dark hair fell down off'n her head in ringlets, smooth and shiny at the top and all fluffy at the bottom, jest like the falls o' the Yellerstone. Her blue eyes were sparklin' like a wind-kissed mountain lake, and all to sudden I got to feelin' all holler and empty just thinkin' whet life'd be like without her. Wagh! This ol' hos come near to bawlin' right thar, he did! It were plumb embarrassin'."

For a few moments then there was silence around the fire,

the only sound the popping and snapping of the burning wood. Overhead the wind, the never-ending wind, whined through the trees, and suddenly Angela felt strangely and unaccountably lonely.

"You really love her, don't you?" Angela said quietly.

"Aye, Miss Angela," the man replied, wiping the tears from his eyes. "Thet I do. More'n words could ever tell, I do. And it air a strange and wonderous thing, Miss Angela, fer Sarah loves me too. Fact is, she's the one whet taught *me* of love."

"Taught *you* of *love*?" Angela blurted in surprise.

"Aye, marm. Fer as purty as my Sarah be on the outside, the more I come to know her, the more I learned thet she were thet much more beauteous on the inside. And thet-air beauty, marm, be love, pure, simple love. Wagh! Why, she be like a bucket of milk from a freshened jersey cow, filled clear up and plumb flowin' over. I never seed a body so purely full of love.

"When this child first recognized her goodness fer whet it was, I asked her straight forward whar she found it all. And jest as quick she answered straight back — from the Lord.

"Weel, thet about knocked me under, it did, fer I didn't understand it. But it got my brain to tickin', and thet were all she wanted.

"Miss Angela," Port concluded, "as time has passed, I've learnt thet my Sarah be right, and slowly I'm learnin' how to love."

The man suddenly broke into spasms of coughing, and Nelson and Angela glanced again at each other, their faces reflecting their uneasiness. Then Nelson, taking the lead, spoke out.

"Port," he said gently, "you need to rest. You'd better stop talking for a while."

"Aye," the deathly ill mountain man answered, gasping for breath, "but first let me s — speak of my son."

The man called Port then spoke earnestly and very coherently, describing the departure of his wife from Pueblo in the spring of 1847. She, her family, and the rest of the Mormons had gone north to meet Brigham Young's party. Together the two groups planned on continuing west until they found their promised land.

"It were not 'til this spring," he said quietly, "thet I learnt they had settled in the Salt Lake country. Thet were also when I learnt thet my Sarah had given birth to a son, a fine boy whose name be Nathan."

"But . . . but Port," Angela asked, confused, "why didn't you go with her? Why did you stay behind?"

"Weel, marm," the man replied, sounding sorrowful, "go with her I sartin should have done, and the Lord has not prospered me fer doin' otherwise. It were a dire and awful decision. At the time, howsomever, it seemed important to trap one more season of plews to build up a stake fer us. With a stake, we reckoned, I could begin the business of bein' a craftsman, makin' chairs and trunks and other sech fofarraw.

"Weel, I done it, and now fer the past six months I been tryin' to get to Sarah and the child. Trouble is, this ol' hos jest can't seem to get the job done. Somethin' seems to all'ays be holdin' me back—storms, brownskins, greenhorn pilgrims, and you name it.

"And now," he said, coughing again, "I be wonderin' if I'll ever see my Sarah agin."

"You must miss her terribly," Angela anguished.

"Oh, thet I do, Miss Angela, thet I do. I bin thinkin' the past little spell thet maybe I could read ye somethin' personal from my journal."

"Oh, would you please?" Angela asked eagerly.

"Ol' hos, if ye could jest hand me my possibles sack . . ."

Quickly Nelson reached over, picked up the man's pack, and placed it at his side.

In silence the man called Port began to rummage through his belongings, looking until at last he retrieved his small leather-bound packet. Then, opening it, and speaking almost to himself, he began.

Oct 18 *It has been well over a year since Sarah left. I've not been writing like I promised her. Most of my days air bein' spent at Bents Fort repairing waggons and not much else 'cept trying to keep my mind off'n my lonesomeness. I promised Sarah I'd write a journal up to this time fer my children and theirs, hoping they'd not need to make the same mistakes whet I've made. I have finished, and will write each days happenings from this time on.*

Oct 22 *Left for Hardscrabble to talk to some old friends. Saw Ol' Bill. We air still not close, but I will kill him with kindness, so to speak.*

Nov 2 *We spent the last ten days with Lupton talking about old times. Bill had so many stories I never found myself tiring of hearing them. Some of the newer boys think Bill is just pulling their leg but I spent a heap o' time with him and know the tales air true.*

Nov 6 *Word finally come that Fremont and his party were close and would be here in a short time. I cain't get any word from Bill if he air going with Fremont or not. Says he won't go if I do. Temperature dropped today and a lot of snow in the high country.*

Nov 15 *Took some trade items down south. Fremont air not expected to be in for another two weeks and talk air he's not going to go on account o' the snow and cold. I bin having second thoughts about going this late and may wait untill spring although having my family so far from me and no way to git to them be almost too much to bear.*

Nov 20 *Stayed with a small group of settlers last night. One of the men had a wife and small son that reminded me much of my own family. Cain't even write how much I miss them. God forgive me for leavin' them, and grant that they are spared any deprivations untill my arrival at the salt lake.*

Nov 24 *Arrived at Bents Fort and found out that Fremont had been there and left. Bill went with them. At this time I find it a hard task to decide what to do. Whether to stay and head out in the spring or go now. If I go I will not rest untill I see my family and pray God that I not perish in the snow on the mountains.*

Nov 25 *Made my choice to try and ketch up to the Fremont party. I long fer my family too much to wait untill spring be fore heading out.*

Nov 26 *Arrived at Hardscrabble and found out that I am two days behind. Lupton and the others tried to persuade me not to go but as the weather has changed and is almost like summer I figured I may make some time on the party. Bill Sharp says he is coming along.*

Nov 30 *Today caught up with Fremont and asked to join. On Bill Williams recommendation we were refused. It were a blow to my hopes. Sharp and me turned back, but tonight I have decided to follow Fremont's trail. Bill Sharp won't do it, but he don't have a family at the salt lake. Tomorrow we separate, and I go on alone. Howsomever, I expect my Rapaho friend will ketch me, as he promised to accompany me west.*

"It were a hard thing to do," Port said, looking up at Angela and Nelson. "But I tell ye, pilgrims, this child could jest not bear the thoughts of spending another entire winter away from my Sarah, whet with her newborn boy-child needin' me more'n more."

"So you actually intended to follow Fremont's trail into the Salt Lake Valley?" Nelson concluded.

"Aye, ol' hos, thet I did. And it were a good plan, too, 'cept fer the snow. I'll read ye a bit more, if ye'd like."

Dec 1 *Got off to a bad start and had to repare my rigging on my mule. Little took place worthy of note. Crossed the summit of the Wet mountains and the going were ruff due to about three foot of snow.*

Dec 2 *Made good time today. Traveled down the lower end of the valley. My thoughts air that Fremont might try to cross the lower end of the Sangre de Christos. It snowed agin last night and is getting colder.*

Dec 4 *The weather turned bitter and it is snowin agin but did manage to make good time even so. Still no sign of the Rapaho.*

Dec 6 *The wind come up and I stayed in a makeshift shelter untill this afternoon. Hands and feet cold so hard to write. Made the summit and decended the other side. The wind be awful strong.*

Dec 8 *I made good time today and figure I am about a day behind the party. Spent a cold night last night. The animals and me air covered with frost and ice.*

Dec 9 *Tonight I am camped on the valley floor. Not much firewood. The wind is scattering my fire and cain't get much rest. Didn't sleep much last night.*

Dec 10 *There is a lot of mist today and I finally had to stop and build a fire to thaw myself out. Still cold and not making much time.*

Dec 11 *I stayed in the valley today to take care of my Flop-ears and Miss Clementine and see if I could take down a deer. I am rested now after many weary nights and my stomachs full. My thoughts air to my family. Tomorrow I will try to ketch up to the others, for there has been no sign of the Rapaho. Fremont won't refuse me now.*

Dec 13 *More snow to day. Made my way down the valley toward willow creek and found where Fremont had struck out past embargo creek and camped at alder creek. It looks like they air planning to make an acent up alder creek. That could be rough with so much snow. Why didn't they take willow creek to the pass? Getting anxius to be with my Sarah and little Nathan. Will they be surprised.*

Closing his little journal, Port placed it at his side, leaned back, and relaxed. "This child never could understand why things were always so hard to do. 'Specially things whet seem to matter the most."

"Oh, Port," Angela cried, her heart genuinely touched. "I'm so sorry! It isn't fair that you've gone through so much, come so far, and have still not made it! It isn't right. It just doesn't make sense that—"

"Miss Angela," Port said, smiling and patting her hand, "it makes sense. It surely do!"

Then, in his wonderful wistful way that was plainly made up of half faith and half hope stuck all together with a good dollop of pure charity, the mountain man explained to Angela that the Lord had taught him a great lesson, and that it would soon make sense to her too.

For a few moments after that there was silence around the fire, for neither Angela nor Nelson could find the words they wished to express.

"But, say," Port went on at last, suddenly brightening, "I asked ye onct afore, and now I be askin' ye agin. Tell me about yerselves, about yer lives together."

For a long moment no one answered. Then Nelson, resigned, cleared his throat and spoke. "My friend," he said somberly, "actually there really isn't much to—"

"Port," Angela interrupted, her face suddenly lit with a beautiful smile, "let *me* tell you about us, about our honeymoon, first of all. Nelson never does tell it as well as I do."

Shocked, Nelson looked over at his wife, who smiled even more radiantly, and then almost shyly held out her hand. Nelson, not yet understanding, slowly took it, felt the firm and steady pressure of his wife's grip, and then listened in wonder as she spoke.

"He took me to Nassau, Port. In the Bahamas! It's one of the most beautiful places in the world. But what *really* made it so beautiful, Port, was the love we shared, a love as 'wonderous fine' as yours and Sarah's, a love that we are learning to feel even more today. I'd like to describe it to you."

And then, while Nelson listened with mounting emotion, Angela described for the dying mountain man the deep and abiding love that she felt for her husband, a love that, she was certain, would last forever.

44

Much later, long after the man called Port had fallen into a fitful slumber, Nelson and Angela lay quietly in each other's arms.

"Honey," Angela whispered, "I'm worried about Port. He sounds awful, like he has pneumonia."

"I know, sweetheart," Nelson replied, his voice choking with emotion. "And I've got to tell you that—that I'm pretty sure he isn't going to make it."

"But why . . . how . . . ?"

"Angie, when I was here with my grandfather we found a grave, an unnamed grave that was marked only with the rotting remains of a crudely constructed cross."

"But . . . that could have been anyone's grave, Nelson. Fremont's men were—"

"Dear," Nelson replied softly, "Fremont lost ten men on that expedition. None of them died even close to here. And as near as I can remember, that grave is right here where the fire is, almost exactly between these three oddly positioned young pines."

Quietly, Angela began to cry. "Oh, Nelson," she sobbed. "Think of his poor wife and son. How will they get by? What will they do without him? Can't we pray for him, Nelson? Can't we pray to have his life spared? He's so good . . . and so pure."

"We can pray, Angie," Nelson replied comfortingly, "but remember, the Lord even allows the good people to die. It isn't—"

Port suddenly broke into a frenzied fit of coughing, and Nelson stopped speaking. When it had subsided the mountain man awoke and struggled up onto his one elbow.

"*Pien Kua Yameh*?" he called out, "air thet ye? Air ye comin' to help?"

"Port," Angela called softly as she hurried to his side.

"Oh . . . Miss Angela," the man breathed, sighing deeply, "this ol' hos were dreamin', I reckon. Thought I saw my brownskin friend, the Rapaho."

"Is that his name?" Angela gently asked, now holding the man's cold hand.

"Aye," Port replied weakly, "*Pien Kua Yameh*. The name means Mountains-where-the-bears-roam. He air a fine brownskin, Miss Angela—as fine a friend as this child ever had."

For a moment the man coughed again, and the two people above him gazed with an aching longing into his hollow eyes.

Suddenly, though, gathering strength from some unknown source, the man struggled again to his elbow. "Ol' hos," he said, looking at Nelson, "fetch me thet-air journal onct more, will ye?"

Nelson searched quickly at the man's side, found the small packet, and handed it to him. Then, in the flickering light from the fire, the man called Port opened it and began, with trembling hand, to write.

Nelson and Angela, at Port's request, listened as he voiced aloud the words that he slowly recorded.

Dec 26 *The cold and snow air worse now, and I fear I cannot continue. My leg air all swole up so I cain't even crawl. My koff be bad and gettin' worse right along. I feel sartin I be dyin and there be still no sign of the Rapaho. If anyone should happen to find me, please make it known to my wife and son that God willing we will meet agin in the spirit. My deeds and intentions were honorable, but the desire to be with my family rushed me to my fate. Should you Sarah or you my little Nathan ever read this, know my love for you air eternal and the time I spent together with you Sarah were the happiest time of my life. Contact Nathan Thomas fer he be a good man to seal you and the boy to me. My family air good people and I desire them to know the things I have learnt to be true. I feel tired but peacified that I had the strength to make these things known. I love the Lord, and know he loves me. All this will work out fer the best, fer with his love it cannot be otherwise. Oh, my family—love the Lord and love your fellowman. As my Rapaho friend told me, that is the path of beauty—of light.*

Am very tired. Will try to write agin tomorrow.

With a long sigh, the man called Port shut his journal, leaned back, and closed his eyes.

"Port," Angela declared, "we'll do it! Nelson and I will get word to Sarah, and—"

"And we'll get *you* there, too!" Nelson avowed, interrupting his wife.

"Ol' hos," the mountain man replied feebly, "Miss Angela . . . thank ye both fer yer care, fer yer love. Ye both be wonderous special, the kind of folks I'd be proud to present to my Sarah. But this ol' hos has him a hunch thet it be too late. I—"

"Port," Angie cried, "don't! You shouldn't—"

"La, Miss Angela," the mountain man gasped, "don't hold onto me no longer'n ye have to. Now s—smile a bit. Ye look about as cheerful as . . . as a bee-stung bear. Wagh! I . . .

"Whoa, it . . . it be gettin' brighter. Hyar, did ye build up the fire, ol' hos? I . . . I . . .

"Stay together, the two of ye! Do ye hyar?"

"Yes, Port," Angela cried. "Of course we will, but . . ."

"Miss Angela, I . . . feel some better. Would ye take my hand, please. Somethin' wonderous be happenin', and . . .

"Sarah? Sarah . . . ?"

And suddenly there was silence on the mountain—silence broken only by the weeping of Nelson and of Angela, the popping of an almost-burned log on the fire, and the lonely sighing of the frigid, never-ending wind.

PART SIX

45

Angela, her eyes squeezed tightly shut against the glare, thought at first that she was dreaming. Port had died, and she and Nelson, both more grief-stricken than either of them could imagine, had at last fallen asleep in each other's arms. But now she was warm, uncomfortably warm, and all around her she could hear the sounds of birds, hundreds upon hundreds of singing birds.

In almost angry frustration she twisted her head back and forth, trying to shut out the sounds of their singing, the happy sounds that had no place in this winter wilderness of pain and sorrow. But for some reason the dream would not go away, and—

Angela, suddenly opening her eyes, sat up and stared transfixed around her. "Nelson!" she whispered in fright. "Nelson, wake up! Hurry!"

Her husband, groaning softly with sleep, finally managed to open one eye. Looking up at her, he suddenly sat bolt upright, his eyes wide and staring.

"Oh, no," he whispered, shaking his head. "Angie, what's happened? Where are we?"

"I . . . I . . . I don't know, dear. I woke up, and . . . this!"

In the early morning light their surroundings were beautiful beyond belief. They were lying alone in a clump of pines, and beyond the trees they could see a meadow, more breathtaking than any garden Angela had ever seen. There was no snow anywhere, and the wild flowers, myriads of them, were beyond description. The early morning dew, heavy upon the meadow, caused the plants to droop a little, and Angela found herself thinking about prayer and about Port.

Port!

Frantically she scrambled to her feet, looking hastily about. But there was no sign of the trapper and mountain man, no sign of their dear friend.

Nelson, now standing beside his wife, suddenly took her arm, squeezed it, and directed her gaze into the trees above them.

"Angie," he said slowly, pointing upward. "Do you recognize that?"

Angela looked up and saw, hanging on a dead limb high above her, the weathered remains of an ancient packsaddle. And dangling beneath it, hanging by a single leather thong, was a small leather bag, black with age.

"It can't be!" Angela whispered in fear. "It just *can't* be!"

"Well," Nelson responded, "maybe it can't, sweetheart, at least logically. Nevertheless, there it is! That is the exact saddle and bag of gold doubloons that I hung there last night. Remember? You watched me do it."

"But it's so high, Nelson. So high and . . . and so *old*."

"It sure is. But then I stood on top of that high snowbank to hang it there, and things age considerably hanging out in the weather like that has done. Here, take a look at this."

Moving quickly, he strode to a spot about ten feet away. Stooping down, he picked an object off the ground. "Angie," he said quickly, turning to his wife. "Do you know what this is?"

Angela took the decayed and lichen-covered object from her husband and examined it carefully.

"It's a jawbone, isn't it? Some kind of animal jawbone?"

"That's right. If my grandfather's knowledge of this stuff was correct, then this is either a horse or mule jaw, an ungelded one. And frankly, I think it's too small to be from a horse. You can tell it was ungelded, according to my grandfather, because of the wolf-fangs, the long teeth that protrude here from the lower jaw."

"But Nelson, what—"

"Angie, Flop-ears was an ungelded mule. So were Fremont's animals."

Moving again, Nelson walked quickly to another spot, back beyond where they had been sleeping. "Over here, darling, beneath these trees, is the grave I was telling you about last night. See? Here's the outline of it, where the earth has dropped a little. Can you make it out?"

"Yes, but . . . oh, no! Do you mean . . . that this is Port's grave? Are you trying to tell me that . . . ?"

"Yes, Angie," Nelson said, placing his arms around his wife. "I am. Somehow we're *back.* Somehow this is now again."

For a moment or so Angela clung desperately to her husband, her face buried in his coat. Finally, though, she pulled away and looked up at him.

"But . . . but was it real, Nelson? Were we really there, or did we dream it, or what?"

"I don't know, sweetheart. I only know that, whatever happened, it brought us back together. That much, at least, was real, and I'll forever thank the Lord for that."

Angela sighed deeply. "So will I, honey. So will I. I just wish there was some way we could thank Port for what he did."

"Well, I guess we can, Angie, just by staying together. For that much of our experience was real. I know that. Port is as real as either one of us. He has to be."

"Oh, Nelson, I hope he was! He was the most kind and loving man I have ever known. And strangely, he didn't even know it. I honestly don't think he realized that he did all of the clean, decent things he did, for they came as naturally to him as perspiring, spitting, using tobacco or fouling the air with vile language comes to most other men."

"Angie," Nelson asked quietly after he had absorbed his wife's statement, "do you remember how we used to discuss the classics?"

Angela wiped her eyes and nodded, and so Nelson went on.

"Port has affected me too, Angie, and the words of Robert Louis Stevenson say better than I ever could, just how, in only a dozen days out of our entire lives, he has managed to affect us so. 'When I met him I was looking downward; when I left him I was looking up.' "

Standing together in silence then, the two held each other tightly, each touched by the deep emotions the other was sharing. Neither of them understood what had happened to them, nor were they at all certain they even wanted to understand. It made no sense, no sense at all. Yet it did. In a way it made wonderfully perfect sense, exactly as Port had told them it would.

Gently Nelson placed his hand beneath Angela's chin, lifting it upward until she was looking directly into his eyes.

"Windows, Angie," he said softly. "Look into them and remember, I *do* love you!"

Angela smiled through her tears. Then she blinked them away and told Nelson that her own windows were finally clear and clean. "Sweetheart?" she then asked, her voice almost a plea. "Can you see my love for you shining in mine? Tell me you can see it, please. It's there, I swear it! With all my heart I love you and pray that you will forgive me. Oh, I've been such a fool!"

"We were both fools," Nelson replied quietly, "and I have even more need of forgiveness than you. For this to work, we must each forgive the other. With all my heart I do. Do you?"

Angela nodded eagerly, and Nelson at last spoke again. "Now, lady," he said teasingly, "let me see if your windows really *are* clean."

Nelson then looked deeply into Angela's eyes, grinned and nodded with satisfaction, and then the two of them drew slowly together until their lips met, softly, sweetly, hungrily, joined in a kiss that at last welded their hearts together in a joyous union of love.

"Angie," Nelson whispered long moments later. "Do you know what I think? Much as I'd love to stay here and do this for the rest of my life, I have a funny feeling that if we climb that little hill over there, we'll be able to see the Lear."

"Do you think so?" she cried. "Really?"

"Yes, I do. I'm serious."

"Well then, come on!" Angela shouted, grabbing at her husband's hand. "Let's get goin', ol' hos!"

"Weel, marm," Nelson replied, grinning back at her. "This child's comin', he be, fer hurryin' shines fine with him!"

Together then, hand in hand, both smiling happily, Angela and Nelson climbed through the grass and flowers of the small hill. And strangely, as they neared the top, both wanted to move more slowly, to savor their last few minutes alone on the mountain.

At last, though, cresting the ridge, they stopped and stared, scarcely able to believe what they were seeing. For there, just as they had left it, was the Lear.

It was lying crumpled against some boulders on the edge of the small mountain glacier, looking tiny and forlorn. The tree that the plane had pushed over, the one that had been burning when they had fled the scene, was only a pile of ashes. Yet, amazingly, the stump was still smoking, and Nelson wondered that it had been burning for so long.

Not far away, at the edge of the glacier, was the cornice over which they had plummeted some twelve or thirteen days before.

Angela, with a queer feeling in her chest that made breathing difficult, took Nelson's hand and started cautiously forward. It was so strange, she thought. Almost like coming home after a long trip. But the plane was not home, there was no one there to greet them, and Port was not . . .

In fact, the profound silence of the narrow valley was eerie, and Angela, in a moment of fear, wanted to turn back, wanted to return to the security of the mountain. For there had been security there, of a kind for which she longed more than any other, the security of a loving relationship with her dear husband.

Suddenly she realized that she was squeezing Nelson's hand, and for a moment they gazed in silence into each other's eyes, each knowing, and each being thankful for, the other's thoughts.

Finally, though, Angela turned, glanced once more at the plane, and then looked back up at her husband, almost questioning. He smiled but said nothing, and so Angela started at last down the long hill, walking beside her husband.

At first her movements were slow, cautious. But then, as her excitement grew, Angela began smiling and moving faster, almost pulling Nelson from his feet in her haste.

"Angie," he gasped, wincing in agony as his leg twisted beneath him. "Take it easy! The Lear's not going anywhere, so slow down a little. Let's at least get there in one piece."

Reluctantly Angela slowed her pace, and the two of them moved carefully down the mountain. As they reached the edge of the glacier, though, Angela suddenly stopped, staring.

"Nelson!" she cried, her voice filled with excitement. "There's the packet I lost! See, over there in the snow? It must have fallen from my purse when I was dragging you across the glacier."

Quickly Angela pulled away from her husband and ran to the spot where the small package lay. By the time Nelson reached her, she had unwrapped the covering and was staring in open-mouthed silence at the small, leather-covered book that had been inside.

"Nelson," she whispered, fear again creeping into her voice, "it can't be. It just can't!"

Nelson, himself dumb with amazement, reached out and took the book from his wife's hands. Slowly then, starting from the back, he flipped through the tiny blank pages.

"Angie," he said, almost unable to breathe, "you're right again. It can't be. Only it is. It's the journal. Listen to this."

Dec 26 *The snow and cold be worse now, and I fear I cannot continue. My leg air all swole up, so I cant even crawl. My koff be bad and gettin' worse right along. I feel sartin I be dyin, and there be*

> *still no sign of the Rapaho. If anyone should happen to find me, please make it known to my wife and son that God willing we will meet agin . . .*

"It is!" Angela exclaimed as Nelson stopped reading. "It's exactly what Port wrote last night. Here, let me see it."

Quickly Angela skimmed through more pages. "It is, Nelson! It's him. It's Port. All of this is what he read to us. And look! Here's his account of saving that Indian's life! See! Here's the Indian's name! And . . . oh, Nelson!" Angela stopped, staring up at her husband. "*What* has *happened* to us?"

"I don't know, Angie. I . . . Wait a minute. His name! Is the writer's name in the journal?"

"It might be. I . . ."

And then, as they turned to the front page of the little book, both stared in total silence, neither able to speak. For the name, the name that the man had placed there a century and a half before, was Sebastian Nathan Westport. And then, in parentheses, he had written the other name, the name he had always used, the name of "Port."

"Port!" Nelson said quietly. "Westport! Of course!"

"My great-great-grandfather?" Angela gasped. "I . . . I remember the name! He was the one who left my . . . Oh, no! It wasn't his fault! Port was my great-great-grandfather, and it wasn't his fault—"

The harsh clatter of a helicopter engine suddenly burst upon their ears, and simultaneously the two spun toward the surprising sound.

Quickly the reverberating rattle of the engine and blades came closer, and seconds later the machine appeared over the far ridge. Barely skimming the rocky ground, the chopper darted toward the Lear, hovered, drifted up and around, and then settled in for a landing on the far side of the jet. And as it did, Nelson was startled to see his company logo on the side of the chopper.

"Angie," he whispered excitedly, "it's Max! It's Max and Jim! They're here! We've been rescued!"

Angela jumped into the air, waving her arms and shouting in ecstasy! But the engine noise was too loud, and the Lear obstructed their view.

"Hold it, Angie," Nelson said, gently constraining his wife. "They can't hear or see you. The chopper's in the wrong place and making too much noise. Come on! Let's go surprise them!"

Smiling with anticipation the two started forward, the journal momentarily forgotten as they ran toward the Lear. With excitement mounting, they raced around the tail of the plane, and then they stopped between it and the helicopter, staring in silence.

"Where are they?" Angela shouted, raising her voice to make herself heard above the clatter of the propellers.

"Shhhh," Nelson signalled, grinning. "They're in the Lear. We'll surprise them when they come out."

Angela smiled in return, pressing against her husband, and together they stood waiting—excited, anxious . . .

Suddenly Angela squeezed Nelson's hand and pointed.

Nelson, still smiling, watched as Max, heavily burdened, backed slowly out of the doorway of the Lear. Jim followed, and Nelson and Angela stared in shocked silence as the two turned and almost in unison laid their burdens in the snow—the burdens of two lifeless bodies.

"Oh, dear God!" Angela cried, her eyes wide and staring. "It can't be! It's not possible! I won't let it! Please tell me I'm dreaming!"

"Angie," Nelson muttered, his voice sounding as shaken as hers, "I . . ." Then he was suddenly shouting, his voice filled with fear. "Max! Hey, *Max! Jim!* It's me! Us! Nelson and Angie! We're alive! Can't you see us? I'm telling you that—

"Hyar, ol' hos, Miss Angela," a voice called softly from behind them, piercing the early morning air.

Spinning, Nelson and Angela stared in total disbelief as a young man walked across the snow toward them.

"Nelson," Angela suddenly cried, "It's *him*! It's the man from Goodwill Industries! It's—"

"Wagh," the man said as his sunburst grin spread across his

face. "It air a fine and wonderous thing, not bein' burdened with whiskers. Miss Angela, ye look beautiful today. Fresh and purty as a mountain meadow after the spring thaw. Ye do yer grandpappy proud. And ye, ol' hos, ye look a whole lot fitter'n my friend Ol' Bill ever did, even on his better days. Now fetch yerselves on over hyar, the both of ye. It be time fer a palaverin'."

"Port?"

"Aye, it be me, sartin as ol' Fetch-um Under had hindsights."

"But—but Port," Angela asked, "are . . . are we . . . dead?"

"Thet be one word fer it," the man replied, smiling.

"But we're not! We're right here!"

"Aye, thet ye be."

"But, Port," Nelson asked, his voice filled with confusion, "I don't understand. What . . . why . . . ? I don't understand the last two weeks. I . . ."

"Ol' hos," the man interrupted, winking at Angela as he spoke, "I knew ye were havin' troubles, eternal ones, and ye were both a powerful long way from solvin' 'em. This ol' coon had a vested interest, so to speak, in yer well-bein', so I went ahead to set things up a mite. I were at yer office, marm, more'n onct, and I were at yer home too. And ye, ol' hos, ye give me a turn in thet fofarraw'n auty-mobile of your'n, ye did."

"It was *you*?" Angela asked incredulously. "It was *you* who was watching me?"

"Aye. Sartin as Christmas follers New Year's it were!"

"And you were in the Countach with *me*?" Nelson asked, his voice reflecting his own shock.

"Aye agin, ol' hos. It were all a part of gettin' ye together."

"But . . . why this . . . this horrible experience in the snow?"

"Because ye wouldn't read my journal. Ye wouldn't even open it. I onct made a turrible mistake in leavin' my Sarah, and I did my uttermost best to stop my loved ones from makin' the same one. That's why I wrote it all down. But if ye wouldn't read it, then ye had to live it, feel it, exactly as I did. It were the only way to get the job done."

"Job?"

"Aye! Afore ye could learn how to be together, ye first had to learn how to love. Folks seem to have to suffer most terribly until they do. I onct suffered and learnt about love on this-hyar mountain myownself, so I reckoned the same sech sufferin' would help ye learn too. Seems I were right."

"Do you mean that none of this past two weeks was real?" Angela demanded, her voice filled with sudden anger.

"No marm, it were real indeed, very real. But it were real in a wonderously different way than ye've been used to. And the time element weren't exactly what ye thought. In point of fact, and without me waxin' loquacious or verboos about it, ye only parted company with yer mortal remains a short time back, a *very* short time."

Angela, still upset, was about to speak again when Port cut her off once more. "Now calm down thet-air Irish temper thet I bequeathed ye, Miss Angela. Cease all them anger-filled roominashuns thet be spinnin' about in yer head, and remember that I love ye, enough even to go through all this misery onct more myownself. Thet were not easy, ye know."

Angela, her understanding suddenly quickened, apologized instantly, sincerely, and just as quickly felt a wave of cleansing love and forgiveness from her ancestor wash over her. It was real! It was—

"They don't even know we're here, do they?" Nelson suddenly asked.

"No, ol' hos. Thar vision be limited most considerable, as yer own will be in a moment or so."

"What?" Angela exclaimed. "But we just—"

"Pilgrims," Port explained gently, "ye have learned of love, which the Good Lord gave His life to teach. Because yer hearts air now right, He's about to give it all back to ye, yer lives *and* yer memories of our little bit of forever spent together. I expect ye'll know whet to do with 'em."

Then, smiling again that wonderful and unforgettable smile that split his face from ear to ear and enveloped Nelson and Angela and the glacier and the entire mountain in the warmth and love of its radiantly happy glow, Port turned to the lovely woman who was his great-great-granddaughter, and gently he spoke.

"I'm proud of ye, Miss Angela," was all he said, and then he was moving away, quickly, and Nelson and Angela were suddenly alone together, tearfully living, learning, loving, going back . . .

EPILOGUE

"Max!" Jim suddenly shouted into the stillness of the mountain air. "She's alive! Angela's *alive*! She's breathing and she has tears in her eyes! She's . . ."

"So's Nelson, Jim," Max replied quietly, his voice filled with reverent awe. "I don't know what happened, unless, unless. . . . Hey, Jim, this is scary! He was dead and now, somehow, he isn't. And there are tears in his eyes, too. Looks to me like they're both going to be all right. I don't understand it, but thank God for great blessings!"

"Somebody up there must like them," Jim said quietly.

"I'd say so," Max responded as he watched Nelson's eyelids flutter a little and push out more tears. "*Somebody* surely does! Now come on, my mechanically-minded friend. I'll notify the FAA, and then let's get these two folks home where they belong. They've surely been through *something*, and I've a hunch they're anxious to get there."

And so, carefully, the two men loaded the weakened and barely conscious forms of Nelson and Angela Armstrong into the helicopter. Then, strapped in themselves, they lifted the craft into the air and turned it toward the morning sun, their hearts filled with joy and gratitude and awe because of what they had seen.

And it was only then, after they were well on their way, that Max and Jim first noticed the tiny packet clutched tightly in Angela's hands, a packet bound in ancient oilcloth and secured with hardened leather thongs, the knots of which had not been loosed for well over a hundred years.

Authors' Note

Because the background of the story *Double Exposure* is in many respects as interesting as the story itself, we have determined to share a little of it here.

Some two years past, a good friend of ours, Richard Jamison, came to us with an idea. He had had some experiences that, combined together, formed the nucleus of what seemed to him a great theme for a story. What if, he asked us, there were a man and a woman, a journal, an airplane, a crash in the desert, an Indian fight, a survival story . . . ? And with that the three of us were off and running.

We had first become acquainted with Dick, one of the nation's foremost outdoor experts, in San Francisco, where we were guest speakers at the same conference. There was an immediate rapport, and we quickly became fast friends.

Dick's expertise in primitive crafts and his knowledge of Native American peoples led us to introduce him to the producer of *Windwalker*, and Dick subsequently worked as the technical advisor to and set decorator for the film. In that capacity he personally constructed and supervised the making of the props. *Windwalker* has since been acclaimed, in great measure because of Dick's expertise, as the most authentic Indian film ever made.

At the conclusion of the filming of *Windwalker*, Dick led us on an expedition to the La Garita Mountains in southern Colorado, where we planned to set the story he had suggested. There, in the tops of the mountains, as we sat shivering around our lonely campfires by night, or crossing the hard-backed and wind-whipped ridges by day, our story began to take form. The characters were each assuming shapes of their own, developing personalities because of, or perhaps in spite of, our own personal discomfiture with the survival experience. With that, at least, we were pleased.

And then, as a spur-of-the-moment aside, Dick talked us into hiking into the 1848 Christmas camp of Colonel John C. Fremont, known as Camp Hope. We did it, and there all things changed. We discovered a grave, an unrecorded grave, and found the lichen-covered, anciently fragile jawbone of an ungelded mule.

Suddenly characters we had only imagined became quite real. The story itself, heretofore only a novel, had taken on a historical form that we had never even considered. Finally we did have a story.

Two years have gone by since then, long years and at times frustrating ones. The story has grown, been trimmed and discarded, and has developed again during that time, almost as though it has had a life of its own. Now, to our intense relief, it has reached its present and fairly completed form.

Since its beginnings, Dick has assisted us tremendously with research, technical advice, and his outdoor expertise. We acknowledge his contribution with gratitude.

Blaine & Brenton Yorgason
Orem, Utah
1982

Blaine (left) and Brent Yorgason on survival, eating berries.

Richard Jamison at Fremont's Camp.